ISLAND FOG

JOHN VANDERSLICE

Lavender Ink
New Orleans
lavenderink.org

Island Fog

The stories in this collection are products of the author's imagination. Every character in every story is either fictitious or used fictitiously. Two of the stories do have their roots in historical incidents. The key event in the story "Guilty Look," the Nantucket Bank robbery of 1795, did happen, and the circumstances of that robbery did suggest some details to the author. But almost every person in the story is an invention. William Pease and Randolph Lovelace are drawn from actual people, but by "drawn" what the author means is that he characterized them in the story as the story needed, not according to the kinds of people they were in real life. The sinking of the whaleship *Essex* in 1819, and the sufferings of its captain George Pollard, did provide useful background to the story "Taste," but the protagonist of "Taste" is by no means George Pollard in disguise. He is his own person, with his own personal history and psychological vicissitudes, all of which have been invented for him by the author. The characters and situations depicted in every other story in the collection are completely fictional, unconnected to any actual person or real life situation. If the characters in those stories bear any resemblance to actual people, living or dead, that is merely a happy—or perhaps unhappy—coincidence.

ISBN: 978-1-935084-41-9

Cover photo: Stephanie Muller.
Author photo: Stephanie Vanderslice.
Book design by Bill Lavender.

Lavender Ink
New Orleans
lavenderink.org

Acknowledgements

Some of the stories in this collection have been published previously: "On Cherry Street" in *Pembroke*, "Morning Meal" in the *Dana Literary Society Online Journal*, "Beaten" in *Oasis*, and "Haunted" (in a slightly abridged form) in *Seattle Review*. The author expresses abiding gratitude to the editors of those journals for first bringing his characters' lives to an audience.

For Stephanie, always.

TABLE OF CONTENTS

King Philip's War

Island Fog

ISLAND FOG

Many hands have been wrung over the tragic dissolution of Old Nantucket, but at this time in the island's (and the country's) development, the idyll of the "peaceable settlement" was proving ever-more difficult to sustain. Although there were some notable individual exceptions, vested interests rather than communal and spiritual ideals had become the driving force behind the proprietary and Quakerism on Nantucket. Indeed, it could be argued that more than anything else, Quakerism was what fouled the Nest of Love, as the religion that had once consolidated a community began to encourage a truly diabolical genius for character assassination. According to one observer, who had much to say about the "depravity" of the Nantucket Quakers: "Unfortunately, the anger which they are forbidden to express by outward actions, finding no vent, stagnates the heart, and, while they make professions of love and good will to their opponents, the rancor and intense malevolence of their feelings poison every generous spring of human kindness." It could also be argued that the effects of this attitude, combined with a knee-jerk economic and social conservatism, were what would ultimately doom the whale fishery to a premature death.

—Nathaniel Philbrick, *Away Off Shore: Nantucket Island and Its People, 1602-1890*

We may reason on to our heart's content, the fog won't lift.

—Samuel Beckett, "The Expelled"

KING PHILIP'S WAR

GUILTY LOOK

Nantucket Island, 1795

In the days following the crime, what Nantucketers find unfathomable is how loud the evening had been and how crowded. With the sheep-shearing festival in full swing, the island was overrun with visitors from America and from the Vineyard—to say nothing of the entire town wandering about—all come to watch sheep get shaved near Maxcy's pond; to see animals judged; to hear airs played on fiddles and flutes and recorders and citterns; to spy the peculiar bony beauty of the local women; to drink the stiffest grog they could find at whatever public house would serve it; to dance with whomever would join them on this Quaker-dominated outpost; to forget their troubles for an afternoon or find occasions to create new ones. They had come to share in and celebrate the growing prosperity of an island which, owing to the whaling industry—and for the first time in its history as an English settlement—had secured wealth that could be called not just noticeable but audacious.

Samuel Oder, the night watchman, was kept busy well past midnight calming a dozen street scuffles, stopping a half-hearted break-in at the nail factory, evicting two drunks from their resting place at the corner of Federal and Main, convincing Johnny Pratt to stop singing "Enraptured I Gaze" at the top of his lungs outside Delia Chalkley's house, and rescuing a variety of strangers who had gotten lost and turned around, headed somewhere they shouldn't, despite the bright moonlight and the number of locals they could have consulted. The islanders and their scores of June visitors carried on for long hours until finally, at some point between one and two in the morning, the streets cleared and the shouting stopped; no more locks were tried or windows broken.

Precisely at this point, a group of four men stepped out of the shadows behind the oil processing plant at the north end of the harbor. They proceeded five short blocks southeast on Washington Street then turned right onto Main. Only four blocks up Main, on the cusp of its intersection with Centre, sat the six-year-old edifice of the Nantucket Bank. Here they stopped. The leader of the four was a man so thin, with joints so pointed, he could almost be called skeletal; certainly he was more than gawky. His face was wide and flat, roughened slightly with florid coloring and lingering marks from a childhood bout with smallpox. His round, wary eyes blinked so often he might have been imitating a nine-year-old. He wore a dark broad hat that covered light, straw-colored hair and a brown coat, no different from the coats many islanders and their visitors wore that evening, except that—unlike this straw-haired man—they were too drunk to remember what they did with their clothes or to care.

On first impression, especially in the well of early morning, the man might have seemed graying and wrinkle-lined, what with his littered face and ancient eagle body. But, in fact, there was not a gray hair on him or a single line cut in his skin. The man was only twenty-eight. His accomplices were even younger.

From the pocket of that coat, the skeletal man retrieved a key, inserted it into the keyhole of the bank's front door, and turned it clockwise. The lithe, practiced manner in which he carried out these motions belied any impression of awkwardness. He might have been invisible as he stood there, so soundless were his motions. When he felt and heard the tumblers give inside the lock, he rotated the knob counterclockwise and then pushed in gently, sending the door away from his hand with the soft ends of his fingers. The thin man watched as the door swung back. He did not turn to offer a victorious grimace to his companions—one smaller, thick-shouldered, and heavy lidded, with a beard that ran up around his ears; the second nearly as thin as the leader, but more moist and sloppy around the mouth, more tentative at the eyes; and the last a squat, stout creature with red hair spilling everywhere around his face, barely held in place by his own broad hat. The lead man didn't nod; he didn't raise his eyebrows; he gave no hand signals. He acted as if what had just happened was perfectly expected, as regular as opening the door to his own home. He stepped through the space and the other three followed. When all were inside, the leader closed the door behind them, applying gentle pressure until he heard the click of the latch.

The four knew what to do next. They had discussed the matter for weeks. They had memorized the map of the bank given to them by the same man who had given them the keys. They memorized it so completely, and had even practiced their steps—for several nights running, moving through an obstacle course of their own making—that they could move through the building without need of a lamp or a candle. With no illumination at all, their feet found the right corridor and the right room and the anticipated vault. They worked as if in a state of déjà vu—more than a metaphor, because in fact they had "already seen" this bank in their own rehearsals. At the vault, their hands found the keyhole. Opening the vault proved no task at all.

By the time they were done, they had secured more than $20,000 worth of gold coins into eight canvas bags. They exited the same way they entered and just as quietly locked the door behind them. They navigated a careful path back to the Old North Wharf, staying close to the buildings, hugging the dark, using shadows and avoiding the broiling moonlight. At the wharf, they loaded their bags into a skiff they had tied up hours earlier. Settled inside, they took up oars, and cut a slow, silent course out of the harbor. At Brant Point they took a hard curve northward and churned for Nantucket Sound. Once in the Sound, they curved again—westward—and the lead man finally let free their sail. Fortunately for them, a passable breeze was blowing. Fortunately, because they had more than fifteen miles to cover before they would find safety for the night.

William Pease is getting nowhere with Louisa Lovelace. Worse, Louisa's girl did something wrong with the tea. For the last thirty minutes, in which he has bravely imbibed enough of the stuff to seem courteous, the concoction has tasted like the water smells that he wrings out of his stockings at the end of especially rainy days. For thirty minutes, he has forced his grimace into a smile as he sips and compliments Louisa on her fine instincts for hiring help; most of all he has tried to keep Louisa's attention on the seven wigs he has brought for her to inspect. But Louisa, who has taken not a single sip from her own cup, has shown none of her usual interest in other women's hair. She has barely glanced at the abundance Pease is showing: a cinnamon brown number that he feels sure would turn her autumnal eyes more lustrous; a scandalous red one as bright as a cherry; three blonde specimens as young and fine spun as any woman could hope for—blonder even than Pease had been at Louisa's age; a rare, raven black wig, the only one of the seven he did not make himself but purchased from widow Chase's daughter when her mother's estate was sold; and, finally, what he has been holding back, waiting for the end of his visit, waiting for just the right moment to spring on her, a mixed creation in which subtle reminders of chestnut and auburn mingle with black and a few currents of silver.

It is a new idea for Pease, one he has great hope for, if only he can convince a few choice women to adopt it: a realistic wig, one that can fool viewers into thinking it is the woman's own hair, except that, because Pease is a master, the wig cannot help but be more beautiful, more dramatic, more heart-stopping and eye-catching than the poor woman's hair on its best day. The black strands are not just dark but an absolute immersion into nighttime; the silver strands are not just silver but shimmering streams of moonlight, visible out of doors. *My, Louisa, I had no idea your own hair was so brilliant. I'm envious.* Unless the woman told, who would know?

So far Pease has held out six of the seven wigs for Louisa Lovelace to inspect, but she has shown no interest. She only smiles palely and asks him idle questions about his wife, about his house. Then she says, "I am curious, William—you haven't—I don't think—shared with me—your thoughts about the robbery." Her eyes grow tense, newly attentive.

"Oh, the infernal event again," Pease begins. "I suppose I am as befuddled as the next man. How could it happen here of all places?" She nods dimly. He's not sure she really heard him. He asks if she, as wife of the bank president, has learned anything new in the two weeks since the crime. She holds her head still a moment; a sliver of worry slides into her expression. Worry, or some new, stronger distraction.

She shakes her head. "You know how it is. A husband rarely speaks of business to his wife."

"I speak about my business to my wife every day," Pease says. "Who else am I going to speak to about it?"

He hopes that this will wake her up, but she smiles as vaguely as ever and says nothing. He thinks of all the replies he might expect from Louisa Lovelace: "Well, what woman is not going to be interested in wigs?"; "Yes, but Sophia is more of the *involved* sort"; "What's the bother; Randolph knows I'm hopeless with numbers." Instead she stares at him and offers a non sequitur: "A few persons I know think it was done by off-islanders, but almost everyone else agrees that the guilty party must be here, in town. Still among us."

Pease puts his product down. Clearly nothing will come of this visit. He feels the need to scratch his face and is reminded again of the rash he's been battling for three weeks. Home grown remedies have failed to heal it. So has stubbornness. He would speak to Dr. Hussey about it, but he dislikes doctors generally and Hussey specifically.

"I cannot imagine," he says, "who such men could be."

"Men? You know them to be men?"

"Surely you do not think they were women?"

"I don't know what to think."

"I think it is a common—and safe—assumption that bank robbers are men."

"How do you know they were 'robbers' and not a 'robber'?"

Pease laughs and begins to stow the wigs in the large canvas bag he uses for these home visits. Louisa is in an odd mood: contrary and strangely uninterested in fashion. "Of course, I do not *know* that," he says. "But you don't think one man by himself could carry off the entire contents of the Nantucket Bank vault?"

"I do not know what to think. I've told you that already." She looks at her hands, at her teacup, at the table, valiantly trying to swallow the anger evident in her last sentence. Finally she looks up. Her eyes have cleared. Her face is calm. "You are the board member with the highest standing?"

"The highest standing?" What an indelicate question to come from the mouth of Louisa Lovelace. "I'm not sure how they measure things like that at the Nantucket Bank. John Coffin and Levi Gardner—and your husband, of course—have served as long as I have. And to speak bluntly, they are both far wealthier than I; as are most of the men on the board."

Louisa smiles as if she is humoring his little lie. But it isn't a lie. Pease closes the latch on his bag and stands. "I see you are not in a buying mood. Shall I return tomorrow, or would you rather schedule an appointment for next week?"

She stares at him: vacantly at first but then with a subtle, burgeoning kind of horror, as if he were a ghost of himself and the real William Pease was hundreds of miles away, on the western frontier of the new United States. "I guess," she says softly. "Why don't we make it for next week?"

"All right then, we will set it for exactly this time next week. That's Tuesday, July 14th. Yes?" She nods, but without conviction. He'll have to remind her. Stop by Monday and make sure she is still planning on him. Louisa Lovelace, after all, is one of his best customers, the woman on the island most eager—or maybe compelled—to spend her husband's money on her own beauty. Louisa Lovelace is a perfectly attractive girl, still fresh-faced and bright-eyed at twenty-nine but at the point in a woman's life when she feels she must fight to keep what she has. For Pease, this is wonderful, especially wonderful because, as wife of the president of Nantucket Bank, Louisa's decisions about her own beauty influence dozens of other island matrons. Pease lifts his bag, turns, and prepares to be shown out of the house. But Louisa stays crumpled—he's tempted to say *defeated*—in her seat. After a second, she says, "I think Randolph wants to talk to you."

"About?"

She blinks. "I don't know." Now she is lying.

"I'm headed over to see Lydia Folger," Pease says. "I'll stop in at the bank and check on him. I think the cinnamon wig might be just what Lydia needs. Her coloring is so similar to yours." He hopes Louisa hears that subtle jab of lost opportunity, but if so it doesn't show in her face. In any case, she stays seated. And the girl is nowhere to be found. Pease will have to let himself out. "Good day, dear," he says and is about to go when he hears footsteps on the front stoop, then the sound of the door opening. He takes a step back so that he is closer to the center of the parlor. He spies the figure of Randolph Lovelace, framed by the front door. Lovelace's flat, gray stare shows neither surprise nor curiosity, as if he expected Pease to be standing exactly there, exactly then.

"Hello, Randolph," Pease says. "Surprised to see you home before dinner." No reaction from the bank president, except that his frown goes deeper. "This is fortuitous. I've been showing Louisa some of my newest items, but she told me not two minutes ago that you needed to speak with me. I was about to find you."

At this comment, Lovelace stands straighter and throws his shoulders back to reveal his full height. At six-foot-three he is taller than any man on the island and strongly built, even now at forty-eight; even with his balding pate and lined skin; even though he does nothing in particular to maintain his constitution. His physique comes to him naturally; which is no real surprise, since his father was the same way. With his dark caste and his intense stare, Lovelace carries the air of a man not to be crossed, a man who could do physical damage if he wanted, though Pease cannot think of a single time Lovelace has ever done so. He has always been more of an internal, self-involved person. A mystery, really. Physical assault is a vaporous threat that gravitates around his being, like the afternoon fog infecting the harbor. A threat that, unlike the fog, never actually takes body.

Pease again wonders at the contradiction of the bank president's famous fidelity to the Society of Friends, especially the group that gathers at the House on Liberty Street. The Quakers: that bastion of pacifism and social high mindedness; firm convictions against drunkenness and dancing and high living of any sort. And yet the bank president lives in obvious luxury in his Centre Street home. To each his own, Pease relents. Lovelace must get something out of his religion; something that Pease, as a committed Congregationalist, cannot understand. But that, Pease knows, does not make the something unreal. Lovelace does not ask after his wife, or call to her. Instead he says to Pease, "I want you to walk with me." Pease shrugs off the distasteful tone of command. "Certainly," he says brightly, as if a walk with Randolph Lovelace would count as the highlight of his morning.

Lovelace pushes the door open and moves down the stairs, still without asking about his wife. Then Pease realizes what a dullard he has been. *He didn't come home to see Louisa. He came to fetch me.* But how did Lovelace even know where he was? Louisa, somehow, must have sent word. He remembers how, almost as soon as he arrived, Louisa looked agitated and excused herself, supposedly to check on the girl in the kitchen. Minutes later she appeared with the vile, sour pot of tea and two cups, carrying the tray herself. It must have been then, in those few minutes she was out of his sight, that she sent a note to Randolph. And who else could have carried the note but the girl? So the maker of the tea must have been none other than Louisa Lovelace herself.

William Pease and Randolph Lovelace were born within a month of each other in 1746, both on the island, but into strikingly different households. Lovelace's father Jebediah was led to the Society of Friends in the 1730s by his wife Abigail, and he soon became the most regular of Quakers. He also became the strongest voice for disciplining errant members: those who demonstrated refined tastes in food, clothes, music, or literature. Those who showed a weakness for dance. He spoke forcefully and often in favor of excommunicating any member caught drinking alcohol. He was, at the same time, famously gregarious, full of laughter and raw jokes and sarcastic political opinions that showed just how much he loved the mettle of the world's business. Not surprisingly, given his combination of shrewdness, energy, and puritanical self-discipline, he was also one of the five wealthiest men on the island, Nantucket's leading shipbuilder and a crucial supplier for the burgeoning whaling industry. So when Abigail was pregnant with Randolph, and again with their later two children, Jebediah had no trouble affording a twenty-four hour cycle of nurses, cooks, charwomen, and laundry girls.

Randolph, the oldest, has always cut a quieter figure than his father: less jovial, more secretive, and with an almost vicious capacity for concentration. While he never treated his father with anything other than ordinary respect, and while he refrained from confronting the loud and dogmatic Jebediah over matters of politics or religion or business, Randolph never showed the man much love either. Randolph was at all times, and in nearly every situation, a private boy, as self-possessed as his father but in an entirely different way: silent, inscrutable, fundamentally cohesive. He had little if any sense of humor but possessed an inborn competitive spirit that drove him to study harder and work longer than anyone his age. He took compliments bestowed upon other boys as a personal affront, as a conscious challenge.

A brilliant study with numbers, Randolph started his professional life as a bookkeeper for his father's business and before long was Jebediah's chief financial advisor and most trusted strategist. It was assumed by all the Lovelaces, by the whole island really, that Randolph would take Jebediah's place whenever the older man finally declined, but in the summer of 1788 Randolph was recruited by a group of investors to head the newly formed Nantucket Bank. They wanted to make him president and director of the board. *No one else has the skills requisite for this job*, they told him. *No one else on the island can take care of our money the way you could*. Then they offered him a truly remarkable salary, less than he would make as owner of a successful ship building operation, but far more than a bank president had any right to expect. Randolph said yes before he even consulted his father, an oversight that some credited with Jebediah's sudden decline and then his death in November of that year, only one day before his son's birthday.

Randolph, who had remained his father's legal heir, sold the old man's business for a famous profit to an interest in New Bedford. Then, over the course of the next six years, he consolidated his hold on the Nantucket Bank—its employees, its board members, its business tactics. He married Louisa Rice and bought his baronial estate on Centre Street, which he outfitted in noticeably elevated style. He purchased furniture from Spain, rugs from Persia, silver from Boston and crystal from Ireland. He paid lavishly for portraits of himself and his wife, for whose sake he enlisted the services of Nantucket's best dressmaker, Jonas Richardson; its most skilled shoemaker, Aaron Rotch; and its only wigmaker: William Pease. But when island craftsmen proved insufficient, Lovelace did not hesitate to send Louisa to Boston or Philadelphia for better outfitting; once he even sent her to London.

About the only comparison that can be made now between

the son and his father is their similar control over the Society of Friends. Following Jebediah's death, Randolph became the leader of a cabal of outspoken members—four women and three men—who came to operate as a virtual senior advisory committee. Or, as some still spitefully deem them, the "ruling council" of the famously democratic Quakers. It is no secret that, now more than ever, no one lasts at the Meeting House on Liberty Street without obliging the favor and flattering the interests of members of the "council." Meanwhile, each year half a dozen members are sanctioned for their excessive worldliness, and one or two particularly hopeless cases are excommunicated. The luxury with which Lovelace and his wife live does not go unnoticed by those within or without the Quakers. But Lovelace's defenders, of which there are several, have a simple and in their minds incontrovertible answer to any possible resentment. Randolph and Louisa, they say, don't actually enjoy their luxury. Only a blind misanthrope could believe that. Given Randolph's profession and his standing in the community, *he has no choice* but to decorate his home and his wife just so. Certain mannerisms, certain comforts, certain standards *are expected of a bank president.* It is the work Randolph cares for, they say. You can see it in his face. It is the work that drives him. Everything else is meaningless. *He is like an Old World monk, spiritual that way.*

William Pease, whose father labored for most of his working career as a passably successful sheep farmer, spent his early years east of the fenced borders of Nantucket town. He can still remember his father's resentment at paying the toll at the Newtown Gate whenever he had business in the village. It was, his father complained, like being "taxed for just trying to stay alive." When William turned eight, however, Jacob Pease, noting the growing prosperity in town, tired of sheep and tired of the toll, abandoned farming to open a dried goods store on Cambridge Street. The family—William's father, mother, sister Mary, and himself—settled into a small apartment above the shop. The business was sluggish at the start, as Jacob had to learn a new set of talents and make friends with a new and wider set of suppliers. But after two difficult years, Jacob's gamble began to pay off. In November of 1757 he made more money in a single month than he had in any other month of his working life.

Then on Christmas Day 1757, Jacob Pease died of a heart attack. He was forty-one. His wife Martha determined that she would run the store, provided she could count on the help of William and Mary. Any notion of a formal education for the children evaporated, a fact that forever haunted the smart, chatty, mentally eager William. Beginning in his late teens, he dedicated himself to a self-styled educational regimen. Every day, with the help of Dr. Johnson's dictionary, he would memorize one new English word, writing out the word and its meaning a dozen times when he first woke and then forcing himself to use the word six times that day in conversation. By this means, and through his own natural cheerfulness, William became known as the most charming conversationalist on Nantucket.

At age twenty-six, he took note of the growing demand for wigs among the women of the middle and upper classes. As there was no wigmaker on Nantucket, he asked his mother if he could try to learn the trade, provided he kept up his hours in the shop. She agreed and three years later, William offered for sale, through private conversation and knocking at selected doorways, his first collection. The entire stock sold out in two days, and for ten times what it had cost him to make them. Thereafter, William Pease did not work another hour at the store.

In the autumn of 1780, at age thirty-four, he converted from being a "nothingarian" to a Congregationlist. About a year later, at church, he met nineteen- year-old Sophia Brewster, whose Tory family had migrated to Nantucket to escape the embarrassment of the war. Sophia's parents eventually fled all the way to England, but by that time she and William were married. It was and is, all things considered, a good, "happy" marriage. Yet thirteen years of conjoined life have produced no offspring for the couple: the one cutting and insurmountable regret of their lives.

In the era of post-war activity, meanwhile, William saw his business flourish. He served on the town council. He became outspoken on such subjects as civic cleanliness and the need for raised walkways, the need for a fire department and a night watch. He campaigned on behalf of the many businesses run by descendents of the "half-share" men who had made the island a hive of commercial success. He threw sparkling soirees for which he kept a stock of champagne imported from the Old Country and at which he loved to see so many women wearing wigs of his own fastening.

William became so well known and loved among certain high-living sets of persons, that it seemed only astute to ask him to join the board of the Nantucket Bank when the board was configured in early 1789. It was said that the new bank would be guaranteed success if it could win the support and approval of William Pease. Whatever Pease lacked in family connections and formal education he more than made up for in social currency, in personal charm, and in his daily access to the island's wealthiest homes. Lovelace grudgingly agreed to Pease's presence, as much as it bothered him to think that someone outside his own Quaker circle was considered necessary for his bank's success. Lovelace was convinced by a few choice board members to swallow his complaint, but he watched carefully as Pease assumed his position. He watched as Pease began to serve with all of his characteristic, unstoppable energy; and his characteristic, unstoppable opinions.

As soon as they are out the door, Lovelace turns left and strides on urgently, as if he wants to leave Pease behind. At the corner of Centre and Pearl, he turns left again and starts in the direction of the harbor. He says nothing for several moments; Pease can do nothing but keep up and wait. That's fine, he thinks, I'm good at waiting when I have to. But he is much more gifted at not waiting. What he is truly gifted with, what has motivated his whole life since the age of eleven, is impatience. He is keenly aware that he earned none of his current prestige through sitting still.

At the corner of Pearl and Water Street, Lovelace turns again—this time to the right—and Pease decides he's had enough of this: being led around silently by Randolph Lovelace as if he were a new hire at the bank, some eighteen or nineteen-year-old ingénue. He is about to announce, "What exactly is this about, Randolph?" when Lovelace stops. They are standing at the intersection of Water and Cambridge. Lovelace is facing the Old North Wharf, only two blocks away, jutting like a stump into the shallow water of the harbor. Lovelace's eyes narrow, fix on something specific and dangerous, as if a monster is working its way out of the murky gray water and into the uneasy sunlight. Pease almost turns to spot the object of Lovelace's fascination, when the banker says, "There have been developments with the robbery."

Pease ignores Lovelace's ungrateful stare. "That's a surprise. Given the paucity of clues."

"You've thought about that then?"

"The clues? Of course. We all have. We all want the money returned."

Lovelace nods. "Yes. I too want the money returned. I want that very much."

"So what are the developments?"

Lovelace hesitates then says, "We know that one of the thieves is Joseph Tyler."

"Tyler!" Joseph Tyler, only three years on-island, works for the bank as a clerk. A struggling young husband with a sick wife, he also performs legal work for hire, and keeps books for a slaughterhouse on Washington Street. Between the three jobs he makes just enough to maintain his household and pay for Annabel's care. He is a famously awkward person, one with mathematical smarts but no social confidence. At the bank he does his job well but avoids all other employees; he avoids society generally. Except for attending Pease's Congregationalist church every other Sunday or so, Tyler's life is one of unending duty to the needs of his jobs and of Annabel. Before the robbery it was considered only a matter of time before Tyler became so disenchanted that he took his wife to America. The only thing stopping that, everyone agreed, was Annabel's extended family on Nantucket.

"Mayhew says Tyler has a guilty look about him." Alexander Mayhew, another Quaker, is Lovelace's second-in-command at the bank and the secretary of the board of directors. "I concur. We informed the sheriff, who has arrested Tyler."

"A guilty look."

"We all know that whoever robbed Nantucket Bank is either an insider or an outsider who received the cooperation of someone inside. The thieves entered without forcing the door. If you consider how financially stressed Tyler is and add the guilty look, I think it's a fairly damning case."

"What exactly is a guilty look?"

Lovelace turns importantly: "I know it when I see it."

Pease shakes his head. "I think you are wrong, Randolph. Wrong and unjust. I know Tyler, not just from the bank but from my church." He notes how Lovelace's nostrils flare at the latter words. "I cannot imagine he would do this. If it's true, he would have to be an absolute fool. And he has never seemed to me like any kind of f—" Pease stops. "Has anyone even searched Tyler's home to see if this suspicion has legs?"

"The sheriff is doing so presently."

"And if he finds nothing?"

Lovelace begins walking again, down the gently sloping Cambridge Street to the harbor. "It matters not at all. Even Tyler is not stupid enough to hide stolen money where he lives."

"But where then?"

Lovelace sends Pease a pregnant glance, as if expecting another sentence from the wig-draper.

"You actually think," Pease says, "he could manage this by himself?"

"No. I do not."

"Have you talked to him, or are you just in the habit of making random accusations?"

"I never make random anything."

Pease feels for Joseph Tyler, for the weeks of internment that surely await him, for the dissolution of a present and of a future that of course looked difficult but at least represented something, some kind of identity on the island. Could Tyler even remain married now? Would Annabel's family allow it? It occurs to Pease that he has no idea why they are still walking to the harbor. What beyond this can Lovelace possibly have to say?

"You should know, Pease, that you have been tabbed as well."

"Me? Who has tabbed me?"

"A conjurer."

"What conjurer?"

"A gentleman named Stafford, from New Bedford. Some contacts

I have there put me in touch with him shortly after the robbery. I actually went to the trouble to travel to New Bedford last week and meet the man in person. I asked for his assistance in unriddling this riddle, which I think you'll agree seems rather titanic."

"And what is a conjurer going to do about it?"

"He told me that four men robbed the bank. One of them was a bony, quarrelsome fellow with a rough face and sandy hair."

Pease's hand went to his rash. "Good god, Randolph."

"Mayhew too, Pease. Mayhew has pointed you out to me."

"Oh, and I suppose he says I have a 'guilty look.'"

"He does."

"Mayhew and an astrologer from New Bedford? What do either of them know about me at all?"

Lovelace raises a palm, as if to indicate that he is the adult in the conversation, and as such he will brook no childish protestations. "In fact," he says, "I do believe you are involved. You have a conspicuous way about you. You have for months, but especially these weeks since the robbery. When I saw you in my parlor right now you looked like an escaped prisoner just caught by dogs."

It takes Pease several seconds to realize the bank president is speaking seriously. Anger begins to limit his vision, to choke the words he needs so badly.

"So can I expect the sheriff to come to my house also? To start turning over my furniture? Run knives through my pillows? Look through my armoire?"

"Yes, you can."

"And this is your idea of a warning?"

"It is my idea of an interrogation."

Pease laughs: brutally, painfully. "You're touched, Lovelace. Your head is full of rubbish. And the sheriff's is too—if he actually believes this. He'll find no stolen money at my house."

"Of course not."

"So why come at all?"

"First things first."

"And since when are you in charge of the actions of Sheriff Fitch?"

They reach the corner of Washington Street and Cambridge. The wharf is only eighty yards off or so. A small merchant ship is docked there. Half a dozen men are busy unloading wooden crates from the cargo hold. Lovelace stops. Again, he focuses his dark, certain stare on Pease. "Since it is my bank that lost $20,000. I think that entitles me to do anything I want."

"Like spontaneously deciding who does and who does not look guilty?"

"You look guilty now."

"Am I to be arrested?"

"Not yet."

"Good. And you may tell the sheriff that if he ever tries to arrest me, I will sue to take away the very little he owns. And when I win my case, I will gather his miserable collection and toss it into the harbor for my entertainment."

For the first time during the conversation, Lovelace smiles: a look, Pease realizes, meant not to pacify but to unsettle. *A quarrelsome fellow.* But Pease cannot help himself: "Why should I want anything to do with robbing the bank of which I am a board member? Why should I want to be involved with that?"

Lovelace cancels his smile. "That is what Fitch and I intend to find out." Instead of crossing Washington and walking all the way to the dock, as it appeared he meant to, Lovelace crosses Cambridge, moving parallel to the water, across the face of Nantucket town. He does not indicate for Pease to follow him, so Pease does not. He can't stand to be in the presence of the banker's watery suspicions a single moment more. It occurs to Pease that he could stride up the dock right now, to where the ship is moored, and purchase a passage to the mainland. He has money in his pocket, after all. He always does. But he won't leave. Because he shouldn't have to. Because it would be wrong. What he has to do is stay on Nantucket and, since the sheriff refuses to, figure out this crime for himself.

"Of course not," Sophia says, "why would he?"

His wife stands at his elbow, more annoyed than flustered, as Pease examines his parlor, with its harpsichord and its settee and its chaise longue, its polished wooden tables and the decorative mantle dressing the hearth. Portraits of his mother and Sophia's hang on opposite walls guarding the room. The chairs appear unmoved and undamaged. The tables have not been overturned. The rugs have not been molested, nor the wooden floor.

"I want you to keep the door locked. Do not open it unless it is I myself calling to you. Make sure it is me, Sophia. Do you understand what I'm saying? Do not open the door just because some man says he is me."

Sophia's brown eyes grow wide with new worry; beneath the blonde wig she prefers, her face takes on a pale color. He has not told her yet, but she guesses it. She is not his wife for nothing. "How could they suspect you?"

"I don't know, but let us say that for now my position on the board of directors looks extremely tenuous."

"But if not for you there would be no Nantucket Bank to speak of. You were the one who talked to Gardner and Coleman. They would not have listened to Lovelace or any of his circle. They cannot stand him. You were the one who told them how vital the bank was for the town. You sold it to them, not Lovelace."

What could he say? Of course it made no sense; none of it did. And that's exactly why he needs to investigate. To find what actual story motivates this nonsensical one. To find what it is that can twist sane men's minds into knots. "Apparently, he has suspected me from the first. He suspected me before it even happened."

"You mean he's resented you. Your influence. The love people bear you."

"Joseph Tyler has no influence, and he too is under suspicion."

"Tyler is not a Quaker either."

"But he is tired, and he is isolated, and he is in need of money—I mean money for Annabel's sake. Perhaps his situation is more desperate than I realized."

"Why are you making Lovelace's case for him? You know it can't be true."

"And he does—or did—have access to the keys."

"So do other employees. So do other board members. And who knows who else?"

Who else. Who else. This, Pease knows, is the crux of the matter. From the start he has doubted that anyone who works at the bank could have anything to do with the robbery, despite the gossip, gossip that surely must be circulating more wildly now. But if not a bank employee, who else had keys? And who would use them for a break-in?

The town jail on High Street is not far from Pease's home on Martins Lane. Established on High Street to be out of the way of the business activity at the harbor, the jail—in a town growing and spreading as quickly as Nantucket—is hardly remote from anyone now. A grown man with a good step can reach it in twelve minutes from even the furthest edges of the defined village. It is bordered by close to twenty homes, some on Pleasant; some on Pine; a few on High Street itself. Perhaps the reason islanders don't mind living close to the jail is that the jail is infrequently full. In fact, on a typical day the jail is empty. The belligerent, grog-soaked whalers who spend the night there are sent on their way first thing in the morning and the cells, two in number, stand fallow through the late morning and afternoon. There will be the occasional petty thief or poacher. For three weeks, four years ago, cell number two housed a man who murdered another on Mill Hill on account of a debt. One year ago, a man out at Long Pond was detained for a month after he lost his senses and attacked his neighbor's cows with an ax. But during the whole one-hundred-and-fifty year English occupation of the island, no one has ever been imprisoned for bank robbery. Until now.

When Pease enters the building, he immediately sees Joseph Tyler in cell 1, on the right. Tyler sits hunched over on a low wooden stool, elbows on his knees, eyes listless and unbelieving. If it were me, Pease thinks, I would be livid. I would be pacing. I would be shouting. *It might very well be you,* he realizes, *and very soon.* He pushes the thought away. Sitting on a wooden chair about six feet from the cell door is Abner Pope: his legs stretched out, his head against the chair back, his cheeks sagging and his moustache bristling, his mouth open in a gasping snore. Pope, an occasional employee of the sheriff's office, has apparently been assigned to "guard" Tyler. The sheriff is nowhere to be seen. Pease is about to check the office in the back when Pope starts. His seaweed green and black eyes open. It takes him a moment to realize what he is looking at. He sits up slowly. He scratches his lower back. "Good morning, Mr. Pease," Pope says. His eyes change: "Is it still morning?"

"Barely."

Pope nods as if this is exactly what he expects to hear. He reaches into his trousers' pocket and extracts a pipe. He searches through the other pocket then a look of alarm crosses his face. "Mr. Pease, I think I left my tobacco sack at Mr. Coleman's. You mind keeping an eye on the prisoner while I fetch it?"

"What about the sheriff?"

"He's out investigating."

"Where?" What he really means is *who*.

"I don't know. But Mr. Lovelace and he seem to think they are on to something."

Of course they do.

"Go ahead, Abner. I need to wait here anyway to speak to the sheriff."

Pope stands, but as he moves for the door his right leg almost gives out beneath him, as if it has fallen asleep. Pope just keeps walking, ignoring his strained gait. If you didn't know better, you'd think the young man was drunk. But as a part-time law enforcer and devout member of the Society of Friends, Pope abstains. Probably for the best, Pease long ago decided. Pope seems like the kind of man who if he learned to drink ale would quickly be drinking nothing else.

Pease cracks the jail door and watches Pope idle up High Street to Pine. He waits until the guard has turned on to Pine before he moves to Tyler, who so far has offered no visible reaction to Pease's presence. Tyler's head remains dropped; he stares at his shoes. *He thinks I am here at the bidding of Lovelace or Mayhew.*

"Where's the sheriff?" Pease asks. Tyler acts as if hasn't heard. "Tyler?"

The clerk's head shifts slightly. "Probably at my home, ransacking it."

"Probably," Pease says and steps forward. He grabs a vertical bar in the cell door; he rests his elbow against the center horizontal and his foot against the bottom. "What's going on with you?"

Tyler doesn't answer.

"Why would you want to put everything at risk for a scheme

like this?"

Despite the fact that Tyler belongs to his church, and despite what he told Lovelace, Pease has no real sense of the man: what he is like to those close to him, how he acts when he goes unwatched. Annabel Tyler is not among his clients; so he has never seen the inside of their home.

"Easy money?" Pease tries.

"I don't think I want to say anything."

"Why?"

Now Tyler looks at him directly. His brown eyes resonate. "Why should I?"

"Because silence will be taken as an indication of guilt." Pease sees a note of surprise in Tyler's gaze: an honest, untutored reaction.

"Protesting," Tyler says, "is taken as a sign of guilt also."

Pease does not doubt this, and he would like to comfort the man with professions of belief in his innocence. But if it is even remotely the case that Tyler knows something—even a little—it is imperative that Pease extract this knowledge, and quickly, before the sheriff returns. He has a feeling that pressing Tyler will yield a better result than comforting him.

"Has Mr. Lovelace been here?"

"No."

"Who has been here?"

"Yourself."

"Your wife?"

Tyler's expression sours. "I don't want her here."

"She is at home?"

"Actually, she's in 'Sconset. Or she should be."

Most of Annabel's relatives live in Siasconset, that small fishing village on the eastern side of the island.

"Her uncle owns a musket and a fierce collection of knives. He will use them on you if you try to bring Annabel back."

"I have no intention of bringing your wife here."

Pease sees Tyler thaw: His shoulders dip; his eyes soften. Perhaps he has scored a point with comfort after all. "I'd like to know why you would cooperate with a bank theft."

The tension returns. "I'd like to know how many people have

been told that I did."

"Ask Mr. Lovelace. He told me."

Tyler does not seem surprised.

"Did you need the money," Pease says, "or did you simply want it?"

"Doesn't everyone need money? Doesn't everyone want it?"

"So that is the reason why?"

"Can you think of any other reason why a person would rob a bank?"

"So you're admitting you were involved?"

"I'm explaining that for need of money scores of people on this island could have done it. For want of money, almost anyone could."

A muscle in Pease's neck clicks. He drops his arm, shifts his weight from his left foot to his right. "That's a fair point, Joseph. Troubling but fair. I will grant it to you."

"Bless you," Tyler smirks. For the first time, his eyes have energy, his square jaw shows fight.

"Hush, man. You're in real trouble if you don't know it."

Tyler gives him a wide mocking look and gestures around the cell, as if to say, *No, I never would have guessed.*

"Somehow," Pease says, "someone got keys to the bank."

"Somehow? You mean besides from a bank employee?"

"Is that who it was?"

"I don't know."

"Who else then?"

"It could be anyone angry enough at the bank—or the island—to want to kick it in the heel."

Now there was an interesting answer. Anger, not need. Not need but anger. Who on the island had reason to be angry with the Nantucket Bank, angry enough to enable a crime? Maybe he is deluded, being a member of the board, but it seems to Pease that the community at large never saw the Nantucket Bank as anything other than a haven and a resource. Businessmen have come to see it as an absolute necessity. If anger was the motivation, the emotion could have come from nowhere but inside the bank itself. Which, of course, brings it back to Tyler. Or to someone else on the payroll. For the first time since news of the robbery broke, Pease stands ready to believe the gossip of island collusion.

He hears the jail door open and turns to see the slight, avian figure of Simeon Fitch: bent at the shoulders, sharp at the elbows, with fine points at his knees and ankles and cheekbones. Almost inhumanly thin, Fitch's skeletal structure and the graying mutton chops that dominate his face only exaggerate the blue-gray sheen of his eyes. Fitch is easily the scrawniest man to ever hold the position of sheriff on Nantucket. But Pease knows he might also be the canniest, despite the clumsy moves he has made so far. Fitch looks surprised to see Pease standing in the middle of his jail. Not annoyed or angry, but certainly shocked.

"Where's Pope?" Fitch asks.

"Good morning, Simeon," Pease says as unctuously as he can. "Abner had to go to Ben Coleman's for a second, something about tobacco." Fitch rolls his eyes and steps inside. Pease can see the sheriff's mind busily working behind his closed look, behind his shut mouth. What to make of the advent of William Pease, latest suspect, standing inside his jail, speaking to another suspect—and without Abner Pope here to witness? What are they paying Pope for anyway?

Though Fitch is a Quaker and thus a de facto ally of Lovelace, Pease still hopes he can trust the man. Pease's earlier anger has burned itself out; so for now he is left with his standing ideas about the sheriff. Quaker or not, Fitch has always struck Pease as a man who is honest out of habit, honest because he knows keeping track of one's lies quickly becomes too complicated. And anything that is a habit will become a tendency, even in a crisis—especially in a crisis. Pease expects that Fitch will not continue to hold Tyler without reason. Nor will Fitch arrest him just on account of some fatuous prejudice of Lovelace's, or some conjurer's word.

"I did not bargain to see you here," Fitch starts. "But I have to admit it's convenient. I was about to start toward your place next."

"You would not have been able to enter."

"Why?"

"My wife has locked the door."

"I'll knock."

"She won't answer."

"Why?"

"Because I told her not to. When one is falsely accused of a crime, one must take precautions."

At this last sentence, Pease hears a shuffling in the cell behind him, a new alertness. For the first time, Tyler has heard what this visit is really about. Fitch's eyes, meanwhile, shine brighter at the word "falsely." But he gives nothing away. He nods. Perhaps he is smiling. Pease can't tell. Fitch starts toward the back room, and gestures for Pease to follow. Pease resists the temptation to glance at Tyler—he's afraid Tyler's smirk will be back in place—and trails after the sheriff. In the small, rear room, Fitch shuts the door and sits at the wooden desk. This desk is historic. It belongs to no one and to everyone. It certainly is not original to Simeon Fitch. Ever since the jail has existed the desk has stood in this office. Pease knows, because everyone knows, that the side drawer contains the only record of prisoners held in the Nantucket town jail since its construction in 1707. Fitch taps the top of the desk, moves a sheet of paper, then motions for Pease to pull up a chair. For the moment, Fitch appears uncharacteristically stuck.

"Mr. Lovelace has talked to you," Fitch says.

"He has."

"I was not going to your house to arrest you."

"I know."

"I calculate, and Mr. Lovelace agrees, that being a member of the board earns you some consideration."

"Innocence ought to earn me greater consideration."

Fitch half-smiles, or rather near-smiles. Because what finds its way onto his face is not happiness. "Besides, I just found out something new."

"What is that?"

"I don't think Mr. Lovelace would want me to say."

"I thought the sheriff of Nantucket works for the town of Nantucket."

"That is true."

"Well, I live in the town of Nantucket."

"So does Mr. Lovelace."

"Lovelace is not the only one who lost money."

Fitch gives him a more serious look. "But he's the one who lost the most." Pease knows what Fitch means. He's not talking about gold. He's talking about the man's sense of control. He is trying to say that Lovelace feels not just robbed but undone: threatened, stripped down. His own work place, the institution for which he is responsible, has been compromised. Pease, like many others, lost money, but he did not have to endure the trauma of such a close, quick violation. For a man as bound up as Randolph Lovelace the trespass must have been critically disturbing. Pease understands this; he has from the start. And he has seen the disastrous result: Lovelace's erratic, grasping speculations.

"When you have been hurt," Pease says, "you should not turn around and arbitrarily hurt someone else. All that does is multiply the crime." Pease can tell that Fitch agrees with him, even if he can't say so. "And it will not get you your money back."

Fitch sighs, scratches his chin. "You should talk to Ebenezer Bunker," he says finally; then he looks at the floor. Pease is not sure he heard the sheriff right.

"Bunker? Why?"

Pease leans closer. He is not going to let the sheriff retreat now. Not when he might find out something that finally makes sense.

But the sheriff only waves him off. "Go," Fitch says. "Bunker. That is all I am telling you. The rest you will have to figure out for yourself." As Pease leaves the jail, he sees Tyler has settled back on his stool and is sulking anew: head down, elbows on his knees. The exact position Pease found him in fifteen minutes before.

Ebenezer Bunker, a retired captain, lives on Water Street. Pease does not know Bunker well, but likes him. Everyone does. Bunker keeps his own counsel, a habit Pease respects, probably because he doesn't do it enough himself. As if in reaction to a long, arduous career at sea in which he had to make thousands of decisions and shout orders to men from a dozen different countries—he even commanded a frigate during the war—Bunker's desire now is to live as invisibly as possible. He spends many an hour at his daughter's house on Lily Street, and occasionally is seen inspecting the most recent imports on display in the shop windows on Main. But otherwise he remains quietly and comfortably shut up in his home. From the window of his second story bedroom Bunker enjoys a perfectly clear, close view of the harbor. He likes to study the activity there, but he rarely walks down for a visit. At one time or another he has received invitations from nearly every island congregation—who would not want a respected sea captain in his church?—but Bunker has declined each invitation, if graciously. When pressed, he merely says, *I worship God everyday from my own station*. No one cares to fight him on this point.

When Pease knocks on the captain's door it takes some minutes for Bunker to respond. From the rumpled folds on the older man's face and clotted look in his eyes, it's clear he has been dozing.

"Excuse the interruption, Captain, but the sheriff sent me over here."

A rare look of fear crosses Bunker's face.

"Nothing like that. Don't worry. You are in no trouble."

"I should hope not."

"But I would hazard a guess that you know why he sent me?"

Bunker nods, then glances over Pease's shoulder at the street. His look darkens with concentration, then he relaxes. "Your testimony," Pease says on a chance, "might be the key that unlocks everything."

Of course, Pease has no idea what such testimony might be, but Bunker seems gratified at the younger man's characterization. Clearly, he believes the same. He waves the wigmaker inside. In Bunker's parlor, the captain settles on his favorite chair and encourages Pease to sit beside him. He apologizes that he has nothing to offer but a cold cup of tea. Pease declines. "It is vitally important that I hear anything you can tell me," Pease says. "Anything that can give me an idea. Because at this moment, in certain quarters, accusations are being leveled against innocent men."

"I know," Bunker says sadly. "I've heard. That is why I wanted the sheriff to know."

"I'm glad," Pease says, feverishly curious. He must contain his nervousness and his need. He has to remember to act the part of disinterested facilitator. Otherwise, Bunker might grow suspicious. "So," Pease says, after taking a moment to adjust his breeches. "Please begin."

Bunker is obviously relieved for the chance to do so. On the night of the robbery, the captain explains, he'd returned late from his daughter's and, agitated from the excitement of the festival, did not feel ready to sleep. He changed into his nightshirt, sat in the reading chair in his bedroom, and tried—again—to make his way through Plutarch. He'd read for maybe an hour when he began to doze. He started; read some more; dozed again. Finally, he shut the book and stood, ready to move to bed. He had just turned the knob to extinguish his lamp, when he happened to look out his window and could see—because the moonlight that night seared the harbor so brilliantly—a boat rowed by four men approaching Brant Point.

"You're sure they were headed out?" Pease says.

"Positive. They were leaving the harbor, intent for the Sound."

Bunker watched the men, unable to comprehend why anyone would be rowing a boat at that time of night toward Nantucket Sound. He was less suspicious of than afraid for them. But there was nothing he could do. It was too late to wake anyone who could help, and they were too far off already to pay attention to a danger signal. Besides, they seemed determined to get wherever they were going. "I've watched too many sailors try too many imbecilic maneuvers in my life. Sometimes all one can do is let them. After they fail, they will listen."

"Where do you think they were going?" Pease asks.

"I can't imagine they intended to row all the way back to America. Maybe they were headed for the Vineyard."

"Still a long way and quite dangerous at night, with the shoals."

Bunker nods; his old man's pink-rimmed eyes focus harder on the question. "I guess it's more likely they were aiming for the harbor at Madaket, or for Tuckernuck. Maybe Muskeget."

Pease agrees. "And in that case, somebody out there ought to know something." He asks Bunker to describe the men, but all Bunker can say is that at least two of them wore hats. One of the hatted men sat in the front of the boat. He was quite thin and seemed to be in command. The other hatted man sat in the stern. That one had long, wooly hair hanging down from the beneath the hat, almost to the center of his back.

"Could it have been a woman?" Pease asks.

Bunker shakes his head. "He was too strong. Burly."

"Is there anything else you remember about them?" Pease watches as Bunker thinks for a moment then shakes his head. Four men—two hats—a thin body—a bulky one—wooly, tangled hair. It was something, but not much, to go on.

"So what did you do exactly?"

"Right then?"

"Ever."

"That night I went to sleep is what I did. I went to sleep and completely forgot about them. Then the next day we all heard news about the robbery. First thing I thought to do was go to the bank and tell Mr. Lovelace. I said to him, 'I saw the men who robbed your bank row away from here last night.'"

"What did Lovelace say?"

Bunker blinks heavily and shifts in his chair, his freckled eyelids and hands—the result of too many hours under merciless tropical suns—as always, summoning the idea of disease. "Mr. Lovelace was not impressed at all. He frowned at me, actually, as if I was giving him a problem instead of a clue, instead of a hope. He said I must be mistaken about the men. He said, 'We think we know who did it.'"

Bunker pressed Lovelace to at least investigate what he saw. It was too late, after all, for anyone to be rowing away from Nantucket for honest reasons. And it must have been close to the hour the bank was robbed.

"What did he say to that?"

"He only became more angry. He told me he had no intention of looking into it, because they already knew who the guilty party was, and they didn't want the facts to get muddled."

"Who is 'they'?"

"He didn't say. But he kept repeating it: 'We know who did it.'"

Moreover, Lovelace told Bunker not to inform the sheriff about the four men. If Bunker did that, Lovelace might have to take legal action against captain "for the sake of the bank." The threat scared Bunker off for a couple weeks, but finally—with the rumors about the robbery getting wilder and with news that Joseph Tyler had been arrested—he couldn't take it anymore. Just that morning he told the sheriff what he'd seen.

"What did the sheriff do?"

"Nothing, sadly. He didn't get angry with me like Lovelace did, but he did not seem terribly pleased either. He just looked at me peculiarly, as if I had told him a joke he could not understand."

"And then?"

"He nodded and said thank you."

"Did he say he would take any action?"

"He said the same thing Lovelace did: They knew who did it, and all the men were on-island."

"He's not going to investigate the boat?"

"No," Bunker says. "It's clear to me the sheriff isn't going to do anything. At least he hasn't, best that I know."

But he did do something, Pease thinks. *He told me.*

Late that week, as soon as he has put away several pressing matters of business, Pease rides out to the western end of the island, where he looks around for a day and spies nothing unusual. He asks the few residents at Madaket if anyone saw four men enter the harbor on the night of June 20 or early the next morning. Four strangers, two with hats, one with long hair. Lots of head shaking; no saw anything. A couple days later, Pease pays a man to sail him to Tuckernuck and then to Muskeget. He has some hopes for Tuckernuck: the bigger of the two islands that sit just northwest of Nantucket and home to a few hearty, isolationist families. But he finds no evidence there of a clandestine boat landing, and his description of the men rings perfectly hollow to the five or six people he consults. Meanwhile, Muskeget—a meager unoccupied strip of sand—reveals nothing either.

Running out of workable options, Pease leaves two days later, July 14, for Martha's Vineyard. He lands in Edgartown midday, and almost immediately information begins to break for him. He meets a man named Snow who lives near the harbor and who, on June 20, received a preposterously large offer from a stranger to rent his fishing skiff for twenty-four hours. The stranger refused to say why he wanted to rent the boat, but the sum he offered calmed any suspicions Snow might have entertained. Pease asks for and receives a detailed description of this man—"blonde and pointy, all knees and elbows, skin pockmarked, blue eyes with a hungry look in them"—a description that does not match anyone who works for the Nantucket Bank; certainly not Joseph Tyler. It is Snow's strong impression that the man had arrived on Martha's Vineyard only that morning, but he can't remember whether the man had literally said this.

"Arrived from where?" Pease asks.

"Based on the sound of him, I would guess the Cape."

It does not take much more investigating before Pease discovers that a man matching the description Snow gave, as well as three traveling companions, arrived on the morning of June 20 on the *Mary Morgan*, a ship from Falmouth that makes regular junkets to the Vineyard and Nantucket. Moreover, on the morning of June 21, the same four men left the Vineyard on the *Elizabeth Hendley*, a schooner bound first for Falmouth and then for Chatham.

Pease spends the night and one more day on the Vineyard waiting to board a ship bound for Falmouth. On July 16, he pays his way onto the *Belted Will* and by that evening is in a tavern called the Maiden Arms, buying a tankard of ale for one Caleb Dawes. Dawes, who Pease estimates as twenty-five or so, has heavy shoulders and thick forearms, but Pease would not call him "burly." And while he sports a messy bush of a beard, one that runs all the way up both sides of his face, his hair is not long and "wooly" but cut fairly short. In fact, based on the thinning fur on Dawes's forehead, Pease estimates the man will be bald before he turns forty. It's not Dawes's appearance but his reputation that pointed him out to Pease. Three different Falmouth citizens told him they had heard talk of Dawes's involvement with a bank robbery. "He's not smart enough to do that himself," they all said. "Supposedly he was helping Isaiah Morse." Pease asked for a description of Morse. The descriptions he heard all fit: "bony," "yellow haired," "blue-eyed," "smallpox face." When Pease asked where he might find either Dawes or Morse, he heard the same thing from all three people: *Morse is gone. No one's seen him for weeks. But Dawes is always at the Maiden Arms.*

To Pease's surprise, the very first time he pulls out an accusation and aims it at the well-lubricated Dawes, the man shivers. His mouth gapes. He sits shocked and silent for a single long moment. Then he weeps. Dawes pleads for mercy. "I just want the money returned," Pease explains; then he adds: "And I want you to explain to Sheriff Simeon Fitch exactly how you were able to pull off this robbery. After that you can go dancing in Philadelphia for all I care." Lovelace, Pease knows, will probably want a good deal more out of the robber than that, but Pease doesn't say so.

"But I don't have the money," Dawes explains. "Morse does." Morse disappeared with the other two thieves—men named John Norman and Patrick Lynde—and carried off the money with them. Dawes can't say where, because Morse refused to tell him. But Morse did say he would return by the end of the week. At that time, Dawes would finally get paid for his work.

"You have not gotten paid yet for helping to rob a bank?"

Dawes shakes his head heavily, his forehead thick with drink. "That was never the plan."

"You mean you men are not going to spend the money you stole?"

Now Dawes looks at Pease as if the wigmaker has a hearing problem. "We aren't supposed to spend it. That was the agreement."

"The agreement with whom?"

"That's hard to explain, because I was never there."

"Where?"

"But he did repeat it when we met him later."

"Met who?"

Dawes licks his lips. His moist eyes try to bring Pease into new focus. He's confused, Pease decides. He thinks he's already told me. Finally Dawes says, "Morse worked it out with that fellow from Nantucket."

Pease sits up straighter. He adjusts his coat. He orders another tankard for Dawes. He has not yet sipped from his own. He waits until the tavern maid sets the ale on the table, then pushes it to Dawes with a flourish and a warm clap on the shoulder. "Now you have my attention, Mr. Dawes," Pease says. "Maybe you should just begin at the beginning."

Dawes sighs tiredly—the weeping and pleading have worn him out. He glances at the door, as if considering making a run for it, but he gives up the idea. He is a man, Pease sees, inclined to take the path of least resistance. Which perhaps explains how he was convinced to participate in the first place. Dawes tells Pease that he'd worked with Lynde several times: minor break-ins, petty theft. "Just for fun and a little pocket money." Nothing real. Until recently, he'd held a job: working at Falmouth harbor, unloading ships. Lynde knew Norman, who worked with Morse. Morse corralled both men to help him on a substantial robbery, a "timely affair." But he wanted one more man. Lynde suggested Dawes, and suddenly Dawes was conspiring to carry out major larceny. When Pease hears Dawes describe the other men, he knows he has his evidence. Lynde, he finds out, is squat as a toad and broad across the shoulders, with long, stringy red hair. Both Morse and Lynde wore hats on the night of the robbery.

The group met regularly to plan and practice the heist. At their first meeting, Morse explained how the operation had come about in the first place. One evening in early May, at a tavern on the other end of Falmouth, Morse had been approached by a man who said he was from Nantucket and that he represented certain "interests" on the island, interests who—for reasons he refused to explain— wanted to see the Nantucket Bank robbed. The man had asked around and learned of Morse's reputation. The Nantucketer wanted to hire Morse to carry out the robbery but under strict guidelines. First, the robbery must be accomplished late on the evening of June 20. No other date could be considered. Second, Morse and his henchmen—he could recruit as many as three assistants—would have to leave the island immediately after the job was done. They must get to the mainland as soon as possible, certainly no later than the following evening. Third, they must take the money and secure it somewhere on the Cape. They must not spend a penny. Then, on the morning of August 9, Morse would meet the man in the street behind the tobacconist's shop in Falmouth harbor. Morse would give the man the stolen $20,000. In return for his services—and for his strict adherence to the guidelines—Morse would receive $5000, plus enough to give each assistant $1000.

The Nantucketer gave Morse one week to consider his offer. In exactly seven days he would return to the tavern to get his answer. If Morse agreed, keys to the bank as well as a detailed map of the building and a current map of Nantucket town would be provided. It should be, the Nantucketer claimed, the least complicated, least dangerous job of Morse's career. If Morse declined, there would be no hard feelings, but the Nantucketer would immediately begin looking for someone else. Morse would not get a second chance at the easiest $5,000 he would ever make.

"So Morse agreed to rob a bank but use none of the profit?"

Dawes shrugs sloppily. "Who turns down $5000? I wouldn't."

"Did you ever learn about the Nantucketer?"

"Did I ever learn about him?" Dawes repeats, as if the question makes no sense. His big, glistening hazel eyes wander for a moment. "No, I never learned anything about him. But I did see him once."

"Where?"

"Here."

"Where?"

"*Here.*"

"Here? You met the Nantucketer here?"

"There, really." Dawes points to a dark corner table half the room away at which sits a man with flaring eyebrows and a soaring forehead. The man is busying himself with an enormous bowl of chowder. Next to his elbow is a tankard, but he pays no attention to it. He eats like a starved person.

"At one point the Nantucketer started to get nervous—this was probably four or five days before the robbery. He wanted to get all of us together, just once. He wanted to see us. If we didn't agree, the deal was off. So of course we came. We took that table over there." He points again, needlessly. The man with the chowder has noticed their attention. Pease looks back at his own table and hopes Dawes will follow his lead. Slowly Dawes's gaze comes back. "Maybe a half hour later the Nantucketer came in."

"How did you recognize him?"

"I didn't. Morse did. Morse recognized him right away." Now Dawes takes a long healthy draught from his ale, as if this is his due. Pease waits. Finished with his swallow, Dawes draws his forearm across his lips. "You'd know him if you ever saw him. I mean—if you'd seen him once already. You can't mistake this man for anyone else." When Pease asks about this, Dawes has to think for several seconds, which Pease can't understand. Finally, Dawes continues. "He's on the tall side, for certain, but he walks oddly—like one leg is shorter than the other—so you don't pay much attention to his height. You just watch him hobble. The hobble gives him away. Another thing is his hair."

"What about it?"

"He has bright yellow hair, brighter than Morse's, and very fine. It doesn't actually match his face, but there you go. That's his hair." Pease asks Dawes to clarify. "Well, the man's skin is regular dark, almost negro. But he can't be a negro, because he has no other negro looks. Not the nose or the lips. I thought at first maybe he was a Spaniard, but he sounds regular English when he talks. The other thing is that he has a deep red bruise beneath his left eye— it's more like purple—the kind of mark you see on a brawler. But the Nantucketer is no brawler. The Nantucketer is a gentleman."

"How do you know?"

"You can tell. Can't you tell a gentleman?"

Pease shrugs. He understands Dawes's point, but he also knows from his own experience that people's backgrounds are not so simple a matter as one might think. What one sees is not always what one has—or what one is. And, besides, how one person defines a gentleman does not always agree with how someone else might. He is actually dubious of anyone who earns that distinction in Caleb Dawes's eyes.

"How old is he?"

"Ohh," Dawes says importantly. He pauses, licks his lips. "That's hard to say, Mr. Pease. He is such a collection of contrary looks you cannot really tell. He might be thirty. He might be fifty-five. Parts of him seem young; parts of him seem old."

This is a ruinously unhelpful statement, even though Dawes seems proud of it. "You still have not explained," Pease says, "why he needed to see you men."

"Didn't I?" Dawes looks genuinely surprised. He takes a quick sip. "That's easy. He wanted to threaten us."

"Why?"

"Oh, you know. He was getting worried about the money. He was worried we wouldn't return it. That's natural, isn't it? He looks around at all of us. He stares at us with his dark eye. He says that if any part of the $20,000 is missing when he collects, he's going to call down the law on us and make sure we are hanged. And if we simply disappear with the treasure, he will pay whatever it takes to have us tracked and found out and killed. This country inn't so big as ye think, he says."

"He said it like that?"

"I don't know. Not just like that. But that's what he said."

"And how did you reply?"

"How did we reply? What do you think? We told him he'd get all of it back. You think I want to be killed?"

Pease keeps his pistol at his side throughout the ride back from the Cape. But he does not cock the weapon until the merchant ship *Amelia* drops its plank at the wharf and his prisoner takes his first step forward to disembark. Dawes's primary occupation throughout the ride has been to scratch at and pet his furry face. Now, however, he is still, almost solemn.

"Remember," Pease says into Dawes's ear, "if you tell the sheriff what you know, I will insist that he redefine you as a witness for the investigation. But if you say nothing, he will lock you up for as long as necessary. And then we will keep you here until we have what we need to prove you guilty."

Dawes's account is truly scandalous. Fitch has to hear it. Pease thinks he knows everyone on the island with any influence at all—he certainly knows all the men with money—but this Nantucketer sounds like no one Pease has ever seen. Fitch will be forced to investigate. Pease wishes he could have snared Morse. Morse could tell far more than even Dawes has, especially where the money went. But Pease could not just go searching for Morse willy-nilly throughout the Cape. If he had he would have risked losing Dawes. So instead of leaving, Pease spent a week with Dawes at the Maiden Arms, waiting for Morse to return. In exchange for Dawes's compliance, Pease agreed to cover all their expenses; but at the same time, he kept his gun at the ready. "If you make any attempt to break from me," Pease said several times, "I'll take you to the sheriff here in Falmouth and have you imprisoned for the crime you have already confessed to." Dawes was too scared and too trapped to run, but Morse never showed. After waiting for eight days in Falmouth, Pease couldn't wait any longer, certainly not as long as August 9. He would just have to return with Fitch in August, so they could spy the Nantucketer for themselves. On the other side of the ledger is the fact that only a day or two after nabbing Dawes, Pease's rash began to shrink noticeably. Last time he checked, Pease would almost call it disappeared. He is as unsure of the cause of the rash's remediation as he is of its coming, but he certainly accepts it as an omen.

For a second, Pease considers the small crowd that has assembled on the wharf. Not even a dozen people. Curiosity seekers? Relatives of the seamen? *If they only knew what I'm bringing back, there would be hundreds*. He turns. He needs to say one more thing to his companion. "If you run, I will shoot you in the back right here. It might surprise a few people, but when I tell them I just shot the man who robbed Nantucket Bank, they will crown me king."

Dawes shudders at the word *back*. He blinks quickly but says nothing. Eager to talk when Pease first met him, Dawes has become increasingly taciturn. And much more sober. Even so, Pease does not actually believe Dawes will run. Why agree to travel all the way to the island only to run once he arrived? And run where? There is nowhere to go. If Dawes was going to run he would have done it on the Cape. If he runs now, on this little bow of an island, he will quickly find himself trapped, out of room. But still, Pease cannot afford to take any chances. He has to pull out the threat. After all, Pease has no authority in this case save for the power of personal suasion, save for the moral imperative of catching and punishing the men who stole $20,000 and a town's sense of itself.

If Dawes had known how thoroughly the wigmaker had acted on his own, he might never have agreed to come at all. Pease cannot even be sure what the sheriff will do with Dawes, but finally a confession—a confession rich in specific, irrefutable details—cannot be ignored by any lawman. The power of truth is what Pease is counting on, because it's all he has. It's unfortunate, Pease muses, while examining the idlers on the wharf, that the sheriff is not a Congregationalist; or better yet a Papist or an Anglican, a man bred on the notion of good form, of form itself containing sacral value and dismissible only at great risk. In that case, there would be no question. Because good form demands that Caleb Dawes be locked up until his story is sorted out and squared away. Without form to count on, the case will depend on the individual instincts of Fitch. Sheriff Fitch is a practical man, of course—and, at least in the past, a habitually honest one—but like Lovelace he is also a follower of the infernally vague "inner light." And who knows what an unformed, undefined light will say to a person; who knows what bad decisions it might justify. If a man actually believes God is speaking to him, does he have the option to deny even the most monstrous proposition?

Pease swats away bad thoughts. Have hope. *Have hope.* There is every reason to believe that this terrible, divisive episode is ending along with his rash. Not that the end will come without detritus, of course. Joseph Tyler's reputation is in shreds, and his careers at both the bank and the slaughterhouse are over. Tyler could simply take his wife and leave the island, but not in her condition, and not when this is the only place she has ever lived. Pease wonders if it's not just Tyler's career but his marriage that is at an end.

Pease knows his own reputation has been battered as well. While his Congregationalist allies all hurried to say they didn't believe the news about him—and even a few Papist and Negro and English women assured him they still wanted his wigs—every Quaker he encountered refused to speak to him. They cut him with their glares or simply turned on him and walked in another direction. Every place he went in town he felt half the eyes hailing him as a beleaguered hero while the other half measured him as one would a man sentenced to hang.

The day before he left for the Cape, Pease heard the news about the board of directors. Israel Purrington, a member of the Society of Friends and Lovelace's handpicked choice, was voted in as his replacement. This meant that six of the board's seven members were now Quakers. And rumors were adrift that Thomas Ballard—an indifferent Methodist and a Federalist; also a ship owner and respected capitalist—was somehow involved in the robbery along with Pease and Tyler. Ballard could not be fired from his own company, but he certainly could be kicked off the board of the Nantucket Bank. He would be replaced, the rumors said, as soon as Lovelace found the right man for the job.

The right Quaker, that is.

Meanwhile, Simeon Fitch had arrested two other people: Peter Pyrs, a twenty-two year old workman who made pitch for John Look, and Phebe Swain, nineteen, a seamstress. Supposedly these two had abetted the thieves in their impossibly invisible getaway. How Pyrs and Swain could have done so, no one knew. And, in fact, no one could explain why two people who were not in any way intimates—and perhaps did not even know each other—could have cooperated in such an affair. Thus speculation flew about furiously. *Maybe they know each other all too well, thank you.* If Pease were not in such a hurry to get to the Vineyard he would have gone to Fitch and demanded to know what Fitch thought he was doing. Pease happened to know both young people and stood convinced that neither could be involved. Phebe Swain's family was too poor to afford any of Pease's wigs, or much of anything else, but since they belonged to the Congregationalist church Pease saw them regularly and had long admired the girl for her ingenuousness. Phebe Swain could no more abet a bank robbery than she could calculate the circumference of Mercury.

Peter Pyrs had been on the island for six years and in that time had proved himself a model of industry. He had no education but an immense amount of Welshmen's energy. He started out doing any variety of odd jobs for whoever would pay him, one of whom turned out to be John Look, owner of the ship works at the harbor. Look was impressed enough to give Pyrs a job at his factory. Since, Pyrs has been made foreman, joined the Federalists, and become engaged to Clara White, a handsome girl from a family of loud and unapologetic Deists who run a dairy farm out toward Capaum Pond. When he'd heard of the engagement, Pease's first thought was that with Clara's beauty and Pyrs's industry, he would soon have a new client for his wigs. Why Pyrs would put his burgeoning future and his reputation for honest work on the line Pease cannot imagine. In fact, Pyrs wouldn't. The charges, whatever their specifics, are as gossamer as any against himself.

Before Pease left, the whole island seemed on the verge of exploding with latent grudges, hurt feelings, and outraged principles.

It was perfectly clear that for the Quakers the theft only revealed the inherent subversiveness of Congregationalism; that the only way to bring the island back to its prelapsarian state was to do what should have been done long ago: make Quakerism Nanucket's officially endorsed sect. Congregationalists, sensing Quaker anger and reeling under the Friends' haute, smelled persecution afoot and began gossiping about drastic responses: boycotting Quaker businesses, locking Quaker workers out of Congregationalist factories, refusing Quaker money in Congregationalist shops. Jared Fanning, a carpenter, had begun broadcasting the opinion that the Congregationalists should write to President Washington asking him to bring a militia to Nantucket just as he had to Pennsylvania the summer before. "If he can use them to collect a tax," Fanning jawed, his face as red from rum as from worked-up righteousness, "why can't he use them to protect the first amendment to the glorious constitution of these most dear thirteen United States of America?" Most Congregationalists agreed with Fanning on principle, but no one believed President Washington could possibly care enough about Nantucket Island to want to send a militia there. *No*, they told the garrulous carpenter, *we'll settle this our own way*.

Standing on the wharf, Dawes looks around as if he expects to recognize someone or catch a signal. Perhaps, Pease thinks, Dawes is merely struck by the sight of Nantucket in daylight. Then at once, Dawes shudders; he looks back expectantly, like a dog awaiting orders. "It's a bit of a walk," Pease says. "But not bad. The fourth street up is Federal. There we turn left. Then I'll tell you what to do." Dawes nods as if he recognizes the street name—he probably does, Pease realizes—and starts, neither hurrying nor dawdling, and with no further prompting from Pease.

After Federal they find Main. They follow Main to Pine, where they turn left and before long reach High Street, a tiny stump of a rue connecting Pine and Pleasant streets. The jail is on the left, just a few steps from the intersection. As soon as he decided to leave Falmouth, Pease sent a letter ahead to Fitch specifying when he would be on-island and explaining that he was bringing with him a "consequential witness." He urged Fitch to leave himself unscheduled for the morning of July 26. But now, nearing eleven-fifteen on that day, Pease tries the handle on the jail door only to find it locked. He calls out for Fitch, then for Pope. He knocks—hard—and then waits, but he hears no one moving inside. He knocks again. Then a third time. Same result. Pease glances embarrassed at Dawes, but Dawes seems perfectly uninterested, as if Fitch's disappearance is to be expected.

"I might have to take you home for dinner first," Pease says, only half-kidding. But Dawes reacts with neither a smile nor a scowl. He yawns. Not knowing what else to do, Pease brings Dawes back to the corner of High and Pine. It is then, glancing back the way they came, that Pease sees two men, all the way down at the corner, idling their way toward him. Their eyes are trained on Pease, but they do not wave or signal. They do not appear to be in a hurry. They do not talk to each other either, but carry an air of having already talked at length, of having talked exhaustively. Of being done with any more talking. One of the men, taller and thicker in the shoulders, wears the costume of his profession: a powdered peruke—all white, with obviously phony curls, not intended to fool anyone; a dark blue cutaway with matching waistcoat; a ruffled shirt, the sleeves of which extend inches beyond the arms of his coat; dark breeches that end just past the knee; bright white stockings and polished buckled shoes.

The other man, not nearly as tall and about half as wide, dresses far more commonly. He doesn't hide his wiry salt and pepper hair under a wig but pulls it back in a rope tied with a black ribbon. The gray muttonchops are as unruly as ever across his cheeks, and his nose is as beaked as if someone punched him. He wears no coat or waistcoat, only an unruffled white shirt that remains half tucked into the waist of his coarse brown trousers. The trousers themselves disappear into a pair of tall musty-dark boots, as if the man has just come from shooting fowl at Long Pond. But Pease knows this man does not hunt anything except an occasional glass of ginger beer and a game of loo. It means nothing that the man is dressed this way—he dresses the same always. The taller man, meanwhile, could change into a different outfit everyday and not run out of clothes for a month. They almost seem from different branches of humankind, and Pease finds it hard to imagine them seated together, on a bench at the Meeting House, eyes closed, listening to some man or woman speak of their inmost revelations. Pease dismisses the cranky notion that the two have lain in wait for him. He's merely happy they are arrived, that they apparently read his letter and paid attention to its instructions.

When Fitch and Lovelace are only feet away, Pease says, "Believe it or not, gentlemen, we are about to get to the bottom of this affair."

Fitch's expression is off-kilter, a mixture of surprise and boredom. "That will be a wonder."

"You received my letter," Pease says.

Fitch hesitates.

"And you read it?"

Fitch smiles, his lips pressed tight. "Every word."

Lovelace, meanwhile, stays silent and angles guarded, wary glances at Dawes. Under the hood of this closed expression, he scrutinizes the thief while at the same time he seems disgusted, even revolted, by the man. Perhaps Pease is only imagining it, but Lovelace actually looks nervous, as if he's trying to restrain one great irrepressible twitch.

"Sheriff," Pease starts, "this is Mr. Caleb Dawes of Falmouth, Massachusetts. He is one of four men who robbed Nantucket Bank on June 20."

This is not news to Fitch, of course. Pease's letter explained why the sheriff needed to meet Dawes. Yet only now, after Pease says what he says, does Fitch begin to study Dawes with serious interest. The smile is gone. For the first time in this encounter, Fitch looks like a lawman. "So that's his claim, is it?" Fitch says, in a low voice. Lovelace says nothing; he only looks on, quietly agitated.

"He can tell you all about it, Simeon. He can tell you every last detail—and some I chose to leave out of my letter."

Pease hopes and expects that the barb will snag exactly where it needs to in Fitch's imagination. But Fitch looks unchanged; if anything, he looks more doubtful. For his part, Lovelace starts as if furious and turns away, too disgusted to stand a second more of this conversation. Fitch digs inside the long pocket of his trousers and retrieves a small metal circle attached to which are three long skeleton keys. He motions to the jailhouse door. "Well, Mr. Caleb Dawes, let us head inside. And then we'll decide what needs doing."

Pease is not surprised when Fitch tells him to wait outside, but he is taken aback by the sheriff's explanation: "We don't let a suspect's friends stick around when we question him."

"I am no more his friend than you are," Pease responds, to which Fitch smiles sadly and Lovelace snorts, a reaction Pease cannot fathom. But as he waits outside the jail and thinks about what Dawes is telling the sheriff and the banker, he feels a growing confidence in the outcome. Surely Fitch and Lovelace will see how impossible it is for Dawes to have fabricated all those details, details that seamlessly explain how the magical robbery was pulled off. And how can the two men not be intrigued by Dawes's tale of the tall, mysterious islander with the dark skin, blonde hair, and purple bruise beneath his eye? How can Fitch not see the need to hold Dawes until a trial can be arranged? How can the sheriff not want to head to the Cape to bring back Morse and Lynde and Norman; to catch the conspiring Nantucketer; most important, to retrieve the missing $20,000? Despite his promise to Dawes, Pease knows the thief will need to remain behind bars for a considerable interval. A competent investigation will take weeks, and a trial cannot be expected before fall. But at least, he thinks, the tide can turn on all the preposterous accusations. *At least we can stop hating each other*.

Pease does not know what to do with himself or how long this will take. He does not know what, if anything, is required of him. He considers heading home for dinner, but is astonished when—only ten minutes after the jailhouse door closed behind the thief, the sheriff, and the banker—it opens again and Caleb Dawes emerges. Dawes blinks, looks bewildered. He steps onto High Street and looks in both directions.

"Where are you going?" Pease says.

"I don't know."

"Where are you supposed to be going?"

This time Dawes answers more strenuously. "I don't know. Home, I guess. Can you get me on a ship back?"

"What are you talking about? You have to talk to the sheriff."

"They said I could go."

"But you committed a crime. A crime here."

Dawes shrugs, looks at the jail door and back at Pease. "They said I could go."

"That is impossible."

"He's the sheriff, Mr. Pease, not you."

Pease does not even look at Dawes anymore but heads inside. The jailhouse is stuffy and midsummer humid. Joseph Tyler is asleep—or at least silent—on a blanket on the floor, the perspiration evident around his neck. Peter Pyrs is stuck in the cell with Tyler. Short, black-bearded, and serious of eye, Pyrs leans against the wall, hands in his pockets. In cell two, a wilted Phebe Swain sits and indifferently picks at some knitting. Pease is surprised they even allow her that, but he has no time to stop and discuss the arrangements. Lovelace and Fitch are in the back room; the door to the room is cracked. Pease barrels through to find Fitch leaning dismally in his chair, staring at his hands. Lovelace stands above him, bent, his mouth close to Fitch's head. Both men look at him at once, a breadth of alertness in their eyes. Alertness but not surprise.

"Aren't you going to lock him up?" Pease asks the sheriff.

Lovelace answers. "What that man says is irrelevant. We already know who did it."

"He can take you to the money—or at least to the man who knows where the money is hidden."

"Dawes is a liar. He has no money."

"But he knows the man who does."

"We don't know anything about that."

"Did he not explain to you about Isaiah Morse?"

Lovelace blinks.

"You are not going to try to find the Nantucketer?"

Lovelace's expression changes to something more aloof. More studied. More peculiar. "What Nantucketer?"

"The one who gave them the keys to the bank!"

As he's speaking, going through useless motions of argument with a man who will not be moved, Pease realizes he needs to reconsider the entire situation. He must think anew over the fact of Lovelace's fixation on Joseph Tyler. He has not understood until now just how baseless that fixation is. And he sees something else too: The picture of the blonde man, drawn by Dawes. The too young, too fine, too bright hair. Hair that does not match his face or his skin. As if he's taken his own hair and dyed it. *Or worn someone else's hair.* Pease wonders if it could have been one of his very own creations, sold to the Nantucketer's mother or sister or wife. He might know the wig if anyone could show it to him. In that case, he knows the woman. And in that case, he knows the man. He may have been inside the Nantucketer's own house. And if the hair was a disguise, why not the bruise mark? Why not the dark skin? Why not the crippled gait?

"Sheriff?" he says, for no particular reason. Fitch looks at him woefully, then he begins to shake his head. *Don't talk,* the movement seems to say. *Not here. Not now.* Fitch looks away. "We can't trust a liar," the sheriff mutters.

"We have no need of that rube," Lovelace adds. "Or any of his friends. If they are truly criminals then they are as unreliable as he." Lovelace nods at Fitch. "And I do not think the sheriff wants to hold him without any proof."

"No, of course not. Not when you are already holding three persons without proof."

A dark flame rises in Lovelace's eye. "That's another matter altogether. Altogether different. You do not know what proof we may or may not have. You are not privy to our investigation. And I don't think you realize how biased you are."

Pease erupts in a laugh. It wheezes its way through his body with hot, hopeless pain; all the way through until there's nothing but hiccups left. Then nothing but faint, oniony breath, pasting his mouth. Odd, because he hasn't eaten an onion in weeks.

Lovelace does nothing but stare at him, unmoved. When the fit is finished, the banker continues. "And you certainly do not realize the extent to which you yourself are implicated." Lovelace shifts his position, stands taller, as tall as he really is. "We have been good to you, Pease. Both the sheriff and I have been abundantly, foolishly patient. More patient than you know. We have deferred to your standing as a board member and as a man of business." Lovelace speaks that last word as if it is a spoiled piece of fruit. "But you are no longer a member of the board. And I don't know if or when you will be able to resume your business. And, besides, there comes a time when patience simply runs out."

Lovelace turns expectantly to Fitch, who only scrutinizes his boots. The sheriff does not meet the banker's eye. But finally he must. Finally he does. And, finally, Fitch stands. He picks the ring of skeleton keys off the desk and gestures to the other room, where the cells are. Pease recognizes, but cannot tolerate the character of apology on the sheriff's bony face. None of this, he realizes sadly, should surprise him.

He thinks of Dawes. Has the thief started for the wharf? Has he already arranged a passage back? But using what for money? He thinks of the $20,000 itself, hidden somewhere on Cape Cod—or perhaps removed from the Cape completely. Perhaps it is headed somewhere else as fast as humanly possible, stolen twice by Isaiah Morse and his henchmen. Would the island ever see that money again? The bulk of its accumulated fortune? Or would Nantucket have to start all over, earn the treasure back, duplicate its own past efforts at prosperity? How long would that take? And what would the island look like then, when it came?

KING PHILIP'S WAR

Nantucket Island, 1823

When I hit him, he bends but does not go down. That's not fair. I hit him with my whole shoulder behind it. And my elbow. And my back. Now my hand stings. I'm not sure if this is on account of his bony face or if my paw just isn't staunch enough. But when he does not go down I've got to do something or risk getting whipped right back. Will Gibbs is not strong—he's two years younger than me—but he's shifty. He will make a decision while you are just standing there. So before he can recover from the surprise of my punch, I lunge for his middle and tackle him. We go down together—belly to belly—in the sandy grass, but because I am taller and have leverage, and he is still surprised, I'm able to lock his arms behind him. I'm not sure what for yet. It's not like I can keep Will Gibbs in a lock permanently. He's small and too nervous, like a kid rabbit. But all I can think now is that I don't want him to attack me. So there is nothing to do but grapple.

I expect the skin beneath his white shirt to feel different and maybe smell different too; I expect his muscles to have a formation unknown to white people. Leaner maybe, and stringier, with its energy going across rather than straight up and down. But I don't smell anything at all—although that might be because I am struggling so hard to keep the lock on—and he feels like any ten-year-old, heaving and bucking. Maybe his hair smells different. It is coarse and dark compared to mine. It almost has to smell different. It doesn't smell bad, necessarily. It smells like an empty barn. One with the horse gone and the hogs and the goats. There is no more dung on the floor mucking up the place; there's no slop whatsoever; but there is still a smell: old and earthy, with an overcoat of cobweb, must, sawdust, and dirt. That's what Will Gibbs's hair smells like. Which is funny because Will Gibbs's father doesn't own a barn. He is a fisherman. The two of them live in a shanty only five minutes or so from Madaket beach.

I figure Will Gibbs's smell would be worse if he were whole Indian, but he is only half. I've never gotten close enough to smell Jesse Gibbs, and I don't want to, but I expect he is more pungent. Jesse Gibbs is full Indian, supposedly the last full-blooded Indian on the island, but everybody knows Will Gibbs's mother was white. They say she was Irish—a house girl, just off a boat, working for one of the businessmen in Nantucket town—though my father, when he's sore, bellows at me to stop wasting my time with that "Portuguese castoff." Father calls Will Gibbs Portuguese not because he knows anything secret about Will Gibbs's background, but because the boy's skin, on account of his mother, is almost honey-colored, like a Portuguese sailor. When Jesse Gibbs first appeared with his fishing smack and his three year old son on Madaket beach there was no Mrs. Gibbs—my father and Mr. Daggett swear to that. Either she died or she ran off. Father says, "What would *you* do if you just gave birth to an Indian child?" Jesse doesn't talk about her—or anything. And no one's about to ask him. The hut they live in used to belong to someone else, a white man named Hale. Father says Hale liked to get swollen drunk at one of the taverns in Nantucket town and then navigate his smack around the face of the island to return home. One day he didn't make it. A year later, Jesse Gibbs showed up and took over Hale's hut.

Will Gibbs shoots his knee into my stomach, and that does it. I can't breathe. I can't even feel my chest. I fall to the ground and stare dizzily up at the water-gray clouds. My stomach feels like it has swallowed my lung and cannot vomit it out. Unless it vomits it out, the lung will stay there. But I don't have time to work my own way out of my own pain. Will Gibbs grabs the front of my shirt with both hands, pulls me up, and shoves me back down, as if trying to hurt my head against a rock. But there's no rock behind me. Then he slaps me once, and as bad as it stings, it lets me breathe. I can move. I stop Will Gibbs's hand just before he slaps a second time, and I yank him down. Clambering to my knees, I manage to get his arm behind his back. *You're done, Will Gibbs.* I push him into the dirt—that gritty, sandy kind of dirt we have out here—and rub his cheek in it. I could, if I wanted, make him taste it.

Will Gibbs goes limp. Stopped. No muscles. I think he is dead.

I think I have killed him. But that's not possible. I let go his arm and jump off.

What?" I say. "What's happened?" Will Gibbs says nothing. I think his eyes are closed. "What happened?" I say. "Get up." Then Will Gibbs starts laughing. That does it.

"What do you think is so funny? That I whipped you?"

"No."

"What then?"

He's still cheek-down against the dirt. If he weren't laughing, and if his eyes weren't open, I would think he was getting ready to sleep. Then he rolls over, puts his hands behind his head, and looks at me. It's easy to see the Irish woman in Will Gibbs: the freckles on both sides of his nose, the shallow eye sockets, the face that isn't long and flat like an Indian's but rounder. Most of all, you can see it in his eyes. Jesse Gibbs's eyes are dark and uniform. They take in a lot but do not give out much, which is one reason I don't go anywhere near Jesse Gibbs. Will Gibbs's eyes are a color more like hazel, although there is not one word or one color to describe them. They look like someone took mud, urinated on it, swirled it around, let it dry for two and a half days, then folded in minced weeds and a cup of water and brought that concoction to boil just as it was hit with breakaway sunshine. Will Gibbs's eyes are a color I've never seen before, and they're never the same from one day to the next. Will Gibbs's eyes make his face look like a lunatic's—or a saint's. And the thing about saints and lunatics is that you never know what they are thinking.

Right now Will Gibbs is smiling at me. That's another difference. Jesse Gibbs never smiles, but when he gives off any kind of expression it goes up and down; it cracks his face lengthwise. Will Gibbs's smile rolls around his face the way a smile is supposed to—the way white people smile—although with those lunatic eyes his smiles can be scary sometimes, or confusing. Like now. He smiles like he knows something about me, and like I do not know anything about him, when I would say the opposite is true. What can Will Gibbs possibly know about me? I stand there looking at the smile and grow angrier. It is a smile with mind behind it.

"You still haven't told me," I say.

"I'm laughing because I think that if I had a knife you'd be dead."

"Nothing doing."

"Say yes, Owen. One second I am face first on the ground and can't move. The next I am free to move any way I want. Free to put a knife in your leg."

"You don't have a knife."

"I could."

"No, you could not."

"How do you think my father guts his fish?"

"I didn't know that he did."

"Shows how much you know."

"Look, Will Gibbs, you better shush. I am two years older." He chuckles, but doesn't say anything back. "Plus, your father would not let you run off with one of his knives."

"Is that what you think?"

"Yes."

"You know my father that well?"

"I know him well enough."

Will Gibbs gives me a long, slow smile. Then he reaches into the side of his boot, extending his fingers all the way down to the arch of his foot. He pulls out a short, single edged knife. It has a midget handle, dark as old leather. The blade is shorter than the handle is. He holds it up like a birthday present and smiles again.

"That knife can't hurt anybody," I say.

"Are you sure?"

"You must have stolen it from him."

The smile disappears. "Father gave it to me."

"When?"

"Last year."

"Liar."

"I am not."

"Why would he give you a knife?"

"I don't know. Because some boy might try to beat me?"

That makes me mad. "I was not trying to beat you. I was just paying you back for what you said." Will Gibbs has decided to be a history teacher lately. Problem is his history is all wrong. Today he told me that the English on Nantucket used to make Indians their slaves by telling lies about how they stole things. I was not going to stand for that libel. Everyone knows it is the English who brought the Indians to God. And to whaling. But I guess they didn't take to God too well, because none of them are left anymore. Only Jesse Gibbs. Regardless, I was just trying to make Will Gibbs shush. If Father heard Will Gibbs talk like that, he would forbid me his friendship. And out where we live, on this part of the island, there's hardly anyone to be friends with. That's exactly why my father built his house here.

"I was speaking the truth."

"I don't think you know truth from lies, Will Gibbs. Who told you that, your father?"

"My father," Will Gibbs says defiantly, "doesn't tell me anything. All he wants is for me not to get into trouble."

"Smart Indian."

Will Gibbs bristles. I see his eyes change to yellow. I'm not sure what that means. He stands up.

"I did not know you were thinking of stabbing me," I say.

"I wasn't," he says and looks away. He slips the knife back into his boot. He looks at me again. "Besides, you're right. It's not sharp enough. That's how I can walk on it."

I nod. "Thought so."

He brushes his trousers, looks in the general direction of his house, although there's no way he can see it from where we are. There's nothing to see but the usual scraggly brush and the dirt road, a few skinny trees moving in the wind. From about a half mile off, I can hear the high tide against Madaket beach. "I am going home," Will Gibbs says, and he starts walking.

Will Gibbs and I have grown up together out here, although I am two years older. Neither of us are in school. We are too far out. Besides, Father says he doesn't want to pay someone actual money just to take away his only helping hand. He is a sheep farmer. But I don't think that's the only reason. He also says he has had enough of the Quakers. If I say to him, "There is a Congregationalist school too," he only says, "Sticking to God because he makes them money." Don't get me wrong. My father pays attention to God. Sometimes on Sundays, especially if it is raining, we sit around and he reads the bible aloud. Psalms or Epistles or Moses. But he says he's not traveling all the way to Nantucket town to hear what a Quaker has to say about God—or his neighbor. The Quakers on this island, my father says, do not do anything but tell on each other. Maybe you can see why my father likes living alone out here. There are a few others in Madaket—Jesse and Will Gibbs, Clinton Daggett, a narrow headed man named Purrington who claims to be raising silkworms, and that woman, Mrs. Marshall—but most of them look like fish stranded on the beach: out of sorts and out of place, just trying to breathe. Without any other choice, they keep living. The fish doesn't have a choice either. But it dies.

You would not know just from watching him that Jesse Gibbs is a full-blooded Indian. What I mean is, he does not act contrary. He does not go to war. Neither does he wander around the island half-naked trying to convince whites to make bad deals on trinkets or medicine for the rheum. He does not put feathers in his hair or crushed berries on his face. He wears the same clothes we all do—maybe his are shabbier than most—and he keeps to his own company. If he reminds me of anyone it's drunken John Bliss who shows up in Madaket around April each year and stays until August, sleeping in the moors or on the beach or sometimes on our front stoop. Drunken John runs if you approach him. Father says this is because John thinks everyone is a constable. But I am sure he just wants to be let alone.

Take the drunk out of drunken John, leave the need for privacy, and you have Jesse Gibbs. The Indian is a hermit. He does not even attempt to be friendly. He does not attempt to do anything except fish. It's like he has given up on people. Watch your back around Jesse Gibbs, Father says to me. You can't trust a quiet Indian. I tell my father that Jesse Gibbs is just a creepy, broken down old man.

That's what he wants you to think.

I never see him. Most of the time if I meet Will Gibbs I meet him on the beach.

Watch the son too.

Will Gibbs and I are friends.

When I say something like this, Father doesn't answer right

away. His mouth gets tight, and the skin on the side of his forehead crinkles. I see ideas gathering steam inside him.

What, I ask.

An Indian—a pure Indian—is sneaky enough. But you take the sneaky and divide it into four different parts, I'm not sure that what you have left is even human. I don't think you can predict anything it does.

What four parts? I say. He has only the one father and the one mother.

Any white woman who would consort with an Indian must have at least three parts in her background. Her three and the father make four.

I guess.

No guessing, Owen. I've seen the world.

Before he became a sheep farmer, my father worked in one of the factories by the harbor, making masts and booms for whale ships. Before he married, he spent two years off-island, traveling wherever he could in America. My mother is dead. From the influenza. Father says he does not want to remarry.

The four-parter is too unpredictable. Maybe he seems white, but there are all these other things inside him. It's like the chicken saying the dog seems friendly. Maybe the dog is friendly six days out of seven, but let the dog taste the chicken's neck and see how quickly the dog turns into an enemy. He can't help it. 'Tis his inborn nature. Maybe his mind doesn't want to kill the chicken, but his blood tells him to.

I go to bed thinking of dogs and blood and chickens. Finally, I ask myself what in the world my father is worried about. There are not enough Indians on this island to make a difference anymore. They had their chance. But now they are gone. All things considered, that's good news.

I'm getting tired of Will Gibbs's jawing and insinuations. I make the mistake one day of offering up the truth that the English proved better than the Indians in using this island. That's why we are still around. Will Gibbs says the English have barely been here at all.

"What are you talking about? We've been here forever."

Will Gibbs says that two hundred years ago there were no white men on Nantucket, just Indians.

"All right then," I say, "for two hundred years."

"The Indians were here for thousands of years."

I don't think that can be true, but I say, "Indians do not get along with anybody. That was their problem."

"They do if they're allowed."

"What does that mean?" I say, but he doesn't answer. He often does not give me an answer. At least not a straight one.

Another day he says something like, "Did you know that the English on Nantucket did not let the Indians graze their horses?" That's daft, and I tell him so. Those early English did not do anything but set up a town the way they knew best. What would they care about the Indians and their horses? If the Indians couldn't graze horses it was their own fault. When I say this, Will Gibbs smiles, but it's the kind of smile that is not happy. It's a smile that says he refuses to admit the truth. A smile that leaves me on the other side of him.

When he talks again about whites making Indians into servants I grow hot. "Look," I tell him. "Anything those Indians had was on account of the English. We showed them how to whale. And some of those whaling Indians got rich." Father says that a lot of those whaling Indians were richer than he'll ever be.

"Right," Will Gibbs says. "They *were* rich. Until they all died."

"'Tis their own fault. Or God's. Or someone's. They got sick and died. That's what happens." Even I know about this. It occurred sixty years ago. Father knows a man, his name is Uriah Alderman, who was alive then. He told me all about it. He was used to seeing Indians around, and then one year there was almost none of them. Less than a hundred. It was just a plague, he says. Sad, but it could not be helped. Uriah Alderman doesn't have anything against the Indians. Seems like he almost misses them. Who is going to dispute what an old man like Uriah Alderman says? I guess, when he's in the mood, Will Gibbs would. But I can't see why he gets so bothered about it. He's only half. Whatever happened to the Indians happened to only half of Will Gibbs. The other half of him has nothing to do with it. So why act like it is important to all of him? Jesse Gibbs never gets into disputes about history. I don't know why that's not good enough for Will Gibbs. So I ask Will Gibbs, "How would your father feel if he knew you were jawing with me about this Indian stuff?"

Will Gibbs grows quiet: a mean little quiet; the hard, consternated kind. "My father," he says, "does not talk about it. My father wants to act like it does not exist."

"My point exactly."

"Wait, no. Not that it doesn't exist, but that there is nothing to be done about it. Not now."

"And he's right about that."

"No, he's not."

"Yes, he is."

"That should not be true."

"Who cares how it should be? That's how it is. That's what your father means."

He turns quiet—another kind, more sullen—and I can't draw him out, not even with a handful of other subjects: Mrs. Marshall's fence, the rabbit that attacked one of Father's sheep, the law that might be passed next year forcing every child on the island to attend school in Nantucket town.

"You ever heard of King Philip?" Will Gibbs says. I'm not sure he even listened to what I said about the school.

"No."

"You never heard of King Philip's war?"

"No. Wait, you mean the Indians who attacked the English in America?"

"Yes."

"I know the Indians lost."

Will Gibbs blinks. "They won most of the battles. They forced English off land that used to be Indian land. They almost forced the English out of America."

"Yes, like I said, they lost."

Will Gibbs makes a motion with his mouth like he's chewing on a rock.

"Why are we talking about this?" I say.

"I didn't know if you knew about it."

"I know plenty," I say. "I know more than enough."

"King Philip was a Wampanoag."

"So?"

"Same as the Indians out here."

"So?"

"And that was not even his real name. His Indian name was Metacomet. Only the English called him Philip."

"Does it matter?"

He doesn't answer me.

The next time I go to find Will Gibbs he's not waiting at our usual spot—at a curve in the dirt road that runs next to the moors on this side of Madaket beach. I know where he lives of course, but I don't like to go there, and I don't think he likes me to, which is why we meet at the curve in the road. I decide to go anyway. The afternoon is blustery. There are clouds. Behind each breeze there is a smattering of wet: little rain seedlings that never quite sprout. We could get a wicked fog in a couple of hours, and I don't feel like standing in the road any longer than I need to. At least if I get Will Gibbs we can do something. As I hike down the lane to his hut, I feel more and more angry. Unless it's really raining, Will Gibbs should be waiting for me. I shouldn't have to fetch him. And even if it is raining it will probably only rain an hour or so—it being May. We can outlast an hour of rain.

I step up to his door wondering if it's worth it—coming all the way here—just to have something other to do than take care of sheep. I hammer the door. No one answers. I hammer again. No one answers. I hammer a third time—longer—and this time I'm determined to wait. I'm not leaving until I see or hear something. I know Jesse Gibbs is not fishing. Jesse Gibbs is on the water all morning, every morning. Because that is when Will Gibbs is unavailable. But by the middle of the afternoon, like it is now, Jesse Gibbs should have returned. I guess I could go down to the beach to see if his smack is moored or out, but I don't feel like walking anywhere else. I am about to hammer on the door again when it opens wide enough to show a face like cracked leather with thick black hair on top. Jesse Gibbs. I don't know if it is worth speaking English to him. Supposedly, Jesse Gibbs knows our language. I've heard Daggett say that he warned Jesse Gibbs to stay away from his spot on the water. I've heard my father brag that he scared off Jesse Gibbs by claiming that he guards his sheep with a gun. They act like Jesse Gibbs knows what they were saying. And you figure that if Jesse Gibbs got along with an Irish girl in Nantucket town they must have been able to talk to one another. But it's hard to believe—as I look at those old dull brown eyes and that cracked, expressionless face—that there's anyone inside capable of understanding anything, much less the dignity of our natural English language.

"You are Jesse Gibbs?" I say. Of course I know it's him, but I want to get him to talk, so I turn it into a question. But Jesse Gibbs refuses to say anything. This is what he does.

"I am Owen Pike. I am here to call on your son, Will Gibbs." I would just say that I am here to call on Will Gibbs, but in the moment I feel I must remind the old crab that he has a son. Looking at Jesse Gibbs, I cannot imagine why any white woman would want to touch him.

Jesse Gibbs grumbles and coughs as if he is recovering from a contagion, but then I realize he is just working his way up to speech. "William is unavailable at this hour." His voice is halting and clunky—mildly ashamed—like the sound you would get if you put mud and stones in a tea kettle and tried to pour. But I'm surprised to find that I actually know what he said.

"Why?" I say.

Jesse Gibbs looks at me blankly. "William is unavailable at this hour."

It is at this point that I guess he's memorized exactly one sentence of English. But if he is going to memorize a sentence why not something useful like, "I want two buckets of milk" or "The heel on my boot is broken." Or maybe something elevated: "This is the day the Lord hath made."

"I understand what you are saying. Do you understand me when I say I need to see him?"

Jesse Gibbs rolls his eyes. That makes me angry.

"I need to see Will Gibbs. Stop this hilarity."

Jesse Gibbs's face stays flat. He softens his voice. "William cannot see anyone. Not at this hour."

"Why?"

I see Jesse Gibbs's eyebrows move. "Good day, sir," he says.

"You may come back another time." He closes the door. Almost immediately voices leap at me from inside. Raised voices. I cannot quite make out what they are saying. The voices stop. The door opens partway. I see Jesse Gibbs's eye, a bit of his cheek, a sliver of his forehead, in the crack. He recognizes me, waves me off, and closes the door again. More voices. First low but then louder. One voice is deep and surly. I suppose that must be Jesse Gibbs, although it's hard to believe he can talk so loud. I know that Jesse Gibbs wants me gone; he probably thinks I am gone. But I stay anyway. Something is going to happen. I want to see what it is.

The voices stop. I wait some more. I am waiting to hear Will's voice, but I'm not sure I have yet. Who else could be inside Jesse Gibbs's shack? For a second I entertain the horror that his Irish girl has returned.

A hand touches my shoulder and I startle. It's Will Gibbs, his head square, his tidy body set. Smiling at me.

"I thought you were inside."

"I was."

"How did you get out?"

"Stealth."

"I didn't hear you."

"I know." I see on the side of his face, that line of skin between his eyebrow and the bottom of his eye socket, a scratch. At least that's what I hope it is. Actually, it looks more like a scar.

"Your father said you were unavailable."

"I was. Now I'm not. Let's go."

"You are sure?"

"Yes."

That's all I need to hear. I start us walking toward the dirt road. "What happened to your face?" Of course I know what happened to his face. Jesse Gibbs hit him. But I want Will Gibbs to explain why. I expect he might feel humbled or embarrassed by my question, but he only looks at me slyly.

"I got in a fight."

"With who?"

"A boy."

"A boy?"

"A boy." Apparently he believes his own lie.

"Which boy?"

"A white boy."

I feel goosebumps on my shoulder. "Stop telling lies. Your old brown dad hit you."

He looks at me funny, like what I said makes him more suspicious of me somehow. But all I'd done is tell *him* about *him*. We are on the dirt road now. In another quarter mile or so we will reach the big curve where we usually meet. You can practically see the beach from there. It is where the road changes from north-south to east-west. If we kept walking from that point on we'd eventually end up at Nantucket town.

"My 'old brown dad' never hits me. He just tells sermons."

"Yes? About what then?"

Will Gibbs frowns. "About being 'realistic.'" He spits the word like it is poison.

"Get on with you. I heard your argument. I was standing outside your door. I heard how angry he was."

"Really? What did we say?"

"I didn't hear that well. The door was closed. But I could tell he was angry."

"He was angry." Will Gibbs lowers his voice. "He is angry. Do you know why?"

"I told you I could not hear that well. All that talking butts up against the doorframe, but it doesn't come out."

"And that's why you couldn't understand?"

"I know it is."

Will Gibbs leaves the road and crosses the stretch of moors in front of Clinton Daggett's house. It looks like he wants to knock on Daggett's door—I thought the Gibbs family and Daggett avoided each other—but instead he moves to the right, to the outhouse. This tells you how deserted is this neck of the island. People do not think anything of setting their privy in plain view. Will yanks open the door, steps in, and lets the door close behind him. What is he doing? Then I hear him yell from inside. I don't catch the first word or two but after a moment I realize what he is saying. He repeats it: *Let me out, Owen Pike. Rescue me from this stinking cell.*

I run over, snappish as a king mackerel. I pull open the door to find Will Gibbs standing there, trousers up, arms across his chest, a proud smile on his face. "What are you trying to do, goad Daggett into shooting us? He will kill you before he'll let you start a ruckus in his privy."

But Will Gibbs does not answer. He waits, like he wants to see what else I might say. But I said what I needed to. I step back, wave him out. I wave again, harder. Will Gibbs shrugs, still smiling, and comes.

"Heard me that time, did you?"

"Of course I did. With your shouting."

"I was shouting with my father."

"Not like that you were not."

"No, actually, we were shouting worse."

He starts walking back to the road. I catch up easily, given my longer stride. No way I'm letting him lead me to my own house. But five minutes later—after we walk through the big curve—I remember: I don't want to go to my house. I'm trying to avoid my house. I've had enough of sheep chores. "I'm shifting directions, Will Gibbs," I say. "Follow me." I leave the road. Not far away on the right is a sand dune, one of the bigger ones. I am going to take us there, to redirect this stalled mission. I don't hear anything behind me, but I don't look back. Will Gibbs does not have any other choice but to follow. And he will. This is what we do when I escape my father's house. We spend our time on Madaket Beach. We watch for smacks. We watch for ships sailing to America. We catch horseshoe crabs. We throws rocks at seagulls and count who has the most strikes. Will Gibbs knows what we're doing. He should want to follow me. But am I going to look for him? I don't go looking for any Indian boy.

I start up the body of the sand dune, straight as a mule-pulled plow, pushing down all those granules with my boots. 'Tis rough stepping; it can hurt your legs to have to push against a shifting surface, but if you don't slow and if you don't let anything stop you, you soon find yourself at the top. Then it is a simple trip down and a straightaway to the beach. I figure by the time I'm standing in the surf, Will Gibbs will get smart and stop messing around. I'm at the top now. I can see everything in front of me, all of Madaket beach, way down to the left where it disappears around some rocks, and also to the right, where it ends at the western tip of the island, the one that points to America.

Then below me, at the foot of the dune, I see Will Gibbs. He takes two steps forward and turns. He tilts his head up.

"What took you so long?" he says.

"Where did you come from? I never even heard you. Have you turned into a devil today?"

He holds a smile for a second then says, "I came from a different angle."

"Why?"

"Why not?"

"Because this is the straight path. The fastest route to the beach."

"It is?" He closes one eye as he looks at me, as if he's staring into a spyglass. He folds his arms across his chest.

"It is if you're not pulling trickery. I could have run like you did, but I just chose to walk it. What's the hurry?"

"You think you can run like I can?"

"'Tis not even a question."

"Then let's try—to the water and back."

I glance at the beach. The water looks like low tide. If I run a straight line from the bottom of the dune to the edge of the closest wave, it might be eighty yards. Until you reach the water line, though, the sand is thick and white, bunched against itself like dirt that has just been shoveled. It will be slow going. Yet no different for Will Gibbs. Sand doesn't stop being itself just because he is running in it. At the thought, I check his feet, to be sure. No, he's wearing his boots, same as me. No Indian shoes.

"We're keeping our boots on, yes?" I say.

"On or off, either way."

I look him in the eye, try to scrutinize the stare he's giving me, but it is too yellow to read. I don't know which way to pick. I just know that no matter what I do pick, Will Gibbs is going to try to steal this race.

"Boots on," I say. "Both of us. Or we don't race."

Will Gibbs shrugs. I hate that expression.

I begin my steady, slow steps down the face of the dune, watching Will Gibbs every second. "You better not start until I reach the bottom of this dune and I say that I am ready."

A silvery idea moves in his eye. "I won't," he says. Now I'm sure he will. He's been acting so queerly today—the appearance at his father's, the trip into Daggett's outhouse—I am thinking I should give up Will Gibbs. Maybe Father is right. Maybe he's more trouble than a friend is worth. But first I've got to beat him. I won't let any Indian boy—even if he is only half—carry around wrong ideas about him and me. When I get to the bottom of the dune, Will Gibbs gapes as if he expects something.

"What?" I say.

"You look ready."

I straighten my back. "I'm ready whenever you are."

"All right, then. When I say go, we'll run."

"No," I say. "We run when I say go." He must think me a fool if he thinks I'm going to let him hatch his plan right at the start.

Will Gibbs shrugs. I don't say anything. I face forward, study the shore line. I see exactly—exactly—where I'm going to stop and turn around. I set myself in running position. I know Will Gibbs will run hard, and I know Will Gibbs is fast, but I am two years older and much taller. One of my steps is worth two of his.

"Go!" I shout as I'm already pushing my first step forward. My left leg follows. Then my right again. I feel good. I feel good! I've gotten a jump on him. The water, a turgid gray color a minute ago, seems cleaner in the moment, almost sunstruck. Already I feel much closer to it. In only a few steps I will be meeting it. But after my next step, it's clear no one is beside me. I thought that surely Will Gibbs would keep it close, at least in the beginning. I'm faster than he is but not that much faster. Then it occurs to me: *He's up to something.* I remember the idea I saw in his eye. He is letting me get ahead so he can ... I look over my shoulder and spy him, back there, at the starting point. His arms are folded over his chest. I stop. I'm breathing hard.

"What are you up to, Will Gibbs?"

He smirks and refuses to answer. His bored expression annoys me, as if this is only a pesky game, an idle amusement. *Fine,* I think.

Now I'm going to have to beat you worse. Then he starts running. Not toward me but leftward, further down the beach, parallel to the water. All I can do for a moment is watch. What he is doing makes no sense. He's lost his wits. But I better get back to business: winning this ridiculous competition. A cold feeling comes over me when I remember that it was Will Gibbs who suggested the race. I said "go," but the whole thing was his idea. What does that mean? What is he doing? *He better not say that the race is to that water over there.* 'Twas never stated. "To the water and back," is all he said. If he tries to say different now, I might have to drub him. I face forward a second time and run. No need to focus on the Indian. The wind hits my trousers, almost percussing; my shirt is outside my pants; the cloth at my elbows snaps and flaps; the sand is snatching at my boots as bad as I expected. My legs don't like this, and I'm afraid I might trip, but I thrust on, one leg after the next. Will Gibbs cannot win if he never reaches the water. And if he avoids the water on purpose—well, that is his own fool fault.

The last few steps, over wet sand, are easier. I reach the water line, an inch or so behind the crest of the last wave. Where we are supposed to stop and return. What we both agreed to before he starting running. I stop. I breathe. 'Tis not even a contest yet.

I practically leap to start on my way back. But as I do, I see Will Gibbs. He's all the way down the beach, fifty or sixty yards further east from where we started. Only now is he breaking for the water. What is he thinking? It doesn't matter. *It doesn't matter,* I shout inside my head. He cannot win. Will Gibbs cannot win. Meanwhile, I stick to my straight line route. Passing this way, I can see the marks my feet left on the sand coming out. I stay as close as I can to those marks. I wonder if I should run back over them, so my feet don't have to delve into fresh sand. No. Too much trouble. Just run. You have Will Gibbs beat.

Run.

After another step or three, I'm halfway to the starting point. Then I see, out of the corner of my eye, something closing on me. Something small, but getting bigger. I can't help but look. Yes, it is Will Gibbs. He's crossing the sand diagonally, heading straight for me, like I am a hog he wants to tackle. If he thinks he's going to beat me this way, he really is daft. Will Gibbs can't tackle me. I'm two years older. But how can he be so close already?

Then I realize how he cheated. How he is cheating. That parallel run was just a trick, a show; exactly what I should have expected. Will Gibbs did not run all the way to the water. He could have run only halfway. Then he turned and came at me, which is why he's so close. Ten yards. Seven. My anger fuels my steps, and I charge harder than I have all day. I'm going to beat him. I will beat the cheating Indian. His cheating won't matter when I beat him anyway. I will beat him anyway and forever swear off calling Will Gibbs a friend. Close to the finish, however, Will Gibbs pulls even with me. My anger somersaults. I am sure he will try to mix his legs with mine. But he doesn't. Will Gibbs just runs. He runs. I do too.

Will Gibbs reaches the dune a step before I do. He stops in an instant and turns. I'm about to dissolve. I am breathing hard: sharp, painful gasps. My lungs hurt. They feel orange. And bleeding. They feel as if someone cut them up in order to give a piece to someone else. I can barely see. But what's worse is my fury. I cannot believe what Will Gibbs just did.

"You cheated," I say, when I can talk. "You cheated and you lied. You are a fraud."

I see his face change. His neck gets stiff. Just let him try to deny it.

"What are you talking about?" Will Gibbs says.

"You did not run all the way to the water."

"I did."

"No, you only pretended to. You went halfway, and then you cut back. I saw you. I saw you do it."

"You saw wrong then." Will Gibbs looks truly incredulous, genuinely and righteously outraged. So I guess along with everything else, the Indian can playact too. I should have expected it.

I sneer. "I'm no fool, Will Gibbs."

His pretend anger catches pretend fire. His green-yellow gaze turns gold. "Not only did I run to the water, I ran toward 'Sconset before I ran to the water. I ran farther than you. And before I did any of that, I gave you a ten step lead."

"Why would you do that? Why would anyone do that?"

"I did it."

"You mean you pretended to."

"I ran all the way to the water and then back."

"No one is that fast, Will Gibbs."

He laughs, but it is not a pleasant sound. 'Tis a mean, spiteful, criminal squeal. His eyes are as lurid as before. "If you do not believe me," he says, "go and look. I scratched my family's initials in the sand."

I laugh. "I'm sure you did."

"Go check."

"I will not."

"Do it, or do not call me a cheat."

"I'll call you whatever I want to call you."

I don't know who hits who first. All I know is that I have to get my hands up. Because Will Gibbs is coming. He grabs my arm and tries to get me into some Indian wrestling hold, but I push him away hard. I'm too strong for the likes of Will Gibbs. And I'm taller. He comes again, lower, like a sneak. He dives at me, crashing me with the full weight of his body, such as it is. We both fall to the ground. He doesn't tackle me, mind you. We both fall to the ground. And he doesn't pin me. I am just turning to get my legs under me. I'm turning to push him off, stand up, and get square. So I can punch him like a white man. I've got him off me, and I am half standing up when I feel a pain in my side, the steely piercing of a blade, a dozen times worse than a wasp's stiletto. That same sharpness but worse. I shout. I fall. The blade comes out. I feel wetness on my back, near my waistline. The blade goes back in. It comes out. It goes back in. There is sand against the side of my face. I don't know if my eyes are closed, but I can't see anything. I wonder if I'm dead. I can't be, not yet, because I hear Will Gibbs say something. He says, "We were talking Wampanoag."

ON CHERRY STREET

Nantucket Island, 1837

Orpha Hussey has only just given up waiting for her husband Reuben when she meets Adella Smythe at the home of a mutual friend named Helene Charlotte Joyner Brayton. At twenty-three, Helene is younger by a decade than any other widow Orpha knows. Unless she counts herself—which she should now, shouldn't she? Helene hardly fits the common notion of a widow on Nantucket: that of a graying mistress resigned to live out her life alone, nostalgic for the years she had with her husband but not a little bitter, even now, that they ended too early. Helene seems almost glad—or at least indifferent to the fact—that Thaddeus drowned, thrown from a rocketing whale boat as it banged and twisted against the ocean swells, pulled by what his mates later claimed was a leviathan of a sperm.

Resigned is the last word anyone would use to describe Helene. Now that the year-long mourning period is over, Helene acts as if she is determined to end her widowhood as soon as possible, certainly no later than her twenty-fourth birthday. To that effect, Helene spreads her network of social contacts as widely as possible, among both male and female, young and old, Quaker and Baptist and Congregationalist, making new "friendships" and renewing extant ones with a dizzying constancy of motion. Better than anyone on this small, sparsely populated spit of ground—better even than the crones who gather every morning for tea at Mrs. Coleman's on Quince Street—Helene Brayton knows about the island's eligible men. If a new one arrives—if any new person arrives—she intuits it with magical immediacy from the perch of her parents' home. She is like a spider who spins her web so tightly that the movement of even the most insignificant creature onto one of its strands sends a clamoring, instantly recognizable vibration. And on an island as small as Nantucket, a spideress does not need to spread her web very far before it encloses virtually everyone.

Orpha does not care to attend another of Helene's private parties, or, rather, her confidence gathering sessions. Because Thaddeus had no money, Helene was forced to return to her parents after her husband died, and these tea parties, no matter how small, seem out of keeping with the introverted atmosphere of the household. They are dress up affairs, tolerated rather than enjoyed by Alice and Mordecai Joyner, two persons who surely love their daughter but leisure in their silence and each other more than anyone Orpha can recall. Besides, on this day, Orpha does not want to be sociable with anyone. Not moderate or diplomatic or pleasantly pleasant. She wants to stew; she wants to be angry; she wants to accuse and shout and enjoy the heady combat of righteous retribution. She ought to feel sadness, she supposes, but it was not sadness that hit her this morning when she finally accepted that Reuben must have died. No, she cannot technically "know" this—there has been no missive from his captain, no gossip among town folk, no gruesome revelation from a whaler recently returned home. The very last communication she received from him was a short, ordinary letter, dated February 11, 1834 and composed while on shore at Valparaiso, Chile. After more than three years with no word from him or his ship there is nothing else to conclude. Conclude it she did—finally, irrevocably—less than twelve hours ago.

No, what she feels is not sadness but peevishness at being uselessly abandoned. She had questioned Reuben two hundred times as to whether or not he really wanted to go to sea. She had said to him, not a week before he left, that she would not think less of him if he changed his mind. Orpha went so far as to say that if necessary she would contribute to the economics of the household: work at her father's tavern, repair clothes for shored sailors, help old Mrs. Pope transport the product of her dairy cows to customers throughout the island. She might even try her luck at one of the factories by the harbor. Orpha would do this as long as necessary, until Reuben had trained himself in a profession he actually cared for and was good at. A career that made sense to him. She would even delay having children—assuming the rumored methods were effective—if that meant giving Reuben more time to hesitate, to debate with himself, to step off the whale ship before it left. But

Reuben, even though she saw in every inch of his face the desire to succumb to her plan, even though she saw a holy eagerness to avoid leaving home, only shook his head.

"You're being foolish," Orpha shot back. "Just because your brothers are in the business."

"No, not just because of them."

"Oh, I would say it is wholly on account of them."

"It is not just my brothers. My father was, and his brother, and two of his cousins. And, you know, my great-great-great-grandfather. Everybody. It's the island, Orpha. It is the business of the island. There is no other. At least for a Hussey." Orpha realized what she was up against. She knew when she agreed to marry him. Reuben's great-great-great-grandfather, Sylvanus Hussey, captained the first ship of Nantucketers to ever snare a sperm whale. Sylvanus became a legend and started the Hussey family on the road to a prosperity they still enjoyed. Indeed, Orpha and Reuben's conspicuous two story house on Cherry Street, built for them at the expense of the Husseys—in fact, at the insistence of Mrs. Margaret Hussey, who did not want to spare her youngest son anything —was only one more revelation of that wealth. And not only did the family pay for the house, they promised to provide Orpha an allowance the whole time Reuben was away. Thus, Orpha's offer to work, however sincere, had been moot as soon as it came out of her mouth. The Hussey family had all the money it needed to support Reuben. They would not have enjoyed funding any "unmanly indecision," but they would have done so anyway, just to keep Orpha from "demeaning" herself as a milk cart driver or, heaven help us, a *bar maid*; she could imagine the word coming at her like a bad cough from the center of Margaret Hussey's outrage. It had rankled her, the week that Reuben's ship was set to leave, how little her offer mattered to him materially. How little he appreciated it. How little he believed in it.

"Just because it's the island's business does not mean it must be yours. Or ours." Reuben looked at her as pitifully as if she had gone wrong in the head. She added, "You don't even like the sea."

He waved the suggestion away. "The sea is what we have."

"So let's move then."

At that Reuben laughed—a sour, hopeless noise—and began

shaking his head just like his father did. This deathly thin, nineteen-year-old who she once thought was so different from his clan. In the moment she hated him. But she only turned away, kept her silence, attended to whatever business their new home demanded of her, this place that must be her sole center of attention until her husband returned.

Orpha wonders now at the strength of her determination and her challenge. She cannot remember her mother ever applying such pressure to her father, albeit her father never came close to becoming a whaler. She knows for a fact that her sister never questions her husband, Captain Asa Wyer, about his choice of profession. Her sister is too content with the income Wyer accrues, and with the house it affords them. Why, she tries to figure now, had she been so certain that something was amiss? She never used to make a habit of reading doom in the air. Was it Reuben's softheaded distractedness, his too evident willingness to be led by circumstances rather than to lead them? His lack of enthusiasm at the idea of hunting and killing sea creatures; the absence of that stupid excitement bordering on idol worship that so many island boys feel toward their whaler-kings? Something—something—would go wrong. A rope catching a misplaced foot; a harpoon stabbing a thoughtless arm; a typhoon attacking late one afternoon with hellish wind and lightning; an assault by a drunken, toothless, pistol-toting ghoul on some South American stopover; a malady spread from man to man in the close quarters of a sailing vessel.

She warned and questioned Reuben to the point that he threatened to leave her, only seven months into their marriage, "on account of her pestering." So she backed off and gave in. She certainly would not be allowed to leave *him*. For what reason, after all? *Because your husband is a whaler*? That would get a laugh. *You and how many others*? Finally there was nothing she could do. Reuben boarded the whale ship *Constance* on the morning of May 3, 1832. The *Constance* removed peacefully from Nantucket harbor around midday. Since then Orpha has played the waiting wife longer and with more exasperation than anyone she knows.

Orpha never had the slightest desire—ever in her life—to take up this peculiar and arduous role, holding herself and her household together for years on end just so she and it can be in perfect condition on the day her husband returns without warning. She does not, and never did, gossip with the other "whaling widows" as to the latest news from their husbands or their plans for his return or when he must next launch or about how much better life was now that he was again safely on-island. Indeed, once it became clear that she had waited an excessively long time without news from Reuben the other wives avoided her like a bad omen. But no matter how much she did not want such a life for herself, Orpha would have accepted it if she had felt certain that whaling was what Reuben wanted to do, wanted it so badly he would be running back to the wharves after six months on land. Reuben had never once run to the wharves. To suffer through this outrageous waiting for a husband who never wanted to sail in the first place seemed inexcusable. A waste.

Now she wants to rage.

She wants to exult.

She does not want any of Helene Brayton's company, or her parents' tea.

She wants to announce her indictment. And that the sad facts of her life are newly permanent. No companion. No helpmeet. No dinner conversation. No bedmate. No affection. The latter had not bothered her much at all; not nearly as much as the other wives hinted it would. Reuben had never been a terribly physical person. And for the seven months they lived together, his need for intimacy was paltry. When he was gone she did not exactly yearn for him to be inside her, but she did feel, as the months stretched on, an undeniable tension in her body, a tension she could only release effectively with her hand. She was always surprised at how pleasant it felt. Better, actually, than when Reuben loved her. She missed his presence, no doubt. The fact of another person inhabiting the house, lying close beside her while she slept. But the act itself, the supreme moment, was higher and sharper, punctuated with actual amazement, when she gave it to herself. This she could not have expected. She was surprised too by the lack of guilt. She didn't— and she never does—feel guilt. But even so months pass before the tension builds to that same bad point, and she must release it again.

Come afternoon, she decides that she will go to Helene's after all. What better way to communicate her new status than to tell Helene Brayton? *I am no longer Mrs. Reuben Hussey. I am free of all that.* Yesterday was the fifth anniversary of her husband's departure. As an exercise in formality, the marking of an official stopping point, and perhaps a necessary last gesture, she had given Reuben until sundown to reveal his location. Either to show his face on their doorstep or by some less direct method to tell her he was alive. Afternoon passed languorously and unwell as the fog came in dripping off the Sound. Dusk arrived, along with the bite of damp May cold. A misty, soaking wetness filmed her windows. She struggled to light a fire in the stove but succeeded after three tries. In no time at all, the funereal, cloud-covered sky turned black. Night took over. Reuben remained as invisible as ever.

Orpha, of course, had expected nothing else. She didn't admit to herself—although it was true—that she had not wanted any other outcome. *All right*, she said aloud, before she lowered the wick on the lamp beside her bed. *It should be clear to you that I was right all along.* She moved her hand to the lamp, then stopped. She sat up straight again. She said one more thing: *And tomorrow, Reuben, will be very different.* She listened, in the elongated fibers of the silence, for a last rebuttal, from wherever he was. She hoped for it, so that she could knock it down, now that she was free. *You had your chance*, she would say. *You had your chance. You had your chance.* But, even though she listened as closely as she ever had to anything, she heard nothing but the sweeping noise of the wind and the childish sound water droplets made when blown against window glass. She turned the knob and lowered the wick; the bedroom was cast in the same blackness as the outdoors. She stretched out, vibrant with her discovery, this newfound reckoning that seemed by all rights irreversible.

It took some time, in her newly agitated state, to fall asleep. Then—at some point in the still middle of the night—she woke with a start. She could see and hear nothing at all. The wind was hushed. The sounds of rain were gone. The universe seemed not just silent, but stopped. Dead. Eradicated. She would not have been surprised to look out the window and see no stars, no moon, not even a landscape beneath her. She was at the dead center of an infernal blackness, and someone was in the room watching her. She could see no actual figure, but she felt it there; some specific, malevolent consciousness: doubting her, judging her, condemning her. Moreover, this consciousness, whoever or whatever it was, had turned the room frigid, as if with every intake it ingested more of Orpha's warmth and replaced it breath by breath with ice. "Reuben!" she shouted. She sat up, daring to meet this thing head on. But as soon as she did so, she felt it evaporate. Blink out. Nothing. The air was cool as ever on an early May nighttime—but not cold. Through the window to her left she could see a newly cleared sky. The brimming moonlight illuminated Cherry Street and every place beyond.

The air feels different at the Joyner's cottage on Back Street. Orpha senses it as soon as she steps inside, before she even spies Helene and her other guest. She can smell it: a straight, swept quality; clean air; air in which hope is allowed and a belief in the future. Air emptied of resentment, of the strained, half-spoken emotions—heavy as chowder—that is the atmosphere at Orpha's; sunlit air, keen on this cool but fogless afternoon.

"The girls are in the back," Helene's mother says, "looking at the delphinium my husband installed last summer."

"Thank you, Mrs. Joyner. I'll wait."

"No need. You can join them."

"No. Thank you. Actually, I would rather not."

Orpha cares nothing whatsoever about flowers, and she would rather avoid another one of Helene's public demonstrations, which are never about the subject itself but only about Helene. But she realizes she has spoken too bluntly. A darker look comes to Agnes Joyner's expression: a coppery, evolving concern. "No word yet from Reuben, I assume."

Orpha hesitates, then says what needs saying: "There will be no further word from Mr. Hussey, I'm afraid."

The woman's soft, jowly face seems to gather inside itself; her gray-green eyes dampen with pity and even alarm, a reaction that actually surprises Orpha. Orpha realizes her own fallacy: that now she has made up her mind about Reuben, everyone on the island should have arrived at the same conclusion.

Mrs. Joyner directs Orpha to the nearest chair and sits beside her. "I am very sorry to hear that. And stupid of me to ask you. But I hadn't heard anything new about the *Constance*. When did you find out?"

"Last night," she says.

"Terrible," Mrs. Joyner repeats. "I really am so sorry." She takes Orpha's hands into her own and stares at the younger woman with a soulful, immaculate attention. Her large hands feel warm and nourishing. Her tall forehead is clear of strain. She must have been so striking, Orpha thinks, when she was younger.

"Oh, I'm not surprised," Orpha says before she can stop herself. "I warned him. I tried to talk him out of going. He had no desire to take up whaling, but he was determined to—to make a mess of things—and only on account of his family."

Mrs. Joyner's eyebrows rise; on that forehead creases appear. The coppery caste has become something else; something tighter.

"Thank you for your concern, but I am not distraught, Mrs. Joyner. Truly. I'm just tired of it all. And frustrated."

The eyebrows again. The woman puts a hand on Orpha's shoulder. "Are you sure you want to be here today? Helene can invite you over again; anytime. When you really feel like coming. When you don't have"—she pauses—"so much on your mind."

Orpha is gratified to see that this is a sincere offer on Mrs. Joyner's part. The woman is not simply trying to get rid of her.

"Thank you. Today is fine. Today, actually, is best of all."

Before Agnes Joyner can reply, the rear door of the small house opens and Helene enters, shaking herself with exaggerated, disingenuous shivers—Orpha knows it's not that cold out—and yet smiling all the same. As Helene steps over to greet Orpha another girl enters. But Orpha cannot see her, her view blocked by Helene and Mrs. Joyner who moves urgently to her daughter. Orpha knows from what Helene told her that the other girl is Adella Smythe, a newcomer "washed ashore" with her father and mother, who have migrated to Nantucket from Boston. Orpha sees Agnes Joyner whisper a low, quick message into Helene's ear. A word of warning and advice. Orpha can easily imagine the content. *Be careful, daughter. She just found out Reuben is dead.* Helene's in-charge look turns to wariness, perhaps even dissatisfaction. As if she's worried her party is spoiled. Orpha wants to set the record straight. She stands; she smiles. "Good day, Helene. Thank you for asking me."

Helene looks surprised at the greeting; she returns the smile, uncertainly. "Mother told me the news. Are you feeling all right?"

"I'm fine, thank you. Really."

"You are sure?"

Orpha lifts her chin. "I've been ready for at least a year now, to tell the truth. The worst part is the not knowing."

The thick-cheeked, green-eyed girl—her face as broad as a baby's, its skin extending all the way above her ears to where it ends in a bonnet of coarse brown hair—nods as if she understands. Because she does. It may be the only thing about her that Helene truly does understand. She remembers Helene in the weeks after she received her own bad news. *She was practically giddy about it.*

"Orpha," Helene says, "meet Adella Smythe. As you know, she has only recently come to the island."

From behind Helene's more substantial figure comes the slight body of Adella: thin-faced, with striking, almost disturbing, black eyes and skin that appears to have never been touched by the sun. A frown is in her brow and across her mouth, and her shoulders are bent slightly, as if she suffers from curvature of the spine. Except that when Orpha looks more carefully she sees that Adella is standing perfectly straight; almost too straight. She stares at Orpha with such strict, analytical force Orpha feels like a specimen before the presence of a brooding, universal intelligence. Adella is not dour, Orpha decides, just melancholic in a questioning way that seems in keeping with her Boston roots. Though certainly if a stranger entered and was asked to guess the identity of the widow and the identity of the island ingénue, the stranger would pick Adella as the former.

"Young women, your tea is ready," Mrs. Joyner interrupts. Orpha did not realize Mrs. Joyner was brewing any. She feels guilty for keeping her. "Please sit—" Mrs. Joyner motions to the broad wooden table at the side of the room—"and I will bring it to you."

The three girls sit at the table and for the next several minutes Orpha witnesses Agnes Joyner playing hostess to her daughter's guests: pouring their tea, asking if they want any honey or milk, sweetening each cup as requested, and then placing it in front of the appropriate person. After she has served each girl, including her daughter, Mrs. Joyner disappears, claiming business next door with Mrs. Gardner, but clearly she just wants to leave Helene to her company. No, Orpha decides, Agnes Joyner is not acting like a hostess but a servant. Helene had sat quietly—still, and vaguely impatient—the whole time Mrs. Joyner carried out the tasks of serving, suffering the ministrations of her mother the way a lady of the house does an inexperienced maid.

As soon as Mrs. Joyner steps out, Adella leans across the table to Orpha. "I am gratified to meet you Orpha, but I am sorry to hear about your loss." The girl must have awfully sharp hearing, Orpha thinks, to have caught that low flung whisper from Mrs. Joyner to her daughter.

"Don't be," Orpha says.

"All right," Adelle says. "I won't."

"I have not actually received formal notice about Reuben. I'm just choosing to make it official myself. Right now. It's my decision."

Helene laughs. Adella allows herself a curling smile. Orpha is amazed at how even that small expression changes the girl's face.

"Well," Helene says breezily, "of all the Husseys Reuben was surely the addlepate."

Adella looks astonished, but Orpha laughs. She laughs, and it feels good. Her shoulders separate, her muscles loosen, a portion of tension descends through her body and sinks into the floor. "Not addled, Helene. Cowardly."

Helene shrugs. "Either way."

"If he was cowardly," Adella asks, "why would he join a whale ship?" It is a straight question. She is not trying to accuse Orpha of underestimating her husband. She just wants to understand.

"Because he did not think he had a choice. But he always did. And I told him so; at least until he ordered me to stop."

At the word "order" Adella shivers. "In that case, he is not merely a coward but a fool."

Orpha squeezes Adella's hand. "Yes, but what's the difference?"

"In practice, none. Usually. In one's heart—in one's mind—a significant difference." She puts her hand against her chest, then releases it. Something about the reserved quality in Adella's voice, that careful diction, moves Orpha profoundly. She feels in the moment that she would like to like to curl herself around Adella's legs, steep in the girl's wisdom. Maybe then she could start to right herself. If she'd had Adella's wisdom in the first place she might never have married. Or at least not Reuben Hussey. She would not have convinced herself that he was so different from the other Husseys: more interior, more homebound, more capable of realizing universal connections. Because, as it turned out, he wasn't.

Adella sees for the first time the collection of scrimshaw on a small table on the other side of the room. She stands and steps over to examine it. "These are lovely," she says to Helene. "From your husband?"

"My uncle. Thaddeus didn't live long enough to collect anything."

"Only you," Adella says. "But then he gave that away."

Helene reacts with a sidewise smile. "Adella is quite the philosopher," she says to Orpha, "as you are finding out." She sends Orpha a long, strict look that Orpha is clearly supposed to understand and return. But Orpha keeps her face blank on purpose. Helene's signal bounces off.

"I am glad for any philosophy that supersedes whale worship. And gold worship."

"I don't know," Helene says. "Gold can be pretty useful." She motions to Adella. "Sit down, girl. You have been standing practically since you arrived."

"If you say so," Adella answers thickly and returns to the table. "But I don't mind standing for as long as necessary." The words, taken alone, are as humble as any Christian husband could hope for, but Adella's tone is completely different. The tone, Orpha notes with approval, implies not submission but the willingness to resist. Once again, the girl has showed a substance that belies her slight figure.

"Adella," Orpha feels compelled to ask, "why are you here?"

A smile enters Adella's eyes. "Because Helene asked me."

"I mean the island."

"My family has settled here."

"Yes, I know, but why?"

"My father already knew Reverend Bunker at the Second Congregational Church. When Reverend Bunker informed him that the congregation wanted to join the Unitarians—specifically the Church of Harvard University—father felt called to assist."

"Permanently?"

Adella studies her a moment, as if she must take care with the form of her answer. "Who can say when inspiration is involved?"

"No, I mean are you here permanently?" At this, Adella shrugs. "Clearly, you're of age," Orpha adds.

Adella chuckles. "As I am reminded of repeatedly by my mother and father—and Helene."

"Oh, stop it. It wasn't like I was trying to hound you," Helene counters. She tries to give her tone the texture of a tease, but the anger in her cheek is unmistakable. It is apparent to Orpha just how much Helene despises her guest, especially the fact that the guest is garnering all the attention, and without even trying.

"You seem about my age," Orpha tries. "Twenty-three?"

"Twenty."

"Ah."

"What?" Helene says. "What 'ah'? What 'ah'?"

"She's twenty. She can stay if she likes, whatever her father decides. Even if he moves back to Boston tomorrow."

"Not much chance of that," Helene says.

"Of course, but I'm only saying—"

"And besides," Helene says before Orpha can finish, "what are you thinking? Where would Adella stay? An unmarried girl? Alone? With her family gone? How would she get by?"

"She could stay with me."

Helene looks at Orpha as if she has lost her mind. Once more, Helene tries to send a message through her eyes, and once more Orpha lets the message bounce off.

"Thank you," Adella says quietly. "That's very kind. But I barely know you."

"That will change," Orpha says. "Soon enough."

"But Orpha," Helene spouts. "What would she *do* here?"

Orpha tries very hard to keep her eyes on Helene. "I am sure we can find some use for her."

The first time they sleep in the same bed, neither knows exactly why or what for—it is simply an automatic thought, decided at once—but they know it is comforting. In shifts behind a screen, both change into nightdresses but decide independently to forego their caps. They lie on Orpha's wedding bed, resting lightly against each other, elbows and shoulders touching. At first they talk about the subjects that have animated them for days: what Adella will do with herself on the island; how she can establish herself independently from her two doting parents; what changes Orpha will make now that her marriage is effectively ended. They are thrilled for their mutual company, nearly too thrilled to sleep, yet after an hour or so, they both do. But all night, Orpha's sleep is light: broken and overexcited by the fact of someone else beside her for the first time in five years. Over the course of hours she moves closer, by sixteenths of inches, to her friend. At one point, deep in the early morning, Adella rolls, and her head abuts Orpha's cheek. Orpha keeps still and smells the loamy scent of Adella's dark brown hair. It smells of leaves and of herbs—of some other continent. Silly thought, she realizes. *Adella's never been to another continent; neither have I.* Orpha wonders what, if anything, her own hair smells like, and guesses that it smells like nothing at all, or only like the Nantucket breeze: thin, perpetually damp, faintly salty, and not always welcome.

She remembers wondering, back in the months of their courtship, what could possibly attract Reuben—as a man—to her. She has never been big-eyed and delicate like Adella or pleasantly plump like Helene—what might arouse either a man's passion or his instinct for protection. Orpha is lean, bony, and vigorous. Her shoulders are too broad and her elbows cranky. Her knees are hard and too apparent, even when covered. Her hair is almost orange, an embarrassment she is eager to hide beneath the widest bonnets she can purchase. She wears the dresses of the day capably, but she does not feel comfortable in them—not the way her mother does or nearly every other island woman. Her figure never shows the dresses to their best advantage; nor do they her. Reuben's desire—no, his obvious need—to marry her could not have had anything to do with a prim nose, golden hair, a promising bosom, or a pretty ankle. Orpha could only conclude that Reuben chose her because she was unlike any other woman on the island. Maybe—she secretly worried—unlike any woman anywhere. As they married and set up a household, the reality of this supposition became more and more true. It became Reuben's blessing and also his curse. Her blessing and her curse too. Perhaps, she thinks now, what was "unlike" in her appealed to what was "unlike" in him, but she doubts Reuben ever let himself realize this.

It is two weeks since she first met Adella. The girl is staying with Orpha because her father has traveled, along with the Reverend Bunker, to Boston for a series of meetings with officials from the Church of Harvard University. Reverend Smythe wanted his wife to accompany him on the journey, but she only agreed when Adella informed her that she could stay with the newly widowed Mrs. Orpha Hussey. It is the third night of Adella's stay; there will be three more. Now Adella has rolled into Orpha and given Orpha the unexpected, even miraculous, opportunity to smell her hair. In the hour that follows, Orpha stretches her arm around Adella, pulling the girl even closer. When she does so, she hears Adella sigh in her sleep.

She will live with me, Orpha realizes. It is so obvious, she nearly smacks her forehead with the butt of her hand. *That is how Adella will become independent. That is the change I will make.*

It is then that Orpha senses it: the return of the presence that watches her in the dark. A specific, tangible entity; a living and focused intelligence; somewhere near the bottom of her bed. Disapproving. Bitter. Petty. Most of all, vengeful. But vengeful for what? And why? The air has turned cold again, just as it did last time, and for a moment she fears for Adella. Then she decides: *No one is hurting her. Not on my life.* Newly calm, she lifts her head to speak this decision to whoever or whatever is watching. But the entity is gone.

In the morning, Adella wakes and slips lightly out of bed. But first she leans into her friend and kisses Orpha on the cheek.

Orpha, drowsy, nevertheless feels the sensation. She is gratefully yanked out of a dream in which Reuben is still alive but floundering in the ocean, without even a bit of driftwood to keep him afloat. In the dream, though, her husband is oddly calm. Some of his shipmates are near, but one by one they drop out of sight. Reuben asks Orpha for help. Nicely at first, but then he asks again: more urgently. She too is there, floating on a plank. He wants a piece of it for himself. Orpha would like to answer him. But whenever she opens her mouth, nothing comes out. Reuben's urgency is about to turn to outrage when Orpha feels Adella's kiss and realizes she is asleep in her own bedroom. There is no Reuben. Reuben is dead. Now it is Orpha's turn to sigh. She moves closer to Adella only to find Adella's place unoccupied. Moments later she hears sounds of activity around the stove downstairs.

The May morning opens damp, chill, and fog-covered. Orpha must show Adella how to start the fire and only then does the air become tolerable. They sit in chairs, sipping tea, smiling at each other, barely noticing the day's dreary cast, the bits of water collecting minute by minute on the window panes. Coming off the thrill of their night together, neither cares a whit about the fog. Indeed, they almost appreciate it, for the privacy it provides. *Underwater weather*, the islanders call it.

Orpha is surprised when in the middle of their second cup of tea a knock comes from the front door. She covers herself with a robe, puts on a sun hat for modesty, and cracks the door to find Reuben's mother standing on the front stoop.

"Mrs. Hussey," Orpha says, croakily. She is unable to keep her hand from running to her throat. "It has been too long. How fine to see you." Orpha waits for a clue, but her mother-in-law's long, still face offers none. "Would you like to come in?"

"Without a doubt," Margaret Hussey says. Her neck ticks upward and Orpha can see how, beneath the woman's hat, the latest round of gray has enervated her once famous mane of auburn hair.

"But what about—" Orpha starts. She opens the door wider to spy the street. She sees no calash—and no son or grandson to act as driver, no man whose thirst or hunger she is expected to qualm.

"You walked out? From town?"

"I did," Margaret Hussey says, sounding less severe than concerned. Orpha has never loved Margaret Hussey, but she has long respected her. It is hard not to. Of all the various and complicated reasons that Orpha consented to marry Reuben, one of the most important was that Margaret Hussey approved of her. As the effective director of the Hussey mansion and the linchpin of a legendary clan that currently tallies one retired sea captain, two current sea captains, a first mate, Reuben, two daughters, two grandsons—the oldest fifteen and impatient to begin whaling himself—three granddaughters, and one of the island's most substantial bank accounts, she has stood at the center of Nantucket's history for the last three decades, easily the most profitable years the island has ever seen. Margaret Hussey is used to being heard and used to being listened to. She is used, most of all, to being served. It means something—and Orpha can only hope something not ominous—that the woman has walked by herself from upper Main Street to Orpha's house on Cherry Street, a mile away.

"It was necessary for me to consider what I should say when I arrived," Margaret Hussey explains.

Orpha doesn't know how to interpret this, so she says, "Of course."

"You said I could come in?"

"Yes. Certainly."

"Yet you still occupy the doorway."

Orpha steps back, abashed. She realizes Adella is still at the table, as underdressed as she and nibbling on a day old biscuit. In the shock of Mrs. Hussey's appearance, Orpha had forgotten about her friend. Now it is too late to tell the girl to run upstairs.

After stepping inside, Margaret Hussey stops at once. She stares at the unexpected figure of Adella Smythe. The older woman's face shows a mixture of bewilderment and controlled outrage. "I did not realize you had company," she says slowly, her voice growing more uncomfortable syllable by syllable. "My apologies."

"You do not need to apologize, Mrs. Hussey. This is Adella Smythe. She's staying with me while her family is off-island." Adella—who after a passing glance at Margaret Hussey, keeps nibbling her biscuit—seems not at all interested in the fact of the newcomer, or perhaps she is actively attempting to show non-interest.

"Smythe," the woman repeats neutrally.

"Her father is the new assistant at the Second Congregational Church."

"Yes, I know." Margaret Hussey studies Adella with some concern, but then nods. "Miss Smythe."

Adella finally lays her biscuit aside. She looks at it with apparent concern and then stands slowly. "Pleased to meet you, Mrs. Hussey." She keeps the pose for a moment but then sits again, throwing Margaret Hussey a long look from beneath a lowered brow.

Mrs. Hussey turns to Orpha. "What I mean to tell you is private, daughter. It concerns my son."

Hearing this, Adella does not hesitate. She leaves the table and picks from a nearby chair the quilt she brought down from the bedroom that morning. She wraps herself with it and moves for the door.

Orpha calls to her. "Surely you are not going to stand outside on a morning like this one." Orpha's guilt comes through her voice as sarcasm. She hears it herself, and this only makes her feel worse. In letting Mrs. Hussey enter she has effectively thrown out her friend, as if Adella were an acquaintance of which she ought to be ashamed.

"I'll be fine," Adella says, but she does not look back. "This will give me a chance to study the country."

"You can wait upstairs, you know," Orpha says.

Adella looks at her. "I'll be fine." She opens the door and steps out. Margaret Hussey watches her leave, then silently shakes her head: a tiny but discernible motion. Orpha, fuming, turns to the woman. "What is it?" she says, with more bluntness than she intended.

Margaret Hussey looks surprised, perhaps even amused. "May I sit?" Orpha nods. "Do not bother offering me tea or biscuits. I am not in the proper state of mind for either."

"Of course," Orpha says. She realizes her answer makes no sense. She has no idea what "state of mind" her mother-in-law has come in, or what she must say. With nothing else to do, she also sits.

"That girl," Mrs. Hussey says, "how well do you know her?"

Better than I know Reuben.

"Well enough," Orpha says, "to do her the favor."

"She will need to leave this house," says Margaret Hussey.

The tone riles her. Orpha will not submit to it. Who is Margaret Hussey to tell her whom she can entertain in her own home? The construction of the house—too big, really, for such a young couple—may have been paid for by the Husseys, but it had been a wedding gift. A gift. To her just as much as to Reuben. And a gift is owned by the recipient. She tries carefully to control her voice, but the single word she speaks comes out as a strangled, sawed off noise: "Why?"

Mrs. Hussey hesitates before answering. "Because soon enough I suspect she will not be wanted here. If it were me, I would not want her here now."

"I am letting her stay with me, as a favor, until her parents return. I am practicing charity for a friend."

Mrs. Hussey holds her eye for a moment; then for what seems the longest time examines the table where Adella had sat chewing on that biscuit. "I understand that you believe Reuben is no longer alive."

Orpha swallows. "I see no other rational conclusion. It has been so long since any word came from him—or about him."

"True. There's no other *rational* conclusion." She sounds the word as if it is an expletive.

"I have not seen my husband for five years."

Mrs. Hussey blinks, shifts in her chair. "I know how you must be suffering, Orpha. You do not know what has happened to him. You want an answer. The infernal day after day of waiting slits you like a handful of briars." She looks Orpha in the eye. "Reuben is your husband, but he is also my son."

"Thank you, yes," Orpha says. "This has not been easy for either of us." She is grateful for Mrs. Hussey's unexpected sympathy, but "suffering" isn't exactly what she feels anymore, if she ever did. Perhaps the first year, yes. But what she has felt for so long—at least until she made her decision two weeks ago—was exasperation and seething. Then today, at last, before her mother-in-law arrived, she felt only a beautiful, perfect joy. A joy she could not have expected in her life, or even, really, imagined. And the one who has brought her such joy is now made to wait outside, shivering.

"Oh, I am not done, Orpha," Mrs. Hussey says. She moves her hands. She leans forward. "I have plenty more to add."

"Of course."

"The way you have dealt with your suffering is disgraceful, a disservice to me, to Reuben, and to yourself. You have wanted an answer so badly that you went out and supplied your own. Without any factual evidence—and without informing me."

"Well—true—that is true—" Orpha struggles.

"You threw my son to the sharks without extending me the least warning."

The truth is it never occurred to Orpha to announce her conclusion to her mother-in-law. It was her own affair, her own husband, her own decision—not Margaret Hussey's. But she realizes now how badly she has erred. She realizes how it must have felt to hear from a neighbor that her daughter-in-law no longer considers herself married to her son. And how couldn't she hear it, once Orpha told Helene? Hadn't that been the point of telling Helene in the first place?

"I'm sorry, Mrs. Hussey. You are right. I should have spoken to you first."

Margaret Hussey's eyes grow flinty in the instant, as if Orpha's apology is insufficient—or irrelevant—or even stupid. "Yes," the woman says. "You should have." She studies her fingers for a moment. "But I am actually more disappointed that you came to the decision at all. I've always thought of you as the heartiest of my daughters-in-law. I would not have thought you'd give up so quickly. I can tell you that *I* have not given up."

Orpha is stunned by the accusation. *Given up?* Easy for Margaret Hussey to say. Her husband is still alive; perhaps too much alive, roaring and slobbering through their prettified, red brick estate. Her two sea captain sons live within a block of her and are both currently on-island; her oldest daughter lives one street over; her youngest daughter—seventeen—lives with the woman herself, in her own house. Her third son is at sea, earning his keep, alive and well by all accounts. With or without Reuben, the woman has a whole family and a whole household to run, as well as half a dozen civic enterprises afoot on the island and a few more involving the

First Congregational Church. But as long as she merely waits for her husband, Orpha has effectively nothing in life to do.

"It matters gravely that you've made this decision, daughter. Even more than you realize. We like you, Orpha. I do. All of us. During these past five years not a week has gone by when Captain Hussey and I, everyone really, has not said how much we admire your courage. We understand long waits. We appreciate their toll. We like to think that your courage mimics our own." Ouch. "But if you insist publically that you are no longer bound to my son, then you have effectively removed yourself from the family's circle. And I don't see how we can—or why we should—support you any longer."

"I have not told anyone I'm not married to him. I said that I believe he must have died. I said that I consider myself a widow." Orpha knows how slight is her logic. While this is technically what she did say, in her heart the result was that she no longer considered herself Reuben's wife. Any bonds of duty to him were cut on the rainy night when she gave him his one final chance and he abstained.

There is no fooling the older woman. "That may be so, Orpha, but I still question whether or not you consider yourself married to my son right now." She moves her head slightly to the front door and then back, a strange, singular motion that cannot be accidental. It is so bizarre, so out of character for Margaret Hussey, that Orpha wonders if she imagined it. "If Captain Hussey and I come to the conclusion that you have abandoned Reuben, then we can only do what seems appropriate and necessary. What to us seems right."

"At this point, Mrs. Hussey, I think you should do whatever you want to. I will accept the consequences."

The older woman's eyes brim with resistance. But only for a moment. After the moment, Orpha thinks she sees admiration there. *The heartiest of my daughters-in-law.* "I think I should tell you something," Margaret Hussey says. "Benedict Pinkham's ship, the *Reliant*, docked on Tuesday."

"I know." She and Adella had stood among the crowd watching. Not for Reuben—not at all—but just to watch.

"Do you know him?"

"Not well." Benedict is about Orpha's age. When they were children, Benedict was known for being a tough, a lout. Someone to be avoided. So she did. Besides, she rarely had reason to go by the Pinkham house on Water Street, and when she did she never stopped. She saw no reason to doubt his reputation, and when he went into the profession it made perfect sense. The boy, unlike Reuben, was born to kill.

"I have let it be known along the docks that I seek any and all news about my son. And I'll pay substantially if the information proves accurate. Benedict came by the house yesterday. He told me that nine months ago he saw a seaman who looked very much like Reuben—identical really—on one of the Sandwich Islands. On a street not far from the harbor where the *Reliant* was docked."

"Really? Did Benedict speak to the man?"

"He tried. He was not fifty yards away when he first spotted him, but the man immediately turned around and began walking in the other direction. Then he entered a shop."

"Benedict?"

"No," Margaret Hussey says in a strained voice. She closes her eyes. "The man. Reuben. Or so Benedict thinks."

"But what did Benedict do?"

Margaret Hussey opens her eyes. She regards her daughter-in-law before continuing. "He followed, of course. He entered the same shop, but the only person inside was an old brown islander. He asked after Reuben Hussey, but the islander did not appear to speak English very well, if at all. Benedict kept repeating himself, to no avail. The old man did not know anything about Reuben or the *Constance*; he certainly did not recognize the Hussey name."

"Did Benedict look in other shops?"

"He did. Unsuccessfully. The *Reliant* left the next day."

Orpha's face and hands have turned cold, despite the vitality of the fire in the stove. She finds herself no longer listening to Margaret Hussey but staring at the boards of the floor, trying to summon in her own mind what Benedict Pinkham, who she barely knows, actually saw, thousands of miles from Cherry Street, on that day nine months ago.

"Did this man," Orpha starts, "did he realize Benedict had seen him?"

Mrs. Hussey's jaw clenches. Clearly, this question has occurred to her too, and she does not like the answer that comes to mind. She responds in a clipped voice. "We cannot know. Benedict cannot know. He says that he did not meet the man's eye directly. But it seems unlikely the man did not see him. Benedict reports that the street, at that moment, was not busy. And, of course as a white man, Benedict would have been hard not to notice."

Orpha considers this new information. "That is not the most unambiguous explanation one could hope for."

"No." Mrs. Hussey pauses. "It isn't." The woman actually seems crushed. Orpha has never seen her face show such abject, honest pain. "But if Reuben is alive, or even seems alive, I hope and expect that you will still claim him as your husband."

"Well—" Orpha stops. "Of course. Yes. Of course."

Margaret Hussey studies Orpha's face. "Because if not, I don't even know what to say to you anymore. If you don't . . . we will be launched, all of us, into a thoroughly shameful imbroglio."

Orpha stalks the house until it feels that the walls cannot contain her agitation, that the whole structure will explode like a powder keg. She must get out. She must—get—out. Only if she is allowed to move, to literally walk off her agitation, will her mind clear, will she understand what to do. At present it is too clouded and fusty and water-logged. Overrun by images; scored by anger. She goes. She leaves. She storms onto Cherry Street and turns right. She does not even think as to whether or not she wears a walking coat, but at some point realizes she is, though she cannot remember putting it on. Adella follows her—somehow Adella is dressed; Orpha does not know when she would have gotten dressed—but within a minute or two Adella pulls even and stays there.

Benedict Pinckham is lying. Orpha has been sure of that almost from the start. It was her very first thought, as soon as Mrs. Hussey gave her the news. He is lying in a mad gambit for the reward money, because that is exactly what Benedict Pinckham would do. And if he's not lying, he must be simply wrong. A second's glance at a stranger on an island in the middle of the Pacific Ocean? How can that prove anything? And don't all those whalers and seamen look alike after years of battling sun, storms, boredom, jealousy, terror?

Months of hunting and killing and barely escaping being killed? They come to fit a type: lean, tanned, oily, coarse, and stinking, their clothes spotted and thinned through at the edges, badly in need of laundering and repair. How could Benedict, with only a second's glance, distinguish Reuben from any other American whaler he might have seen? She could barely tell the men apart herself. When they came home from their long expeditions, when they stepped smiling onto the ground of the harbor, she literally could not tell one from the other: Leander Story, Stephen Jenks, Edwin Arthur, Israel Morrissey. None of them looked like the young men she remembered from before they left, even less like the boys she grew up with. They were coarsened and darkened; hollow-eyed; ravenous. Despite the smiles and embraces, they looked isolated within their own minds—where they had been living so long—and potentially dangerous for it.

No, Benedict is lying. Or wrong. She clings to this line now as she and Adella take their customary route to the center of town, zigzagging from Orange Street to Mulberry to Union to Coffin. The day is as wet as earlier; the sky as clotted as before; the rain cannot decide whether to come or go. But in fact, Orpha barely sees it and does not feel it at all, nor the occasional rise in breeze or the dampness that promises more fog by afternoon.

To Adella's credit, she keeps silent, ready with an opinion when asked, but otherwise letting Orpha form her own. Back at the house, when Orpha asked Adella straight out what she thought, Adella agreed that they could not take Pinckham's report at face value. "It is too easy," Adella said, "to mistake a stranger for someone you know. Especially if you dearly want to see that person. If you need them."

Orpha nodded and stored Adella's wisdom, glad—relieved—to have her suspicion verified, not asking herself the obvious question: Why would Benedict Pinkham dearly want to see Reuben, so much so as to invent Reuben out of nothing? But now, as they walk, the more Orpha thinks about it, the more shades of meaning are revealed. Whale ships, those vessels dominated by Nantucketers, regularly stop and resupply on the Sandwich Islands. It is certainly not impossible that on the Sandwich Islands Benedict would meet Nantucketers from other ships. In fact, it probably happens regularly, but no one comments on it—unless one has spied a ghost. And isn't Reuben a child of one of Nantucket's most recognizable families? But if the story is true, if it might even possibly be true, what does it mean? Only one thing for certain: that Reuben Hussey was alive nine months ago. Not now. It doesn't—it cannot—automatically mean that. Not automatically. Because, Orpha knows as well as anyone, anything can happen in nine months.

But if Reuben was alive nine months ago—and in port—why didn't he write? And why had he walked away from Benedict Pinkham? Orpha could imagine a scenario in which Reuben ducked into a shop run by an island friend, a man he knew would lie to the other American, perhaps even pretend ignorance of English, just to get Pinckham to leave. After all, what shopkeeper on the Sandwich Islands does not speak at least a little English, what with all the British and American currency to be had? If the man Benedict saw truly was her husband, it seems incontrovertible that Reuben did not want to be found. Reuben had gone into hiding. But from what? The profession he never wanted in the first place? His family, who he feared would abandon him if he made another choice? Orpha herself? But why? *Why, Reuben?* Because she'd been right? Because she had understood and predicted better than anyone, better than Reuben himself? Is her husband really that petty? The more she thinks about it, the more easily she can see Reuben giving in to the impulse to run. Just so he will not have to return home and endure the inevitable confrontation. Just so he will not have to look her in the eye and listen to her. Yes, Reuben would prefer to play possum. To play dead. But it could get even more complicated than that. What if he had fallen in love with a black-haired, brown-toned, near naked Sandwich islander? What if he married her? Is Reuben Hussey the father of a clan of mulatto children? Or perhaps the perpetrator of some other, worser, darker sin, a sin so shameful he can never return home, never tell his parents who he is and what he's done? She can see it—all of it—perfectly clearly. Reuben would run. Reuben would hide. Reuben would avoid them all.

"He's hung me out to dry," Orpha says, watching the ground proceed before her feet but not seeing the streets themselves; not seeing anything actual. "And he's protected himself. He's left me waiting for over three years—and he's going to go on letting me wait—so he can give up what I told him to give up in the first place." Adella nods as if she has had the exact same thought.

"He may be too ashamed to see you," Adella says.

"Why?"

"Because he would have to admit you were right. And he would have to do something about it."

"So he strands me instead?"

Adella's voice grows cooler. "He also would not want to face others."

"So he strands me," Orpha repeats.

"Apparently." For a few steps, Adella says nothing. Then: "Remember, this all assumes that Benedict Pinkham saw what he says he did." Adella bites her lip and in the moment Orpha understands—how could she not have seen it earlier—that her friend has been placed in an even more difficult position than she. She takes Adella's hand. Recently, Adella's hands are the only things that have calmed her. "Only a little while ago," Adella says with difficulty, "we were both sure he was lying."

One can hope, Orpha finds herself thinking. And she realizes that the end she wishes for more dearly than anything is for Reuben to be dead. Not just gone but deceased. It is what she has been counting on; not just since her announcement at Helene's party but for months. Even years. By not dying, by allowing rumors to persist, by being merely gone, Reuben is keeping her chained even as he affords himself perfect liberty. If he is gone but not dead her life on Nantucket, or anywhere, can never truly begin.

Instead of working their way to Main Street, as they might on another afternoon, as they might have done just yesterday, in order to avoid the stink and the industrial ugliness of the harbor, all the machineries and factories of the whale business; instead of moving in the opposite direction from the water, far enough so that the stench of burning animal flesh lessens, far enough that they can inspect the storefronts of Morrisey's and Pratt's, spying items newly arrived from the mainland; instead of that, they head directly to the harbor. Orpha's feet wend that way without her asking them to, and Adella follows. Not fifteen minutes after leaving Orpha's house they stand on the South wharf, staring at the cold gray water. Somewhere over there lies Boston; over there lies America, the New World from which Adella's parents will soon be arriving, to which Orpha wishes she could run. Anywhere to get off this lonely little bow of earth, which has never seemed more closed—and more closing—than now.

For minutes on end, both women stare at the water. Then, so slowly the words seem to come as if tortured out her mouth, Adella says, "Orpha, why are we here now? Do you hope to see Reuben on the next ship?" For the first time since they have known each other, Orpha shouts at her friend. She calls Adella a traitor. She calls Adella stupid, a nincompoop. She calls her a scourge and an ingrate. Then she leans on a post and begins to cry. She covers her face. She is ashamed to be seen this way, not just by the steady number of people who pass by—dock workers and factory workers and sailors and would-be sailors—but mostly by Adella herself. Adella herself. Adella, for her part, stays silent. She looks at the water. She looks at the clouds. Finally she steps over and encircles Orpha's shoulder with her arm. Orpha does not draw closer, but neither does she pull away. Adella apologizes, tries to explain, stops, apologizes again. Orpha's breath finally steadies.

"If you want me to go, I'll go," Adella says. Orpha wags her head. "I can walk back to my parents' house. Nothing will happen to me there. You know that."

Orpha feels a droplet sting her face; then a larger one. She imagines in the moment's mental distortion that the water of Nantucket harbor has been watching her all her life, just waiting for the right moment to ridicule her, to deface her happiness. To actually make that happiness impossible. To tell her, by the most direct means possible, that she should never expect to feel joy again. Then Orpha remembers it is merely raining. Or was. Now is again. A wispy, ghost-like, island kind of shower, a mist more than a storm, barely noticeable—until the water thickens and one feels a spatter against one's cheek. A wound in one's eye. Until one realizes that one is slowly and inexorably getting soaked.

"I'm not letting you go anywhere," Orpha says numbly. "Not on account of Reuben Hussey." She would like to think that that puts an end to it, but in Adella's concentrated stare Orpha sees as much pity—and as much resignation—as she does confidence. Orpha sees that nothing is at an end. All the things that had become something else were about to become something else again.

TASTE

Nantucket Island, 1846

The death he is able to forget about. It rolls past his memory like a shuttling breeze off the harbor; like the notion of a United States anywhere but on this island; like the possibility that somewhere in the world people might be joyful and at peace; like the ideas that as a youth he thought were worth risking his life for: *esteem* and *ambition* and *wealth*. Like the image of himself as he was in late summer 1818, those weeks before his whale ship, the *Northampton*, unmoored from Nantucket harbor to begin a voyage intended to last two years. The heady time of hiring and stocking and scrubbing and inspecting. The countless hours of anticipation. Those days in which while he still walked on land his mind was already sailing for the horizon, a sensation so strong he could be struck with vertigo just navigating from Quince to Hussey Street. He would have to pause, settle, take moments to feel square again, to reconnect with the cobblestone beneath his feet and the mind inside his head.

The image that tests itself inside his imagination looks like this: a thick-jawed, straight-backed, thirty-three year old captain named Gideon Mitchell, no longer a novice commander after three successful voyages but not experienced either, because so far he has encountered nothing out of the ordinary, nothing that he could not overcome through the force of prior knowledge and preparation; nothing close to the bizarre stories of despair and danger told him by Captains Worth and Chalkley and Coleman in those months before he assumed his first command; nothing he could not have expected from his earlier assignments as whaler and first mate; nothing he could not have predicted from the rows of seafaring books that stuff the massive, newly installed shelves in his captain's house on Orange Street. As of September 1818, he has never been forced to summon an ingenuity—or simple daring—that he may or may not have. He has never been forced to get along merely through bullheadedness or charisma. He has so far followed the customary procedures, the common practices, and the unwritten rules of the sea. His ship has suffered only passing damage; none of his crewmen have died; best of all, each voyage has garnered hefty profits for Messrs. Macy and Bunyan, owners of the *Northampton*. In turn, he has been rewarded handsomely. The results indicate for Gideon a life ahead that will be as uneventful as it is successful, a combination he prefers and even feels proud of.

That image of himself—now twenty-eight years out of date—does not haunt him on this April day, but neither has it dissipated. It is more like seeing a drawing of some stranger dressed in clothes from earlier in the century. A seaworthy and self-satisfied captain, stocky but not overweight, cheerful in his way—if not exactly loquacious—and optimistic for the future, secretly hoping to own his own whale ship and retire one day to a baronial estate on Pleasant Street, paid for cash out of pocket. The stranger is as incredible to Gideon as is Jared Worley or Daniel Coffin, two of the three fellow Nantucketers stranded with him on that whale boat in the North Pacific after the *Northampton* sank. Or the other four that weren't Nantucketers but suffered with him too throughout those terrible ninety-nine days. Their names he has trouble remembering as much as their faces. This is how insubstantial their deaths seem to him now: banal and unterrifying, not even worth considering, really. As fictional as their lives. Did those men really have homes and families, worries and aspirations? The very idea seems preposterous. It seems to him now that they were born merely to live out their deaths, which to Gideon is not a particularly drastic or gloomy thought. Just an informed one. For nothing is more common than death; it is commoner even than life. In every man's life he suffers a thousand deaths, the cessation of one's heartbeat being only the final and not even the most painful.

No, the deaths do not haunt him or the men who suffered them. For twenty-six years, since he returned from his last and only failed command at sea, he has worked as a night watchman. It is the only job he wanted; also the only one ever offered him. As he strolls the streets in and around the harbor every evening, eyeing alleyways and storefronts, reading the eyes of the sailors and whalers who stumble out of taverns late, studying the shadows that obscure the doors and windows of the homes of town magnets—ship owners and captains, merchants and factory owners—his mind does not whisper to him that he has played a greater part than most men in bringing death into the world, that in escaping it, because of escaping it, he bears its cumbersome red mark squarely upon his forehead. He hears no such whispers; he feels no blood red mark.

What he does remember is the taste of human tissue. Sometimes the memory of it incarnates into a kind of gamey skin on his tongue; it lingers in his mind so long and so badly he is driven to near hunger-madness, as he felt so often during the ninety-nine days, the whale boat lashed by the unbearable sunshine and constant high heat; his last meal as long as a week ago; his last good quaff almost as long. The meal being the skin and muscles of one of his former crewmen; the good quaff coming from that whaler's blood. The sensations return, the need returns, as it has so often over the course of these last twenty-six years. It returns so often it can be called the theme of his island life. Even while his wife was alive and they sat down before one of her usual good meals—her chowders or hams or roasted potatoes; her freshly baked bread and handmade jellies; her elaborately buttered beans; her roasted corn or baked chicken or grilled bluefish—the memory came back, along with the terrible skin on his tongue. He thought not of the meal in front of him but one he endured seven times on that drifting whale boat: an acidic but not overly acidic taste, stringy but not unbearably so, an almost smoky flavor imparted subtly and gradually to his tongue, because the actual amount of flesh to be had from those skeletal bodies was small. By the time the men died—or, in some cases, were voluntarily executed—they had all but dried up. Even so, it was a taste Gideon got used to; one he grew to love, if only because it kept him alive.

The madness came back even more painfully those times he made love to his wife, when his mouth accidentally found itself on Sarah's shoulder and he tasted her skin. He could have ripped out her bone with the square mandibles of his jaw. All he had to do was bite. And how much better would her tender flesh taste than the undernourished, sapless flesh of those men in the whale boat. How much juicier a repast! In those moments the madness almost blinded him. The only way to stop it was to move his mouth away and shake his head, try to concentrate on the least toothsome items he could imagine: the Book of Leviticus, the price of tea leaves at Mrs. Coleman's, a worrisome crack in the right hand wall of their dining room. The strategy worked. His fever dimmed. His breath slowed. The hunger passed. But too his member shrunk. The love, never entirely started, was not completed, leaving neither of them satisfied—especially Sarah. Gideon didn't care about his own genital gratification. On these occasions, all he felt was that he had averted disaster. This was more than enough. But he knew the disappointment festered within his wife and grew worse every time.

"How come," she would say, "you never finish? It is as if you talk yourself out of it. Or do I disgust you somehow?"

"You never disgust me," he would say, not meeting her eyes.

"Then why do you stop?"

He would hesitate, shake his head.

"Is it the tragedy? *Still that?*"

"Yes," he would say quickly, knowing exactly how she would interpret the reply, knowing how it must keep her from criticizing him.

Sarah would go silent and studious. Then she would sigh, a deep soul-searing noise of fatigue. She would stare up at the ceiling and say something like, "Well, that is entirely *too bad*." Then she would turn her back to him and try to find sleep, leaving him to face his madness alone.

His wife has been dead for ten years—gone at forty from an eccentric strain of diphtheria—and in that time he has made love to no other woman. For ten years, he has been served no meals at any woman's table. Yet the haunting returns. Not just on his nightly tours of the harbor, not just on this April morning, but potentially anytime and anywhere. He can be stopped at Mrs. Coleman's for an afternoon biscuit and observe the neck of a delivery boy; he can be sitting on a bench at the Quaker Meeting House, Eldon Chase's leg or Polly Wyer's shoulder too close to his own; he can be in line at the cobbler's, waiting to drop off a pair of damaged boots, when he sees the lithe hand of Elizabeth Pollard gripping a pair of her husband's creaky shoes. It can happen even when he is alone, inside his own house. He can be in his bathtub, simply trying to clean himself, when he stares too long at his flabby stomach or his oversized thigh, and the memory returns, the sensation, the skin on his tongue. He thinks, *I wonder how I taste?*

When he finally made it back to Nantucket in August of 1820, it was clear exactly how far his story preceded him. A crowd of a thousand or more gathered at the wharf when the whale ship *Lucy* docked. A thousand intent, snooping, murderous pairs of eyes. While he waited to step upon the gangplank and shuffle down to the pier, he heard chirps and murmurs, even open debates. *What do you think he will he look like? What should we say? I wonder if you can smell it on him.* But the instant he appeared the crowd went quiet; the thousand merely stared. Gideon lowered his head and decided to look no further than the toes of his boots. When he reached the bottom of the plank and stepped on the solid ground of home, he glanced up to see that the crowd—like two conscious wings—had parted to let him through. This was not necessarily an act of respect. It might very well have been a measure of their repulsion. He didn't care. He supposed he expected no less. He walked directly to his home on Orange Street, where he was relieved to find a wife and a twelve-year-old son who asked not a single word about what happened to him. Why should they? They already knew.

But in the months that followed, as he took up his duties as night watchman, as he tried to grow comfortable again in the body of his house—and to know the wife he had not seen since September 1818—person after person knocked on his door for one invented reason or another: to pass on news about whalers Gideon used to sail with, to see if the family was sufficiently stocked with eggs or flour or lye, to donate clothes to Caleb. Gideon would have been offended by these implicit recognitions of his reduced income, but he realized that what people really wanted was just a chance to see him. And what he thought he saw in their eyes was not repulsion or fear but a compassion that bordered on pity. Or even naked sorrow. A keenly felt empathy for what it must have done to his mind and to his soul to eat another man's flesh, to gnaw on his grizzle. And not just one man but seven, and not even all of them men; no, not all. If he was a monster—these visits seemed to say—then he was a guiltless one, a monster forced into actions by circumstance, as much a victim as any of the whalers he consumed.

For twenty-six years Gideon has accepted their compassion and been grateful for it; yet all the while he has kept his secret hunger a secret. He apes sobriety in public; he keeps his back straight, his gait active, his eyes clear and focused on what lies before him. If anyone talks to him, he answers with a controlled calm, a pitch that fairly imitates how sane men speak. The hunger grew worse after his wife died, then better, then worse again. On especially keen days he feels like a predator haunting the body of a doddering and genial old seaman. Days in which when he sees a woman, any woman, he wishes he could gnaw on the points where her hip joints meet the tops of her legs. Or if it's a man, especially a whaler, he longs to know the taste of the flesh atop his kneecap, that thick fatty morsel. He stiffens himself, clears his eyes, tells himself these are *innocents*, that the man or woman he pines for *might not even have been born* when the *Northampton* went down, when one Gideon was lost and another's future began.

It is not as if he has nothing to distract him. For the last twenty-six years he has watched Caleb grow into a youth and an apprentice, then into a man and a craftsman, one with his own tailoring business. He has seen Caleb make enough money to move from the room above his shop to a quiet cottage house on East Creek Road, removed not just from the town but from nearly everyone. He has seen Caleb marry Rebecca Morrissey, a handsome but rather stern woman, a woman Gideon is determined to like regardless. He has seen Caleb, a year ago last April, become a father to a milky boy named Jasper. Caleb's house is too far from the harbor to be included in Gideon's nightly circuit, yet he walks by his son's shop every evening. He checks the doors, he stares into the window, he takes a long look down Rose Lane to see if he can spot potential shopbreakers. He never sees any, but he tells himself that when he does he will battle them to the death.

On this day—an abnormally sunny Tuesday, the seventh of

April—as he leaves home to resupply a few items at Mrs. Coleman's, he sees one of the island's many wooly-headed, impatient young boys lumber by. The boy is carrying a circle of cheese for his mother, who walks beside him. Gideon, at the end of his walkway and about to enter the street, decides against his journey and turns back for his house. He is three steps on his return path when he hears the boy say matter of factly: "There's the cannibal."

"Hush," his mother says, embarrassed, maybe even panicked. She speaks in a stage whisper so strong it flies past Gideon and strikes his window. "That's a poor man who had to do something terrible to survive a tragedy. I am sure that his wife and son were very happy he made it back."

"But he is a cannibal. Tom told me so. He ate the men's bodies instead of throwing them to the sharks. The sharks were everywhere, Tom said, and they wanted the men's bodies, but he ate them instead."

"Did you hear what I said?"

"But the sharks were right there!"

"Shush now! You don't know what you're saying."

"It's disgusting, I think. Doesn't it seem disgusting to you?"

All Gideon can do is to move as fast as his legs will allow. He cannot blame the boy for his opinions. He actually admires the boy's willingness to express them. He wishes everyone on this island were as honest.

"Shush," the mother repeats. "You never know what you're saying."

"Oh, so that's it, eh? He's the cannibal, and you blame me?"

"Do not speak to me that way," the mother says. From behind him, Gideon hears a muffled cuff, a hand meeting a clothed piece of body: a shoulder or an elbow or a backside. Not terribly hard—more for demonstration than actual punishment.

"What's that for?"

"For passing on lies. For laughing at a perfectly good man."

"I wasn't lying. And I wasn't laughing at him either."

"You were. You know it."

"I wasn't. I never once laughed. Ow!" That time he heard skin.

"You need to understand."

"Hitting me is helping me to understand?"

Gideon enters his house, closes his door, and the argument dies from his hearing. He feels mortified and outraged and giddy at the same moment. Found out and nailed down. Almost set free. *He wasn't laughing*, he thinks at the woman. *And he is telling the truth.*

Now that his wife is dead and his son is fully ensconced in his own home, Gideon has little to do each day but wait for the night to come. He makes dinners of tasteless carrot soup and Mr. Pickford's thick black bread. He makes suppers of salt pork or an egg. He stays in bed and reads, not about seafaring anymore but histories of ancient wars or tracts of stoic philosophy. He naps. He listens to his house. He walks to Mrs. Coleman's or occasionally to the harbor, though he sees the place every night on his watchman rounds. He steps outside and lets the weather strike him as it may. He is as happy to be hit by a sour dog of a fog as he is by summer sunshine or a brisk autumn wind. Anything to wake himself. Some days he considers if he should just end his own life, since it has effectively ended already—not just the first but too this second Gideon Mitchell existence. He decides against it. Not because he fears death—he does not fear death in the least—but because, in his middle 60s, he has become lazy and a coward about pain.

After he hears the boy on the street, Gideon decides to visit Caleb's house. Though it is not really as far a walk from Gideon's as a map might make it seem, his son's house is in an isolated spot. Only one other home stands on East Creek Road; and the neighbor Caleb and Jasper visit most often is no human but a little inlet three hundred feet from their house, where the harbor has cut into the shore. Gideon knows that such an inconspicuous location is where he should live—where he should have moved as soon as he returned from that disastrous last voyage. It is his son, with his steady work and growing business and a clientele that love him—with his history of having never once left the island—who belongs in Gideon's spacious house on Orange Street.

Gideon once half-heartedly offered the house to Caleb, but before Caleb could answer his wife tomahawked an unequivocal *No*. Rebecca wants nothing to do with the house, with her father-in-law, with whatever moneys might be leftover from his apocryphal days as one of the island's most successful whalers. (While Gideon will not say so, there are no such moneys. But Rebecca never asks.) When he made the offer, Gideon tried, albeit not as strenuously as he could have, to explain that he did not mean Caleb and Rebecca would live in the house with him, but that the two households would swap residences. It didn't matter. Rebecca would not allow the conversation to go any further. Any idea of muting the distance between her home and Gideon Mitchell's, between their lives and Gideon Mitchell's, brings a visceral reaction from the woman. To his daughter-in-law, Gideon is a stigma, nothing more. A cause for shame—maybe even suspicion—and something to be endured. As a consequence, Gideon does not visit his son nearly as often as he would like, and Rebecca allows him in only because she has no choice. When there, she shows him no warmth; she offers him no tea; she avoids being in the same room with him. When Gideon goes with Caleb and Jasper to the inlet, Rebecca stays behind, but not without whispering strenuous warnings to her husband, warnings that must, Gideon assumes, involve himself. If Caleb is not around, she refuses Gideon the trip altogether. She makes up lies to send her father-in-law away. *The boy is ill.* Or: *He has just set down to nap.* Or: *I am off to my mother's. She likes me to bring Jasper.* Her lowered brows, her nervy brown-black eyes, and her immovable chin are too easy to read.

Gideon shouldn't have to knock, but he does anyway. He hopes that demonstrating respect for protocols will earn him Rebecca's acceptance, or at least her tolerance. *I am not forcing myself on you. I am letting you choose to not let me in.* At this hour, Caleb will almost certainly be at the shop. Gideon knows he should just stay away, but he needs to see his grandson. Even more than usual he feels dispirited. Useless. Perhaps this one time Rebecca will relent. This one time she will accept that he is not a threat. Or a disgrace. But it is not Rebecca who answers.

"Oh," Caleb says, surprised. "Hello, father."

"Shouldn't you be working?" Gideon says, a mockery of remonstration. In fact, he is thrilled.

"Rebecca asked that I come back for a few hours. There is some women's meeting."

She could have asked me to come, Gideon thinks, but he knows that would be expecting the impossible. The good thing is that she is gone.

"Another meeting, is it?"

Caleb wags his head and feigns vexation. But Gideon can tell his son is perfectly happy to have been called home. As always, Gideon can't help but see how indebted his son's looks are to his mother. The dark eyes, the pronounced lips, the hair that in this damp and salt-riddled air refuses to lie flat but curls and bends at the sides of his face. Yet it's more than his son's features that remind Gideon of Sarah. He sees his wife too in Caleb's careful expressions and gently clipped speech; the dry humor that can turn quickly to consternation, an irritation he will not express but instead try to navigate by laughing it off or moving the conversation elsewhere. After a career at sea, no matter how abbreviated, it still surprises Gideon when a grown man does not release his anger or express his opinions. That is not the seaman's way. A seaman lets his anger out—sometimes violently—and then lets it go. It is no wonder there are so many scraps aboard a whale ship, and even more when the boat reaches shore. This is what comes when anger is let out. But as a captain Gideon would rather have had the open scraps than interminable leagues of whispers and back-stabbing; of seething, low level resentments. A captain needs to see what emotions there are aboard a ship. It's what he can't see that threatens him.

But Gideon also knows that the seaman's way is not everyone's. Why should it be Caleb's? Caleb was never a sailor. And until the disaster happened that forced Gideon permanently to the island, he spent remarkably little time around his son. During the first twelve years of Caleb's life, Gideon lived a combined three and a half of them on Nantucket. It was Sarah who raised the boy. Yet another lance of regret, but this at least is a common one. What whaler or sailor—the married kind at least—does not regret his time away? Certainly Gideon knew captains that after eight or nine months on-island were demonstrably agitated, eager to get back to the sea. This, he always believed, had nothing to do with the state of their marriages but their commitment to adventure. The thrill of the hunt. The desire for money. Or perhaps the addictive power of ruling a watery planet. (Although it was true too that in his time Gideon heard stories of captains who kept "wives" at various ports of call; men who fathered children of all colors and even provided those children with homes and clothes and education. Men who never knew the sadness of leaving spouse and family because they were forever sailing to others. On the other hand, neither did they ever know the intense, sweet relief of returning home.)

"Come in. Jasper will be happy to see you." Gideon wonders if he hears the strain of a lie in that last remark. In fact, Caleb's son has always looked at Gideon as if not quite sure how to feel about the old man. How can Jasper not have heard and felt and implicitly absorbed Rebecca's scorn for her father-in-law? How can he not feel that his grandfather must be avoided?

Gideon steps inside the cottage and finds Jasper lying still on his side in the crib Caleb built for him. It looks like something one might import from the mainland, every piece fitting cleanly against the next, every line straight; even the paint—a calm shade of blue, deeper than the sky but not nearly as dark as the ocean—has been applied with a professional's unnoticeable stroke. Caleb has always been good with his hands: building and shaping, cutting and repairing. Taking rough pieces of nature and putting them in order. No wonder he never felt the call to leave land.

"Is he—" Gideon starts, in a whisper. "I don't want to wake him."

Caleb shakes his head. "He's up. It just takes him a bit to feel fully returned to the world."

Gideon often feels the same way, even when he isn't coming out of sleep.

Caleb gently urges the boy's name. Jasper moves his head at once, then his whole upper body. He stumbles to his feet and rubs his eye with a thick left hand. He sure seems to have just woken up. He scans the room for a face, passing over his grandfather's almost without looking at him. It is Rebecca he wants. But failing Rebecca, his father is an acceptable second best. Jasper extends his arms to Caleb, who pulls him with a grunt out of the crib. The boy rests his wide, bald head against his father's chest. His face points to Gideon. The hard stare he sets on his grandfather—as if he's never seen the man before and is fairly certain he does not want to—confirms Gideon's fears.

"Do not worry, young Jasper," Gideon says and steps over. "Your grandfather is here for a visit. We'll have a grand time."

"He's not worried, father. Just sleepy. Like I told you, it takes—"

Just as Gideon reaches a paternal hand to pat Jasper on the back, the boy shrieks. He pulls his head away and then leans to his right, so that Caleb has to struggle to keep Jasper's heavy body from toppling onto the floor. Finally, Caleb manages control of his son and sets him down. "Oh how now, little one?" Gideon intones. "You are flesh of my flesh. Blood of my blood." But the boy only grips the leg of his father, his brown eyes round with alarm. Gideon comes one step closer, but this only makes the boy back away. Jasper stumbles and falls, bottom first, on the hard planks of the floor. More crying.

"Come on, come on," Caleb soothes. "Surely no one can be afraid of grandpa."

Gideon says nothing, only feels the air grow close against his skin. Then he manages to speak. "That's right. I am no risk."

"You are hungry, I expect," Caleb says to Jasper. "We never did get around to taking care of that." He picks up the boy and brings him to the table, where a cup of milk and a piece of bread wait for him. Caleb hands Jasper the cup and the boy drinks lustily. He drinks as if drinking can chase his fear away. He eats a bit of bread. Soon his mood improves. The next time Caleb puts him down, Jasper toddles about the room, grabbing and manipulating whatever he sees at his feet: one of Caleb's boots, a small wooden horse Caleb carved, the leg of a side table. It is hard not to be impressed with the boy's physique, his tall upper body and chunky shoulders. The beefy white splendor of his thighs.

"He's as big as an Indian king," Gideon says, "and only thirteen months old!"

Caleb smiles at Gideon's appraising stare. "Yes, he's a lad now, isn't he?" Caleb says. "A thick, powerful lad." Before Gideon can reply, Caleb shouts at Jasper to leave alone the fireplace poker. The boy drops it, but it makes a rude clatter against the hearth, loud enough to start him crying again.

"To be a lad he'll have to stop shedding tears," Gideon jokes.

Caleb frowns at the comment. It appears that he is about to speak, but then he doesn't. They both stare silently at Jasper, who is not yet calm. He refuses to settle until his father picks him up. Caleb says, "We should get him out-of-doors. Less trouble to be had."

The two men dress the boy. Given the unusual warmth of this April morning, they decide a short-sleeved shirt and trousers are cover enough to keep away a chill. Caleb grabs a quilt for them to sit on and they set out for the inlet. They cross over eighty yards of moors before they reach their stopping point. There, atop the clotted and rocky sand, they settle in to spy trade ships entering the harbor. They tell Jasper about these "water mules" that bring so many wonderful goods from so many distant places. "If you keep an eye, I bet you'll see one," Gideon says. "Yes, yes," Caleb seconds with a drummed up enthusiasm. "Perhaps several. Especially on a day like this one. Keep an eye, Jasper." But as the hour goes on, all they spot are two aimless fishing smacks having no success in the shallow water near shore. They fall silent. As happens so often, Gideon grows tongue-tied around his son. The feelings he first had so long ago—that Caleb is a stranger to him, not kin to his own soul—have only worsened with time. He loves Caleb and is proud of the contented life he has made for himself. But now more than ever Gideon only sees Sarah in him, and if so to what part of his son can Gideon connect? How will Caleb ever feel connected to him?

"Father," Caleb says, "can you watch Jasper for a minute? I should have left a note for Rebecca. She will want to know where we are."

Shouldn't she be able to figure that out herself? Gideon thinks. *And doesn't she trust her own husband?* But he says nothing except, "I'll be glad to. You go on."

Gideon fears that Jasper will throw a tantrum as soon as Caleb is out of arm's reach, but the boy merely wanders a few feet away, searching for what he can find in the sand of the cove. He picks up the odd shell or a bit of a stick, brings it close to his face. Gideon waits for Jasper to begin gnawing at the stick—Gideon will have to take it away then—but Jasper resists the temptation. He collects his clumsy armload and toddles back to the quilt, where he sits and picks carefully through his collection, examining each item intently before moving on to the next. So much like his father,

Gideon thinks. *This one won't go to sea either.* Gideon scoots closer. The boy either doesn't notice or doesn't care. After one more move, Gideon is close enough to put his arm around the child. He does so lightly, barely grazing the boy's back with the arm of his jacket.

"That's not really the way you go," Gideon says, pointing toward the harbor and the water beyond it to the west. "That's only for the merchant ships and their unending back and forth to America. If you want to hunt whale you come around this way." His motions pull him even closer against Jasper. "When you reach the far side of Siasconset you start east. And you keep going east, more than halfway to Europe, until you reach a little place called Corvo. It will take you a few weeks to get there, but it's a good place to lay in supplies. And you can stretch your legs."

Jasper looks up at him as if almost understanding what Gideon is saying. No sign of crying either. Apparently, the boy is no longer afraid. Encouraged, Gideon continues. "Then you start the long trip south. There's one stop more along the way, in the Cape Verde Islands. The last chance—for many months—to resupply. But after that you go. You go way far to the south—stopping to kill any whale you spy, of course. You go all the way down to the bottom of South America. Do you know what South America is, Jasper?" The boy cocks his round head and squints. "'Tis a continent—a land mass thousands of square miles 'round. It's shaped like a big arrowhead, with the tip of the arrow down near the bottom of the world." With his free hand he tries to demonstrate the figure. "You have got to get to that tip in order to sail around it, right? There's no way through a continent, eh? Not with a whale ship and dozens of men. They can't lug the ship on their shoulders." Gideon laughs, a forced, over-jolly sound. Jasper makes a noise and then starts exaggerated chewing motions. But with nothing in his mouth all that results is a smacking of his lips.

"So, my dear, you go around the tip." Gideon pauses. "Then guess what you do?" Jasper squeaks; he frowns. "That's right. You go back up again! After sailing from Nantucket to nearly the bottom of the world you have to go back on up. But this time on the western side, the side that faces the Pacific. Yes? You leapfrog along the west coast of South America, looking for whale. You go out a ways for months at a time; then you come back in, to this port or that. There's Talcahuano. There's Arica. There's Atacames. Strange names, I know. Eventually you find yourself near the top, off the coast of a place called Ecuador. And now Jasper, tell me what you do then." The boy makes a different, high-pitched noise, more like a yap. He shakes his head. He shakes it again. "You don't want to guess?" Jasper shakes his head again. Gideon sees a ball of saliva slip out from the corner of Jasper's mouth and slide down his chin. He wonders what the saliva would taste like if he were to lick it off. Slurry, he supposes, with a slight fizz atop a texture of oil. Gideon looks over his shoulder, checking—he realizes only after he does it—to make sure Caleb is not coming back, to make sure he still has the boy to himself. Even so he decides, regretfully, not to lick the saliva. Instead, he squeezes Jasper's hip, feels the roll of flesh there, the thick, milk-fed padding against hip bone.

"Well, I'll have to tell you then, won't I?" Jasper tries to stand, but Gideon pushes him back down. Jasper cries, more from surprise than pain or sadness. He tries to stand again, but once more, if gently, Gideon sets him back down. "Do you turn around, little Jasper? Is that what you do? Huh?" Gideon hopes the boy will listen instead of wrestle. He would rather keep Jasper's attention through questions than force. "Do you finally head home? Not at all. Of course not. You have only been gone a year. What you do, my dear, is go *west*!" Gideon tries to amplify the word, to make it sound like a birthday surprise. But Jasper is not assuaged. "A whale ship wants to reach the Offshore Ground, west of the Galapagos. Plenty of good whaling to be done in the Offshore Ground, at least in my day. Not so much anymore. These days the ships must go much farther than that to find new whale. These days the ships sail well past the Sandwich Islands. The Sandwich Islands, Jasper." The boy stares at him sharply and makes an urgent, whiny noise. He wants to get up. He wants to escape. He wants to be elsewhere. "The Sandwich Islands are *thousands of miles* from Ecuador. And they are so so so far from this little island here. Halfway around the world. Can you imagine that, Jasper?"

It's no use. The boy is more intent on moving than listening, so Gideon gives up speech and focuses on physical restraint. But, even as he struggles to keep Jasper close at hand, his mind wanders. In his time, even when the Offshore Ground was a new discovery, it wasn't enough. Even then the *Northampton* had to push further out into the Pacific. Or at least Gideon felt they had to. It was his captain's opinion and his rightful decision. The men would have been happy to turn back. After a year and a quarter, the casks were 70% full. On the voyage home they surely would have spotted more whale, enough to get them to eighty or ninety percent. But Gideon did not want to leave the economics of the expedition to chance. After three straight commands in which he returned home at 100%, he did not want to risk disappointing Messrs. Macy and Bunyan. 100% was what they expected. Gideon knew that once he declared they were heading home the men would stand only so much dawdling. They too were eager to make as much as they could off the voyage, but how long, once they turned for home, would they be content to remain at sea for the sake of that last 10%? Nine months? A year? Two? As long as Gideon? Never.

It had seemed an automatic decision. His right as the commander and his duty as the chief representative of the owners of the *Northampton*. They would sail further west. They would not turn back until they were closer to full. That was Gideon's call. And if not for this decision, the *Northampton* would not have met and drawn the ire of that malicious, unnatural sperm. They would not have been rammed twice by her. They would not have had to abandon ship and every ounce of its hard-earned oil. Twenty-seven men would not have been left stranded on small boats in the middle of the godless Pacific, haunted by sharks, battered by the sun, deadly afraid of monsoons, uncertain how to make their limited supplies of water, jerky, and hardtack last.

Jasper is straining harder now and whining worse, whining so badly he might be heard back at the house. It is a whine of strenuous effort, of young determination; the spirit inside a healthy body; a well-fed and fattened persistence. For the first time in several years, maybe even a decade, Gideon thinks of his cabin boy, Billy Holbrook. Fourteen; blonde-haired; blue-eyed; sweet-chinned. Gentle of voice and smooth of shoulder; delicate throughout his limbs. Billy was the son of his cousin Lydia, who lived with her husband Oliver

Holbrook on Mill Hill. Billy was so full of excitement when they started the voyage—his first—his cheeks were almost as pale as a woman's. Billy ended up as one of the eight passengers in Gideon's whale boat. And by the time the boat's supplies had run out; by the time they despaired of ever catching another sea turtle; by the time Coffin and that other one—Rawlings—had died and they made as a group the fateful decision not to toss the bodies overboard to the anxious sharks but instead to feast on them themselves; by the time it was clear that the only way for some of them to survive was to eat some of the others; by the time they decided to let a lottery determine matters, it was Billy Holbrook who drew the shortest piece of rope. Billy offered no resistance or even complaint, only a sunken, deflated expression. Gideon thought that as captain he must perform the terrible duty, although at that point any real difference between captain and crewman had become meaningless. It took one bullet from Gideon's pistol to Billy's head. The boy dropped instantly, and then the rest of them fell on him. They had to act fast before the meat spoiled or the blood ran out.

He remembers how sweet Billy's skin tasted. Not like the earlier skin off Coffin and Rawlings, not such a smoky, sour taste. Billy's skin was mellow, his gristle almost fatty, even after so many malnourished days. Like eating lamb. Gideon remembers how clear his head felt when he finished his meal; he remembers feeling hopeful again and not at all ashamed. Stronger, if not actually strong. For days after, he and the other men sucked on Billy's bones. One of the men—Shattuck, Gideon remembers now—tried to argue that they should throw the bones over: a kind of burial at sea. The least they could do. But Gideon overruled him. *If we are to do what we're doing, we should get the most out of it. Otherwise there is no point.* A sonorously worded explanation, befitting a captain. Truth is, he just wanted Billy's bones. He would have brawled Shattuck for them. He would have shot the man. But as Gideon spoke, the other three whalers nodded their heads in unison. Shattuck scowled and gave in.

The deaths didn't matter. The deaths didn't matter. No death matters. Life was the point. The point then was singular: *stay alive*. They'd thrown over, by necessity, every other principle, every other consideration. But what he remembers so fondly now is the lovely, supple taste of Billy's body. It and survival were irrevocably the same.

Gideon hears Jasper cry: a real cry, brazen and pained. He feels the boy strain with all his power. Then he realizes why. Jasper's fat upper arm, the juicy area just above his elbow, is in Gideon's mouth. Gideon is sucking on it. And it is miraculous: the sensation his tongue receives as it moves on Jasper's skin. The sweet, dough and milk aroma of year-old child enters Gideon's nostrils and sets his head spinning. Gideon wants to dig his teeth in. Gideon wants to bite. Gideon wants to chew. He's waited so long. But to taste Jasper he must first hold the boy down, against the force of his struggling. If Gideon wants to get his teeth in, the boy must not be allowed to escape. And Jasper has to stop shrieking.

"Stop it! What are you doing? Stop!"

The hysterical tone of the woman's voice stuns Gideon numb. His arms drop from Jasper's body; Jasper's arm falls from his mouth. Gideon can't move. Jasper, meanwhile, pushes himself up and away. He moves as fast as his chunky, stumbling legs will take him—to this woman charging at him as fast as her leaner limbs can move. In moments, their bodies meet. She scoops the boy up and into her grasp. She checks his arm. She turns to Gideon, shielding the boy with her whole left side.

"You're mad! You should be hanged! You should be locked away!"

Gideon has never seen a woman's face so taut with rage, so demented by venom. Her hairy eyebrows are almost inside her eyes. Her teeth are bared. She would kill him if she could. She would tear him apart.

Someone else, a man, approaches. "What's going on?" he says. "What is the shouting for?" The man stops beside the woman. He is brown haired; smooth of cheek; much calmer in eye than she. He is strangely pretty for a man and younger-looking than his age, but at the same time he does not look like an inconsequential person. He looks like someone with inner order, a broad and hard-earned valley of calm. A contrast with the woman. A contrast with Gideon himself. This noble, confused man peers at his wife, then at Gideon, then back at the woman. He is eager to comprehend, to moderate, to settle whatever is the dispute.

"I'll tell you what I'm shouting for: Your father had Jasper's arm in his mouth and was about to bite him."

The man is so stunned all he can do for a moment is stare at Gideon. Then, with this new set of facts, whatever settlement the man had imagined disappears. It becomes impossible. Not even worth considering. Gideon sees all chance of it evaporate as the man's eyes begin a dark and drastic reappraisal. The woman continues her litany, but the man does not appear to hear her any longer. The man is involved in his own quandary, a thornier dilemma at play inside his mind. She knew it, the woman says. She always knew it, but she couldn't say so because no one would have believed her. Her husband would not have believed her. Her husband would not have backed her up, with his mad devotion to his father. But she knew. Oh, she knew. She could sense it. She could feel it. She could *smell* it.

And this proves it. This proves it to the world.

She was right about him.

She knew it all along.

So, Gideon thinks, apparently she did. And a little part of him is glad it's not his secret to keep anymore. But as he looks harder at this woman with the imploding features—her crinkled brow, her bared teeth, her face creased with fury—he realizes the greater, truer part of it that she can never know. What no one else on this island, save for him, can know. And even he doesn't know it completely. Not even now. Not yet. Because for now he has done nothing but put a milk-fed arm into his mouth. He did not even get to find out what it tastes like.

HOW LONG WILL YOU TARRY?

Why art Thou silent when the wicked swallow
Those more righteous than they?
Why hast Thou made men like the fish of the sea,
Like creeping things without a ruler over them?
--Habakkuk 1:13-14

Nantucket Island, 1920

"Mrs. Ogilvy," Allen Pile says, "this is not something I want to do right now."

You lift your hand from the test you are marking. Sixth grade fractions. Sally Jenks just scored a 58.

"*Miss*," you say. It is the fourth time in two days you have corrected him. Allen Pile: this snub-nosed, dark-haired, black-eyed, boy; so polite, so surprised, so ingenuous when you confront him, so willing to fix whatever it was he was doing but who inevitably repeats the behavior as soon as you turn your back. You wonder all the time whether Allen Pile is merely stupid or playing a diabolical game of torture. You have not decided on an answer, but you know that most of the time he does not seem stupid, just ordinary.

"Yes," Allen Pile says and blinks. "Miss. Excuse me, ma'am. Miss Ogilvy."

"*Mrs.* means you are a married lady."

"I know."

"I am not married."

He does something with his mouth. A smirk? A spasm? A sigh? The beginning of a yawn? Whatever it is, it stops—then it's gone—before it can tell you anything. "I know," Allen Pile says.

You are very tired. It is a gray, chill, wet October day, more like winter than autumn. You can see out the window on the far side of the classroom the afternoon failing and the accumulated clouds mimicking nighttime. It is 3:40. Most likely you will have to walk home in fog, because Allen Pile has barely even started his assigned punishment: copying the chapter on "Our American Manners" from the social studies textbook. You did not give him this work because he called you "Mrs." again—although that certainly made you testy enough—but because he kept poking Vivian Fanning with the metal tip of his fountain pen. Prick, prick, prick. You watched it happen. Four times over the course of two minutes. To her credit, the girl did not squeal or scream, but she did keep jerking, and finally you had to put an end to it. You had to call Allen out. Sometimes you try to ignore Allen Pile, and occasionally that works. Not today. Now it is 3:40, and he has barely started on his punishment, and you cannot let him out of it, because what respect would he show for your punishments the next time around?

You have learned in seven years of teaching sixth graders to be firm—or else. It is not actually in your nature to be firm, to be harsh, but you have learned that a teacher has no choice, at least a teacher with less than ten years experience in this building and whose skin is many shades darker than the boys and girls under her instruction. You must stay firm or you will drown beneath the swell of these mocking, canny animals. You know this. You have learned it. So you don't know why you are sitting here explaining the difference between *Mrs.* and *Miss* to Allen Pile. It is not as if he cares and, besides, he knows the difference already. He is just trying to aggravate you with his *Mrs. Ogilvy*s, maybe even punish you for detaining him. You know that what he deserves is a swat on the can or an increased assignment or, at the very least, an icy reply on the level of: "Don't approach this desk and call me what I'm not," replete with a red-eyed stare and a strict cast about your lips. But you are tired—in many ways and of many things, one of which is pretending to be something you are not.

"I know you're not married," he repeats.

"But I was once engaged to be married," you clarify. "To a young man named William Hawkins. He used to work on the railroad, but he left the island. He lives in California now."

"Is he coming back?"

You can't help yourself. You smile. You see that, for sure this time, Allen Pile does not understand the foolishness of his question. "No, he is never coming back. Even if the railroad started up again—

which it won't—I am sure he would not return."

You are telling the truth. In 1910, seven years before the railroad closed and its tracks were ripped up and sent to France to support the war effort, William fell into a fatal argument with a customer. The man had just bought a ticket to travel outbound from the harbor to Siasconset. William, whose job was to keep the locomotives in good repair, had stepped into the station house to deliver a report to the new manager, Lucas Rose. Before William could get anywhere near Lucas Rose, the customer flagged him and explained that he wanted help with his bags. "I'm not a porter," William said, "but I know where the porter is." William thought it should be obvious he was no porter. He was dressed in his mechanic's shirt and dungarees. His face was salty, his shirt soaked, his whole aspect testy and energized after struggling for an hour to restart the gasoline car, which the railroad had purchased three years earlier. So far it had given the railroad—and William specifically—nothing but headaches. "A locomotive does not need to be a car," he used to tell you. "Plenty of coal left in the world."

If this white man actually thought the Nantucket Railroad let its porters get this disheveled and this malodorous, William wondered what kind of porters the man was used to. Maybe none, William mused. Maybe this white man had never ridden a railroad before. That would be a first. "Let me get the porter for you," William said and pointed toward the window, beyond which it was easy enough to spy Lower Orange St. There, Zachary Fitch was loafing with another boy, a kid so young and blonde and bland he could not be more than midway through high school. Zachary himself had graduated only a month earlier.

"He's right outside," William said.

"Look, you lazy scamp, I know you're the porter," the man said.

William was not used to having his word doubted when it came to railroad matters; nor did he like being called a "scamp." Yet, according to what he told you an hour later, when he showed up at your house looking as agitated as you had ever seen him, he managed to trap his rising anger and simply repeat that he would fetch the *actual porter* if the man still wanted one. But the customer only became more adamant. He refused to let William leave. He again accused William of lying. Not being trusted, you knew, riled William worse than anything, worse than being called a name, worse than losing money, worse than being cheated. So the gloves came off. The argument escalated until the white man shouted, "I don't care whether or not you're a porter. You're supposed to carry my bags."

It was not the first time William had heard this during his six years with the Nantucket Railroad. He had complained to you before. In the past—in his first year or two—he might have given in and just taken the bags onto the train. The difference this time, he explained, almost choking on his anger, was that with the retirements of Orville Pratt, the former manager, and Eudora Thurlow, the matronly ticket seller, William had seniority over anyone else in the station house that day. William was not going to do Zachary Fitch's job for him, especially after struggling so hard with the gas car, and especially seeing as how at the moment Fitch was only loafing, shooting the breeze with a witless fool on the street outside. William shouted at the man in return, something he claimed to not remember but which an eyewitness later called "racially insulting." The man's face went pale and gravely cold, as if he were not merely angry anymore but deeply nauseous, bodily disturbed. He stalked back to the ticket window and demanded to know who was in charge of a railroad that allowed random niggers to insult its passengers. It took William only forty-five seconds to realize that Lucas Rose would have no choice but to fire him. So he quit instead.

As strenuously as you tried to convince him to do otherwise—you were engaged, after all—William took a boat to the mainland the next day. He was leaving the island. He had told you for many months that the railroad was failing, too many people driving cars now, that it couldn't possibly last until the end of the decade. (Indeed, the Great War provided the railroad with just the excuse it needed to dissolve with dignity.) More than that, William said he could not live trapped in a nuthouse anymore. "This island," he said to you, and you were not to take this personally, "feels like some mad doctor's lab experiment."

He told you he would write you soon enough. He told you that when he settled permanently you could come join him. You had no choice but to agree—he was too angry, too determined to leave—but secretly you hoped he would fail on the mainland, and settle nowhere, and eventually return. In all, William wrote three letters to you. One straightaway from Boston; another a few weeks later from Omaha. The last letter came nearly a year after the second, and it came from Bakersfield, California where William had taken a position with the Southern Pacific Railroad. In none of the letters, not even the last, did he say anything about you joining him. If he truly wanted you to, he would have said so. And, besides, how easy would it be for anyone, especially a man as shiny handsome and gregarious as William, to meet someone new in California.

Over the years it has crossed your mind to go find him, to assert your rightful place as his one-time, and maybe still, fiancée. But you are not someone who believes in chasing other people, and you know in the base of your spirit, as if reading a page stranded there, that if you suddenly showed at his residence in Bakersfield—if that is even where he still lives, if he is even alive anywhere, for that matter, and not another casualty of the war—he would smile a greeting at you and hug you as quick as a water bug, but at the first available second he would run. Ten years ago William thought he knew the pattern his life had taken. He was glad for it. You'd like to think he was proud of it. But you can imagine that after having the pattern punctured several times, William no longer believes in the idea of patterns and possibly even resists them. So you do not go.

"What's so great about California?" Allen Pile asks.

Again, you smile. Because you have asked yourself the same question. "I don't know, but a lot of people think of it as the place for new beginnings. I think it's always been that way. You know, the excitement of the west? In the middle of the last century lots of people left Nantucket for California. They heard stories, and they wanted to find out."

Allen Pile looks at you, confused. His black eyes, almost fearful, tremble over a question. "What if you don't want to go west? What if you want to stay here?"

"Then you stay. No one's forcing you out."

Allen nods, but he seems unsure. He seems ready to refute the statement. In fact, you yourself are not sure you could live in

Bakersfield, California—or anywhere outside of the island. You never have, after all. You are, through your mother's side, the great-great-grandchild of Absalom Boston, once the wealthiest and most charismatic Negro on the island, the prince of the community of "New Guinea": a self-contained neighborhood of negroes and Indians and itinerant Portuguese just east of Nantucket village. In 1845, Absalom Boston sued the village so that his daughter Phebe could attend high school. Absalom Boston won, and in 1846 the girl took her rightful seat. Relatives of yours have lived on this island as far back as the middle of the 18th century. William, however, arrived on Nantucket only six months before he started working for the railroad, a lark of a trip suggested by an out-of-work friend. Both men were willing to take a dare on better fortunes than they could find in Brockton. The friend lingered for eight months, picked up only piecemeal manual labor, then left. William found a job and stayed.

He always seemed happy, you reflect now, but at the same time, given William's quicksilver, impatient nature, his cheerful impetuousness, his eagerness to know and learn and see everything, it was something of a miracle that he ever agreed to marry you. You always were waiting for the other shoe to drop. And this, in the end, is the real reason why you cannot head off to California in search of William Hawkins. Because William does not want to marry you, and he probably never did. If he did, he would have brought you with him in the first place.

But are you actually going to admit this to Allen Pile? And if not, why is the boy still standing in front of you instead of copying the social studies chapter like you told him to? "Why don't you sit down," you say. "This isn't the right time to talk about my past. Not when you have work to do."

Disappointment infects Allen's expression. His eyes tick in search of a new thought. Then they look you square on, his face sick with sincerity.

"Both my mother and my father told me this morning that I must not dawdle coming home."

This is almost certainly a lie, but you can work with it. "Then how much more important for you to behave well in class, right?"

He blinks.

"So you don't have to stay after? So that you don't disappoint them?"

His mouth squirms slowly. He is considering a reply. You know you should have said something like, "Too bad—sit. You made your own mess." You know this is what the boy deserves. Maybe a year ago you would have said exactly that, or said nothing, only pointed imperiously at his seat until he slunk to it: defeated, hang-tied, and ill-dressed. A year ago you would have taken Allen to task for his damaged trousers, the right rear pocket of which somehow ripped and has been hanging down all day. To make it worse, at recess he was trying to splatter his classmates by stomping a puddle, the only result being that he sprayed his own leg, the back of which is now dotted and caked with chunks of clinging, tan mud. A year ago, you would not have stood for it. A year ago, you would have sent him home to change immediately after recess. A year ago, you would have brooked no excuses. Today, you are just tired. You are deeply, unfathomably tired—as if you are drowning in your own private lake of fatigue.

All you can think about now is the remains of a pot of pea soup that you stored unceremoniously in the ice box last night. You will go home. You will take out the pot. You will light the gas burner on the stove. When the soup is reheated, you will sit at your kitchen table and eat straight from the pot with a spoon leftover from your morning coffee. You think about how good the soup will taste on a misty, chilly, foggy day like today. Especially when chased with a jigger of whiskey. Your students would be scandalized to know you keep a bottle in the rear of your cupboard. Or maybe they wouldn't. You would hazard to guess that at least three-quarters of your students' parents defy the Volstead Act with regularity and conviction. Or, rather, they defy it in spirit. So far none of them need to buy or make liquor, because they all stocked up in the year between passage and enforcement. The whole island stocked up. Except, perhaps, Allen Pile's father. Everett Pile is a merchant seaman and travels off-island so frequently he can find alcohol in dozens of ports of call. Looking at the man, those few times you have seen him, you have no doubt that his relationship with liquor is as good as ever.

You think about the pot of soup, the lonely jigger of whiskey, and you realize you are in danger of becoming a cliché to this community. The spinster schoolteacher. No, something even more particular than that: the spinster Negro schoolteacher. An active member of the African Methodist Episcopal Church; friend to dogs and seagulls; wearer of efficient yet supremely inelegant dresses; hoarder of her own privacy; occasional dabbler in perfume; never a nuisance; the kind of person who might be called invisible except for the memories of her former pupils, who in their recollections will make her out to be more commanding or cranky or supercilious than she ever was in real life. Not one of those students will ever actually know you. In this moment, on this day, perhaps Allen Pile knows you best of all.

"I'm supposed to help my father with the house," Allen says. "Before he leaves. He's going to Canada tomorrow."

You have spoken to Allen's mother and father exactly once, earlier in the year, after one of Allen's mishaps. They did not want to keep it a telephone matter but arranged an appointment with you the next day after school. You took their eagerness as a sign that they regarded their son's behavior as a serious matter. *This should nip it in the bud*, you remember thinking. How different the actual meeting went. Everett Pile only listened when he was talking—bursts of galloping, off-center opinions, striking at the edges of the conversation. When you talked his eyes flitted and his head turned; he played with his jaw as if to dispel the abiding need for a cigarette. As if whatever you said didn't need tending to, because it couldn't possibly be legitimate.

Lottie Pile, meanwhile—a tiny spit of a woman with sulfurous yellow eyes, a ruddy tinge at the top of her cheeks, and sunburned blonde-brown hair—listened better, but in her responses she only wanted to talk about her son's fine qualities. Lottie Pile, born not on Nantucket but in Charlestown, Rhode Island, wanted to explain all you needed to know about young Allen. It did not take long for you to realize that their motivation in setting up the appointment was not to absorb your account of Allen's behavior but to refute it. And perhaps also to let you know that you were on notice. You left the meeting far more troubled than when it started. Now you had more than Allen Pile's behavior to worry about. Lottie Pile, you quickly gathered in listening to her, had barely any education at all, but you knew from reputation what a social force she was, allied with several mid-island cliques, including the First Baptist Church, the YWCA, and a sewing circle that met every week at Flora Bunker's house on Backus Lane. If she wanted to, Lottie Pile could turn several opinions against you.

"What exactly are you supposed to do?" you ask Lottie Pile's son.

Allen thinks about this question. You see him mentally considering and testing different possible answers. You see that he never expected to get this far. He expected that by this point you would have yelled at him or doubled his punishment. Or called his parents. He did not anticipate civility. He did not expect a discussion.

"The roof is cracked, because of the storm. You can see straight through to the air. The rain comes in."

The horrible thought hits you that what Allen says might be true. The storm that struck Nantucket at the beginning of the week before—with its gale force winds and improbably large hail—not only savaged houses in the various pocket communities rimming the island but battered many central island homes. You know a man from your church who still has a telephone pole on the floor of what used to be his living room. You have seen several cars pockmarked with hail dents. You heard that a woman in Surfside was killed when a shutter from a neighbor's house came loose in the wind and struck her in the head as she ran up her driveway. It is perfectly possible that there is a hole in the roof of Everett Pile's house. In your mind's eye, you can see it. And if Everett Pile is leaving the next day on another three month merchant marine adventure, there is every reason for him to want to have the roof fixed by tonight. But you can't simply succumb; not when you don't know for sure.

"Surely on a nasty afternoon like this one your father will not try to fix a broken roof."

"It's because it's nasty he wants to fix it. He doesn't want any more rain getting in. Or the air, now that it's cold. He doesn't want to leave mom and me like that. He says he's getting it done one way or another." You can just see Everett Pile saying that, accompanied by a wild arm gesture: *One way or another*.

You lower your head. You stare at your hand. It holds a rust-brown fountain pen, almost six years old now, with which you once scratched scores at the top of your students' math tests. You no longer know whose test you hold or what the tally is. You look at the knuckles on your left hand, the skin stretched across them: so dry, so coarse. You are only thirty-four; yet your hand could be your mother's when she was fifty-five or sixty. Sterile; papery; giving off a faint smell of dust and ruination and a useless douse—hours old—of hand lotion.

"Go home," you tell Allen Pile. "But you will have to make up this work tomorrow after school. No excuses. Tell your father and mother I said that."

Allen smiles once—a loud, singular sneer—and nods. He immediately turns his back to you and scoots to his desk. You see the ripped pocket. You see the muddy leg. What will Everett and Lottie have to say about those? He picks up his satchel and surges for the classroom door. He does not say, "Thank you." He does not say, "Don't worry. I'll be here." He says exactly nothing. You hope you will hold him to his assignment tomorrow. You certainly plan on doing so. But you can't be sure of it.

The damp, frosty teeth of late afternoon nip your cheek as you walk home along York Street. You pull your scarf tight across your face, but it makes no difference. This morning, when you walked this same street in the opposite direction, sunlight poking and probing around clouds, you told yourself it felt like September. By midday, during recess, you would have called it early November. But now that the fog has taken over, blocking and blinding your own island from you, it is December. Perhaps even early January. You will have to start the stove as soon as you get home. You will have to eat that soup. You need reinforcement against this bleary contagion. As you pass the cottage houses on your right, you think of how many of these homes are empty. It's true that a few—but only a few—are empty because they belong to absentee owners: northeasterners from Massachusetts or New York or Connecticut whose lives elsewhere are so prosperous they can afford to abandon them for the summer months and live here instead. You wonder for the thousandth time what it is they do in their professions. Your summers are free too, but you do not make enough money to go anywhere. You stay shut up in your tiny house during the warm season, reveling in the freedom from the responsibility for other people's children. The freedom to read what you want. To think what you want. The freedom to relax. The freedom not to have to hector and test and correct and lecture. The freedom from being Miss Ogilvy.

And if you did have money? Would you spend it to come here? A sandy bow of land twenty-nine miles offshore, a glorified fishing village whose golden days are several decades, even a whole century, behind it and whose modernity never quite arrived? The island's population inexorably dwindles year by year, so much so that you fear one morning you will wake and find yourself the only remaining person. For a lark, an escape, an adventure, where would you go? Paris? (Because shouldn't everyone go to Paris?) Montreal? (Because it's closer.) Mexico? (Because it's warmer.) Madagascar? Actually, you would love to travel to Madagascar. Someplace that different. That far away. You would like, if only for a month, to experiment in throwing off Stella Ogilvy entirely. Bakersfield, California? No, you can never go there.

You pass the house where Elizabeth Barnard lived while she waited for her son to return from the war. When Elizabeth found out he would never return, she locked herself inside. She retreated from her church, from shopping, from Christmas Eve parties and New Year's celebrations. Within a year she abandoned Nantucket entirely, and her house too, which has stood unoccupied ever since. A number of these houses are ownerless. Drains on some bank somewhere. Or, even if paid off, lifeless structures containing no one, not even in summer, emitting no particular energy except the scent of decay and implosion; no longer tended to, no longer repaired; only gnawed on—season after season—by the fog. Each morning and every afternoon, trudging to and from school, you wonder which house will next be abandoned.

You hear sounds behind you—illiterate, shuffling steps—blurred by the encompassing mist and by the scarf hooding your ears. You turn as quickly as you can and barely make out the tail ends of black coats, a couple crops of hair. Boys—perhaps two—disappear behind one of the empty houses. You don't know who they are, those bound up bodies. More bored little boys. Good god, aren't there enough of them on this island? Feral like rabbits. In the old days, they could lionize the whalers and imagine careers that would take them to South America and to Hawaii and to New Zealand, where they would drink the local grog and do unspeakable, delightful things to dark-skinned, naked young beauties. They could commit as many sins as their wills and their money allowed, things they would never admit to their mothers and their sisters and their ministers and their wives. And along the way they would merely put their own lives at risk time after time after time, chasing and killing gigantic, warm blooded sea mammals, the largest creatures that have ever existed on planet earth. What red-blooded boy would not yearn after such a life? What boy would not sacrifice everything he had—especially his boredom—to make that life real? But these twentieth century boys, these disconsolate island mutts, don't have a single comparable dream. They have literally nothing to do here; nothing to aspire to; nothing to believe in. There is nothing to keep them busy. *Except for bothering you.*

You hear another sortie of noises, but this time they are far ahead and possibly across the street. Maybe it's someone's dog who, confused by the mist, is unable to keep a bearing on home. More than likely, though, it is just these boys. They have stealthily charged ahead and currently study you from a new outpost, using the fog for camouflage. You know that for some of them you are endlessly fascinating and essentially inexplicable—the Negro schoolteacher— like something from a freak show. Or an animal act. *See the elephant perform calculus. See the cat make an omelet. See the Negro speak the Queen's English.* They can't help themselves. They can't help but stare at you. It's gotten worse since your mother died. When your mother lived you walked everywhere together, two dark-skinned women forming an alliance, operating as a team. The boys, and some of the men—even some of the women—might glare at you, might act as if they would like to do or say something. Yet they would refrain. Whether out of intimidation or lack of convenience or simple confusion, you never knew. But now you are alone, an isolated target. Fair game. The same runty, small-eyed, sharp-boned white boys who ninety years ago would pine in their imaginations for a fifteen-year-old girl with skin the color of yours now act as if that skin is universally worthy of disdain. Not that these fog boys mean you any harm, necessarily. They are bored. They have nothing to do and, it being mid-October, have no work waiting for them at home. They want to see what they can get away with.

You hear a chuckle from across the street. You look to your left. No one. The air feels more wet and more cold than even five minutes ago, a thicker texture of gray. You are in the high tide of afternoon fog. You can't see these boys, wherever they are, no matter how you try. And they know you can't see them. Something hurtles past your head, something rectangular or oblong, something that buffets the cold air with a clunky, percussive sound and lands on the sidewalk ahead of you, skittering to a stop. You look again across the street. How can you not? No one. The rock did not actually come close—these hoodlums are only trying to tease—but, even so, now you're angry.

"Why don't you let me see you?" you shout. "Brave, aren't you?"

You don't know if the snickers you hear are real, or merely the breeze that has pulled this fog onto the island, or a piece of an old house speaking, or just your own relentless cogitations. You step off the sidewalk and into the street. You want to get closer. You study the other side. You take another step. You squint. A car, possibly a Studebaker, turns from South Mill Street onto York, its headlights so impotent against the webby, occlusive brume that you know the driver cannot see you. You step back, and seconds later the car barrels over the exact spot in which you'd been standing. You look to see if you can recognize the driver, but the vehicle is enveloped into the skin of the mist. Jupiter Williams, who like you lives on South Mill, owns a Studebaker, but Jupiter doesn't drive that fast. Does he? Not when someone might be out walking in this muck. What if you'd been crossing the street?

You shiver. It's colder still. Colder than it was a minute ago. It can't be that the temperature has dropped any further. It's just that the fog has insinuated itself into your coat, your hair, your scarf, your hands. With every passing second you are losing your insulation. You hear feet shuffle rapidly somewhere on the other side of York. Perhaps behind houses. Perhaps between them. A porch light comes on, but you can't see anyone. The light, drowned and distorted by the fog, does nothing but make the dying day seem more hopeless.

"If you were in my classroom," you say out loud, "I'd show you what for. Whosever class you *are* in, I'm ashamed of you. I will find out, sooner or later. Believe me, I will." You won't. You won't. You know that, but you feel like saying it anyway. No reply comes. No answer. Not even snickers and the scurry of feet. Maybe your warning actually touched them. Maybe. But truth is, even if you find out who they are, you don't know what you can do. What you can do depends on who the parents are, and there's no telling with these boys. They might come from quietly desperate houses, from disheartened and unemployed parents, people living off charity and whatever liquor they can scrounge. But they could just as easily come from one of the best families, one of the unimpeachable ones, set up in stately harbor homes. They threw a rock at your head. Sadly, that tells you nothing.

Grace Allison, who teaches fifth grade, has developed an easy formula: normal parents=crazy kids; crazy parents=normal kids. It does, indeed, seem true enough to accept as an axiom. You consider how weird it is that Grace Allison knows more island families than you do. This seems wrong. It always seems wrong, but on this fog-crossed, chilly afternoon, with these bored little boys playing their mysterious game, it feels more wrong still. Grace was born in Carlisle, Kentucky. You were born here. Here. *I was born here*, you feel like telling these two lurking, invisible brats. *Just like you*. But you don't say it. Not only because you can't see where they are, but because you don't know how much it finally matters. Your father was born here, and he died of a stroke at forty-three. Your mother was born here, but in her final years she was so bitter with arthritis and bursitis and her neighbors' cold shoulders that she never left the house, except to go with you once in a while to the AME Church. Your mother's mother was born here, but she spent most of her adult life sweeping floors for Abraham and Delia Coffin in their Union Street mansion. Phebe Boston was born here, and in

1846 she was allowed to enter Nantucket High School because her father was willing to sue the very town he lived in. But three years later Phebe Boston was dead from dysentery. That was the closest anyone in your family came to completing high school until you finally did so sixteen years ago.

Another car—this looks like a Ford— turns from South Mill on to York. Once again, you retreat to the sidewalk. The car passes. It honks. Possibly—probably—it's a friendly honk, but you can't see this driver either. You can't know. Is it possible, you think, to be born in a place and not be from it? Is it possible that a person born elsewhere can turn out to be the true native? But in that case, what do the words *native* and *foreigner* mean anyway? For some reason, you think of the American South. Terrible troubles down there now. You have read about them in the newspaper. You have heard about them from others at your church. You know what Dr. DuBois says. But for a crazy second you wonder if it might be better to live in a place like the American South. In a place like that, you know exactly who your enemies are. They don't hide, because they don't have to. You can see them in plain daylight and react appropriately. You can take cover while there's still time. You shake your head. What are you thinking? When in your life have you ever wanted to live in the American South? The furthest south you have ever traveled is Bridgeport.

Someone is on the sidewalk ahead of you. For a moment or two they seem to be coming your way, albeit very slowly. But then it seems—you're virtually positive of this—that they are moving on. The same direction as you. You hear the slow scratchy shuffle of old shoe leather against concrete. The sound does not sound like any hoodlum, or like any boy. You study the figure carefully, until it finally separates itself from the mist and solidifies into a tall, narrow person in a dark coat and complicated head covering, possibly involving feathers. You think it might be Mrs. Rotch. Mrs. Rotch is tall. Normally, you would call hello to Mrs. Rotch, but that feels wrong today. Something looks and feels all wrong. Mrs. Rotch is not that tall. She has no elaborate hats. And the sound of these feet is too heavy for her, almost too heavy for a woman. But if it's not a woman, what is it? You look again. You can't be sure if this

136

thing is a man or a woman, white or Negro, reality or phantasm. Only that it is on the sidewalk and apparently moving in the same direction as you. At least this presence makes it less likely the boys will throw any more rocks. No vandal wants an eyewitness. You pull your scarf tight around your face. *Please*, you pray to it, *give me just a bit more warmth*. But all you feel is the same kiss of wetness, chill and slimy against your cheek. You glance at your feet for a second. When you look up, the figure is gone.

A rock strikes the sidewalk a yard ahead. You hear feet move not far behind you, on this side of the street. So they crossed, did they? They crossed, and you had no idea about it. You heard absolutely nothing. You're scared now. Angry and scared. You stop, turn full around, and see a shadow sprinting from your side to the other side of York. Something small and nimble and feline. Not more than ten yards away.

"Scaredy-cat," you spit out, and you know immediately it's a juvenile thing to say. The shadow chuckles and disappears. Then you hear another noise and you swing around once more to face the direction you were walking, the direction home. You see, because he is not far enough ahead in the fog to be disguised, a second boy, this one just as small but more solid, dashing across the street, as if to mock you with his proximity. You see dark hair. It could be any boy's dark hair. But before this boy disappears you notice the back of his pants: a ripped pocket, a mud-splattered leg.

There's another noise, some other human sound, and now you see, approaching on the opposite sidewalk, encased by the weather, a new person. Not as tall as the last person, but tall enough. Tall enough to not be a child. It's a woman, you think. There's a certain telltale delicacy in its shoulders and its stride. But you know that could merely be an effect of the fog. You start to cross the street. You can't even guess who this woman might be. But you want to be on her side of the street; you want to be where she is. You want to wave to her. You want to stop her. You want to ask where she is going.

ISLAND FOG

MORNING MEAL

Nantucket Island, 1999

The eggs were overdone, but that was the way Carpenter liked them: hard yolks more blue than yellow, the whites ribbed brown with fried grease and black at the edges. His bacon was as crisp as matchsticks, his sausage so well done it was juiceless, his toast charred. Here at the Downy Flake, where Carpenter ate almost every morning of his life, they knew precisely how his meal ought to look and taste. Which is why he kept returning. He couldn't make breakfast half so well himself.

He turned over a salt shaker and pumped it five times. Six. Next came the Heinz. He stuck a knife in the opening and let the ketchup run. It formed a soggy red lake on one side of his plate. Into this bloody liquid he would dip his dry eggs, his black bacon, his juiceless sausage, and his burnt toast.

Carpenter was forty-five. He was five foot, eight and a half inches. He weighed 257 pounds. His blood pressure was 159 over 112. His cholesterol was 288. He drove a twenty-year-old van that said *Island Plumbing* on the side. He lived in an ancient mid-island fisherman's shack, not much bigger than a living room, that he inherited from his mother. Except for the plumbing, the shack had not been upgraded in any fundamental way since the 1950s, but the price was right, and the location convenient: a minute's drive to the Downy Flake. Within a stone's throw too were the bank, the post office, and the Stop and Shop. His wife—the only woman who ever told him that she loved him—died in May, 1996, along with their infant daughter, when she fell off a ferry midway between Nantucket and Hyannis. They had been married for two years. She was taking the baby to visit her sister in Newton. Carpenter remembered that blurred, nightmarish time only in brutal flashes, rare seconds of clarity knifing at him out of a fog of soporific recollections: calls from the police, calls from the newspaper, calls from a lawyer. Weeping in his bathroom.

A few months after his wife's death, Carpenter adopted the Downy Flake. He ate at the restaurant Monday to Friday before he went out on his first job, and on any Saturday morning when he didn't feel like fixing a cold bowl of cereal or reheating pizza. Which was about every Saturday. Every morning he ordered the same thing: two eggs, two strips of bacon, one sausage patty, two pieces of toast, coffee black. He always sat at the counter rather than a table. Those, he figured, were for the families. It took him exactly nine minutes to finish the food and drink one cup of coffee, during which time he spoke to no one. It took another ten to smoke a cigarette with his second cup, during which time he would speak but only when spoken to. Which was almost never. When the cigarette was consumed and his cup empty a second time, Carpenter lingered a few moments more, dreading the day ahead. He always hoped that somehow, if he just stayed in place a little longer, when he walked out the front door he would find the normal terrible day scheduled for him erased, and in its place a different sort of life. But of course that never happened. In the final act of his ritual, he ground the butt into a tray until it was nothing but obliterated pulp: deathly gray with shabby scabs of black. Then he stood up, threw five dollars on the counter, and left.

Most days, after struggling with leaking pipes, inoperable toilets, and backed up sinks all morning, Carpenter ended up at the Downy Flake as well for lunch. A cheeseburger well done or a deep fried cod sandwich. Lots of french fries either way. At five o'clock he would head home, where he fixed a frozen Salisbury steak dinner and watched television. When he felt his neck tilting and his eyes closing against their will, he pulled out the sofa bed. On most days—most days, mind you—he fell asleep within minutes, stunned thoughtless by the long hours of viewing, to say nothing of the exhaustion of his life's work.

If Carpenter wanted to sleep though, he had to not look at the photograph on the shelf behind his sofa, the photograph showing a brown haired woman with a big square face and chubby nose, clear smiling eyes and a soft grin. He could not look at this picture, but neither could he bring himself to take it down. To hide the picture of the only woman who ever told him she loved him would mean the conclusion of their existence together. Carpenter was too afraid of what came next. So he left the picture up, but forced himself to ignore it. He trained himself to not spend every evening mooning at her familiar face and warm gaze. Nights when he gave in, when he didn't have the strength to keep himself from the comfort of her, when after two hours of staring he would finally be moved to say out loud, as if she were still alive in the room with him, *Why?*—those were the nights when Carpenter never slept, no matter how tired.

But whether he slept or he didn't, every morning he drove one minute in his twenty-year old van to the Downy Flake, where he sat at the counter, protected by the company of frivolous island chatter. Meanwhile, in the base of his throat and behind his lungs and beneath his heart, stabbing up at its exposed underside as with a white-hot utensil, the fact of his wife's passing burned him with every mouthful.

Carpenter finished his toast. He tugged once on his blue cap and scratched the crumbs out of his moustache. A waitress came quickly to refresh his cup. While she was pouring, a man sat next to him. The man told the girl he wanted an omelet and coffee. Something about the voice sounded familiar. Carpenter checked. Nope. A stranger. He was a thin man, maybe forty, with crew cut blond hair and a hard, tanned, angular face. He was wearing a pale blue Steamship Authority shirt. The uniform. The man met Carpenter's eye.

"Morning," he said indifferently. He had a copy of the *Globe*. He was set to read it.

Carpenter nodded and looked away. This was going to be difficult. He reached into his jacket for a pack of cigarettes. He heard the paper open beside him.

"You work on the ferry, I guess," Carpenter said, his voice in his own ears sounding jammed and rusty.

The man muttered something, but he was obviously not paying attention. Already, he was reading. Carpenter looked. The sports page. Carpenter rolled his eyes. The string of an old inadequacy twanged within him. In grade school he was the fat kid who couldn't play football worth a damn. The last one picked. *Fatty fat ass.* High school was worse. In high school he lost every prospective date to guys like this: lean men who read the sports page. And it was not as if on Nantucket Island in 1971 the number of girls available were infinite. He didn't go on his first date until he was twenty-one. Even now, the sight of a sports page filled him with an actual if quiet nausea, an instinctual revulsion. *Isn't it about time you grow up?*, Carpenter thought out at the stranger.

Of course, Carpenter had seen more potent kids games than football in his twenty years as a plumber. Every day he entered other peoples' houses; he met residents and visitors, tenants and landlords. He heard conversations. He watched the drunk and the rich and the whiny and the garrulous shout their demands at each other, as indifferent to his presence as if this were the Old South and he the house nigger. Spoiled children, every last one. Whether they were quiet or talkative, cold or charming, dull or bitter, middle-aged or young, the same air was about them all: persons used to making demands and used to having those demands satisfied. There were a few games Carpenter saw all the time: *I want one of each* (most popular), *that's not my responsibility* (a close second), *I want you gone* (the loudest game) and (most disorienting) *let the other guy take the fall.*

These games could get quite dangerous. He saw vacationing wives come home to find vacationing husbands with nineteen-year-olds. He saw the fights that happened. He heard commodity trades muttered tensely into cell phones from living room couches. He saw the ferocious silent pacing that always came next. He heard thin-voiced landlords throwing college student tenants out of their houses, only to have the tenants shout themselves back in with threats of lawsuits. He saw a famous summer resident—a used-up Hollywood actor—in a spat with his lover, stalk naked around his living room destroying every decoration with a baseball bat.

The island had changed enormously since Carpenter was in high school. In almost all ways for the worse. Off-islanders had flooded the place, taking it over, molding it to a resort that fit their tastes and their bank accounts, not those of the 10,000 people who actually stayed on the island year round, some of whom could barely afford a gallon of gas. Nantucket was no longer owned by its natives but by tourists. Of course, the only woman who ever told him she loved him had first come to the island as a tourist. Ten years younger than himself, he met her only because he saw her stranded with a flat tire on Surfside Road and decided to help. Carpenter still counted that as a plus.

"Can I ask you a question?" Carpenter said. The man looked up, uncertain, alert to some danger forming. Carpenter lit his cigarette.

"I don't mind if you smoke," the man said quickly. He tried to put his head back in the paper.

"That isn't it," Carpenter said. "But thanks." He would have smoked regardless. "I was wondering what a big ship like a ferry would do if somebody was to fall off. You know, all of a sudden, in the middle of the ocean."

The man's eyes narrowed, as if trying to put Carpenter in new focus.

"We'd stop the boat."

"And how long would that take?"

"Not long. We don't ever get up too fast. It's impossible carrying that load."

"But it's a big ship."

The man shrugged. "Not a problem."

"How long you worked for the Authority?"

"Five years. Why?"

"You ever worked a boat when someone fell off?"

"Never."

"But it happens."

"Pretty rare."

"Oh yeah."

Carpenter took a drag and blew it away. The man waited a moment and then returned to the sports page.

"So from the time, you know, that a body's in the water till the time that the body is out of the water and into a dinghy—how long is that?"

The man snapped his paper.

"No more than fifteen minutes I should say. If it's an emergency."

"Fifteen?"

"Maybe twenty."

Carpenter nodded.

"What if it was to take forty-five?"

The man's face changed. "There a reason why you're asking?"

Carpenter shrugged. "Just heard of it happening once. Always been curious about that. Seems like a long time to me. Forty-five minutes."

"You talking about that woman?"

Carpenter squinted at him.

"A few years ago?" the man asked.

"Was it a few years ago? Seems longer."

"It was three years ago."

"You would know."

"I know very well, because I had some friends working that boat. Good men. And they got into serious trouble."

"Like I said, you would know."

"No, you're not hearing me. Those guys followed procedures to the letter. They did nothing wrong. Still they end up being suspended."

"Rough," Carpenter said.

"More than rough. Can you afford to lose a month's salary? On top of all the publicity? Would you like to have your name in the paper because of something like that?"

"No."

"All right, then."

Not good enough, Carpenter thought. "So maybe they didn't do anything wrong. But, I don't know, forty-five minutes?"

"That one was different."

"Was it?"

"The woman wanted to die. It's not easy to save a person when she won't let you pick her up."

Carpenter smoked.

"People have strong wills," the man said. "You know?"

Carpenter didn't answer.

"You can get them out easy if they want to come out. If they don't, it's next to impossible."

"But," Carpenter said, "I don't think that was ever proved, from what I hear. I mean her wanting to die. She was a new mom, after all."

The waitress set an omelet, toast, and a mug of coffee in front of the stranger. He scooped up his knife and fork, threw a paper napkin on his lap.

"I don't know where you heard it wasn't proved," the man said. "Because that's what the police said. That's what the coroner said. That's what the newspaper said." He took a bite of omelet.

Carpenter's snatched his coffee cup, but he didn't drink from it.

"You got a wife?"

"Sure," the man said.

"She ever have a baby?"

"Three."

"Anything like that ever happen to her?"

"Never."

"Okay then," Carpenter said.

Okay what? That was the problem. Carpenter could never decide.

"The nurses said they had to tie her to the bed."

"They never tied her," Carpenter answered immediately. "Never. I don't know why people say that."

The stranger eyed for him for a second; then he shrugged. "I'm not denying whatever it is you heard," the ferry man said. "You may be right. But that's why my pals were reinstated finally. The cops said the lady wanted to kill herself. And the baby."

Carpenter winced. The words pounded into him one after the other like solitary nails.

"If they had done something wrong they would have been fired." The stranger was talking with his mouth full. "At the very least. And if they'd really messed up they'd have gone to jail. I mean, when two people die. That's a crime. But every last one of them is still working for the Authority."

"I know," Carpenter whispered.

"They're doing okay. They're good guys, if that's what you're getting at."

"I'm not getting at anything," Carpenter said.

He felt overheated now and a little woozy. His tongue was slightly swollen. "I just asked you some questions," he tried to say but couldn't form the words right, so he stopped. Spit dribbled on his chin.

His forehead was beginning to bead with sweat. And his palms, and his shoulders. His chest felt like it was sinking; his fingers went numb. He couldn't feel the smoke that rose from the cigarette and twined around his face. He couldn't feel the cigarette itself in his fingers. He couldn't hear the scratch of the stranger's knife against his plate, or his teeth bite into a triangle of white toast. Then the sides of Carpenter's vision pinched and he seemed to be viewing the counter in front of him from a great distance. Or in a dream. As if the Downy Flake and the waitress and the man and the omelet and the plate and the newspaper weren't actual but only imagined by the plumber while he had been somewhere else: his shack, or the Stop and Shop, or in a bathroom on Long Pond Road, or standing in St. Paul's graveyard staring at a single naked stone. Perhaps all those locations and many more at once: a wandering spirit, at home nowhere, the smell of burnt tobacco and paper his only surviving sense.

BEATEN

Nantucket Island, 2001

I was thirty minutes into a fifty minute run along the cramped and hilly Madaket bike path: that last serpentine quarter of it where bends become sudden, straightaways few, and there's little to notice on your left or right except scrub brush and the occasional, meager throng of box elders or hemlocks. I was headed back to the condo—my wife's aunt's place, modest by Nantucket standards. In exchange for two weeks before the season started we agreed to perform a whole list of minor improvements. So far we'd fixed the chain on the upstairs toilet, repainted a bedroom, waterproofed the deck, changed out two of the light fixtures, called in a repairman to look at the dryer, and wasted a day trying to find Marion an affordable sofa. We spent an hour on the phone with her that night, describing her options, none of which she liked. There was more we were to get to in the days remaining—the list was potentially endless—but we also needed to take time to do what we hadn't yet: enjoy the island. Watch ferries appear and disappear at the far end of the horizon, drink wine at restaurants, saunter slowly through shops on Main Street, linger on benches at the Athenaeum, drive to barren beach-hugging coves and listen to the surf. After all, how long had it been since we simply enjoyed anything?

He was just coming out of a bend in the path when I saw him, three steps away, moving at a good clip: a firmer, longer, more confident stride than mine. He ran bare-chested, showing off a tanned torso, not ripped or overly muscular but slim and conditioned in the natural way of runners. He was about forty, I guessed—based on his balding top and the burgeoning gray in his moustache—but an obviously healthy forty, healthier than me at least. Even the gray in the moustache seemed a sign of vigor, contrasting so vibrantly with his coppery skin. He was oiled with a first innocent sweat—the kind that has no scent and only lightly dews one's body—wrapping him in a swelling, friendly glow.

He motioned at me with his head, what I took to be hello. "Hey," I said bluntly, my standard greeting to fellow runners, accompanied by a nod that couldn't be misinterpreted. I believed in being polite to the rest of us, whether we're faster or slower, slimmer or fatter. We were all part of the same company, this little club of morning exercisers. A lot more joined than separated us. He didn't answer, though, and in a second passed me, headed the opposite way down that narrow alley.

I had been concentrating on what we were supposed to do that day in the condo, but the sudden appearance of the stranger startled my mind out of the box I successfully held it in. My thoughts went in their own directions, errant and conniving; to what I most didn't want to see. Ann in a hospital bed, sweating and exhausted, pale but unable to rest, crying as I held her small, bony shoulders. My holding her made no difference at all. I had no comfort to give. I had no control, no explanation, no perspective to offer on what had just happened. No one did. Not even the doctor. Not even God.

It was not our first time either. Our first one lasted only until six weeks. And the second nine. But this baby had only a week or two to go before being a viable, sustainable life form with the help of those machines in the PICU. Only a week or two more and the machines would have been enough; our bad luck and our bad timing and the apparent curse put on us from Somewhere would not matter anymore. We would have beaten them. Us and this marginal human know-how. Potent and collusive as those other forces were, they could not have stolen our baby. She would have been safely out of their reach.

We held our breath every day of that pregnancy, just waiting for the bottom to fall out. Waiting, fretting, thinking, doubting. The first time we got pregnant it took a year, a specialist, and significant money. The second time took longer and cost us more. This time it had taken three years, two specialists, and all the money we had. This was our last chance. There would be no fourth. Ann was thirty-nine; I was forty-one. What else could we do but hold our breath?

But when the day came that this third child lived longer than our second I celebrated, if against my will and solely to myself. I didn't dare breathe a word of joy to Ann. I was not that stupid or that reckless. Not yet. As the ballooning spirit of victory spread through every limb, I waved a brain finger at myself. *Don't get your hopes up. Anything can happen.*

But I celebrated all the same. Surely it meant something that this child held on longer. It must indicate some superior strength, something regular and healthy in its DNA or in Ann's body or in how the baby settled there than was true the first two times. The doctor said Ann's pregnancy was progressing normally. The word never sounded so monumentally, even inhumanly, impressive. *Normal.* And every day that we traveled safely beyond that black, terrible number in our memory was a day further along this new road of normalcy, a day further from godless tragedy. Might we be allowed to travel all the way? Could we actually start to think that?

As we neared three months, Ann and I began to share glances, little smiles, automatic hand squeezes, furtive looks of confirmation. But not a word of optimism, not a hint of planning, not a single spoken sentence about the concrete life we might expect to fill our house in half a year. Then came the day—we both knew exactly when—when the first trimester passed and our baby was still alive. After an ordinary dinner I said to Ann, "I'm pouring a glass of wine, and for you an O'Doul's." The biggest smile broke out across her little body. She understood. She consented.

Every day after that was better, surer. I knew we'd won. Against what, you ask? Maybe just the odds. After all, if there is no god then it's the odds that rule, right? And what are the odds of the same tragedy happening three times in a row to the same physically healthy couple? The odds had to be low. If not, how did babies get born in this damn world? Plenty of them do, after all. Hundreds of thousands, emerging each year in bedrooms and taxi cabs and shanties and rice paddies. Wanted and unwanted. Fat and scrawny. Red and black and yellow and white. Irrepressible unstoppable life. Though I tried to counter every mental picture of a happy birthing room with *Don't get your hopes up*, I couldn't keep out vibrant images of conquest: The baby came. The baby was alive. The baby was more beautiful than the world.

Don't, I told myself. *It's your last chance.*

Forgive my presumption, I thought out one day, stuck in traffic on my way to work. I didn't know to whom I was speaking: which spirit, which deity, which invisible and theoretically benign power that theoretically respects prayers. I didn't have a clue as to what power I needed to appease. It wasn't a matter of specific religiosity but just hedging my bet. Expectation asserted itself in me daily, like my heart against my chest. I could barely suppress it. I had to do something. In case it wasn't only a matter of odds. And who knew? Throughout history there were a lot more and varied explanations dreamed up than the orderly God of my Presbyterian parents, a being I had more or less dismissed even before our first daughter died. The Wheel of Fortune, the Killing Fates, Shiva the destroyer, jealous Jehovah. Better to pacify them all. *Forgive me,* I brainwaved toward the roof of the car. *I won't get my hopes up.*

They went up all the same. At least until the day at end of the eighteenth week when Ann sat in that hospital bed howling and insensible, unable to speak except in shrieks, while I kept my arms around her, my arms that felt like stick arms because they were so inadequate. Because I didn't have the power to summon what didn't exist.

You did this to her.

So far on our vacation I had to shake my head and beat my temples half a dozen times to chase away the picture of that hospital room. I would insert instead some neutral, functional idea, one that forced me to plan ahead: chicken or fish tonight, remember to take Ann to Surfside, pick up a gallon of white at Marine Home. They worked, these little detours, for a while, as long as I was vigilant. But inevitably there would be another day, another reason, another minute when the hospital room came back. I could only fight so hard.

I was nearing my turn off point: East Cambridge Street. One long uphill slope remained. At East Cambridge I would turn left, then a right onto Arkansas Avenue: a sandy, unpaved path with rocks at every other step and potholes the size of small lakes, a veritable invitation to sprain an ankle. After a minute on Arkansas Avenue I would turn left into a driveway and be at the condo. I would kiss my wife. I would begin a new day. From behind me I heard steps: steady, determined. Faster than my own. As if whoever was back there was charging, and had been for a while. Seconds later, a shirtless black-shorted man passed me, his muscled legs pounding the pavement, his arms working tightly, his bald head shining in the risen sun. He was sweating more openly. While before he had been only dew-covered, now whole rivulets flowed down his cheeks, over his neck, along the gullies formed by the muscles in his back.

So, he managed to catch me. Even though when I saw him before he was headed the other way. Even though he must have run further in that direction before stopping, turning, and coming back. More power to him. If I was twenty-five and a lot better runner, maybe my competitive instincts would have stirred. But I wasn't twenty-five and hadn't been for a long time.

He waved as he went by, a kind enough way to dispose of the tension that happens when one runner passes another.

I grunted and continued at my snail's pace. He kept pumping and soon was far ahead. He disappeared over the top of the hill and charged on toward Madaket Beach.

I looked for Ann in the bedroom on the first floor, but she wasn't there. Odd. She's not up before nine if she doesn't have to be. But the sheets were thrown off, her bathrobe gone from the chair by the bed. I took a step back toward the front door, where the stairs were.

"Ann?"

No noise anywhere. Not even the refrigerator.

"Ann?"

As I moved up the stairs, I felt the living strain in my legs, each separate muscle doing its ordinary work.

"Honey?"

When I reached the top I saw her at the far side of the room. She was in her bathrobe, still as a respirator, looking out the big window at the newly christened morning.

"Ann, you all right?"

I didn't move any closer. Neither did she turn.

"What are you doing?"

"This place," she said slowly, still looking out the window, "is infested with rabbits."

I nodded—a stupid motion. She couldn't see it.

"How is that?" she said. "It's an island."

"Isolation. A safe breeding ground. They don't have enemies."

She moved her head. Something.

"I guess. But it's . . ." There was no word out there; not the one she needed. "Infested," she said again.

"Right."

"And they're brown. That terrible ratty color. I thought they're supposed to be white. Aren't rabbits white?"

"They change color in summer."

"They do?"

She looked at me finally. Her auburn hair was a wreck; her eyes were too dark for this time of day. I didn't know if rabbits changed or not. I think I once saw something about this on a nature program. But the program wasn't about Nantucket; I remember film clips of frozen tundra.

"Since when?" she said.

"It's camouflage."

"For what?"

"Protection."

"You said they don't have any enemies."

I shrugged and glanced away. "You want coffee?" I asked.

Her head dipped but she didn't really answer, only ran her tongue listlessly over her lips. Then she spoke, "How was your run?"

"Okay," I said.

"What's happening out there in the world?" She said it numbly, as if it were a place to which she never expected to return.

"More of the same. You know."

"Yes." She pulled the two sides of her robe closer to her chest. She put her hands back in the pockets. She turned to the window. I went to the kitchen and made as much noise as I could trying to find the coffee maker.

I was surprised to see him the next day. At a place like Nantucket, in the summer, nearly everyone you meet is a visitor. They are on vacation. Their schedules are turned off. They let themselves go. They drink too much; they sleep late; they exercise irregularly. You see someone on the bike path one time and never again. But the next day there he was: shirtless, black shorts, white shoes, bald head, graying moustache. Moving in the opposite direction: toward town while I was headed back. Except this time I was much closer to home than when I saw him the day before. Maybe ten minutes were left in my run. If he ran as far as he did the day before there wouldn't be time enough to come back and catch me. No one was that fast. It didn't matter, of course, but I was glad; I didn't want to be caught.

As we passed each other I gave the usual firm nod. I said hello as loudly as I could. I respected his wave from the day before. I wanted him to know I held no grudge. His eyes met mine, but it was as if I hadn't spoken. They were a hard brown-black, his brows knotted above. He offered no greeting, not even a smile, not even a tip of the head; only a confused, constipated gaze. Staring at a ghost. Or someone you never expected to see, at least not yet.

Feeling burned, I looked past him and ran on. *Fuck him.* Probably the last time I would ever see him anyway. I tried to make this final part of my run count. I'd been too sluggish and distracted that morning. So now I focused on each step, feeling my legs moment by moment: how they pushed off, how they landed. I tried to make my stride longer, which I'd read makes you faster. I don't know if I was running any faster but I was working at it harder—and keeping my head well occupied.

I was no more than fifty yards from the intersection with East Cambridge, nearing the end of that long incline, when I heard steps. I didn't think anything at first, but I realized soon enough who it must be. And then he passed me. His stride was the same, as was the stiff posture of that bared chest, the discipline in his motions. He was raining sweat under the strain of his exertion; even worse than the day before. This time there were no waves. He was disciplined, close-mouthed, even stern. He pushed on as hard as he could, and at almost the exact spot he passed me the day before he did so again. Then he seemed to dig in even harder, as if trying to leave me as far behind as possible.

I couldn't believe it. I was astonished, yes, but the astonishment was born of anger. This jackass had turned around early just so he could pass me. He must have. I remembered my nod, my hello, my deliberate show of friendliness. *And then he goes and spits on it.* He decides I am merely someone to be beaten. *He actually goes out of his way.* It was the most gruesomely unsportsmanlike move I'd ever seen. Not even competitive really—I mean truly competitive—but more like a desecration of the competitive spirit. After all, I lectured hotly to myself, if competitive sport is about two reasonably matched contestants playing under an agreed set of rules with the understanding that only one of them can win, his passing me ranked as something else entirely. *This is no goddamn road race.* We were dopey has-beens, all of us. On vacation. Besides which, I wasn't reasonably matched against any runners, certainly not that guy. I'm a slow, back of the pack jogger, who runs only because if I didn't my weight would soar past 220 and my doctor would start warning me about my blood pressure. I don't race; I've never raced; I've never wanted to race. I run because I don't like looking in the mirror and seeing my father's body blooming in the glass. I run because I like the satisfaction of being done with a run, of having it over: sweating and spent and spitting saliva as I open the door to my house, feeling like I've accomplished something genuine for once. I run because after that third trip to the hospital with Ann, I had to do something or else lose my soul.

Asshole.

The worst thing was that there was nothing I could do about it. He'd beaten me. I couldn't reverse it. I couldn't change it. I couldn't catch him if I tried. I couldn't fetch Fairness off whatever dilapidated bench she happened to be sleeping on—stoned drunk and useless—and drag her back into the world. Her and her kissing cousin Justice. I turned off Madaket Road onto East Cambridge, then onto Arkansas, cursing this self-glorifying, yuppie creep, hoarding his measly victories over defenseless pluggers. I would tell Ann all about it, what a rape it was. But then I saw I couldn't. Because the real reason it felt like an atrocity would be apparent.

I stopped. I was outside the house. I swallowed a stream of sweat, closed my mouth, pushed the words aside. I opened the door.

I better not see him tomorrow.

I didn't. It was a Monday; I hoped that meant he was a weekender, safely ensconced in Northampton or New London or Providence. Manhattan, maybe. Probably Manhattan. There was a good chance I would never see him again. Which was a relief, not just for being spared the humiliation of him beating me, but spared too that terrible moment of seeing him approach from the other direction, of having to meet his eye. I didn't know how I was supposed to react.

Ann and I worked on the first floor bathroom. We were hanging paper over dreary, lime painted walls. We'd been putting this job off for as long as we could, more afraid of it than any of the others because it wouldn't take mere mechanical effort but a kind of artistry. The risk of failure and Aunt Marion's disappointment ran high. As deliberately as we'd done everything so far, we slowed to a snail's pace—taking hours to inspect and clean the walls. We worked in silence, as had become our habit. We probably should have had a radio on. We should have gone out and bought one if necessary. But neither of us thought of it. Ann had the same flat look on her face she'd had all week: her cheeks still, her mouth set in a line, her forehead holding back the crinkles of worry, as if by an act of will. Her eyes stayed fixed on each square of work, concentrating on that single section, inspecting it for dirt or dents or bumps that later might cause obnoxious bubbling in the paper. Her small arms moved as cautiously as her eyes, not allowing herself one sudden action, not one movement that wasn't planned well in advance and tightly orchestrated by her controlling mind. I tried not to watch her. Watching her threw off my own rhythm. But it was hard to get used to, even after a week and a half of doing these jobs: standing side-by-side in a tiny space and not talking.

By early afternoon we were ready to hang the new paper: a creamy white brand with a subtle seashell pattern, something Marion had selected. Since neither of us were confident paper hangers we worked even more slowly: minute by minute, section by section, aware of an awful responsibility. I couldn't really be sure how it was going and was afraid to step back to check. I was half-certain that if I did I would see a mess far worse—and less fixable—than the one we stepped into hours earlier. So I kept going. It took us almost to four o'clock, but eventually there was no more wall to cover. There was nothing to do but look.

Ann glanced around, almost surprised, not really believing. She narrowed her gaze to a tunnel of suspicious focus. She saw something. She went to one corner and ran her hand over the paper. She made a tiny satisfied motion with her head. She stepped back. She frowned.

"I think Marion is going to like this," she said.

I nodded.

"She really hates this room, you know. She says she wants to blow up the condo every time she sees it."

"If I were her I'd get a new toilet. That thing is a disaster." I pointed at what surely must have been an original fixture: a murky rotted white, stained brown inside the bowl and around the bottom, rust showing at the metal connections, dewy cobwebs coexisting with toilet moisture.

"One thing at a time," Ann said.

I moved my head; my mouth opened. "I know," I said.

She looked once more at our work. She breathed out. "Well, this is a start."

"It is." I brought up my brush and touched her nose with it. "Nice job, Mrs. Meyers."

She gave me a parental look. "Thank you," she said.

Then there it was, making its first tentative entrance across her face. I saw my wife's teeth. "You too, Mr. Meyers." I smiled back. That was all. I didn't know what else to do. And nothing else was required. With each moment her expression loosened. There was something shyly hopeful in her look that I hadn't seen for a long time. She raised her brush and touched my nose in return.

"Let's have a drink," I said.

All we had in the fridge were a pair of Bud Lights, but that was enough for a celebration. After working hard all day the beer tasted better than champagne. We opened the sliding door and let the June breeze settle around us as we sat on the couch, leaning into each other, heads touching, resting against the good firmness of our bodies. Eventually we put down our bottles and reached for each other. I for Ann's waist, she for my back. Both of us for lips.

We made love for the first time since we'd arrived on the island. A mindless love, which was the best part. Love that was not about getting over a wound or working through a wound or even accepting the wound. Love that had nothing to do with the wound at all. Love that was a thoughtless hymn of satisfaction with our work.

"This has been a very good day, Mrs. Meyers," I breathed in her ear. She looked up at me and smiled but didn't say anything; as if she were holding back, afraid to gamble on a yes.

We did nothing then but hold each other, drowsy and drifting and content. I'm not sure for how long. Not long enough. Then I felt it: Ann stiffening, becoming flat and unresponsive. Not because she consciously changed her body, but because her consciousness had gone somewhere else. I looked at her. She was staring across the living room, a dead, vacant look in her eyes. It wasn't the living room that absorbed her. She didn't even see it.

"Ann," I said as softly as I could, but with an edge of admonishment. *Don't*, I wanted to say. But I couldn't. It was still too early. It wasn't fair. All I could do was survive with her through these long, pointless stares. A half-dozen times a day.

She shifted. She entered her eyes again, back where we were, on that sofa. She moved her arms so that they were around me again.

"I know," she said. That's all. We held each other for a little longer, but we were no longer drowsily twined. More like two girders thrown together on a pile. We broke it off and stumbled to different bathrooms to pee.

My heart sank the next day when, almost done with my run, I heard the footsteps again behind me. I didn't get it. Where had he come from? He hadn't passed me coming out. Maybe it wasn't him, after all, as much as the steps sounded like his. I almost turned to look but couldn't. What an admission that would be: He'd managed to get inside my head. He'd made me paranoid. I wasn't going to be drawn into some perverse, personal battle. Let him pass if he wants.

And he did. The steps came. It was him, exactly as before. Pounding the hill. He grunted something as he passed, something not the least bit friendly. I have no idea what the words were but the tone sounded like *Gotcha*. I started to sprint. I pushed my tired, fat man's legs to go faster. I would catch him with sheer willpower. That tone of his—whatever he said—was the ultimate condescension. I pushed myself to sprint speed, barked at myself in my mind: *Just hold it*. In a minute I would be at the turnoff. The race would be over. I would have won.

But I wasn't fast enough. Not when he had a head start. For a few tense seconds I managed to draw close, but finally he pulled away with the same set stride. Just before I turned at East Cambridge— my lungs red and ready to burst, my breathing raw as rocks—I saw him make a gesture. Not the finger. Not that. Some quick sidewise motion with his hand. I can't really typify it because I'd never seen the gesture before. But I understood it all the same.

From the couch, Ann watched me worriedly. I was moving around the condo like an animal with a brain disease: taking off my shoe, staring at the insole, carrying it to the living room, sitting down, taking off the other shoe, carrying them to the kitchen, checking the window, opening the refrigerator door, closing it without removing anything. Opening it again. The weird thing is that the whole time I thought I was still.

"What is it?" she said.

"What?"

"What are you thinking about?"

The fear was vibrant on her face.

I shook my head. *No, it's something else.*

"Close the refrigerator," she said.

Only then did I find my hand on the door handle. "Oh."

"Tell me," she said.

"It's nothing."

"Tell me, please."

"I told you already. It's nothing."

"*Tell me.*"

"Ann—"

"Why can't you just tell me? Is that asking so much? God." She hugged herself, her mouth pulled tight. All at once I heard her breathing.

"It's nothing, Ann; I swear to you. I didn't run well today. That's all."

She nodded. She didn't believe me.

"I'm scared," she said. "I am so scared." She stayed on the couch clutching herself. "Nothing feels the same." Then I heard the horrible sound I knew so well, the sound I could not physically bear anymore, not now. My jaw dropped dumbly on its own. Maybe, somewhere in the charcoal recesses of my mind, I had thought to say something. But my tongue was a corpse in my mouth. I stood paralyzed, the open refrigerator door in my hand.

The next morning I began with a plan. I was not going to be taken by surprise. Not this time. All the way out I ran with a tight, controlled energy, disciplining each step, keeping a serious and strategic reserve. When I was halfway back I still hadn't seen him, but I kept up my guard. I was not going to be humiliated again by that Wall Street vermin. I stayed under control. I waited for him to show.

And there he was. Approaching me from ahead, running toward town. My discipline became even tighter. I kept my eyes fixed straight ahead. No games with gestures or faces. I wasn't even going to pay him the homage of checking on his expression. He was invisible. He wasn't there. He was nobody worth wasting a glance on. I was someone with better things to do. I heard nothing and saw nothing as he passed. Then I fought like hell to keep from looking back.

I waited thirty seconds. I actually counted them off in my head. A half-mile from East Cambridge I started to sprint. I quickly reached my upper speed limit and committed myself to maintaining that pace no matter what. Shortly, my legs were complaining; my thighs too, and my knees. But I had prepared for this pain. I had thought long and hard about it since the night before, since I formulated my plan. I knew it was coming. I knew how bad it would be. I blinked the pain away and tried to run even harder. Over the next five minutes, any time I felt my body tighten I just pushed it worse. Soon my lungs felt loud pink, then rose, then cherry red, then white-hot and painfully thin, as if they were being stretched by hands reaching inside my chest, the passageways squeezed to nothing. Meanwhile, the throbbing in my upper legs became like a hammer. It occurred to me that my body might just explode: my arms landing on the edge of the road, my legs sailing into the brush, my head rolling onto a passing driveway, patches of skin strewn everywhere and slicked with pints of blood, my heart shattered beyond recognition—not a vessel anymore but a bloody knot of ruined muscle wheezing one last time in the dead center of the bike path. I saw the image like a photograph in front of my eyes, and it so reminded me of another that I almost stopped. Then I heard him. He was coming hard. He realized what I was doing. There was no time to reconsider anything.

I dropped my head and concentrated every ounce, every thought, every idea of available energy into my dying legs. They didn't need to run faster than him. I had given myself the head start. They only needed to run fast enough. East Cambridge Street was a hundred yards away if uphill. The finish line. All my legs had to do was get me to East Cambridge first and I'd never ask another thing of them. I wouldn't run on the island again. I wouldn't give the man another chance to beat me. We were leaving soon anyway, Ann and I. We had accomplished what we came to do. Right?

When I was almost at the turnoff I couldn't breathe anymore my throat was so small. Spots were flaring over my vision like gamboling fireworks: blue, purple, orange, submarine. Whirling and gyrating and bouncing, almost blinding me. But it was there. There it was. Twenty yards ahead, fifteen. He was almost a body length back. Ten yards. Nine. Seven. He was just over my shoulder. He could reach out and tap me. I was still a step ahead. Two. One.

I cut to the left, onto East Cambridge, rejoicing. I'd gotten there ahead of him. Our race was over. There was nothing he could do now but go on sulking toward Madaket, nursing his beaten pride.

Chew on that, Yup Boy.

But I hadn't a moment to relax when I realized the horror. He had turned off too. He was following me.

He was going to make me lose.

There was nothing to do except keep sprinting. When I got to Arkansas Avenue I took the right turn hard, hoping to surprise him, trying to force him to reset and come back. But somehow he managed the turn without faltering. As if he had guessed it, or he had spied on me this whole time and knew my routine. We were nose to nose, fighting it out on that sandy, ugly stretch of island road. It might have been disorientation on my part—I had been sprinting far too long—but it seemed that he was slowing to my pace, becoming fixed there next to me, his breathing as hard and ragged as mine. His body wincing from the exact same pain. Like I said, maybe it was disorientation. Maybe he wasn't even there with me, much less moving at my speed. Maybe he was up on Madaket road: slowing down, breathing easier, giving up the silly contest.

But if so who was this: this shoulder to my shoulder, this step to my step, riding me like some damn demon I could not put behind me. At least until we reached the condo where—if I got through the door first and moved just so—I could shut the heavy thing on his alloyed face and lock him out: this sweating, molting, bleeding, disintegrating mess of a man on my doorstep. If only I could.

HAUNTED

Nantucket Island, 2004

He drank the last of his Costa Rican and thought about the letter. He didn't have much time. He should be at the Athenaeum now, collecting cash and looking inscrutable. But he didn't want to. It was cold. Another fog had come in, turning the streets invisible. After his 5:00 tour he had no choice but to duck into The Bean and hide out with a warm cup for as long as he could make it last. Maybe there wouldn't be anyone for 7:30. This early in the season, with the few meandering tourists punished by a dank nipping mist that made notions of any walking tour ludicrous. But there was always someone. There had never been no one, not even on his first day.

Back then he worried that a Nantucket ghost tour was a flaky lark of an idea that could never generate sustainable dollars, not over time. It was an experiment, a start, a try at something other than what he'd always known: working on houses. It was a way to raise some extra cash on the weekends and have fun at the same time. He wasn't about to quit his day job. But at once he hit an astonishingly deep vein. Even in that first season, with no publicity except for those cheesy xeroxed flyers featuring a screaming woman he cut from a soap ad, even then he got upwards of sixty people on a midsummer night willing to pay fifteen dollars apiece and follow him around town center for an hour and a half, trusting that at each stop he could marvel. In four years, he'd expanded from one tour a night to two, from two nights a week to four. He gave up the construction work—at least during the season—and become a new Nantucket institution, profiled in the *Inquirer and Mirror*, the *Cape Cod Times*, *Nantucket Life*, *Yankee*, even *Victoria*. For the last two years he was named Most Entertaining Ghost Walk in the *Globe*'s Best of Boston survey. If he were to stop now someone would have to take his place.

But then there were nights like these. When even wearing a sweater and lined windbreaker the dampness found a way onto his skin. When he had to worry about a client stepping off the sidewalk into the vapor only to be hit by a delivery truck that hadn't turned its lights on. When he must tell the same old stories to three or four shivering, underdressed visitors caught unawares by the mid-May dip in temperature. When he had to work to keep their attention, to make the stories suspenseful and mesmerizing, to invest in them all the power they had originally when he first heard them years ago: the fiery-eyed man glaring at two kids from the altar of the Unitarian church; the organ music sounding from a deserted home once occupied by a famously tortured musician; the strangely dressed child whom the young Jill and Harold Isley played with every day near the Quaker graveyard. Twice a night, four times a week, four months out of the year. And on nights like these, while he made his eyes go wide and his voice dip with manufactured drama, all he felt in his heart was the cloying desire for a hot shower and a double scotch.

But tonight, too, sitting in his small seat at The Bean, there was this letter, arrived in the morning mail. He carried it around all day, afraid to open it. Also afraid not to. So, after his 5:00, after he escaped into The Bean, after he'd sweetened his Costa Rican and taken off his windbreaker and straightened his sweater and scratched his armpit and checked his watch and drunk his first draught of the bitter, eye-opening brew, he finally did it. He broke the seal.

Dearest Matthew,

I hunted for an e-mail address on you but found none. I uncovered this snail the old fashioned way: through the phone company. I hope to God it is current and this is you and you are reading these words right now.

Forgive me. Okay? Please? That's what I'm saying. Should I grovel? Okay, I will. Please, please, please forgive me. I didn't know what I was doing. I was a fool. I was a tart. I was a whore. I was dazzled by all those superficial things. By watches, and haircuts, and slacks, and boats, and restaurants. I was dazzled by cocaine. And Cuban cigarettes. But he's gone now. I swear. I've thrown him off. The old rag. Fifty-something lizard of a human person.

What I think about now is You. I think about how good we were together, how much I enjoyed you even if we were just watching television. And of course I remember how stupid I was to ask you to leave. I can't believe I did that. I ruined it for us, for me. And now I'm getting what I deserve.

Please come back to Boston. I promise you I am different. I promise I'll never be so stupid as break us up again. Please believe me. Goodbye. I miss you. I love you.

Truly yours, Alan

P.S. FORGIVE ME! PLEASE!

It was an assault. An insult. To think he could forget the past and jump back into Alan's arms at a moment's notice. And just because Alan, having fallen out with his glamorous beau, was feeling lonely. Maybe Alan had "thrown him off," but that was probably a lie. More likely was that Alan, dumped and in a fit of self-pity, was searching for an easy mark to assuage his wounds. *Move back to Boston?* He was going to broach that in an e-mail? It was too crazy, too out of the blue. Matthew nearly ripped the letter in half. He put both hands at the center—one above, one below—and started the yank. But then different emotions came, swelling beneath his anger like a surf, staying his hands.

I won. I beat him.

And in the moment's sweet victory, he actually felt sorry for that pathetic, needy gadfly Alan Worthington. For Alan to apologize, to grovel even, he surely must be in a bad way. Finally, drinking off the last of his Costa Rican, Matthew's pity blurred and sunk and mutated into something like a strand of buried affection. He stared at the letter in front of him, confused.

It was almost 7:30. He had no more time to think about it. He raised his cup and threw it back one more time, hoping for a last watery line to warm him. No luck. He stood up, and for a second had the most disturbing sensation of vertigo: he couldn't remember who he was or why he was here or where in the world he thought he was going.

Nantucket had been Matthew's refuge when Alan threw him out. He had never lived there, but had come regularly with Alan in the mid-90s: brief weekend excursions to "soak up the shopping and the prettiness," as Alan put it. Matthew hadn't cared about that: the gilt-rimmed, hyper-hygienic, Disneyland slickness of the town center that drew such crowds in July and August, sunglasses around their necks, coffee cups in hands, shopping bags holding thousands of dollars worth of merchandise. What impressed Matthew was the awful weight of history pressing down upon the island, throbbing outward with the sea at the harbor and back again with each arriving vessel. Palpable in the cobblestone streets and the gray shingled houses and the widow's walks. He felt on certain moments on select narrow streets that time had stopped or had circled around on itself, that he was back inside that living spiraling body, that awful protean force. He felt alive in another reality than that which existed back in Boston, at a juncture with other realities: of whaling ships and money interests and functional Quaker hypocrisies and lamps that emitted real smells when one passed them; when time as he conventionally knew it had no meaning because he, on that street, at that moment, had no past and no future. He was outside his own life with Alan, merely visiting it on the wave of this newfound time, like a spirit from the future or the past.

But these were such short excursions. They would arrive on Saturday morning, take a late ferry back on Sunday, and be up early the next day for work: he on another of the remodeling jobs that were his career, Alan to work for the Boston Lyric Opera. Matthew could never get over the awful sense of disorientation when he stepped off the boat in Hyannis, of feeling thrust into literally another world: America, the 90s, his job, his commitments, his time-bound, hide-hounded life.

Two people showed for the 7:30: a man and a woman, both in their forties. They were dressed in shorts and unlined windbreakers. They hunched at the shoulders, bent their necks, kept their hands submerged in their pockets. Their faces, strained and shivering with discomfort, poked out from beneath thin brown hoods, accenting their teeth. They looked like two anxious groundhogs.

"Would you like to come back on Friday?" Matthew said. "You don't seem very comfortable."

"No," the man answered. "We're leaving tomorrow morning. It's got to be tonight."

But why does it have to be at all? Matthew wanted to ask. He looked at the woman. Perhaps there was a chance with her. But he saw no softness there either, only the same haggard, intent expression. Her forehead was plastered with damp brown hair, her nose royally arched. Her small eyeglasses glinted in the fogged light cast by a street lamp. She nodded at him silently. She wanted this too. They must have been told, Matthew thought. Someone said to them: *Don't come back before you do the ghost walk.* So, damn it, they would, come hell or—

"Fifteen dollars," Matthew said. "Each."

The man thrust his hand out. He had the money ready, dewy and crumpled in his paw.

He returned to the apartment house on Cherry Street at nine-thirty. He carried his bike upstairs and stowed it in his living room against the wall. He was chilled and feeling fog wet, so he took a shower. He turned up the heat. He put coffee on. He changed into thick sweatpants and a dry t-shirt. It took a second for him to realize which of his shirts his hand happened upon: "We Sing, Therefore We Live. The Boston Lyric Opera." He took the shirt off and threw it in the trash. He put on another: "Cisco Brewery, Nantucket Island, Massachusetts." Someplace Alan had never been. Matthew gave up on coffee and poured himself a whiskey instead. The letter was still folded in his fanny pack.

Would Alan really expect a reply? More to the point, did his missive really represent a sea change? Matthew knew that if he called Alan in Boston he might only be greeted with, "Forget the letter. I was out of mind when I wrote that." He could actually hear Alan's voice say those words, the precise timbre. And even if Alan had changed, even if he did say he still wanted Matthew back, so what then? Even then, what business did Matthew have trusting him? After six years, his heart still carried the scar of what Alan had done. It was there like a literal rip in the muscle, turned white only because the initial scab had flaked away. But a scar all the same. It was a lie, Matthew knew, that time healed all wounds. What it does is disguise them. The hard scab disappears but the real cut lasts as a shadow entity. You can't see it unless you really look for it, and sometimes even if you're looking you still can't. You have to know what to look for. It's not bold red or black, but dim and frosty as an eidolon; invisible against the busy background.

Around two a.m. Matthew woke. Someone was in the room with him. A presence, beyond the end of his bed. Matthew knew it had eyes, even if he couldn't see them, and the eyes were looking at him. He felt palpable movement, as if ocean air were circulating through his apartment. But that wasn't possible. All the windows were closed and locked. And this air was no mere air either, not just blank, ordinary wind. More like a conscious presence gorging on warmth, stealing oxygen, making the bedroom fatal by an unstoppable act of will.

Matthew tried to remember how the victims in his stories escaped, but all he could think of were the ghosts and how they perpetuated their horror: they threw knives and bottles; they sat on your chest until you almost passed out; they laughed at you with red, accusing eyes. Perhaps the worst story he told was of a strange little girl who appeared every night for two weeks to a childless middle-aged woman. The girl might have even been beautiful—what with her straight, clean brown hair and nineteenth century dress—except that she always wore a sarcastic smile. She approached the woman slowly, pointing at her a long, extended index finger. She mouthed one word: "Mama." Finally, she pounced, beating and scratching and pulling hair so badly the woman cried for her to stop; except the ghost never did. It never left until the woman passed out from pain. Had any of the victims ever died from a ghost attack? Matthew didn't think so, but in the moment he couldn't begin to feel certain. His brain was blank. As if half his mind were stolen, leaving only the brute ability to perceive a living terror staring at him from the end of his bed.

Matthew threw off his covers and ran from his bedroom into

the living room. Within seconds he was outside, on Cherry Street, dressed only in his underwear, looking up at the sky and feeling the sting of a freezing May nighttime. The fog was gone, but the wind blew. Stars were out, burning fiercely above the tepid nimbus of street lamps. He looked up at the apartment house: a bulky, two story mid-islander, constructed in the early 1830s and remodeled several times after, the last in the 1979, when it had been converted into four separate units. He looked at his own window. The lights were off. There was no sign of movement or occupation. No evil figure showed against the pane. Matthew shivered and convulsed for minutes, till even his tears started to chill him and he decided that it had only been a dream, coming on the heels of an awful day. He went inside and up the stairs to the second floor. The apartment felt so much warmer than the night outside.

The next evening the weather was better. No fog. His 5:00 tour totaled nine. A good number for that time of year. He might have twenty for 7:30. And his five o'clock was a good group too. They stayed alert, asked questions, passed around ghost stories from their own hometowns. Matthew should have been pleased, but he was too distracted to notice. Not from the previous night's haunting. That, he decided, was pure illusion, a function of whiskey and stress. He'd managed to fall back asleep quickly, and he woke at his regular hour. What distracted him now was the pressing question of Alan. He could make Alan wait for only so long. He eventually must write him. If not, Alan would never stop badgering him. When attention was the issue, Alan would never stop until he claimed it fully. But *what* should he write? Matthew still didn't know. It peeved him that in a letter of apology, a letter of actual begging, Alan was still trying to define the relationship on his own terms. To even assume, first of all, that after six years, Matthew would be available and willing. As if Matthew had done nothing with himself that whole time but wait for the call from Alan. *I've had a lover, Alan. Do you know that? A kind man who was kind to me.*

Of course, maybe Alan couldn't help himself. It wasn't just that Alan was beautiful—strikingly, astonishingly beautiful, an only slightly feminized version of the young Christopher Reeve—it was that Alan had been his first. It was Alan and no one else who had made Matthew who he was, what he was. Before Alan he was still fumbling through awkward, unsuccessful dates with women, too much the coward to act on the truth of his own nature. He would have stayed that way, stuck and scared and possibly married, if Alan had not hired him to work on his kitchen. Alan said later he immediately recognized Matthew's secret. So it was not difficult to bring it to the surface. Two weeks into the job, Alan insouciantly suggested they go out: dinner and a movie. They were both bored, single guys, Alan said. Why not be bored together? Matthew understood the consequences—or at least he recognized Alan's intentions. One look at Alan's home had told him what he needed to know. He accepted the invitation. And at the end of the evening, after what happened between them happened, he found himself in Alan's arms, dissolved into a moist hurry of tears and confessions: a puddle of stupid gossipy appreciation. For almost three years, this was how Matthew remained: scared, grateful, inferior, eager to please. Because, after all, Alan had done something so huge and meaningful that it seemed a debt Matthew could never repay.

For better or worse, those three years in Alan's house had defined him—had ended some more dangerous confusion—even if too he was nearly destroyed at the last with pain. Perhaps, eventually, he might have to do it after all: go back to Boston. And *maybe* it could turn out differently. Maybe. Now that Alan knew what it is like to be the one without control, led around by his heart, and by his heart made to suffer that one excruciating torture.

"So what happened to him?" a man in front said. He had a rocky, mountainous face, big eyeglasses, a craggy bearded jaw, thin graying hair. A camera around his neck. Matthew blinked, confused as to how this stranger knew. Matthew almost said: He's still in Boston and says he wants me back. But then he saw the man's expectant look and remembered what he was doing.

This was one of his better stories. For weeks, in the early 60s—when the mansion behind him was being restored by the Nantucket Historical Society—a newly installed alarm system had the police scrambling. Three, four times a night they were called to the site, but they never found an intruder. And there was no sign of forced entry. Something is wrong with your building, the police told the contractor. Fix it. After inspecting and re-inspecting the alarm system and finding it in ordinary working order each time, the contractor decided to spend the night in the building himself. He brought along a clock and a gun. It was a spring evening, not unwarm. The contractor sat in one corner of the dining room, his weapon ready. Hours passed. Repeatedly, the contractor nodded off and woke up, each time finding his arm resting limp against the floor, the pistol almost fallen from his hand. He would look hurriedly about to see if he had missed anything. Finally, around two in the morning he heard a telltale click from upstairs. A lock had turned. The contractor's hand stiffened around the gun. He sat up on his haunches. He held his breath. Ten seconds later, a shivering white and liquid figure—a human figure—appeared at the bottom of the stairs: cloudy and plasmatic, floating and rotating and yet dead still. The figure pulsed and ticked like a satanic parody of heavenly light. It had no face; it had no eyes; it had no identity. Worse, the air on the entire floor had turned unearthly cold, as if the frozen acres of hell had coalesced into a single throbbing form. The figure raised its arm. Then it moved. The contractor dropped his gun and ran out the back way. He didn't stop running until he was halfway to Madaket and could not take another step.

"Nothing happened to him," Matthew said. "There was the fear, and then nothing else."

"So the thing, whatever it was," a woman said, "it didn't get him?" She leaned in, her eyes wide, genuinely alarmed.

"No," Matthew said. "He left the building and never came back."

The woman breathed out, relieved.

The first man shook his head. "I'm afraid that would have scared the life out of me. Literally."

It's just a story, Matthew wanted to say. I heard it from a guy on a ferry. And that guy had gotten it from a neighbor. I don't even know if it really happened.

Instead, he gathered himself, put on his most authoritative, dramatic voice. "There are no documented cases of a human being ever being killed by a ghost. They may terrify us. They may make us uncomfortable. And confused. And lonely. But they do not seem to hold the power of life and death."

The man nodded slowly. He raised his camera and snapped a picture of the mansion.

"And sometimes," Matthew said, "sometimes they even love us."

He drank three beers and watched the tube. Matthew was tired of thinking. He didn't want to make any decisions or even consider any decisions. He didn't want to ponder what he owed Alan or what Alan owed him. It was all too difficult to understand and the ramifications too broad. He drank and watched, watched and drank, the combination thankfully removing him from the world.

He woke hours later on the same couch with a sharp real weight pressing down on his chest. Hands were on his shoulders holding him in place. At the same time he felt an incongruous wet stain on his thigh and something hard against his leg. He tried lifting his head to see who was attacking him; but instantly the hands were at his forehead forcing his neck against the couch. The air around him was frosty, like refrigerator air. Lips—cold and lifeless, but lips for sure—pressed against his forehead.

Matthew tried to call out, but his mouth hung suspended on his face half-open, like a hinge, the words caught in his throat. All he was allowed was to keep his eyes open, but this revealed nothing. He saw the same old ceiling of his apartment, the same old fan overhead. Then his vision grew dim. He seemed to be heading out of his body, out from his life, out from the earth. He saw the galaxy surging and pulsing and flaring before his eyes, stars strewn across the vastness of space, the colors of supernovas. He saw billowing sheets of gas; he saw explosions; he saw matter swirling at infinitely high speeds, making moons and planets and asteroids. It was life; it was active; it was beauty in its widest, most awesome form. And then, all at once, he saw this universe being covered by a single black hand. Dark fingers extended over the vision, fingers that were nearly as delicate as a woman's and yet seemed to be able to stretch indefinitely, blocking the light. The broiling galaxy was nearly eliminated, replaced by a blackness so pure that light wasn't just absent but could never live there.

The next thing Matthew knew it was six o'clock in the morning.

A numb silver sheen budded in the living room. He was lying on his couch, a beer bottle beside him. The windows were closed. His leg was still damp and smelled of yeast and grain. Matthew made a shaky pot of coffee and drank as much as he could, all at once, as if the ghost were a toxin he could piss out. He sat at his kitchen table, the dried sweat on his skin stinking up the air.

"I'm going crazy," Matthew said out loud. But he knew he was only parroting the same old hopeless excuse embraced by anyone faced with what they didn't understand. His own speech, delivered at the start of every tour, rebuked him: *When faced with the inexplicable, our reaction is to reduce it to what we know and therefore can accept. But as the stories I will tell you show, some phenomena are so startling, so impossible, that they force us to consider them on their terms, not ours, opening us to a wider mystery and perhaps a wider knowledge than we have ever contemplated.*

He put on a sweatshirt and clean jeans. He went out into the street. It was a cloudy morning. It might rain or it might not. Matthew didn't care either way. He began to walk in the direction of town center. He looked neither left nor right, only straight ahead, only the way he wanted to go. Twelve minutes later he stood on the ferry dock, staring at the span of Atlantic Ocean separating Nantucket Island from America. Over there was Massachusetts. Over there was Boston. Over there was the whole larger United States he had not seen in six years. Suddenly he very much wanted it to rain. Not merely a shower but a torrent. He wanted and needed to be washed; not just washed clean, but washed away, like poisonous runoff from some sordid manufacturing plant. Not sightly, not useful, not worth preserving. A bad reminder of what actually goes on in the world.

In the afternoon, another letter came from Alan. The man, Matthew thought, must really be getting desperate. Or at least impatient. Haughty for an answer. Yes, that was Alan. *It's only been two days,* Matthew thought at his former lover. *Doesn't getting shucked warrant at least that long?*

He dropped the letter on the table. Matthew needed a smoke. He hadn't had one in years, but he couldn't possibly read what Alan had to say until he settled himself with a cigarette, or something.

He looked in the old shoe box in his closet where he had stored an end-of-the-world supply of Camels, the lid sealed tight with almost a whole roll of duct tape, and then two extra layers of packing tape—so he would have to really think about it first. *This might be the end of the world right here*. With a pair of scissors and earnest yanking, Matthew ripped away the tape. He threw off the lid. The box was empty. Matthew didn't understand. He had no memory of ever touching the box after he sealed it, much less throwing the cigarettes away. And even if he had, why would he save an empty box, with a taped lid? He went to the refrigerator. He remembered seeing three Sam Adams after he'd taken his last one the night before, the one that ended up on his leg. He opened the door. No beer.

This isn't funny.

This is seriously not funny. Whoever's doing it.

He inspected the apartment. His television was still in the living room. And his DVD player. In the kitchen he saw his microwave and imported coffee maker. In the bathroom, he looked under the sink. There, in a paper envelope, he kept his cash earnings from the tours until he got around to depositing them. Some weeks he stuffed thousands of dollars into that envelope. After last night, there should be at least three hundred. He checked. $420.

Why would a thief take five-year-old cigarettes and three bottles of Sam Adams, but leave a television and his own private Fort Knox? This was a nasty, punishing robber—one who didn't steal to get richer but to inflict a little extra heartless pain at the weakest moments of a person's life, at the weakest point in his soul. This thief didn't care what he gained, only how much he hurt you. Because it made him feel better to see you grovel. Matthew looked up into the mirror and saw his own dark eyes staring back. He fled the bathroom.

The letter was still on the kitchen table. Matthew needed more time. Alan needed to give him time. What was it anyway? What could Alan possibly have to say now that Matthew wouldn't be hurt by? *You haven't contacted me yet, so I'm withdrawing my offer.* Or: *Benjamin said today that he loved me after all. He wants me back!* Or: *I've heard some really weird gossip about what you're up to there, on Nantucket. Come back to the real world.* Matthew cleaned the sink and emptied the dishwasher. He started an onion bagel in the toaster. He cut a tomato. He checked his watch against the clock on his microwave to make sure the watch wasn't fast again. The watch was okay. He looked out the window to inspect the sky.

He needed more time, damn it. Alan had to learn. Alan needed to be taken away and reprogrammed to not be so pathologically self-centered. Use hypnosis and flash cards and movie clips. Electric shocks, doggie treats, scream therapy. *Fact is, the fact really is, that Alan secretly believes all men and women have been placed on this earth to anticipate his needs. Even if those needs are totally conflicted.* Six years ago, Alan needed to be rid of him. Then, on Thursday, Alan needed him back. Now. *Now?*

The bagel popped up. He went to the kitchen. He laid the two halves on the counter and put the tomato slices on one half. The other half he covered with a neat line of yellow mustard. He pushed the two halves together. He found a plate. He sat at the table. This is what happens. *This is what happens.* What? He didn't know. He ate his bagel without tasting it. When he saw that he was done he was surprised. He didn't feel the sandwich anywhere in his body. He felt completely empty, nearly transparent. He looked to see if he'd dropped it on the floor. No, nothing there. Only crumbs on his plate. Matthew stood up. He walked the plate to the sink. He checked his watch against the oven clock. His watch was okay. He opened the letter.

> Thank you for reading this. Thank you. Thank you! (Kiss. Kiss. Kiss.) I love you, Matthew. I love you. Please forgive me. I really was wrong, and I really am sorry. May I come to see you? Is that where we should start? Forget what I said about coming to Boston. That's not fair.
>
> You have a life where you are. Just tell me when and tell me where I should go. Tell me to move to Nantucket for you. Tell me to go to hell, and I'll accept it.
>
> Thank you for reading this. Please forgive me.

Matthew couldn't feel himself breathe. His lungs seemed stymied

174

in his chest: tight, hot, constricted. His head was light, his fingers
tingling. He hit his chest with his fist and heard a numb, dead,
wooden sound. Maybe it was a delusion: that he was sitting there
awake and alert. Maybe he had blacked out. Maybe he was dead
already. Maybe he was haunting his own home. He put the letter
down; he went to the kitchen; he found a spoon. He could feel the
spoon. It felt like a spoon. Ordinary tempered metal. Concave.
Not cool or warm. Hard enough, but finally not all that hard, not
hurting hard. Not able to damage. His fingers, if tingling, sensed
matter. Then he breathed. He felt it: the air going in and coming
out. His chest moved.

He saw the letter lying on the table like a stranded body waiting
for a final home. Even as he breathed, Alan's words came back to him
and circulated like dreamy whispers. Then he had a vision: clear and
in color, present before his eyes like any movie in a theater. Alan sits
in his office, midmorning, talking on the phone to the director of
the BLO. "No, Jeremy, I can't. I'm leaving early. Noon. That's right.
Thanks." Alan hangs up slowly, a frown indenting his forehead.
He stares at a calendar pinned to the wall behind his computer;
not at any particular date in any particular box; in fact, Alan sees
no numbers or boxes at all, only a maze of muzzy, blended shapes.

New scene: Alan takes the T. He sits on the hard brown seat,
holds his briefcase to his chest, and stares at his feet. The conductor
calls out stops loudly over the P.A. Alan does not realize his own
stop has come until a woman beside him pushes his shoulder and
says she must get off.

New scene: At home, Alan packs a weekend bag, talking to
himself. He packs a pair of red socks, then unpacks them. He packs
them again, thinking they are green. But they aren't; they're red.
He sees this, shakes his head, takes them out. He goes to his sock
drawer. He puts the red socks back. His hand looks for the green
socks but falls upon the red. He brings out the red and carries them
to the bag. He packs them. *No matter what*, Alan says to himself.
Okay? Done with the bag, he walks to his front door: stiff-legged,
wary, like a prisoner toward his legislated doom. He opens the door.
He takes a long step out. He's on the front stoop. He surveys his
neighborhood. He records the world as it looks at the moment,

committing it to memory. He breathes; he turns. He locks his door.

New scene, last scene: It is late afternoon, plenty of light left in the May sky. Alan steps off the fast ferry, the one that takes only an hour from Hyannis. He is dressed in tan slacks and a dark polo shirt, his black hair trimmed, his hands and wrists and knees and waist moving with the same old elegance. But his face looks older and bothered and penitent. His brows are crossed; worry darkens his blue eyes. There is much more gray at his temples than before. But these are all good, fetching developments. Alan, a middle-aged man, grips his weekend bag like a kid clutching his knapsack on his first day at a new school. He scans the crowd on the dock. He does not see Matthew. In the moment he believes no one has come to meet him. Matthew sees Alan's face fall. Then Matthew steps forward. He calls Alan's name. Alan sees him. Alan smiles. His head dips. His expression moves in a moment from surprise to relief to gratitude.

When the vision cleared, Matthew found himself sitting on his couch in the same position as the night before. His chest was calm, his breathing regular, the air inside his apartment as fresh as any he had ever had the pleasure to taste. He checked his watch. 4:30. An hour had passed. Time to get going. He had a job, after all. He had a life. He would pedal down to the Athenaeum. He would meet an eager if unfamiliar crowd: trusting, decent, likable human faces. He would accept their money. And he would tell them a ghost story.

NEWFOUNDLAND

Nantucket Island, 2004

The day was sunny but the bags weighed in his hands, the thin paper handles pressing his flesh like chords. Their hotel was just around the corner, but his wife wanted to make another stop. The last one. She promised.

"Just let me look," she said. She noted his expression. "I said look, not buy. And so what if I do buy? It's not like we can't afford it."

"We've already afforded these," he said. He lifted the bags.

"Yes, we have. And we definitely can afford those." She flitted away before he could respond, leaving him stranded on the sidewalk as the first of the late afternoon breezes sliced Centre Street. He checked his watch. 4:25. She had also promised they would be done by 4:00, when—as he'd discovered during this week of determined real estate hunting—the warm, late spring afternoon could change to a simulacrum of a blowy autumnal one; and any tourist caught in a knit shirt and shorts suddenly shivered in place.

He descended to the bench outside the gift store. He had to shift his position immediately as the Swiss Army knife in his pocket pressed into his thigh. The knife, a gift for his fifty-second birthday, was the one purchase by his wife that he respected, even now, more than ten years later. He'd used it for a gallery of small chores, so many that he learned to keep it on him like a wallet. How much cheaper too, and how much more like him, than the prissy five bedroom on Wyers Lane Dorothy had decided on a few hours ago. Robert choked when he saw the asking price but said nothing; in truth, he had so long prepared for this eventuality that he almost—almost—met it without visible reaction. He spent the rest of the afternoon avoiding her eyes because he knew if she looked into them with any attention she would read his disgust, his heart-stopping anger.

The breeze barreled through, setting his thinning hair astray, canceling his thoughts. He patted the hair with one hand, but as soon as he took the hand away the strands were dancing again. He looked at his palm. A purple-red slash lay evident across the middle, like a burn. Thirty-seven years in the car business just so he could be a shopping bag caddy. He fantasized about dumping every overpriced kitchen gadget, perfume bottle, handcrafted brooch, silk scarf, and marine-themed geegaw on the sidewalk. Let them go. Let them break. Then tear the bag apart for good measure. Watch the wind push the pieces up Centre Street toward the Pacific National Bank. Then he would cut out. Take a taxi to the airport and board a plane. Better idea: Charge down to the harbor and buy the first boat he sees. Steer the thing into the Atlantic, back to the Cape. No, better idea: up the coast. All the way to Maine. Further. Newfoundland.

When Robert was two-and-a-half his father left boot camp at Fort Bragg, North Carolina and traveled with hundreds of other soldiers to North Africa to participate in the invasion of Italy. When Robert was three, his father, as part of a forward patrol operating outside Arno, was shot in the heart by a sniper. The man died in three minutes. When Robert was three-and-a-half, his mother took a job as a night desk clerk at the Wareham Hotel on 18th St. in Philadelphia. While she worked he slept, guarded by a seventy-five year old neighbor who would take only a dollar a night for her services and whom he learned to call Auntie. When he was five, Auntie died of a stroke while listening to the radio in the living room of his mother's apartment. When he came out of the bedroom that morning he saw the old woman sitting stiffly on their couch, slumped to one side as if asleep. Nothing unusual. Until he saw her strangled face, that is, and her eyes open.

At nine, he played tricks with Eddie Jordan and Cecil Cassidy: slashing tires, tossing eggs, making stink bombs, lifting gum and sodas. At fifteen, he was stealing hubcaps and radios. Occasionally a whole car if the circumstances were right. He never kept them, just stole them. Because he didn't need any car, just the vitality he felt in the act of theft. During every second of the hurried maneuver—busting the window, unlocking the door, slipping into the driver's side, digging under the dash, locating the wires, making the engine erupt—his body seemed to beat with a double heart, his lung possessed double oxygen and his arms double blood; thoughts felt doubly clear in his brain. Not just his life but the entire world in which he existed seemed more acutely colored than it ever had or ever would be again. When the theft was over and the joy ride through, it took him hours to get the high out of his bloodstream. And the memory of it only egged him on to another more daring heist. They were nabbed when they tried to steal an Imperial in broad daylight, two blocks from a police station. Only because his mother was sleeping with a cop at the local precinct did he escape juvenile detention. Eddie didn't. Cecil got hit by a car. At eighteen, Robert decided he would finish high school.

At twenty-two, he applied for a job as a car salesman at Cecchini Motors on North Carlisle Street, because he heard you got to drive the new cars for free. That was true, but he soon found himself too busy hustling customers to care about testing the merchandise. In no time at all he learned the pattern of the sale: the customer's initial caution; the torrent of smiles and words that could earn a break in that wall; then that opening, almost possessive, look that told him the customer had caught the idea, the idea that the car—this very one—this sassy beauty—could be his. If he only said yes. It was then that Robert felt that old familiar vitality, the surge of double blood. And with a new torrent of words, his brain surging warmly through the high, he pushed on for the kill. He repeated the pattern time and again in those first years, so many more times than he had ever stolen a car. And so much more profitable.

At twenty-five, he sold a Bel Air to a stunning young woman named Dorothy Schaefer: her features thin, her figure pointed beneath the snug dress, her eyes an alluring yellow and green, her accent from someplace richer. She seemed so self-possessed and so not from the neighborhood that Robert felt his rhythm fall off, his confidence flutter. The entire time he talked he didn't know if he was getting an inch closer to a sale. As he showed her the new features on the '65 she maintained a poker face, her eyes narrowing with analytical prowess, as if this were a laboratory and he were explaining to her the method for converting hydrogen to oxygen—and, strangest of all, he didn't quite care if he sold the car or not. Yet he did. And when she came to pick up the new Bel

Air a week later, Dorothy found a dozen long stem red roses in the front seat. She smiled as if not quite surprised by the gesture, thanked him genially—if not quite personally—and drove away. It was only then that it occurred to him that she must have left a phone number on the sales papers. At twenty-seven he proposed to Dorothy Schaefer, who for all her exotic qualities and the whisper of money in her background, worked as a secretary in city hall and grew up only two blocks from where he did, with a father who was a butcher. When Robert asked the question, a satisfied look crossed those cutting eyes; then for a second she stared over his shoulder at the door of her apartment. Her eyes came back. "That would be a clever idea," she said.

At thirty-three he opened his own Chevrolet franchise on 29th St. and immediately began outperforming every GM dealer in the Philadelphia metro area. At thirty-six, he opened a Pontiac/Buick/Oldsmobile franchise a mile from his first dealership. At thirty-eight, he moved with Dorothy and their nine-year-old daughter to a gated estate deep in the suburbs west of downtown. When they took over the place, Colleen immediately scrambled through every room, chirping and exalting at the space; his wife, on the other hand, stood stock still, and surveyed the mansion like an exiled queen returning to her ancestral home. "Not bad at all," she said.

At thirty-nine he opened a Cadillac dealership a mile from the McCall Golf and Country Club. Robert decided to sell the first car himself, which he did, to a Mr. and Mrs. Henry Edel, a short, graying, yet cheery couple, their skin too white perhaps but the faces healthily plump and their blue eyes bright with trust. Robert led the Edels so smoothly through the old moves that in a half-hour he had them committed to a purchase. They didn't even ask for a test drive. Twenty minutes later, inside his office, he stood and shook both their hands. He smiled. He demonstrated. He laughed, as if in the presence of old friends. A contract had been signed. He escorted them to the parking lot and watched as they pulled away. The old couple waved vigorously. He raised his hand and motioned back. He stood there until they were out of sight.

* * *

At forty, and again the next year, his Chevrolet dealership lost money for the first time ever. Big money. He had to do something, so he fired most of his salesmen. But it wasn't their fault, and Robert knew it. No one could sell those cars. The word was out and the word was true: Chevys were junk. Pontiacs were junk. Buicks were junk. For that matter, so too were Cadillacs. The finish was terrible. The frame was terrible. The brakes were shaky. The axles were unreliable. And the engines were a complete joke, not lasting past 50,000 before blowing a gasket. The insides were waxy plastic crap that would scratch or break or warp in a month. The A/C and starter and alternator all went the second the car was out of warranty. American cars were glorified soup cans. Go carts were better engineered. Robert knew this as well as anyone. He lived with the cheap ass things every day of his life. If he weren't a GM dealer, he would drive a Toyota.

At forty-five, he suffered his first heart attack. Serious enough to do damage; mild enough not to kill him. He spent a week in Bryn Mawr hospital and then was sent home: weak, pale, and tired. His wife served him toast and oatmeal and bananas, decaffeinated tea and worried looks. "You're not leaving me," Dorothy said. "I committed to you, so you damn sight are getting better." He sat on the sofa, watched *Donahue*, and wanted to die. But he didn't. Colleen, a sophomore at the Gilman School in Baltimore, was two hours away. Finals week. Her mother told her to stay put and worry about exams. Her father was still alive.

When he was forty-seven, his daughter received an acceptance letter from the University of Oregon. She also received letters from the University of Pennsylvania, Villanova, Brown, and Georgetown. Dorothy campaigned for Penn or Villanova. "They have immaculate reputations," she said one Saturday evening when their daughter came home for the weekend. "Whatever it is you want to study, they will give you the best for our money." And how convenient that they were also the two closest schools of the five. Colleen, who had flowered into a stunning combination of her parents—with her mother's petite waist and brilliant eyes, her father's softer, more balanced facial tones—nodded before Dorothy's reasoning but never indicated if she agreed with it. This wasn't the first time she had been given her mother's opinion.

"What?" Dorothy said. "What?"

Robert knew: Colleen wanted to go to Oregon. And he understood: she wanted out. She'd been free of them, more or less, for four years. And now she wanted to be freer. Not only of them but the whole east coast. Of the privileged, private school network. She wanted to set her own course. On the phone, he'd heard the loony thrill in her voice when she told him of the acceptance, even though that one had been in the bag since the moment she mailed in her form. The other four were the toughies. Unfortunately, Oregon was also the only choice Dorothy deemed unacceptable.

"I think," Robert said, "that you should go to the school that makes the most sense to you." Dorothy savaged him with a slashing glance. Colleen, meanwhile, broke into a bearish smile. "I'm glad to hear it," she said.

At forty-nine, his Chevy dealership had its best year since the early seventies. When the fiscal year numbers came in, he took his wife out to celebrate. He had steak and a potato and a house salad. She had breaded veal over spaghetti and grilled vegetables. They both had champagne. He lifted his glass to toast.

"To General Motors Corporation," he said. She made a face. "Which," he said, "has basically paid for our lives."

"And almost ruined them."

"Just those two years."

"They were a spectacularly hard two years."

"Granted, but they're over."

She said nothing. She shrugged, noncommittally. Neither of them had taken a sip of champagne.

He felt a second's flush of anger. "GMC has bought us everything we own, Dorothy."

"I'd rather not be reminded of that fact, thank you."

She put her glass down and stared meanly at the vegetables.

Robert sat still, holding his glass but not drinking, a slab of brown meat in front of him getting colder.

Shortly after he turned fifty-three, his daughter died. Married a year, pregnant, ready to quit her job at MCI's Portland division and become a mother, she was driving on Route 5 when her car was hit head on by a Suburu that had crossed into oncoming traffic. The driver of the Suburu, a diabetic who had overlooked his morning insulin injection, had first lost consciousness and then control, weaving in freeway traffic, a motorized fatality begging to happen. Dorothy's first reaction was to scream. Then she began slapping Robert. He had let her go out there. *He* had let her go out there. And now this was the result. In the moment, overwhelmed by the news himself, trying to avoid his wife's flailing palms, it was impossible for Robert to realize what he did minutes later—when Dorothy retreated to their bedroom and gorged herself on shrieks; when he, as if propelled by a force outside his body, started up his Cadillac and for next four hours drove the same tight circle around the city: 76 to 95 to 676 to 76—that an accident like the one that took Colleen could have happened anywhere. In Rhode Island. In Washington, DC. In Philadelphia. And though realize it he did, he never spoke this truth to Dorothy; not during that interminable first day when she remained stricken and hiding; not during the terrible silent trip to the west coast for the funeral; not during the equally silent trip back; not during all the hard weeks that followed when Dorothy's resentment seemed to grow only larger, so much so she could not be in the same room with him without bristling. Her anger seemed to well up like actual fluid in her body, brimming her eyes with red oil. He never spoke that truth to her because he knew precisely what would be her response. *It didn't happen anywhere. It happened out there.*

At fifty-four, he discovered that Bill Lagana, the manager of his Buick dealership, had stolen $157,000 from him over the course of two years. The man had reached his target goal and fled the country. No one knew where. Robert was floored. He didn't understand. He'd liked Bill Lagana. He liked him better than anyone he'd ever interviewed. Bill Lagana had been a superb salesman. He'd been a good employee. He'd been a friend. And what good was $157,000, anyhow, compared to a career? How long could a $157,000 hold out these days, living on the lam? He wished he could find Bill Lagana, not necessarily to prosecute him, but just to ask him what he was thinking.

At fifty-five, at work, he had a scare: shortness of breath, weird movement in his chest, numbness in his arm. He dialed 911 himself and was in the ER in fifteen minutes. They examined him crown to toe. Nothing wrong, they said. Maybe it's just stress. To be safe, he spent two days at home, watching *Geraldo*, *Montel*, and *Jenny Jones*. His wife served him toast and juice and tomato soup and salads. In the afternoon of the second day she said, "I'm sure they must miss you at work. I'm sure they need you there." He resisted the impulse to shake his head.

When he was fifty-nine, they celebrated their thirty-second wedding anniversary with a long weekend on Nantucket Island in a hotel that charged $500 a night. "Costliest fuck we'll ever have," his wife said, smirking, as they walked up the stairs to their room. Not really, he thought. His costliest fuck was getting married.

Dorothy had become infatuated with the once-upon-a-time whaling hub. Eight months before, she accepted a friend's invitation to spend Labor Day weekend there, while Robert was tied up with business. She returned jubilant. The weather was clear; the beaches were gorgeous; the island was filled with all the right people. And the shopping was heavenly. He didn't ask how much. But when the Visa bill came he couldn't keep from looking. She spent $11,000 in two days. We must go next season, she said. I want you to come with me and see it. He swallowed and nodded his head.

"I think we should move here," Dorothy said to him. They were having their anniversary dinner at the Jared Coffin house. "After you retire. Who needs Philadelphia? We've earned our way out of that dump."

"We've been out of the dump for twenty years. What do you call the house we live in?"

She wrinkled her nose.

"Common," she said.

"Come again?"

"Oh, it's fine, of course. It's huge. It's pretty. But it looks like everyone else's huge, pretty house. We live our neighbors' lives."

He hesitated before responding. "I thought I was living my life."

She smiled pityingly at him.

"Of course, Robert. And you are. But I think to have an actually distinctive life you have to think harder about it. You have to plan."

"I think hard enough," he said, "just getting through each week at the dealerships."

Her expression was like a sprung trap. He'd said exactly the right thing.

"I agree. So let me think about it. Let me examine the alternatives."

He took a curt drink of red wine. "Which alternatives?"

"Like, for instance—just for instance—those homes we saw today. The ones I pointed out."

"You mean near the beach?" Five million at least. Maybe seven. "I'm not spending my life's savings on a goddamn beach house."

"Don't be sour, Robert. I'm just asking. Wouldn't it be fun to have Tommy Hilfiger as a neighbor?"

"Tommy Hilfiger runs a worldwide clothing business. I operate three car dealerships in Philadelphia."

"Very successful dealerships."

"Tommy Hilfiger can afford a beach house."

She waved a hand. "So can we. You're just being cross. You need to be more imaginative."

"I'm being sensible."

She bulled right past the word. "I think it would be delightful."

"But it wouldn't make any sense."

She brought her face back, like sheathing a sword. Her smile was gone, the light which for a moment almost turned her hazel eyes emerald. She put her hands in her lap.

"Not to you, maybe."

"No, not to me."

"It's only one option. There are others."

"Like living in Philadelphia."

She stiffened. She drank some of her own wine now, a measured sip, her face smothering a twitch. She lowered the glass slowly to the table and pressed the base into the tablecloth.

"Yes, that is one option," she said.

At fifty-nine, sixty, and sixty-one he went regularly with his wife to the island. Short, weekend jaunts to search out potential real estate and speculate further about retirement. So far it was all talk, an expensive game that he put up with for two or three days at a clip before being allowed to return to the regularity of his business life. When he left the island at the end of one of those long, cash-heavy weekends he felt the woozy, discentered relief of someone escaping a nightmare. Yet it was a nightmare that was gradually, relentlessly encroaching. His wife was determined they would live on Nantucket. No other "options" were ever discussed. So he tried to avoid the issue of his retirement altogether. But it was out there, looming closer, a swinging scythe that was already altering their positions in the relationship. In only a couple years, he would be retired: out of the world—stripped of command—dead as a man. Every day he worked at the dealerships brought retirement one day closer. He felt it; Dorothy felt it. He was soon to be decapitated. She meanwhile, in the graying years of her life, seemed to have doubled in strength. She had taken the upper position. She had found her platform. It was now, and it was them.

Robert understood that in its early 21st century form, Nantucket Island was the territory of middle-aged white women from the eastern seaboard states. Shopping was the primary local sport, followed closely by enviously eyeing new constructions (or wagging one's head at the "degradation"), followed by guessing which outrageously overpriced restaurant would be the scene of that night's meal, followed by waxing cheaply about the past glories of the island. Yes, he thought bitterly, when it was actually inhabited by normal people; when the grime was palpable and it literally stunk from the business of the whale business; when the harbor was ringed with active factories, labored in by half-literate but aspiring men; when full-blooded American Indians still existed here; when each year people came from the mainland not to retire but to live; long before it became an isolated, gentrified lab experiment in exclusion and price gouging. Waxing that is, about a Nantucket Island that these women wouldn't be caught dead on, because it would not have flattered their ambitions for superiority. Finally, there was the sport of meandering past store fronts on the cobblestone streets in town center—a tea or latte in hand—soaking in the pleasure of simply being there and feeling wealthy for the fact. There did not seem to be much for a man to do on this prettified outpost; even the beaches had little of the essential roughness he preferred in living things. No wonder the men who lived on the island seemed out-of-focus and feminized, their edges rubbed off like bits of beach glass. The male college students, for all their buffed, blabbering, and insufferable arrogance, at least had life.

He would have to stay inside his home—wherever that turned out to be—and watch ball games on cable. Baseball in summer, football in fall, hockey in winter, basketball in spring. He would have to buy the most elaborate package available. That and become the permanent handyman for the new home he couldn't afford: repairing, painting, caulking, soldering, replacing, cleaning. Something to do, while the lady of the house, with a free mind and a free checkbook and a half-dozen similarly vigorous, immaculately coiffed companions, pillaged the island for sales and deals, ornaments and antiques.

It was a great relief, when on a Sunday evening on a plane pointed toward Hyannis, he'd watch the island dissolve below him, then disappear. Tomorrow he would be at work, on the job, making a living, managing actual men in an actual world. The island a memory. But when he looked at his wife—eyeglasses on her forehead and coffee cup in hand—poring over real estate magazines, he saw his doom clearly enough. This was only a temporary reprieve.

Early in his sixty-second year, he suffered a second heart attack, minutes before he would have left the office to drive home. His secretary, who happened to come back for the coat she forgot, found him on the floor, still breathing. The ambulance came in three minutes, oxygen ready. He lived in ICU for a week, then in a recovery room resting and being monitored. He was asked all over again about his family's medical history.

"My father was gunned down by a fascist. He was too young

to worry about his heart."

The young Asian-American nurse was soft in cheek and voice but she worked with a determined courteousness, regarding him through small, wire framed glasses.

"Your mother?"

"She dated assholes her whole life."

"Sir."

"What?"

"Is your mother alive?"

"No."

"When did she die?"

"1986."

"Of what?"

"Loneliness."

The nurse sighed. She scratched the side of her head. She wrote something on her pad. "Grandparents?"

"Might as well not have had any."

Which was true, if not exactly what the nurse asked. Growing up, he didn't see his father's parents. They didn't visit; didn't write; didn't call. It was as if their son's death erased the grandson as well, as if Robert too had been shot in Arno. As a kid he didn't really care, and later he tried to understand—they must have been too broken at the loss of their handsome young man—but finally he couldn't get around the fact that their behavior was lousy as hell. It didn't help, of course, that his mother told her own parents to stay away. But for that he couldn't blame her. About the time Robert was stealing hubcaps with Eddie and Cecil, they told her it was her own fault her son was becoming a delinquent. *Boys don't get that way if parents don't let them. Parents who are home.* Get out, she said to them. Robert was in another room but he heard her easily enough. *Get out of my place.*

"Are they dead?" the nurse asked.

"Of course. But I don't know how those turkeys took it."

The nurse sighed again. "I'll have to call the doctor in."

He shifted his head, looked out the window. He would have turned his back on her if that were possible. No more questions, he would have muttered. He had no family history.

The doctor urged Robert to retire. He couldn't find a plausible reason to deny the request. Six months later, he sold the whole group of dealerships for a whopping price to an even bigger collective. He met with his investment analyst and his accountant. They came up with a sound plan for the money. His financial future was secure. His fortune was guaranteed. He could rest. You can take it easy now, they said to him. You did it. You won. Kind words, but spoken—every one of them—from behind lying, impatient smiles. He knew what they really meant. He could hear the other words beneath their spoken ones, as relentless as their polished shoes, their Italian neckties, their tiny newfangled phones. *Time to get out of the picture, old timer, and let guys like us take over.*

He'd been sitting so long on the bench his ass hurt. He shifted, looked at his watch: 4:55. He opened the shopping bag and glanced once more at the trinkets inside. Another blast of wind barreled up Centre Street and hit him like a body in a hurry. He stood up and went to the big glass window. He looked into the shop for his wife. He saw a fortyish woman with a pale, featureless face studying glassware. An infant slept on her back in a backpack. He saw a graying blonde woman—perhaps fifty—in a crew neck sweatshirt and rain slicker move slowly from table to table with a concentrated frown, lifting merchandise and setting it down, lifting and setting down. Never buying. He saw two twenty-somethings with bored expressions looking at a painting of a whale ship in stormy seas. One of the young women said something. The other smirked. Then she answered. The first girl started chuckling. He looked all around the shop—what he could see, at least, through the window. His wife was nowhere. Maybe she was in the back; if there was a back. Then he saw her, suddenly appearing out of some nook he hadn't recognized, a large glass item in her hand, a keen smile on her face. She talked excitedly to the saleswoman at the counter. He knew the expression. She was telling the tale of her discovery. His wife and the woman stood and talked, recounting and replaying the moment, forgetting the necessity of ringing up the purchase, while he stood outside, attacked by cold air.

He dropped the bag at once. He heard a smashing noise below him, but didn't look. He walked as fast as his retired, heart-damaged legs could down Centre Street, to the intersection with Broad. At Broad he turned right. He walked that whole sloping cobblestone avenue, almost to the ferry dock. He turned left at Beach. He passed the Whaling Museum on his left, a bike rental shop, and an ice cream stand. On his right were intermittent boutiques; behind them the ocean. He reached the Children's Beach, where the smaller boats were moored. He felt in his pocket. He still had it. The only thing his wife gave him that he ever loved.

He moved with short, hard strides across the sand. When he reached the water, he stopped to take off his shoes and socks. He discarded them and then headed on. The first boat he reached, he cut its mooring line. He used the flathead screwdriver attachment to pry open the dashboard. He looked at the linguine of red, green, and yellow wires. Engines hadn't really changed much in fifty years. It occurred to him that he might be watched, at that moment, in the act of committing a crime. But he didn't check over his shoulder. Let them watch. He heard no one shout, no one sound an alarm. What he heard, in fact—the blood doubling in his neck—was an engine come to life under the command of his working, nimble fingers. He sat back, put a firm hand on the wheel, and opened up the throttle. The boat jerked ahead a foot, then smoothed out, inching ahead. He turned the wheel and pointed the boat toward Brant Point, the exit from the harbor. Now, he thought, which way to Newfoundland.

MANAGING BUSINESS

Nantucket Island, 2005

For the third morning in a row the fog hung like spun glue. Tameca zipped her windbreaker against the dank, then she shifted her overloaded backpack so that the straps did not bite so keenly into the tips of her skinny shoulders. Too much Chemistry. Too much Trigonometry. Too much American History. She took a step down from the doorway to the cracked sidewalk.

"Remember," her mother said. "Don't come home this afternoon. Go to the shop."

Tameca nodded. She held her hand up straight to imitate a wave but didn't look back.

"I'll find something for you to do."

A surge of seasonal wind blew across the tiny parking lot and cut her face, a momentary assault. Tameca lowered her head to wait it out.

"Girl," her mother shouted. Tameca looked back. She saw exactly what she expected: the eternal worry that weighed Hosanna's face, that pressed her cheeks, that bottomed out her jowls into doughy flaps of skin. That and the same old mote of confusion in her eye, as if every moment of her life on this island the woman was trying to figure out the next, still astounded that she transferred herself—and them—from Jamaica to this cantankerous northern outpost. Hosanna Lloyd pursed her heavy lips and kissed the air.

"You my baby," she said.

"Yes," Tameca said. She saw her brother appear behind her mother, his long thin frame miniaturizing Hosanna's round one. Demont yawned, scratched his head, looked at her with puddled eyes.

"Get going," he said. "It's witchy out."

"I'm out. You're not."

"Yeah, but you're dressed for it."

"Get dressed then."

"You crazy? I'm going back to bed."

"It's seven-thirty, Demont." With that she begged a half-smile from him.

"Middle of the night," he said. Demont slept downstairs, which he liked for the isolation, but every morning he shouted at her, usually with the covers over his head, to close the door so he could get back to sleep. Demont drove a cab and didn't get home until 2:00. At least that's what he said. Neither Tameca nor her mother were ever up to hear him come in.

"The shop," her mother repeated, more adamantly.

"I know. I heard you." Tameca put her thumbs through the backpack straps and walked away to meet the wind.

Hosanna didn't understand why the Americans wanted the shop open with seasonal hours. It was the first week in May. It was a Wednesday. Daytime temperatures reached only into the middle 60s; nights were in the 40s, sometimes the 30s. The wind was raw. The fog was thick. Tourists were few. We want to be at full stride on Memorial Day, they said. *Full stride*. How was that even possible before the college crowd descended? Before they showed up half-stoned and half-naked, ready to take over their jobs from the summer before. The jobs they needed not to earn money for school—their parents already paid for their private colleges—but just to have a few more bucks to spend while they summered on-island. Beer, sweatshirts, condoms. Drugs. But then again, Hosanna knew she was jaded—maybe unfairly so—by her own experience as manager of Magpie's, a combination ice cream/ sandwich/coffee shop tucked away on Water St., not far from where the ferries docked. The Americans always insisted she hire three or four college kids, because—as they put it, a spoonful of guilt weathering their voices—"they get along well with the tourists." Which of course meant: "They make the whites feel comfortable." Yes. The whites. All those tanned, sportily dressed middle-agers from the eastern seaboard: Boston, Providence, Bennington, New Haven, Hartford, Albany. The Great Pale Goose of Tourism Dollars that every shop and restaurant fought to attract and then keep loyal from season to season.

For the sake of these customers, Hosanna was charged every

summer with the oversight of blonde, blue-eyed twenty year olds with minimal skills, poor work habits, and no genius of any kind, save the talent for issuing perfectly transparent excuses in almost convincing tones. No wonder they had their parents pocketed. These were employees who regarded her—the manager of the place—with either barely suppressed sarcasm or droll nods. Boys and girls obviously not used to taking orders from a forty-year-old woman with nappy hair, a Caribbean accent, and skin as dark as licorice. *They just assume I am stupid.* If Hosanna had real control over personnel, she would refuse to hire most of them, and she would fire about half the others. But the Americans would brook only so much dissent. Every year, for the last two weeks of May, they abandoned their headquarters in Medford for the island, where they lingered around the shop, asked too many questions and interviewed countless young, white applicants. Whomever they hired formed Hosanna's crew for the next three months. Until they came and gave her these employees she would have to tread water with a skeleton crew, serving almost nobody. *Full stride.* She decided on the spot to open at noon instead of eleven: a small rebellion no one would notice, because she hadn't even posted the new hours yet.

Of course, these same Americans had seen fit to hire her so many years ago, when she first came to the island, leaving ten-year-old Demont and six-year-old Tameca with her mother for the summer. They even appointed her manager after their own son—a stringy-haired, pimply lout named Aidan, who ran the shop for all of two months—emptied their account of $80,000, took a puddle jumper to Logan, and then a 727 to Auckland. Hosanna had suspected the boy might be up to no good. She tried to warn the Americans, but the subject proved too delicate. It was not something you could just come out and say about the owners' son. Not when you are black and not even a U.S. citizen. Besides, she reasoned, if the Americans remained blind to the boy's thefts, it must be that they wanted to remain blind. So she let them lose their money.

The shock of Aidans's heist seemed to wake the Americans to Hosanna's value. Clotted with shame, smarting from the betrayal, living with the specter of their blood turned into a permanent fugitive, they were in dire need of a trusted hand. So they offered the manager's position to Hosanna, who by then had worked six straight summers. She let them sweat a whole day before responding. And even then she enunciated demands: If she were being asked to live permanently on Nantucket island—because in the off season the shop opened Friday through Sunday—she would need to bring her son and her daughter up from Jamaica. Moreover, she would need an affordable place to live; and by that she didn't mean a single room in somebody's basement, or an abandoned fishing shack astride an inlet, or a house that would become an orphanage for rowdy students in the summer. She meant a place suitable for raising children, according to American standards. She was being asked, after all, to take an American's job. The owners must not be allowed to think they could get her on the cheap.

At first, the Americans protested. All right, she said, then pay me triple what you did Aidan, so I can afford to rent here. Soon enough they admitted to owning a townhouse in Madaket. Instead of letting it week-to-week to tourists, they would rent it to her year round—at half the going rate. Half the going rate still seemed like naked thievery, but on a manager's salary Hosanna could just make the payment. She accepted. In the four years that followed, Hosanna was forced to put up with a platoon of dimwitted white boys and girls, but the Americans also allowed her to hire, at one time or the other, her sister, her sister's daughter, her sister-in law, and her sister-in law's cousin. She even put Demont on the payroll part-time. The college kids would always be there, regarding her with the same bland faces, blonde hair, infant voices, and needing eyes. But Hosanna had developed a functional strategy: stick them out front, where they could be seen and heard by others of their kind. Give them little to do, and the moment their shift ends send them on their way. Meanwhile, reserve the real work of preparing, clearing, cleaning, planning, and ordering for herself, her children, and her relatives. They were the ones who could really take care of business.

* * *

At the bus stop on Madaket Road, Tameca waited alone for ten minutes before the McConnells joined her. Tom, a lanky junior with a narrow chin, shoulder length hair, and a pocked complexion had not yet grown into his 6'2" body; it did not yet fit him, as if the sunken chest, jutting elbows, and fence post shoulders were only a costume he might shrug off at any moment to return to his normal, younger form. Presently, he stared at the fog, his brown eyes as dark as soil, his expression opaque. It wasn't just the early hour. This was Tom's usual expression. At school all the kids called him a stoner. Tameca wasn't sure.

"Hi, T," Tom's sister said.

Tameca nodded. "Sarah."

"You ready for Chemistry?"

"I think so," Tameca said.

"I am so not ready." She looked at Tameca meaningfully. "Not at all."

Sarah—a blonde who, if nature had its way, would be as brown as her older brother—was more social than Tom but not as interesting, not nearly as mysterious. In fact, Sarah wasn't mysterious at all. At any given moment, her whole personality was on the surface, gesturing and articulating. But this, and the fact that she had a conventionally pretty face and that she fit easily into her taut, compact body, meant she was popular. She had a devoted consortium of friends and was connected at several points to the power centers of the sophomore class. For this reason, Tameca always felt on guard around the girl, though Sarah had never been other than welcoming.

"Julie called me last night," Sarah said. "That's why I'm not ready. We were up to like 1:30 talking. You won't believe what she told me about Lynna."

Sarah looked at Tameca knowingly, as if she expected a response. Tameca shrugged.

Sarah only mouthed the word, her eyes aglow with the power of the secret she must have sworn not to speak aloud: "*Pregnant*." Sarah held her hands in front of her, a clumsy imitation of a swollen womb. Sarah checked to see if Tom had witnessed her gesture, but the boy only stared down the road in the direction where the bus would appear.

Tameca nodded. "That will change things for her."

Sarah's face opened exultantly, but then her eyes dimmed, as if she realized there might be something other than collaboration in Tameca's words. She shook off the doubt like a nuisance.

"I know. Think about how many phone calls are going to be about her from now on." Sarah smiled, wide as a Christmas party. Then she too looked for the bus. For the moment—only that one—Sarah's face as dully expectant as her brother's—Tameca saw a similarity between the siblings. So maybe they came from the same parents, after all.

Tom and Sarah were the only other high schoolers in the complex, yet Tameca barely saw them except for the bus stop. Even after four years on Nantucket she hadn't gotten used to the paucity of companionship. In Jamaica, their neighborhood had been a poor one—the whole island was poor—but it always overflowed with children. And yet, it seemed, there were never too many. Seeing so many children and so many neighbors was simply the rhythm of life. But in this neighborhood of gray-shingled townhouses, used primarily as rental properties for summer tourists, only a handful of owners, like Tom and Sarah's parents, passed the year here. Their slight number meant that the neighborhood was bare for nine months out of twelve. Tameca hesitated to say this to her mother, but the complex was a bore: dozens of identical units, backed by acres of scrub brush, beset with knifing winds from the ocean half a mile away. But it was safe, as Hosanna constantly liked to remind them. And quiet. You do not know what a luxury quiet is in this world, Hosanna said.

Quiet, yes, Tameca thought as she spotted the fat headlights of the school bus luminous against the spooling fog. But sometimes she would not mind distraction.

The cappuccino machine was in pieces on the floor; the glass jar of the blender lay beside it in slivers while the bottom section had been drowned in a full sink, its circuits ruined. Six or seven pieces of silverware were jammed into the garbage disposal; and the refrigerator—its glossy stainless surface exploded into craters and river-sized fissures—looked like it had been brutalized with a sledgehammer. All the coffee mugs had been destroyed, their pieces scattered nonsensically throughout the shop; the lemonade and fruit punch dispensers were broken and lying on the bathroom floor, their electrical cords cut in half. The worse mess, however, was the food. Two tubs' worth of chicken salad were smeared across the front counter, rank after hours in the open air, the flecks of grape and walnut and raisin looking like the remains of cat vomit. Pounds of luncheon meat—ham, turkey, pastrami, salami, pepperoni, roast beef—had been chucked slice by slice everywhere: on tables and chairs, against the front glass, across the floor, on the counter, underneath the prep table against the wall. The vandals had done the same with cheese. The ice cream freezer had been turned off; its contents were all but melted. They even removed a few containers and accented the general mess with scoopfuls, now nothing but colorful, sticky puddles: mint chocolate chip, blueberry, marshmallow-caramel swirl. There were open gashes in the hardwood floor—four or five glaring rents—as if someone had attacked it with an axe. Hosanna could not begin to understand what she was looking at, or how it happened. There was no sign of a break in: no shattered windows, no busted glass in the front door, nothing different about the locks. In the middle of her astonishment, Hosanna managed to wonder why the vandals restrained themselves to only four or five thrusts against the floor. Not as fun as smearing chicken salad across a counter, she guessed. If they had stopped to think about it, maybe they would have kept on axing. But obviously these weren't thinking people.

Soon enough, the consequences of the vandalism occurred to her: 1) Aidan was back from Auckland and would have to be located; 2) the summer opening would be delayed for weeks. Maybe months. The Americans would complain not only about the repair bills—though surely they had insurance for that—but how much money they were losing by not being open. As if there is anything she could do about that. As if it is her fault the place got wrecked. Of course, they would deny Aidan had anything to do with it. Why would Aidan do that to us? they'd say. *Were they kidding?* When there is a warrant, initiated by his parents, still outstanding for his arrest? But no . . . not Aidan. They would never consider that.

Instead they would blame her. Because she was on-island. She was their ears and their eyes. She let them down. Finally they would claim they couldn't afford to pay her, not until the shop reopened.

The Americans, Hosanna knew, were already growing uncertain of her. Sales had been flat the last two summers. They quizzed her last September on a Labor Day stopover. *Why aren't we growing? What are you doing with the place?* The real answer—that the recession bottoming out many businesses on the island had inevitably affected theirs—they did not accept. When she mentioned this, their expressions turned sour, as if she were a child trying to put a lie past her parents. This was not a high dollar business, they reminded her. They weren't selling jewelry or fine art: stuff that people will put off buying when times got hard. This was ham sandwiches and chocolate ice cream. Sandwiches and ice cream sell no matter what the economy. *Or at least they should.* Their eyebrows arched meaningfully. So in other words, Hosanna heard, it was all her fault.

And this would be her fault too, even though the day before she'd taken all the normal steps to protect the space: locked the doors, secured the windows, turned on the alarm. She did what every other shopkeeper on the island does, no more and no less. So she was just supposed to know, in the middle of the night, from her home six miles away, and even when the alarm fails, that someone was wrecking the shop? So that's how it was? They might even use this as an excuse to fire her. And without the job, of course, she couldn't keep the house. She would have to leave the island, uproot Tameca, abandon her plans for bringing her smart girl up in America. Demont could stay if he wanted, if they let him. He was old enough, a man. But not Tameca; the girl would have to leave.

Calm yourself, she thought. *None of that has happened yet.* None of it. *Only this.* And this absolutely had not happened because of her. She gripped her cell phone and reviewed the coming, unavoidable conversation. She wouldn't mention Aidan. She'd let them suggest him. For now, just the facts: *Someone busted in. I don't know who. I don't know how. They've ruined the food; they've destroyed the equipment.* She had already punched the number into her phone when she realized what she was seeing atop the stainless surface of the prep counter: a message put where only employees and managers have reason to look: the letters drawn in pink ice cream, melted almost beyond reading, but with a discernible, encrusted residue. FUCK OFF H.L. She canceled her phone call and made two others instead.

Only once did Hosanna lobby the Americans to hire a white girl. The owners had left for the day when the young woman came by with her application, so Hosanna initiated the interview herself. Before the girl spoke, Hosanna knew this one was different. This one she liked. Her eyes weren't lazy blue but black and guarded and rarely met Hosanna's, yet her cheeks spoke of determination. Her hair wasn't blonde and layered but thin and near-dark, the color of polluted water. It was cut rawly, as if the girl might have performed the operation herself with kitchen scissors. She dressed for the interview in gray sweatpants and a plain, white t-shirt, the shadow of a tattoo showing just out of the end of the sleeve. Her narrow nose was catarrhal and ran throughout the whole interview. She coughed once. She sneezed. Hosanna was about to ask her about this, but the girl offered her own information.

"I'm sick a lot," she said. "But I'll work."

"What are you sick with?" Hosanna was careful to express the question in a non-accusatory tone. As if she were merely curious.

"I don't know. The doctors can't seem to figure what. So I live with it. I don't have any other choice. Don't worry—I'll work."

Hosanna nodded.

"You've worked on the island before?"

"Never," the girl said. "Back home."

"Home is . . ." Hosanna glanced at the girl's application.

"Troy. New York."

Hosanna nodded neutrally. The place name meant nothing to her.

"Rather be there than here," the girl said.

"Why?"

The girl's smile was like a razor; then it disappeared. She looked away. She tilted her chair back.

"Because this island is for pussies."

"Who do you mean?"

"You don't see them? All these spoiled rotten punks? It's like one big fashion show, all summer long."

Hosanna's heart moved inside her. She moved her head slightly.

"You don't go to college?"

The girl shrugged, met her eye for one second.

"I went to community college last fall. One semester. I might go back. I don't know. I prefer to work. If I go back to college it's got to be for something real."

Hosanna read over the whole application. "So in Troy you worked at a carpet store."

"Yep."

"You didn't like it?"

The girl turned her head. "No, it was okay."

"Why did you leave?"

The girl studied Hosanna for a clinical moment. "To come here," she said.

"But why, if you detest the island so much?"

"Because my father said I had to."

"You're nineteen."

"Tell him that."

"What does he do?"

Hosanna had developed a tourist's fascination for the high power jobs held by those who visited the island every summer.

"He's an oncologist. The big cheese of Troy cancer. He's decided that our family should summer in Nantucket, even if he can't be here."

"Why?"

"Because he's got to work back in Troy. Which is what I'd like to do, except no, I have to join mama and baby sister just to satisfy my father's patrician idea of summer."

"And you didn't work last year?"

"You mean last summer?"

"Yes."

"We were only here for a month. A trial thing. This year we're in it for the duration."

"I understand," Hosanna said. She told the girl to come back the following morning to meet the owners. Which she did, dressed exactly like she had the day before, except her t-shirt read "East Greenbrush YMCA." It was a short interview, as blunt as the first. The Americans did not want to hire her. They didn't like how she looked. Or dressed. Or coughed. They said she didn't fit the culture of the shop. Hosanna agreed, but that's precisely why she wanted her. She pressed the girl's case harder than she thought she could. The Americans finally relented, but only because Hosanna—three years into her tenure as manager—had earned the benefit of the doubt. It's a smart move, she assured them. You won't regret it.

The message came during fifth period study hall. Tameca's head was lowered over a history book, reviewing what she'd read twice already. Mr. Wittenburg quizzed his class nearly every day. Tameca had a 100% average, which impressed but also seemed to surprise the short, dark-eyed, hirsute man. He visibly stiffened whenever she spoke aloud in class, as if her accent was something she'd invented to torture him with. As if it was all he heard when he heard her. Tameca knew the only thing that kept her out of his doghouse was the 100% average. So she had no choice but to keep reading and rereading the same facts, making sure she wouldn't slip up when the time came. Tameca felt a hand on her elbow, then a voice. "This just came from the office." The librarian held out a small square slip of paper. It read: "Your mother says to go directly home today and wait for her. Do not go to the shop." Tameca couldn't imagine what brought about this change, but neither did she care. Her day was suddenly made free. She wouldn't have to keep herself busy in that cramped back office while her mother circulated and fretted, growing progressively testier and nervous, snapping at Tameca about her homework and, after a refrain of exasperated sighs, setting her to work cleaning toilets. Now Tameca could just ride the bus home. At home, Hosanna was calmer.

The white girl from Troy—her name was Alison Phelps—showed every day for the first two weeks and worked harder than any three other employees combined. She volunteered to scrub bathrooms; she cleared and wiped tables without being asked; she never let a customer stand at the counter for more than five seconds without an offer of help. Almost immediately she began getting looks from the other kids. Soon they were whispering to each other, whispers usually followed by head nodding and crooked, lippy smiles.

Hosanna got so tired of this infantile behavior that she couldn't help but intervene.

"What's wrong?" she said to one of them, a boy with spiky brown hair accented with blonde streaks. His eyes were as wide and fat as plums.

"Nothing," he said. He seemed astounded she had spoken to him.

"I'm glad," Hosanna said. "Let's keep it that way." She'd followed with a long, lingering look, so fierce the youth had to turn. *Watch out for your job, rich boy.*

After that, Hosanna intervened nearly everyday. "What's wrong?" she asked. "Nothing," they always said. "I'm glad," she'd say. Or: "Exactly." Or: "I hope you don't think anything's wrong with what she's doing."

Instead of fear, however, what she started to hear when she turned her back were snickers. The college kids were laughing at her. At both of them. Hosanna began getting calls from the Americans.

That girl you hired is turning out to be a problem. Make sure she doesn't run off our crew. Make sure you don't.

Who told you she was a problem?

Oh, you know. You just hear things.

She wondered which of the babies had whined.

In my opinion, Hosanna said, she's the only one around here earning her pay.

In your opinion.

Yes.

Don't lose your crew.

Demont dropped the Taurus keys on the kitchen counter and moved to the fridge. Breakfast time. He couldn't eat when he first woke—11:00 or so—and today he'd had to drive his mother to Magpie's almost as soon as he was out of the shower. The sign of summer again. That's how it would be every morning for the next four months. Drop her off; take her home whenever her shift was done, pretending he had a fare to Madaket. Then head back toward town to scrum up enough business to keep life interesting until he could knock off at 1:00 and catch a drink at O'Riley's, if anyone was there. Most times, these days, there was no one. Just that fat, corn-haired bartender frowning at Demont when he came through the door because now the man would have to stay open another hour. Usually Demont thought *Fuck him* and ordered a drink anyway. If the bartender was especially ornery Demont ordered a rum cocktail from back home. The bartender couldn't ever remember how to make it—or maybe he refused to remember—and tried to beg off. In turn, Demont would say, *Then I'll tell you how to make it.* The bartender rolled his eyes. I'm not sure we got the stuff. *You got rum?* Of course. *You got limes?* Yes. *You got bitters?* The bartender nodded reluctantly. *You got coffee liqueur?* The bartender didn't answer. *You have coffee liqueur, man,* Demont would say then; *I drank some last week.* The bartender sighed. His blonde-brown eyes looked orange in the dim light; his Nazi skin jaundiced. Whatever, the bartender said. If he was feeling less ornery, Demont would just order a beer. And some nights he didn't feel like a fight at all; so he left without asking for anything.

There was nothing in the fridge but milk, a few apples, and something in a Tupperware carton. He opened it: brown meat, caramelized and spice-smelly. Jerk chicken, leftover from the night before. He loved jerk chicken but not for breakfast, so he settled for coffee and a few pieces of rye toast. He'd have to pick up groceries before he went to work. He considered doing that now, so he could have a real meal. Nah. He ate his bread in front of the tv, flipping channels. All he found were sailing shows, Nantucket real estate bits, soap operas, and American news networks. Island cable sucked. Just once he'd like to see a channel that carried programming originating from below latitude 30°N. He settled for a Hepburn movie on AMC but could only take fifteen minutes of it before turning off the machine. Maybe he would get the groceries after all. Then the phone rang. Hosanna was talking so breathlessly he could barely understand her. All he got was that he was supposed to come back to the shop. Now.

After the Americans issued their warning, Hosanna called in the entire staff. Mandatory meeting. She closed Magpie's for a full hour in the middle of the day. "If you don't actually want to work here, leave," she said. "I'm not holding anyone against their will. So who wants to quit?" She stopped, crossed her arms, held her breath. There was nothing really, at that moment, to keep her from losing the entire group. Nothing except intimidation and lethargy. But she gave them the chance. She had to for the sake of her performance. She gave them ten slowly ticking seconds. They fidgeted; they glanced at each other, they shifted weight from one foot to the next; they looked at the floor; they sighed. No one walked out.

"All right," she said. "So you want your jobs, after all. Good. But there will be changes—if you want to keep them. The biggest change is that Alison is now senior staff. When she says something, it is the same as when I say it. That is not an opinion. That is policy. She now outranks every one of you."

Hosanna glanced briefly at her favorite. The girl was smiling dimly but avoided meeting her eyes or the eyes of the crew.

"You don't get to say no to her. If you say no to her, it's the same thing as saying no to me. And we'll have to deal with the consequences of that. But it seems to me the wiser choice would be to just do what she says and keep your jobs."

They were glowering; they were simmering. They would explode as soon as they hit the sidewalk. Hosanna didn't care. She was enjoying this too much. She was sure their parents never talked to them like this.

"Any questions?"

They heard her but said nothing. They'd gotten the real message: She didn't want any questions. Nor any "suggestions." She wanted no lip of any kind. What she wanted, for once, was straight, unadulterated obeisance.

Afterwards, she met with Alison in the back office.

"I need to give you keys," Hosanna said.

"Senior staff, huh?" Alison said it as proudly as if she'd tricked the taxman. "That was sudden, HL." "HL" was a new moniker for her that Alison started using only a couple days earlier. Hosanna didn't really like it, but she let it go. The girl meant no disrespect.

"I've been thinking about it for a while."

"I didn't know there was such a thing as 'senior staff' here. Except for you."

"There isn't. I made it up."

"Cool."

"You're the only one around here I trust. You're the only one I understand."

Alison nodded, the smile smaller and slyer now. In the expression Hosanna sensed a personal residue the girl was holding in reserve, something Alison was not telling her. This made Hosanna pause, but it was too late now. She'd already chosen sides.

"I will try to get you a raise," Hosanna said.

The smile disappeared. "You'll try?"

"That has to go through the owners. They are notoriously frugal." *And they already don't like you.*

Alison moved her head: a noncommittal, inexplicit motion. Her face was blank.

"If I have to," Hosanna said, "I'll pay you a little extra out of my own salary.

Or maybe—" She was about to say "Or maybe take it from the till," but she stopped herself. "Something. I don't know. You'll get more."

The girl nodded once. "Okay."

"And I'll get you your own set of keys—so you can open and close."

"Yes."

"The important thing is to let those kiddies have it. Hard. Don't let up on them."

"Oh," Alison said, a shadow of the earlier smile curling her mouth, "you don't need to worry about that."

Tameca sat across from Tom McConnell. Sarah stayed rows ahead, closer to the front, talking in so loud and nasal a voice that it carried backward, vibrating along the steel roof. Out of the corner of her eye, Tameca noticed Tom's hands move: precise, practiced motions. She turned to see him fold a piece of rolling paper into a taut cylinder, then twist the ends. On his lap was a baggie, containing crushed green leaves. It looked like the chopped basil her mother threw into her fish stews and bully beef. But Tameca knew it wasn't chopped basil. Tom put the finished joint in his coat pocket. He looked at her, his eyes as flat and indifferent as ever, as if she had just witnessed him setting his watch. Tameca didn't quite know how to react to this stare. She had no quarrel with Tom—in fact she had real sympathy for him—but she'd said almost nothing to him in four years. She couldn't imagine how to start now, in this situation. Tom's eyebrows arched, as if in the first intimation of an idea. He reached into his pocket, retrieved the joint, extended it a few inches in her direction. The eyebrows again. *Would you like one?*

Tameca faced forward, embarrassed. She interpreted his offer as a rebuff, an attempt to shock her into not watching. Well, it worked. Except that now that she had seen it, she couldn't help but look again. This time she saw the whole maneuver. Tom pulled four fingers' worth from the baggie and placed them at the edge of a piece of rolling paper, which he rested as flat as possible against his thigh. He lifted the edge of the paper and brought it forward, covering the leaves in that first fold. With a smooth one handed motion he finished shaping the paper—like running a rolling pin across a marble counter—licked the other edge, sealed it, twisted the cigarette's ends, and stowed it in his jacket pocket with the others. He examined the contents of his baggie. All gone, as far as Tameca could see. Tom folded the plastic flap of the baggie under, locking it shut. He then folded the bag in half, and in half again. This flat, translucent square he placed in the same coat pocket. His eyes met Tameca's. This time—for the first time ever—he smiled at her, a shocking phenomenon. "Hi," he said, in a low breath. "Hi," she said back. Then Tom faced forward, put his hands on the seat in front of his, and settled: a picture of unsuspicious ease.

"What is that supposed to mean?" Demont said, pointing to the ice cream scrawled message. Hosanna had considered scrubbing it before calling her son, but then decided against it. The police might need to see.

"I can take a guess," Hosanna said, not meeting his eye.

"So guess."

She took a breath.

"I had a bad crew last summer, remember? I had to fire some of them."

"Like who?"

"I fired two white boys for smoking dope on their shift."

Demont frowned, eyes pinched. "And they were surprised? Surprised enough to wreck the place?"

"I'm not saying they did it."

"Who then?"

Hosanna shrugged.

"You think someone would come back nine months later just to do this?" He spread his arms, rotated in a semicircle.

"I don't know, Demont."

"Are they even on-island?"

"How would I know?"

"Mum, what the fuck is going on?"

Hosanna gave no indication of having heard him.

"So what now?" Demont said. His hard eye said he needed an answer quick—and it better be the right answer. He was supposed to be on call in a few hours.

"What do you think? We've got to clean this place up. You do the windows. I'll keep working on the counter. There are buckets and rags under the sink."

Demont checked his watch.

"Nobody needing any cab now," she said. "This time of year."

"I had fifteen fares yesterday."

"Who?"

"I don't know who they were."

She rolled her eyes. "Where were they going?"

"'Sconset, a couple of them. One to Surfside. No, two. A couple to Long Pond. And the airport. A few in town."

"Were they tourists?"

"I don't know."

"Did they look like tourists?"

"I guess. Maybe. No, actually. What difference does it make?"

Hosanna's eye's flicked to the ceiling. "What do you think the owners are going to say when I tell them we are going to miss weeks worth of business? Have you looked at these machines?"

Demont shrugged—more like a squirm. He knew the answer—he got the picture—but he didn't want to admit it, not yet.

"My only hope is to tell them that nobody is here anyway. The place is barren."

"The place is not barren."

"I said that's what I will tell them." She stepped to the front counter, began scraping. "Did not say it was."

"And you think they're going to believe that?"

Hosanna glanced up, then lowered her head again. "I don't know."

"You going to mention your little message?" He pointed a thumb. Hosanna didn't answer.

"Mum?"

"If I do, then it won't matter what else I say to them, will it?" She looked her son in the eye. Demont nodded: once, curtly.

"I guess that's right."

"The windows," she said. He moved to the sink. Hosanna bent over the counter. She tightened the muscles in her forearm and her shoulder, readied for a renewed attack on an encrusted corpse of chicken salad.

The balance lasted until Alison stopped showing. First it was only one day. Hosanna waited until Alison was an hour late and then began calling. She called her every half-hour all day long at the number the girl had written on her application. No one ever picked up. But the next day, Alison was back. She claimed to have been sick. She did look tired, even drawn, so Hosanna simply forgave her. Then, over the next three or four weeks spaces of two and three day absences were strung together repeatedly. These came without forewarning, and when Hosanna called the number there was never an answer. When Alison returned, it was with the same excuse.

"Why don't you see a doctor," Hosanna asked, a reasonable response, she thought, especially since she could have blasted the girl.

"I've seen doctors," the girl replied. "My father's a doctor. Why do I need another one?"

The worse part of Alison being gone was that, having chosen sides, Hosanna was now stuck with supervising the enemy. And it wasn't working. Floors were not being mopped, meat was not being put away, ice cream machines were not being wiped down.

"Hey," one kid dared say to her, "where's the real manager?"

Hosanna fired him immediately. But she had to take him back after the boy's parents called the owners.

When Alison returned to work after being absent for an entire week, Hosanna took her to the office.

"Look," she said, "I like you, but this cannot go on."

The girl's face was noticeably red, more than usual. Not the apple-cheeked coloring of a healthy complexion but darker, like a suntan gone bad. Her nose was running as in her interview, and she looked greased, as if she had just been, and could not stop, sweating. Hosanna tried to remember if she ever looked this bad before. As Hosanna reproved her, Alison began to smirk: as thin an expression as any of the college kids gave her.

"I told you I get sick."

"And you told me you would work anyway."

"I work hard."

"When you're here."

"Of course. I can't work when I'm not here."

"You're here almost never."

"Not never."

"Almost never. Lately."

"Fuck that. I'm here."

"Lately, you're almost never. And I am left with the babies staring at me like dead fish."

"I'm not the one paid to manage this place."

"You're paid to work, not stay home sick. Or whatever."

The girl stood up. "Are you done?"

"Are you working?"

"I'm not going to stand here and be insulted."

"Who insulted you?"

"You said I lied about being sick."

Hosanna leaned back in her seat. "I did?"

"You sound like my father now."

"And?"

Alison started out of the office. She stopped, turned. "All right, fine, good. You can deal with these idiots. Instead of forcing your job on to me."

It took Hosanna a second to recover, to realize just the right thing to say. Fortunately, she said it before the girl was out of earshot. "At least they come to work."

Tameca walked with Tom and Sarah down East Cambridge. As usual, Sarah conducted the conversation all on her own. Tameca knew her place: to listen attentively and nod at Sarah's more exuberant announcements. She was supposed to say nothing unless asked a direct question. Since she didn't want to talk to Sarah anyway she was happy to oblige.

"Justin Mayberry just asked me to the prom," Sarah said, her hazel eyes brimming yellow with self-satisfaction. "Can you believe that?" Not only could Tameca believe this, she didn't see how Sarah anticipated any other outcome. For the past month, Sarah had focused on almost nothing else but winning an invitation from the boy: one of the captains of the lacrosse team. In an academic way, Tameca understood Justin's attractiveness: the blonde hair, the square jaw, the broad shoulders. But personally she felt none of his pull.

"I know that's what you wanted," Tameca said. Sarah smiled and nodded, but then stopped.

""Who's going to ask you, Tameca? I don't mean this year. It's too late for that. I mean, you know, when you have to go."

"I haven't thought about it," Tameca said. "Not one little bit."

Sarah frowned: a soupy, exaggerated expression. "That's so sad," she said. "Let's try and think who to set you up with. There's got to be good candidates. Who is there?" She went silent. "There's Rico." Rico was a light-skinned boy, half-Dominican, half-Hawaiian. A nice enough kid, Tameca thought; he smiled constantly, but was completely immature, even for sixteen. At sixteen Rico looked and acted more like twelve. Tameca said nothing. "No? Okay, how about Jeff ?" A dark skinned boy, new this year. Distant and difficult. Jeff simmered with a low-level, never explained agitation. Even after months, no one could tell why. He came from Worcester and lived with an in-law—that's about all anyone knew. "He's kind of cute."

Tameca looked at her.

"All right, all right, all right," Sarah said. "So not Jeff either. But I don't know who else. I really don't." Tameca stared fixedly at the ground, a meager if actual attempt to disguise her anger. *She means she can't think of any other black boys*. Tameca didn't care about the prom—she had no plans of ever attending such an expensive parade of idiocy—nor did she harbor a secret interest in dating whites. But she cared if she was seen as only a skin color, when she, looking outward, never confined anyone to such a box.

Tameca lifted her head, swallowed a mouthful of briny spittle. Then she breathed out. What else did she expect? This was Sarah. Sarah. What else had she ever been to Sarah anyway?

"Shoot, I forgot," Sarah announced. "I've got to get ready. I'm supposed to be at Jessica's in an hour."

Without looking back, she lifted a farewell hand then trotted up East Cambridge, thumbs hooked to the straps of her lime colored backpack.

Tameca stared until Sarah was nearly a hundred yards away; the dyed blonde hair, the Calvin jeans, and her cream colored blouse turned to patches against the orange dirt. Only then did she convince herself to give up the anger.

"Sorry about my sister," Tom said. "She's a douche bag."

Tameca couldn't help herself. She beamed. "It's nothing," she said. Which wasn't true, and she knew it. She kicked herself for emitting such a predictably deflating statement. But that's who she was; that's how she handled social tension. At least since she came to Nantucket. She denied herself the right to open anger, partly because of the discomfort the anger would cause other people; mostly for the attention it would bring.

"If it's nothing," Tom said, "it's because she's nothing. Because otherwise it would be something."

Tameca took one step. Another. She turned her head toward Tom McConnell, but at the last second she looked at the ground. "I know."

Tom said nothing. He was thinking hard. Or maybe, Tameca considered, he'd just used up all his conversational energy for one day.

"Hey," Tom said then, "you want to smoke some of that shit with me?"

Tameca saw a line of nervousness in his cheeks, a coppery light blooming in his dark eyes, the nickel's other side of doubt. Maybe this afternoon will be different, the look said, not the same old oppressive bulk. The same old life.

Hosanna watched as a stranger tried the doorknob, frowned, looked through the glass.

"Demont, hang a sign. Tell them we're not open."

Her son paused in scrubbing a window. The pane was almost bright again, almost virginal. Another spot or two, then a water rinse, and it would be new. "Just let me finish this," he said.

The would-be customer studied the two black people inside. His eyes met theirs. He held Hosanna in his gaze for seconds—as if studying her for later recall to the police—then he continued down Water Street.

"Now," Hosanna said.

`Demont threw his damp cloth in the bucket. He breathed a watery sigh.

"Don't fuss with me, Demont."

"I'm not fussing with you, I just—"

"What?"

"When are you going to call those people?"

"Who?"

"They have to know about this, mum. It's their shop."

"I know whose shop this is. That's one thing I don't need to be told."

"So call them."

"Once we get a start on it."

Demont shook his head.

"What?"

"It's only going to get worse if you wait." Hosanna looked away. "They'll blame you for the damage—and for the waiting."

Hosanna's face went dead, drained, as if struck with a bullet.

"And besides which," he said, "who else is supposed to be working today?"

For a moment, Hosanna couldn't remember. "That Kiley girl, around five." Kiley Hall, a senior at Nantucket High, worked the end of the last summer and said she wanted to return. Hosanna agreed immediately. She knew the Americans would be happy; and she needed someone local to rely on.

"Well, I think she should be here, cleaning this place up in order to save her job. That way I can go and save mine. Why am

I stuck doing this?"

Hosanna dropped the dough scraper. "You're stuck with it, Demont, because we are." She pointed back and forth between the two of them. "We are. Not the Kiley girl.""I don't think so," Demont said and moved to the door. He opened it to find on the sidewalk a man and a woman, both tall and angular, retirement aged. The man wore a thin jacket, navy blue. Despite the lines of years around his eyes, the man's hair was blondish red, only veined with gray on top. The woman was jacketed too. Like the man's, hers fit snugly, albescent white. Her hair, meanwhile, had turned full snow, a lustrous, queenly color she displayed proudly on her stiffly held head: chin out, nose raised. The pair could be models for Lands End. They seemed shocked by the sight of Demont. Their first reaction was alarm, which turned instantly to suspicion: lowered eyebrows and mineral hard stares. Then the suspicion devolved into confusion. They frowned and—as if in a planned, coordinated movement—turned their backs on him and walked up the sidewalk in the other direction.

Demont closed the door. "I'll make that sign," he said.

"Look in the office," she said. "There are markers." She had removed the last of the chicken salad and thrown out all the deli meat stranded on the front counter. Now she needed to thoroughly wash the area. She began filling a bucket at the sink. She made a decision: she would get rid of the ice cream message.

Demont came out from the back, empty-handed. "So what am I supposed to write this sign on?"

"You've never heard of paper?"

"There's no paper back there. There's nothing of anything."

Hosanna frowned. She turned off the faucet, and stalked directly to the office, arms at her sides. At the doorway, she stopped, her mouth open. The tiny room was completely stripped, save for two pieces of office furniture. Both the computer and printer were missing, but that really wasn't surprising. She should have checked on them earlier. What she couldn't fathom was all the rest that was gone: the chipped and dented particle board desk the computer sat on; the cheap ass desk phone; the wall calendar and clock; the poster advertising Nantucket Nectars; the plant someone left last summer but Hosanna hadn't seen fit to throw away; the framed 4 X 6 picture of Demont and Tameca taken several years earlier in Kingston. The bigger, heavier, metal desk on the right hand side—the place where Hosanna actually did her work—still sat against the right wall, as did the single metal filing cabinet, but the cabinet had been cleared of its half-dozen or so magnets, and the top of the desk had been wiped clean: reams of printer paper, three coffee mugs, a stapler, a roll of duct tape, a container of Tic Tacs, an assortment of clip boards with blank schedules she had prepared for the coming weeks, a calculator, a dinged up radio with a broken antenna. She had seen that desk just the day before. She knew exactly what should be there.

"Who steals paper," she said. "Who steals coffee cups?"

She took a step inside; she opened the top drawer of the desk. She should have spotted a half dozen markers, perhaps twenty pens, an assortment of stray pencils and old staples, a bigger clip or two, a few 3.5 inch disks. But there was nothing. She had a thought: the file cabinet. As her arm reached for the pull, she recalled all that was contained in this one unit: copies of invoices; copies of receipts; copies of employment applications; manila files for each of the service companies they've had to call over the last ten years; manila files containing bank account numbers; manila files with social security numbers, addresses, telephone numbers and performance reviews of anyone who had ever worked at Magpie's. Manila files with personal information about the owners. The cabinet was empty.

She took the same step, but stiffly and in reverse.

"Go home," Hosanna said to her son. "Find your sister."

Weeks after Hosanna fired her, Alison still haunted the shop: lingering across the street, watching the door, moving in and out of view, speaking briefly and furtively with some employees, avoiding others. When Hosanna finally expressed aloud her befuddlement, one of the crew laughed: a bony, black-haired girl who had been with her since May.

"What?" Hosanna said.

"They're still her customers," the girl said.

Hosanna looked at her.

"I mean, even if she doesn't work here anymore, that shouldn't matter. Should it?"

Hosanna went over every one of the girl's words twice and still could not make sense of them. More confusing was that the girl acted as if Hosanna should understand.

"You can always call the police," the girl said.

"Why should I do that?"

The girl looked at her swiftly, as if sure Hosanna must be pulling her leg. She laughed again. Hosanna opened her mouth, about all she could manage. She shut it.

"We figured you had to know. How could you not know?"

"Tell me what Jamaica is like," Tom McConnell said, as he lit the first joint.

They were sitting behind a storage shed at the far end of the property. Resting their backs against the body of the shed, they saw in front of them acres of sandy, weed-cluttered dirt, shaken now and again by a wind that rose and fell every few minutes. There was a forecast for rain, but that didn't seem possible anymore. Instead the front left schools of horizontal, gray-white clouds, mobile in the breeze. Every few minutes the sun showed itself in silvery half-light, but then just as quickly was blotted out. From the near distance, they could hear the papery rumble of the Atlantic Ocean.

Tameca said the first thing that came to her.

"It's a lot warmer."

Tom nodded, distracted. He was more intent on the joint. He brought it to his lips and took a long, slow, steady drag. Done, he kept his mouth shut, rested his head against the shed and closed his eyes. Slowly, he lowered his arm, all the while holding the joint with delicate care between his thumb and index finger, his wrist bent so that the front smoking tip of the joint pointed downward and away, letting loose its string of steam a half inch beyond the curled fingers of his hand. It would not be wrong to call his movements graceful. For at least five full seconds, he did not speak, did not breathe. Then he opened his mouth and released what little was left of the smoke. He turned toward Tameca. Already he looked more at peace, far less lanky than the shy, stiff boy who waited with her at the bus stop.

"We get pretty warm in the summer."

Tameca snorted. "August. July—sometimes. The rest of the year feels frigid to me." As if to emphasize the point, she crossed her arms over her chest and clutched her elbows with the opposite hands. But it wasn't really that cold. Not when the wind died.

Tom nodded: a slow, dark expression. Then he looked confused, as if forgetting what should happen next. He extended the joint in her direction. "You want some?"

"Not yet," she said.

He nodded, slower than before, and took another hit.

"What do you miss?" he said.

"Miss?"

"I can tell you miss it."

Tameca was incredulous. Did it really show that bad? Because, truth was, she wasn't sure how much she missed it—not always. After four years, they were so established on Nantucket island. Demont worked. She was an Honors student. Her mother, meanwhile, claimed that for all its trouble her job at Magpie's was better than any she could find in Jamaica. The condo they rented was a bigger, more comfortable space than they could hope for back home. Her mother was shamelessly proud of the place. Yet, at the same time, coming on unexpectedly like the flu, Tameca was beset with pangs of longing for a climate, a life, a people that for twelve years were all she knew. Even so she did not indulge herself; she cut the pangs almost as soon as they came; she moved her mind elsewhere. Because the longing made Tameca feel guilty, as if she were blaming her mother for trying to improve her own life. She did not want to deny Hosanna that satisfaction. Demont, meanwhile, never talked about Jamaica at all. He never reminisced. He never called up old friends. He never ordered Jamaican CDs from Amazon or talked Jamaican politics or dreamed about opening a Caribbean-themed business in America. He acted as if he had always lived on this cold, quiet, foreign island, as if he were born here.

"I miss not being different," she said. She took the joint.

Tom's eyes narrowed. "You're not different. People just think you are."

Tameca nodded. She nodded again. Something had begun inside her she hadn't expected. She felt herself shake. She tried to stop it. She lowered her head and let it pass through her like an inborn fire. When she raised her head she felt her cheeks wet. She didn't wipe them.

"Hey," Tom said.

She brought the joint to her mouth and sucked. An acrid fire surged down her throat; it entered her chest. She was coughing, all the way from the bottom of her lungs.

"That's too fast," Tom said, with what sounded like fear. "Be careful. If this is your first time, just take a little. Hold it in your mouth. Don't swallow."

Tameca brought up the joint again, but hesitated.

"This is good stuff for your first try," Tom said. "Mellow."

Tameca offered a smile. The tears were gone, wind-dried. "My mother will be happy about that," she said.

Tom smiled back. Tameca took another drag. This time it didn't burn. Instead she felt a succulent sleepy smokiness move inside her, across her tongue, against her uvula; she felt it start in her throat. She closed her eyes and let the sensation go anywhere it wanted. The delicious warmth; the languid tingle; the opus of relaxation. A smile she couldn't stop became a grin and with the grin smoke escaped between her teeth. She opened her eyes and saw Tom looking at her with pride. She saw too that in those few moments the wind had carried off the clouds. The sky had settled. She was staring into it now: the vast unbothered expanse, cobalt blue.

Even after the girl told her about Alison, Hosanna waited a week before she called the police. She wanted to give Alison that long to disappear. And when she did call, it was not for revenge but because she knew that drug-dealing outside her door would lose her business. She went to the office and called the police station a couple blocks away. She gave an exacting description of Alison—the red face, the bad hair, the runny nose—who at that moment happened to be across the street sitting on a bench outside a t-shirt store, looking directly into Magpie's. "Get her gone," Hosanna said.

She hung up, thought for a second, left the office. She walked out of the shop and straight across the street.

"I just called the police."

She saw the nervous jump in Alison's expression, the tick of worry, but then, with barely any difficulty, the old defiance. "You lie, HL."

Hosanna smiled. "I'm giving you the courtesy of a warning."

Alison shrugged, a look of contempt so fixed on her that it came out as a grin. She looked over Hosanna's shoulder into Magpie's, as if trying to spy someone in particular.

"What are you still doing here, anyway?" Hosanna said. "Why don't you go back home?"

"I could ask the same thing of you."

Hosanna dropped her head. She struggled to check her anger. The comeback hurt worse than she might have expected. "I have a job. You don't."

"Maybe not there I don't." She pointed at Magpie's. "But I make money, believe me."

"You don't even like this place."

"You like it less than I do."

That might be true, but at the moment Hosanna couldn't know. It was hard to separate her feelings about the island from her feelings about this head strong nineteen year old who had decided to set up across from her place of employment, the place Hosanna was responsible for.

"Actually," Alison said, "I'm starting to think Nantucket is all right. I can take it." She stretched her arms across the back of the bench, looked calmly down Water Street. Then the grin returned. "But if I were *you*, this is the last place I'd want to be."

Hosanna's back stiffened, her chin came up. So that's what this conversation was about. She was stunned, but she didn't know why. Why in the world should she, of all people, be stunned? She turned her back on Alison Phelps and moved for the shop.

"Hey," she heard from behind her. "Did you really call the cops?"

Hosanna stopped. She stared at Alison Phelps for a long moment, smiled, and shrugged. The girl laughed and relaxed against the bench. Five minutes later, a policeman showed up. Hosanna watched the confrontation from the door of Magpie's. She couldn't hear what the cop said, but she did hear the girl's last exhortation, issued not against the policeman but Hosanna herself: a strangled curse, a bite of words, all she got out before the policeman forced her—red-faced and blinking—to the concrete and stopped her voice.

Demont was pissed. Fixing the flat on the Taurus only put him further behind, to say nothing of exposing him to a swarm of west island speed demons. Far from town, and with no real influx of tourists yet, drivers were using Madaket Road as their own personal raceway. Demont was almost cut down by a Rover, then a Lexus, then—the biggest insult of all—a Sanitation department truck. 5:05. He was late starting his shift, and on top of that he had to babysit his sister, just to make his mother feel better. The girl was in high school. But his mother, in best of times merely suspicious, was in the full middle of a meltdown. She still hadn't called the owners yet. Even after he warned her twice: *The longer you wait, the more they will have to blame you for.* Something more than the job was at stake here. It was as if she were afraid for her life. And theirs. All right, all right, he said. I'll watch Tameca. But not for long.

He careened onto East Cambridge, the Taurus practically hopping off the crater-sized pot holes in the dirt road. Let's keep this place pure, old fashioned, he thought to himself, mocking the sentiments of town planners. *So I can crack up my damn car.* A minute later he was outside the condo. He could tell straight away no one was there, and no one had come home. No lights on. Door locked. Now he started to worry. When he entered, he shouted Tameca's name up the stairs. No response. He took the steps two at a time. A few moments' survey told him what he already knew: the place had been unbothered and unvisited since he left hours before. He considered calling his mother to find out if Tameca had gone to the shop after all. Bad idea. He didn't want to panic the woman any further; besides, if his sister wasn't there, he'd get an earful. As if it were his fault Tameca didn't know how to follow orders.

He went to the next unit and beat hard on the door. The old man who lived there, Ronald Lassiter, couldn't hear well. Most of the time his tv was turned up to full volume. Demont calculated: Tameca liked the old man, or at least she tolerated him. Was it possible—possible, mind you—she went to visit him? No. She'd never actually spent time with Lassiter, only smiled at him. Why would she change her pattern now? Still, Demont beat harder on the door.

He heard movement. Finally. But the movement was struggling, slow. It took a full minute for the door to open. Lassiter stared at him, tufts of white hair astray on his head, his thick-lensed glasses fractaling watery blue eyes, dissipating their pale color and leaving only one expression: astonishment.

"Yes?" Lassiter said and shifted his shoulder suddenly, as if on the other side of the door he had grabbed the knob more firmly, readying himself for danger.

"Mr. Lassiter, have you seen my sister?"

Lassiter stared at the young man, more blank now than astonished, as if the question hadn't quite sunk in, as if his mind could only process one word at a time.

"I'm Demont Lloyd. We live next door?"

The eyes changed: a spot of black, a questioning.

"De—?"

"—*mont* Lloyd. I live right there, in 213, with my sister and my mother?"

Demont saw no sign of recognition.

"I work late, so maybe you don't see me much these days. But you know my sister?" He stuck out his hand to suggest her height. "She's sixteen; she goes to the high school? You've seen her with all her books?" No response. He changed tactics. "Mr. Lassiter, you know my mother, right? Hosanna Lloyd?"

Surely the old man would react now. Demont's mother had introduced herself at least three times when they moved in. And over the years she had helped Lassiter with grocery bags, signed for his packages, even accompanied him to the veterinarian when his Pomeranian needed to be put down. Hosanna never saw Lassiter without saying hello, part of her policy not to get kicked out of the lily-white environs. But now the old man did not answer. His head stayed still; his mouth hung open. The mote of black in his eye darkened.

"Mr. Lassiter. I've lived in unit 213 for four years. You don't recognize me?"

The old man moved his arm again behind the door.

"I don't understand what you want."

"I want to know if you've seen my sister Tameca. She was supposed to come home after school, but there's no one in our unit."

"Your unit," Lassiter repeated.

"*We live right there*." Demont began pointing and gesturing. "Right next door. My mother and my sister and me. Have you seen my sister anywhere?"

The old man stared a second longer. His mouth moved up and down mechanically, like a fish snared from the water gasping for drinkable air. Then he formed words. "I haven't seen anybody," he said. He closed the door.

Demont walked away fast. Fuck the senile, donkey-faced fart. After all the studied generosity from his mother. To act as if her son was going to jump him. Worse, now Demont had no one else to ask. Except for 213 and 214, the row was empty. He could ask at the office, but that would be as useless as asking Lassiter. The whiskey-cheeked lard-ass over there paid attention to nothing else but collecting owners' fees. Demont wasn't sure the man even knew what Tameca's last name was. So instead, Demont circled the row of units, looking for clues. He checked the concrete slab outside the back door. Nothing new: the same, round rusted white metal table; three plastic chairs; a bike his sister had outgrown; a green hose neatly coiled; a pair of flippers; two small cans of paint leftover from trim work Demont did in the fall. He turned and examined the back expanse of the property: the acres of scruffy, apricot-tinted dirt, the lime-colored weed trees. Nothing. Then he noticed a straw line of smoke wavering, barely discernible, above the storage shed four hundred yards away.

"How come you let your sister do all the talking?" The pot—even what little she'd taken—was making her not just giddy but daring.

Tom shrugged. "It's just noise."

"It's noise that tells people what you're thinking. It tells them who you are."

Tameca could see cogitation working behind the bloody lines in his eyes. But his composure was the same as ever.

"What does my sister's talking say?"

"That she's a fool." Tameca giggled.

Tom nodded. "I knew that anyway."

"So?"

He stared ahead, as if studying the curve of the breeze. "Sarah's meant to dominate. I'm not."

Tameca found herself on her feet, giggles gone. "Bullshit."

Tom mooned up at her, openmouthed, as if he had missed some crucial intervening sentence in the conversation and had nothing with which to fill it in.

"You're going to let her dominate you, even though she's stupid as a rock? Just because?"

"I didn't say me, I—"

"It's the same thing. It's the same thing in the end." She took a breath, lining up exactly what she wanted to say. It seemed extraordinarily important for her to say this right now to Tom McConnell—and to say it just so.

"People don't get to dominate other people. They're not allowed to bully them or harass them or talk about them or play mind games just because they want to. They might try to—they might even succeed—but they don't *get to*."

Tom stared a moment longer. Then he focused on the dirt at his feet, his face trapped.

"Here they do," he said. "I thought you would have figured that out by now."

Tameca was about to shout at him, when she heard distinct steps on the other side of the shed. Then she was looking at the figure of her brother—or someone who looked exactly like him. Demont should have been driving a taxi. He was always driving a taxi. So how could he be here, staring at her and Tom McConnell, his gaze returning repeatedly to the joint in the boy's hand?

"What the fuck you doing?"

Tameca couldn't be sure to which of them he was talking. She answered anyway.

"Nothing."

Demont laughed a laugh too ragged to be real: a mean, tired noise that accidentally escaped from his snarl. He studied her as if he could rearrange her with the look alone.

"Fine day this is."

"What are you talking about?"

"Well, for one thing this." Demont kicked Tom's hand, his foot landing squarely, sending the joint flying in a smooth airborne arc. Tom yipped, waved his hand.

"Stop it," Tameca said.

"Smoking ganja with this loser."

"That's not true."

"So what are you doing then?"

"I mean he's not a loser."

Tameca eyed Tom. The boy stayed frozen. Apparently, he was not going to admit that the whole thing had been his idea. That she had not asked to be included. Not that Demont would care; but her mother might. And Tom ought to say it regardless.

"He's . . . all right," she said.

Demont refused to look at McConnell anymore. "I don't know about that, but that's not what I asked you anyhow."

Tameca lifted her arms as if to grab invisible handles in the air, but then she brought them back to her sides. "I don't know what I'm doing, Demont. Something different. Something no one wants us to be doing. Why not?"

With those words, Demont's anger disappeared, or rather devolved into something else: something looser, less pointed, less actionable. His shoulders fell. He made a motion with his head. He took a step away. He turned back.

"I want to go home, T."

"Me too."

"You do?"

"Mum doesn't."

"She might have to now."

"Why?"

Demont hesitated; he blew a weary mouthful of air. "Come on, and I'll tell you." He nodded in the direction of their unit.

Tameca glanced at Tom, who remained as precisely fixed in place as moments before.

"I've got to go now, Tom. You want to walk back with us?"

Only a slim movement from Tom's ear indicated that he heard what she said. He did not answer. Instead, he scuttled on hands and knees across the dirt to reach the joint where it lay smoking against a nub of grass. He picked up the artifact. He examined it. He tried to suck from it. All he drew was a cough.

ISLAND FOG

On the Steamship Authority's Eagle ferry, Hyannis to Nantucket, 2005

The light inside was a flinty red, the color of the sunset against the clouds. Doug didn't look to see the orb dip into the water. He could tell just by inspecting this cafe: the yawn from the dark-skinned woman who clutched a plastic bag to her lap and let her eyelids dip; the squinting expression on the hard-boned older man at the window, his eyes fixed on the water, his hands folded as if in prayer; the indifferent calm of the redhead at the table next to him, her nose in a book, her paw around a pale gray coffee cup that sent up no steam. The day was dying. Doug put his head against the back of his booth. He wanted a beer. He really wanted a beer. But he had to save money. Even the pisswater coffee occupying that woman's cup was too rich for his wallet.

It was the third year he'd made this trip: leaving school in Amherst, driving his Jetta not north and home to Andover but three hours south to the Cape and finally to Hyannis where, dressed in a green U Mass sweatshirt, purple shorts, and scarred brown loafers, rank from the trip and still hungover from a last night of partying, he maneuvered his car onto the ferry that would take him thirty miles across the water to Nantucket.

The first two years this passage was nothing but a kick, a thoughtless transition from the business of school to the careless excess of summer. A ceremonial Sam Adams in front of him, Doug would silently toast his friend Joe's generous brahmin parents who offered to take care of the deposit and the rent for whatever house Joe found. He would then pass the trip eyeing girls, watching far off boats, and idly wondering what sort of place Joe got for them: how close to town, who were the neighbors, what would be broken when they got there and what would they break; most of all, what unfamiliar young woman was at that very moment in a dorm room or off-campus apartment in some northeastern city preparing for her own passage and eventual rendezvous with Doug at a yet to be realized island party. Who would it be that summer? The first year it was Karen, a dark-eyed cs major from Tufts, her body as tight as a snake, who gave him a full month of her uninterrupted company before her boyfriend showed on-island in August. The second year it was ditzy, hyper-permed Rachel, a would-be junior at Middlebury, who because she had no major and no plans for one never questioned Doug about his own; better, she gave him hummers that made his head spin.

Sure, he'd work—they all did—but after his share of the booze and the pot and food, after buying gas and condoms and lightbulbs and new clothes and all the other assorted shit a person needs to live somewhere for three months, he wouldn't make any money. None of them would. But they knew this from the minute they decided to go. Doug knew this even as he sipped those ceremonial beers aboard ship. Money wasn't the point of working a summer job on Nantucket. The island was the point; the ocean was the point; the girls were the point. The point was the doing it at all instead of something pitifully banal like lifeguarding at the country club, or waiting tables at Chili's, or—God save him—helping out at his dad's law office. You go to the island. You get a tan. You see and are seen. You hang with old friends and you make new ones. You drink. And you drink more. You worry about precisely nothing. You return to Amherst fifteen weeks later, having successfully avoided your parents all summer: better, tanner, happier, but certainly no richer.

This year was different, though. This year Doug was making the passage a week early. So early that the Italian restaurant where he would work did not even want him yet. So early he was missing final exams. But that was okay. Doug had subterranean Fs in all five of his courses. The exams were pointless. He could ace any one of them and still be twenty points from a passing semester grade. Besides which, at this point in his college career, acing an exam was impossible for him. Doug didn't know exactly what had gone wrong. That's what he told his father when he finally bucked up to the inevitable phone call. *I don't know what's gone wrong this year.* The old reliable methods he used for two years to pull out last minute Cs and Ds, even an occasional and remarkable B, were simply not working. Quizzes constantly stung him; tests he never understood much less passed; the few papers he wrote were slammed. He tried being apologetic; he tried being charming; he tried pleading troubles at home. But the same cellar-bound grades kept coming back at him, deaf, cold, and punishing. Even the papers he bought—those carrying a *money back guarantee of success*—didn't satisfy his profs. Doug suspected they had grown to doubt any and all signs of accomplishment from him. But rather than accuse him of cheating, which they couldn't prove, they simply gave him Fs and ridiculed the papers mercilessly, judgments with which he couldn't contend because he didn't know the subject matter. The end result was that he would not return to U Mass: not in the fall, probably never.

"We're not spending thousands of dollars for you to jack off," his father put it with characteristic bluntness. "You want to go, go. But you pay your own tuition from now on." Of course he couldn't—which his father knew damn well. He packed his bags as soon as the phone call was over. He had five tests scheduled for the next three days and one late term paper, but those challenges had just been rendered meaningless by his father's announcement. He drove in one straight shot to Hyannis. He had fifty-seven dollars in cash and a credit card that was perfectly maxed. It was a good thing he'd bought his ferry ticket months before.

The past two summers on the island had been animated by a buoyant belief in himself and his prospects. These party-filled forays among the youth of the northeastern upper crust were, he always assumed, just pauses in his inexorable push toward a million dollar future. Had that not been his father's destiny, after all? Had it not been the destiny of so many people he knew back home? But Doug had no sense of a future anymore, except in negatives. He would not graduate from U Mass. He might never graduate from anywhere. He would not go to law school. He would never follow in his father's footsteps. (That had been a stupid idea anyway.) The future draped before him like an island fog: dank, listless, and inscrutable. Possibly even dangerous. Only his next step was visible, nothing beyond. He was going to Nantucket. He was moving into a house with Rick and Joe. In a week, he would start at Marconi's.

Past that there was nothing to anticipate or believe in. He just hoped that no wreck was coming at him from the fog's other side.

For Doug, right now, taking this ferry ride wasn't just leaving America; it wasn't just abandoning academic headaches back in Amherst or avoiding his parents in Andover. It was running in the fullest possible sense. But when you run, Doug knew, eventually you run out of room. You hit a wall. Or a fence. Or a dead end. You reach a place you can't escape from. Doug was afraid this island might be exactly where he ran out of room. And then? He pushed even further into his seat, as if he could become invisible if he only tried hard enough. *And then?* He didn't know. And it didn't much matter. Because right now he didn't have any other choice.

The sea was rough. It had rained in the afternoon, turning the waves metal gray and triangular. No one was out on deck. Instead, they were collected in this room with him, bits of continental refuse, going to the island in an out of sync time. Doug gave into himself and spent three dollars of his little hoard for a Sam Adams. If the beer didn't satisfy him, he decided, he would buy another. If he was going to be poor he might as well be poor and buzzed. If he ran out of food money he'd live on Ramen noodles and tap water until payday. The beer was more important. It calmed him. More important, it gave him something familiar to do, and an identity: a man enjoying a beer by himself. Nothing strange about that. He tried to drink it slowly but found himself gulping. Old habit. What the hell, it was only his first. He could afford to take it fast. Now the second one—that one he would conserve.

The woman with the coffee noticed him noticing her. She laid her book down and stared at him quizzically. Doug moved his glance away. *No, I'm not looking at you. I just needed a place to put my eyes.* The last thing he wanted was more complications.

She was older, late thirties at least, with strands of damp stringy hair cluttering her face. She'd let it grow too long: erratic and untempered, like a hippie girl's. Crow's feet were budding at the corners of her eyes, and he saw one long wrinkle on her neck she'd done nothing to hide. In contrast with her disordered hair, she was dressed unremarkably: a green windbreaker that looked a size too big, and a comfortably aged pair of blue jeans. New Nikes on her feet. Her face was her most noticeable quality; amazingly lucent, it seemed to broadcast light. Her cheeks were shockingly white save for a pattern of freckles on both sides of her nose; and her eyes were practically violet. They flashed with bright precision, as if backlit by strobes inside her head, a roaming, restless mentality that for the moment shone upon him. She was one of those women who, even in middle age, could have been deemed sexy if that were important enough to her, if she'd taken the time and trouble to work on it. But clearly she hadn't. It must have been a decision, a matter of will. Doug didn't know if he pitied or respected that. Both, he guessed. There wasn't a single girl he knew at Amherst who wasn't obsessed with her body. Lots of guys too. Perfectly thin young females on radical low-fat diets; guys with decent bodies compelled to hit the weight room four times a week and stock up on nutritional supplements at GNC. Endless worry. Silly, yes. But, on the other hand, he had to admit, the worry paid off. To a man and a woman, all of his friends were handsome people.

No, I'm not looking at you that way.

Her quizzical stare was done. Apparently, Doug did not hold her attention. She picked up her book again and for the first time he noticed the title: *The Seven Habits of Highly Effective People*. He almost laughed out loud. He had to turn to keep from chortling in her face. She wouldn't understand; he wasn't laughing at her. He took a long drink and finished the bottle. He looked over again, but her nose was back in the book.

Doug was curious now. He would speak to her. But he needed that second beer to steel himself. At the snack bar he laid out another three dollars. Maybe, he decided as soon as he had the bottle in his paw, he shouldn't sip this one either. At parties he was generally useless until he'd downed four. He returned to his table and took a long first swig. Abruptly the woman snapped shut her book and set it down in front of her. She took a sip of coffee, checked her watch, rapped her fingers on the table. She glanced at him, then away.

"Boning up?" Doug said.

"What?"

"Your book."

"What about it?"

"I don't see too many people reading stuff like that."

Her look was withering.

"Millions of persons have bought this book."

"Oh," he said and took another drink. He wondered if she was a professor.

She started to read again, a hard thing to do once the ice has been broken. But Doug didn't care. She was under no obligation to entertain him. The woman faltered, closed the volume once more.

"Go on," Doug said, "if you want to read."

"No, it's not that. I'm wondering if I ought to get some work done before we pull into the harbor."

"What kind of work can you do here?"

Half a smile secreted across her face; then it disappeared.

"You'd be surprised how much work there is to do when you own your own business. In fact, there's never not work. Not this time of year."

"You run your own business?" She moved to a new plateau of regard in Doug's mind. The woman nodded: firm, quick.

"On the island?"

"Yes."

"What's it called?"

"The Treasure Box."

"Not Treasure Chest?"

"No."

"Box is more ambiguous."

"It is," she said.

"And more tempting."

She smiled silently.

"So what is it? Like antiques or something?"

She reached under the table into a heavy leather briefcase at her feet. He wondered how he hadn't noticed it before. He had seen her shoes, after all. She brought out a business card. With a shrug, he reached and took it.

THE TREASURE BOX
"Hopes and Promises"

Fourteen hundred and fifty-two
South Beach Street
Nantucket Island, Massachusetts 02554
508-370-8842
Ms. Leigh Warner, Ms. Jeannie Gert

"Hope and promises?"
"Right."
"That's what you sell?"
"In a way."
"Nobody can sell hopes and promises."
"Why not?"
"They're not real."

For a moment she only smiled: the same aloof expression that increased their distance instead of halving it. She seemed to pity his stupidity or even loathe it. Loathe him. In a crazy moment, the thought occurred to Doug that she might be a spy sent by his parents.

"I'm not sure our customers would agree with you," she said. "Besides, doesn't every business barter in hopes and promises?"

"I don't know about that."

"Sure. A hope on the buyer's part, a promise on the seller's? The seller extends the promise prior to the transaction; the buyer transforms his hope into trust; i.e., he believes the seller's promise and then transfers that trust like an invisible token—or the real payment you might say—to the seller. He pockets the merchandise, along with the promise the seller extended. That goes in the bag too. And it is the far more important item in the transaction. What the buyer leaves with is not merchandise as much as a promise of happiness."

Doug tried to absorb her tortured proposition. When he bought stuff he was buying stuff. At least that's what he thought.

"Think about it," the woman said. "Why do so many people, especially dissatisfied, pestered people, like to shop so much, even if they do not have the money? Is it because they actually need all the silly trinkets they buy?"

"I don't know," Doug said. He was still chewing on what she said before. "But think of all the times you end up unhappy with what you buy."

"I said promise, not guarantee. Guarantees are meaningless because they are impossible. They are lies. No one can guarantee your happiness. No one knows you that well, even yourself. Fortunately, all of us—most of us—are pragmatic enough to understand this, so guarantees have very little power. We discard them as the scams they are. The promise actually has more allure. It is not a shut door but an open one. Thus we believe it. And thus our anger when what we buy fails to satisfy."

"The promise has been broken."

She closed her eyes importantly. "Exactly," she said. She opened them.

"You feel used," Doug said.

The smile again. Slightly less loathing.

"See, you're understanding now. You deposit hope, in the form of trust, into the hands of someone who returns what you finally realize was a faulty promise. Chicanery, you say to yourself."

"Well, yeah. They acted in bad faith."

"It seems to you, in that moment, a personal insult."

"Sure. 'Cause it is."

"As if you were thought to be too stupid to have caught on immediately. As if you were just a mark."

"That's the word. A mark. I hate that feeling."

He drank more of his Sam Adams and more cheerily. What luck, he thought, to have found someone on this longest ferry ride of his life to distract him from the mess he'd made.

"But are you, really?" the woman continued. "Were you? Or do you only suppose yourself to be?"

"Be what?"

"As I said before, you were trading a hope for a promise, not a guarantee, which does not legitimately exist. It is in the nature of promises to sometimes go sour through natural causes; on their own volition, if you will. But still we are hurt. We are more hurt in fact by the broken promise—which we believed in—than by the broken guarantee, which we never did. So, as counterintuitive as it might seem, a promise has more emotionally binding power than the guarantee."

"I guess."

He took another swig, as much to cover his face as to taste the grainy ambrosia.

"A promise, therefore, is viewed by buyers as being inherently in good faith, while the guarantee is not, because of the element of chance embedded in the promise. By not guaranteeing, the seller admits to the mathematical possibility that the buyer will be unhappy. This admission is interpreted by the buyer as a sign of honesty, fomenting trust; while because the buyer dismisses a guarantee as a negative certainty—i.e., it can't possibly be true—the seller who guarantees is never trusted. The inherent possibility that the buyer will not be completely happy with a purchase actually draws the buyer to that seller. Indeed, the element of chance even increases the excitement of buying. What is more exciting after all than buying a lottery ticket, in which there is not only an admitted possibility of not winning but an admitted likelihood?"

Doug had nothing to say. He was reasonably sure she had lost him.

"But—and here is my final point—because the buyer's trust, however misguidedly, was transferred to the seller in the conduct of the purchase the buyer feels anger on finding that trust violated. He feels that the whole network upon which our economic and social life depends has been undermined by a bad faith promise."

"Right," Doug said. He jutted his bottle at her. "That's what burns me up."

The smile again.

"But, in fact, as I've said, a number of promises—because they are and can only be promises, because they are inherently endowed with the element of chance—will on their own go awry; not because of bad faith on anyone's part. Shit happens, if you will."

He shrugged. It didn't matter to him why a promise failed. It still failed.

"So all I'm really trying to say," she said, "is that you may not be a mark after all. Just an angry, misguided customer."

She settled the tiniest measure into her seat. She was done. There was none of the smile now, only contented poise, like a lawyer who has just killed a closing argument. Her hands formed around her coffee cup. Her shoulders relaxed.

"Why do I get the feeling," he said, "that you've had this conversation before?"

She sat all the way back and drank fully from her cup. Then, in one deliberate motion, she came forward and placed the cup back on the table. She reached again into her briefcase, this time bringing out a few legal-sized sheets.

"I have it everyday," she said. She extended the papers. She nodded for him to take them.

A CONTRACT OF BUSINESS, he read on the top sheet. What followed was single-spaced legalese, only occasionally comprehensible. He understood one or two passages:

> Whereas the nature of the promise is inherently tenable even if offered in good faith and with the actual intention to fulfill such promise in a timely manner satisfactory to the buyer, the buyer named herein agrees to not hold the seller responsible, legally or personally, if the buyer feels that compliance with the buyer's expectations from this agreement are less than one hundred percent. Specifically, the buyer named herein agrees to forego the right to sue The Treasure Box Inc. or its owners. The buyer named herein agrees to not threaten, harass, or otherwise inconvenience The Treasure Box Inc. or its owners. The buyer named herein agrees that upon completion of the currently purchased operation the buyer will not visit, linger in the vicinity of, or otherwise impinge upon, disrupt, or delay the daily business of The Treasure Box Inc.

"You make them sign this?"

"A necessary protection."

"Kind of extreme."

She looked pleasantly puzzled, perhaps amused. "Hardly, I think."

"Yeah?"

"Not when you realize that a promise has more power than a guarantee. More power to be misunderstood and misinterpreted. More power to hurt finally, even if the giver of the promise has only and truly the best intentions, and does his or her best to fulfill that promise. A number of people who do not get what they want leap to the conclusion that the promise was extended insincerely. And this they simply cannot stomach. They are incensed. They turn to what for them is the most powerful and inscrutable system of all: the law. They don't understand the law and are mortally afraid of it; if it threatens them, that is. But if the situation is reversed—if they hire the law to threaten someone else—they feel like kings. They feel empowered to right every sort of imagined wrong, even if trivial, even if not a wrong at all. They lose their heads. This contract—which they must sign if they do business with me—blunts their charge, breaks their sword, sends them off wasted. The system itself, they realize, has been on my side all along. I have prepared for their charge long before it ever occurred to them to make it. That is mortally disheartening to any combatant."

"Must be some business you're running."

She shrugged, then after a thought bowed her head, as if to a round of applause. But he intended no applause.

"What are you doing this week?" she said.

"Don't know. Getting the house set up, I guess. Visit my job. Why?"

"Perhaps you'd like to see for yourself."

"You mean The Treasure Box?"

"Of course."

Doug hesitated. He shrugged. "Sure," he said tepidly.

"When will you visit?" she said. She was leaning toward him.

"I don't know. Friday? Saturday?"

"Fine." She leaned back. "I'll look forward to it. I'm Jeannie, by the way."

He stared at her.

"Jeannie Gert. On the card."

"Oh. Right."

He thought she had said 'I'm a genie.' Which would have fit, sort of.

"Leigh Warner is my partner."

"Right."

She gave him a short, smart, formal shake of the hand. As if they had just agreed on something important.

A muzzy voice in the speakers overhead informed them that passengers with automobiles needed to return to those automobiles.

Doug drank off the last of his beer in a swig.

"Gotta run," he said.

"Yes," she said. She went back to her table, lifted her briefcase. "You go. I'll be right behind you."

He stumbled numbly downstairs to the bottom level of the ferry, as if pulled out of some strange, nagging dream. Not a nightmare, not by any means. Just a skewed and outlandish fantasy, but near enough to reality to convince you while you're in it. It felt good to take hold of the familiar steering wheel of his car, to put his key in the ignition, to feel what he knew so well solidly about him. He looked in his rear view mirror but did not see the woman, not in or around any car. He opened his door, got out, and looked back over the snaking lines of vehicles in the barn of the auto bay. Under the garish halogen lights he could make out many of the drivers. But not her. He had the sudden discomforting notion that they had never actually spoken.

The next day, Wednesday, Doug lay in a tiny supply of groceries and went to the beach. It was not yet summertime warm, but he didn't care. He dressed in a sweatshirt and long pants. He just wanted to relax at some place that was not home and not school and not work. But instead he found himself worrying all over again about the fall. What would he do? What would he have to accept? What would be asked of him? He was not prepared for any kind of life than that of a slacker student. How would he handle the transition? How could he handle his parents? Would he fail at that too? And if so, what then? How would he get back to college? It was useless. There were no answers to be picked up like baubles in the Nantucket sand. After an hour he tired of the wind and the solitude. He gave up and drove back to the house. He'd be glad when the rest of the crew arrived and his job began.

On Friday, just before eleven, he went to Marconi's to tell his boss he was in town, just in case she needed him. Maybe the place would be a mess with customers: impatient weekenders waiting for tables, the ones already at tables stewing about their orders, the cooks sweating and overwhelmed, the single waitress—an island teenager—scuttling from kitchen to table trying to understand what *bolognese* or *carbonara* meant, the owner abandoning her station up front to ease customers and bitch at the cooks. *Hurry up. These people are hungry.* She would see Doug and scream. *Thank God you're here.*

Not likely. She had told him weeks ago exactly when she needed him. Now wasn't it. He parked on one of the side streets near the Athenaeum and walked toward the harbor. As soon as he saw the restaurant he grew worried. It was lifeless, completely dark. He went to window and put his face against it. Inside, tables stood unoccupied: white, stiff, and empty. Vacant cloths lay like shrouds over the wood. There were no water glasses, no silverware, no plates. Not a single person. He didn't understand. Marconi's ought to be open for lunch. It was Friday, the start of the weekend. Besides, Marconi's was one of those rare island businesses that stayed open through the winter. He moved to the door. A sign was posted with duct tape. Hastily cut white poster board, with a message scrawled in fine-line black magic marker. *Marconi's is closed. It will reopen in July under new management.*

Doug tried the door. Locked. He dialed the restaurant's number on his cell. Someone would be inside. Someone had to be. Someone had to tell him what the hell was going on. As little as two weeks ago he'd talked to the owner. He confirmed his arrival date. She hadn't said a goddamn thing about new management, or July, or gypping him out of his summer's sustenance. An electronic shriek blistered his ear. Then that unforgiving voice: *The number you have tried to reach is no longer in service. Please hang up and—*

Doug pounded the cancel button with his thumb. What to do. What to do. This was just such pure ungodly shit. Why hadn't anybody warned him? How could they just go and do something this drastic without telling him? Doug didn't have the owner's home number, but he sure as hell knew her name. If there was ever a time to bother someone.

He dialed 411. He gave the operator the name. Hold a second, the operator said. No problem, Doug told her. He kicked the sidewalk with his heel. A beefy woman in sweatpants and a raincoat strolled by with a sausage dog on a leash. The operator returned.

"No one by that name in the listing."

"What do you mean? She lives here. She lives on the island."

"No one by that name with a Nantucket number, sir. I'm sorry."

"You mean she's got an unlisted number?"

"That would mean she has a number, wouldn't it?"

"I guess."

"Sir?"

"Is there anybody with a similar name? I mean a name that sounds like hers?"

"Sir."

"I know. I know. Forget it."

He hung up, sat on the stoop of the restaurant, and stared at the harbor. A ferry, heading out, was only a speck against the volume of dark water. In a second it would be invisible. She was gone, Doug thought. She'd evaporated into the clear blue sky and took with her his job. Probably his summer. You don't just get good jobs like that one—or any jobs—at the last minute. He knew as well as anyone how far in advance these things were arranged. For the first time he considered going home. He could prostrate himself in front of his father, beg the man's forgiveness, plead for one more semester to prove himself. He'd go to summer school, make up the hours. He'd stay in his room like a nerd and earn all As for the first time since ninth grade. He would swear to it. He would promise with all his bleeding, spilling, cream-orange guts.

Mercy was about all he could hope for now. But he could not count on it. Not from his father. Not after he bent and pushed and stretched and abused his parents' patience for three straight years. Doug would never forget the pleasure he heard in his father's voice when he'd delivered the sanctimonious bomb he'd been holding back for so long. "You can pay your own way." He spoke each word with blatant, almost sexual, urgency. It was the ultimate consummation: ripping the rug out from under the boy's future. An eminently satisfying sensation which he must have replayed to himself dozens of times in the hours that followed as he imagined his son cringing by his bed, cell phone in hand, a puddle of stinking remorse. *Got him. Got him GOOD.* No, there would be no going back to his father.

It occurred to Doug that he must still have that business card on him somewhere. He checked his wallet. His jeans. He finally found it in the pockets of his hoodie, folded over and breaded with sand. 1452 South Beach Street. What else did he have to do on Nantucket just then, or anywhere?

He almost missed it: a small, square, two story building with the same weathered gray shingles and fishing village aspect as every other structure on the island. White shutters, which at the moment were closed. A slatted, wooden welcome mat at his feet. Beside the door a small sign cut in the shape of a coat of arms. Letters were carved into the wood and painted gold. THE TREASURE BOX, HOPES AND PROMISES. That was all. No building number. No street address. No business hours. No invitation to enter. But it was here, after all. That's what mattered. It wasn't a dream.

He tried the door, but the knob wouldn't budge. He knocked. No answer. He knocked louder. Very loud. He stopped. For a second he thought he might have heard a shuffle of feet inside. He stood rigidly, bent an inch, listening with all his body. The wind moved over his head and on the back of his neck. Footsteps moved on the sidewalk behind him. Someone shouted at a passing car. He tried the knob again. No luck. He didn't understand. She said Friday. She had specifically invited him for Friday. It was almost eleven-thirty. The middle of a business day. He knocked one more time for the hell of it but didn't wait for a response. He turned and took a step or two in the direction of the sidewalk. He examined South Beach Street as if it might hold clues to the mystery. Across the street was a fancy ocean shop: overpriced sand buckets and beach umbrellas. Its huge glass window featured a kite display. An OPEN sign in lemon letters hung on the door. Through the window he could see the owner—a short-haired, pear shaped, fiftyish woman—moving behind a counter, taking something off a shelf. On the sidewalk was another woman: younger and thinner, wiry brown hair, wearing a sleeveless mauve dress with a blue sweater draped around her shoulders. She stopped, pulled open the door, and went in.

On his side of the street to the right was a moped rental shop, doing no business at the moment. To the left some yards down was the intersection with Harbor Way, a private drive that led to what Doug knew was a compound of expensive rental units: rows of flashy townhomes, an enormous hotel with towering glass windows and a carriage parked outside.

Doug heard a noise behind him. He turned back. The door was open: only a crack and behind that darkness. He trod forward until he was so close he could have put his nose against the wooden panels. Still he heard nothing.

"Hello?" he said. No response. "Is someone here?"

Could his knocking have loosened the lock? Had the wind pushed it open?

Doug peered through the crack. His shoulder glanced against the door, nudging it open another inch. All he could see was an empty floor: planks of hard wood painted white. He pushed the door. It opened, exposing the whole room. Against the back wall was a counter, white too, holding but one item: a small, old-fashioned cash register. A single bar stool, also painted white, was in front of the counter. Behind the counter, affixed to the wall, were some shelves, but these were empty. All four walls of the room were bare: white and pristine, like the inside of a padded cell.

Doug stepped in. He noticed to his left a brown, slat-backed wooden rocker turned just askew, as if its occupant had gotten up in a hurry, only moments before.

Jammed against the right wall was a narrow stairway. He walked over and glanced up. He saw nothing except the white ceiling of the second floor and some sunlight evident through whatever windows were there. He took each step slowly, not sure if this counted as trespassing. Can it be trespassing if you're invited? And if the door is open? With each step he grew more anxious at what he would see when he reached the top. This place contained too still a silence. A silence you could hear. A silence like the wind against your earlobe. A stillness that was a conscious force occupying the room, moving about it, watching him like a ghost. Covering something. But what?

On the second floor he saw a mere home office. Or what looked like one. The floor was painted bottom-of-the-sea blue. In the center lay an oval throw rug—Pier One quality—the kind of thing he'd seen in so many undergraduate apartments. Tones of sky blue, dark red, and some black. Farther back, at the far rear end of the room was the bathroom. The door was open and he could see the ancient, cruddy and cracked black and white tile, the toilet. Against the wall opposite the staircase, under a small round window, sat a metal desk and a well worn brown office chair. The desk was comfortably cluttered: phone, pencil cup, stapler, letter opener, In and Out boxes, portable typewriter, a small stack of mail ripped open, a coffee mug ringed brown at the bottom, a pile of manila folders. The folder on top was open. He saw what looked like the floor plan of a house. Photocopies of architect drawings. To the left of the desk, from where he was standing at the top of the stairs, were two black metal file cabinets. He decided not to test them.

Against the "front" wall—which he realized must be the back side of the building—squatted an old couch: a lumpy heap of thing with grotesque brown and gold fabric discolored and grown thin in spots. Someone's old but useless favorite. A throwaway. Salvation Army. Or not even. No one in Nantucket owned a couch like that: the beaten up bulk, those hideous 70s hues. In front of the couch lay another, smaller throw rug. The same quality as the other, but flecked loudly with lime green and coral pink. In the right corner of the room, a few feet from the top of the stairs sat a stereo system, clean enough but clearly dated: a turntable, cassette player, receiver, tuner, ogre-sized speakers. Huddled together like a little town. Every piece earth brown, not black or silver, as they are these days. The kind of equipment you might find in a college student's room thirty years earlier.

It was a comfortable if tacky space; humble; a space one could step in and occupy with ease. But the weird thing was that, unlike the bare downstairs, Doug didn't have the sense that anyone had been here recently. It felt more like a museum piece. Assembled for show. A room kept in a time capsule, perhaps dusted once in a while but otherwise left unaltered after the girl or guy who occupied it had died or run away or disappeared in mysterious, heartbreaking circumstances. The room was waiting for his or her return. In the meantime, no one should touch it because it was not meant to be functional. He had a sudden idea. He walked to the desk and picked up the phone. The buzz of a dial tone startled him. Okay, so maybe he was wrong.

He tried to think what else to do. He didn't want to leave. Not only because he had nothing to get back to, but because he wanted an answer to a question he hadn't even formed. He felt stymied, the unmade formulation pinning him in place. But Doug could dawdle for only so long. With his luck, the other owner—the one who didn't know him—would appear and call the police. Doug headed back down. He noticed one odd thing downstairs. The rocker was no longer by the front door but in the center of the room and facing the stairway.

Doug walked out, his head riddled, trying to remember when he had dragged the chair away from the door.

The telephone rang as he entered the house. Then it stopped. Good. Doug was afraid it might be his father. The old man might have found out by now about the skipped exams and tracked him to Nantucket. Not able to reach Doug on his cell, he bullied Joe or Rick for the house phone number—or Joe's or Rick's parents. Then he called to berate his son for his betrayals. Doug turned his cell on again. No messages. He rang Rick in Amherst to tell him everything was okay with the house; he hoped his friend would say that he'd just called. No luck. Instead, Rick said they would be delayed coming out. Joe's parents wanted them to do some work on their pool. They could hardly refuse. Then there was the Rock Island Music Fest. Doug should expect him and Joe in about ten days, still enough time to get into full island swing before Memorial Day.

"Dig the privacy while you can," Rick said.

"Sure," Doug said. "I will." He didn't explain about his job. He felt embarrassed, as if it were his fault Marconi's failed.

"Gotta cram," Rick said. "One more exam this afternoon. Accounting."

"Sucks."

"Yeah. But then I'm free. Free as a bird."

"Yeah," Doug said, remembering the feeling, what a clean sensation it was.

"All right," Rick said. "Later, friend."

Doug couldn't think of a single thing he wanted to do. So he cracked a beer and stared out the window. You know, he thought, I should be hungry. But he wasn't at all. Dread had canceled his appetite.

The house phone rang. He gave it three rings. He decided to answer.

"Doug?"

A woman's voice. He didn't recognize it.

"Yeah?"

"This is Jeannie."

"Oh," he said, but couldn't for the life of him think of any Jeannies he knew.

"Jeannie Gert," she said.

"Oh! Jeannie. Right. Hello."

"Calling to see if you're managing."

His mind roved. Had she seen him in the building? Was she going to threaten him? Bring charges?

"I'm fine. Getting my life in shape. You know, for the summer."

"Yes," she said, flatly. She was silent, as if waiting for more. Then: "How's that job of yours look?"

"Great. It, you know, starts soon. Not yet, but soon. As soon as the season gets underway."

"Of course," she said. She sounded unconvinced. He wondered why he was lying to her. What did it matter if she knew? But these questions were second to the more pressing mystery of how she got his phone number. He couldn't remember even telling her his name.

"Just thought I'd check on you," she said. "You seemed a tad frazzled the other night."

"Me? No. I'm fine."

"You're sure?"

"Yes."

"You have a friend on the island. Remember that."

"Sure," he said. "Thanks. Thank you."

Silence.

"Okay," she said. "I'll talk to you some other time."

"I went to your place today," Doug said.

"The Treasure Box? You did?" He couldn't tell if her note of surprise sounded forced.

"I knocked, but there was no answer."

"What time?"

"Eleven, eleven-thirty."

"Curious. We were definitely in this morning. Working. As you say, the season is coming."

"Well, I did knock. Swear. I—" He was ready to tell her that he'd searched the building, but then he knew better.

"You what?"

"I knocked, like I said."

"Uh-huh. Curious." He had the feeling that she knew exactly what he had done there, step by step. "Did you look in the window?"

"Couldn't. The shutters were closed."

"Really. And you're sure it was our place?"

"The sign said *The Treasure Box*. It was on South Beach."

"Weird. Okay, tell you what. Come by again this afternoon. Four? I guarantee you that we will be there." She hesitated. "Unless you have to work that job of yours."

"Not today."

"Good," she said. "Good." More waiting. Doug was now certain she knew about his job. "Okay. See you at four?"

"Right."

"It will be good to see you again, Doug. You won't regret it."

It was impossible that this was the same place. At once, he backed out through the doorway and onto the sidewalk. He examined the shape of the building, the condition of the shingles, the sign next to the door. These certainly were what he had seen that morning. But inside was utterly transformed. The walls were a pale, colorless blue; institutional carpeting—gray with repeating geometries of red—covered the entire floor. Framed posters of world destinations dotted the walls: Alaska, Rome, Amsterdam, Cairo, Sydney, Rio. If he hadn't known better he would have thought it was a travel agency. The counter across the back of the room was gone. In its place was a heavy and expansive desk, cherry red wood. A thin, young, blonde woman with narrow eyeglasses and pendulous earrings sat behind the desk staring intently at a computer screen and talking lowly into the phone. The desk was disciplined, clutter free. An in box. An out box. A stapler. A paper clip holder. One plant. A computer. Her nameplate read Doreen McAlister. Immediately behind her, on a stand, was a broad electric typewriter; on the wall above, a clean white clock with black hands and no numbers.

Against the left and right walls of the room, below the level of the framed pictures, were small tables like library carrels, the same wood as the secretary's desk, each holding a computer and small printer. At one table a thin, drawn, brown-haired woman, perhaps thirty-five, tried to type with her left hand while managing a struggling infant on her other shoulder. Evidently she was not used to typing with her left hand. "It's all right honey, it's okay, just wait," she intoned distantly, reaching with her pinky. The infant, its expressed wish for escape ignored, began to howl. At a nearby table a man and woman, about retirement age, huddled so close to the screen Doug couldn't tell what they were looking at. They studied for whole moments before turning to each and whispering fiercely. Apparently they were having a disagreement. At the table nearest the secretary sat a young man not much older than Doug, dressed in a dark sport coat and blue jeans, his hair moussed so that it sprung this way and that in soft tangy leashes. He did nothing but tap a single key every five seconds or so, looking fixedly at the screen, as if he were being tested on how much information he could absorb in those prescribed periods. Every so often he showed a wiry smile; then his face went blank and intent again.

Doug couldn't guess what all these people were doing here; he was so astounded at the change in the room he had no space in his head for anything else. A woman came in behind him, nearly pushing him aside. She waddled quickly—short, jerky, muscular steps—to the secretary's desk. She was stocky and big shouldered. She had short thick-tangled orange-red hair, brown eyes, a windburn across the pale skin of her nose and upper cheeks. Wearing a green nylon jacket and long tan shorts, she looked thoroughly the part of a no-nonsense, SUV-driving New Englander. She leaned into the secretary and spoke something low and insistent. Doreen McAlister, who just that second had gotten off the phone, took the attack with only a hint of reaction. A flash of surprise blossomed in her eyes but in the moment was gone, replaced by coolness. She kept her voice even, her face flat, her attitude polite but perfectly indifferent. Doug could not help but admire the effort.

"She's not in right now. In fact, she's off-island. Can I take a message? She'll get it as soon as she returns."

"That's what you told me last time. I did leave a message. And I haven't heard a thing."

McAlister paused, reflecting on the information. She tried again.

"I see. I apologize if formerly there was any miscommunication. I can promise you that as soon as I take your message I will go and put it in the center of her desk. It will be the first thing she sees when she gets back."

"I gave you a message last time."

No reaction.

"Over the phone," the woman said.

McAlister's expression did not change. "I'm afraid I don't remember. But I certainly would have given the message to her. If somehow I did not, or if it got lost, I apologize, although I don't see how that could have happened."

"You apologize."

"Yes."

"Lotta good that does me."

The receptionist blinked.

"Besides which, you know goddamn well that's a misdirection play. She got the message, but she just doesn't want to call me. That's what I think."

"Ms. Gert returns all her calls, ma'am."

Doug's ears stood up at the name. Jeannie Gert was off-island? Something else that had changed since the morning. Perhaps he should leave.

"Her office is up there, right? Right up those stairs?"

As the orange-haired woman's voice rose, the whole room stopped to watch this face-off.

"Yes, ma'am," the secretary said. "But she's off-island today."

"Off the island. I tell you what I think. I think I'm being avoided. I think she's giving me the blow-off. I think if I climbed those stairs right now I'd find her waiting at the top, behind a desk, smirking. That's what I think. I think I should go and see for myself. If you really want to know."

The perfect reply to that last sentence hung in the air like a fat gold coin dangling on a string. He could see that McAlister knew it. He could see the awareness in her eyes. But he also saw her resist the response, her professional instincts so refined that it was not even a matter of biting her tongue. Her tongue was never tempted in the first place. One hell of an employee. She looked only slightly older than himself, if more professionally dressed. He wondered how someone that young found herself here, and endowed with such singular poise. He would have been shouting at the stocky woman's first insult.

McAlister blinked once; she made a supple gesture with her left arm. *Be my guest.*

The orange-haired woman stared at her, hesitating. She took a step toward the stairs. She stopped. Evidently, she was afraid of following through on her threat. Perhaps it had never been a real threat in the first place, only a bark.

"I'm not kidding," the woman said.

"Yes, ma'am."

"If this is the way a person gets treated around here."

The receptionist blinked again. The woman's face fell.

"All right, just leave her the message," the woman said sorely. "But you make sure she gets it this time, okay?"

"I will, ma'am."

"You put it on her desk, or wherever."

"I will."

"All right, then."

The woman turned to leave.

"And the message is?" McAlister said.

"What?" The woman turned back, wild with irritation.

McAlister spoke slowly, calmly. "What do you want me to tell her?"

A ragged hollow show of victory spread as a smile on the woman's face. Her cheeks grew fat and blustery. Her back stiffened. "You tell her that Denise Brubaker came here to see her. Tell her that. And tell her she better call me back, or I'm going to call my lawyer."

"Yes, ma'am," the receptionist said. She reached for a pen and faithfully encrypted the words on an office pad. She looked Brubaker in the eyes. "I will make sure Ms. Gert gets the message as soon as she returns."

Brubaker paused, looked sullen; an exhausted force outmaneuvered by a more disciplined enemy.

"When will that be?"

"Next week."

"When next week?"

The receptionist stiffened, her blue eyes as bright and unwelcoming as ice cubes.

"I cannot say for sure, because she isn't sure herself. But we anticipate the end of next week."

"Friday?"

"Probably, yes."

Brubaker nodded. "Okay," she said. "I'll wait till then." She moved away, her eyes cloudy, her shoulders caving. She opened the door. She was gone.

Doug expected Doreen McAlister to allow herself a sigh or a roll of the eyes or at least an embittered stream of air blown through her cheeks: a private moment of relief any normal person would have taken. But she didn't. Her face relaxed not at all from the courteous stiffness she showed the departed woman. She turned those hard blue eyes on him.

"Can I help you, sir?"

He took a single, embarrassed step forward.

"Probably not," Doug said. "Ms. Gert—Jeannie—called me this morning and told me to come by. But it sounds like she's left the island again, so—"

"And your name?"

"Doug Durkin."

"Right." A tiny but real nod. "Ms. Gert will see you now. You may go up the stairs."

Doug almost guffawed. What balls. Concrete balls. He wondered if he should be offended by her unabashed lying to that Brubaker woman. In front of everyone, after all. No, it was just too damned impressive. This McAlister had the secretary's role down to a science. Like a forty-five-year-old. Except she wasn't. She was like him. Sort of. But now he even wondered about that. Clinically attractive though she might be, he couldn't picture her in a bathing suit, relaxing on Jetties beach. Her skin, if there was any beneath that shrouding blouse and skirt, would be alabaster and as stiff as marble. A bony statue in a bikini. Forget the beach, he couldn't even see her meandering down Main Street window shopping, or digging an ice cream cone at the Juice Bar, or so much as filling a grocery cart at the Grand Union. He couldn't see her existing anywhere on the island except that desk.

"Thanks," he said.

McAlister blinked, then returned to her computer screen.

He went up the stairs, certain of what he would find at the top. But here again, like on the first floor, his expectations were riddled. He did find Jeannie Gert, reading glasses atop her nose, hawkishly studying the contents of a manila folder. Her distraction afforded him some moments to look around, but it took only a second to see that the upper room was as thoroughly altered as the lower. The dull blue walls were now viridian; the painted wood flooring was silver tile: cold and courtly, covering the entire room. The furniture was placed in familiar locations but the dilapidated pieces from before were gone, replaced by sleeker ones: an executive desk and tall leather chair for Gert, computer station and office phone, a licorice leather sofa and glass table, a coffee bar beside the sofa complete with a Krups cappuccino machine, a series of husky egg white mugs, and four varieties of whole bean coffee displayed in tubular glass jars. The stereo system was gone.

More startling, the window that existed above the desk had disappeared. The space now was just another part of the newly green wall. And at the sofa end of the room, where there had been no casement at all, was a long rectangular pane through which Doug saw in panorama the west side of Nantucket city center as it slanted up from the harbor: successive streets of old-fashioned, weather-grayed shingle buildings, their tall slanting roofs, the spire of the Congregational church, the gold dome atop the Pacific National Bank; beyond, in the distance, Madaket Road; and finally, above it all, a stretch of sky as marketably cerulean as china. Again, the thought insisted itself: I must be in a different building. He turned to check—yes, there, in the same place, was the bathroom door. At least he assumed it was a bathroom. The door was closed. And it was painted red.

Somehow two week's worth of remodeling had been accomplished in half a day. He imagined an army of island workmen springing on to the property the instant he left it that morning; working with historic ferocity, until just minutes before he returned. But even that, he knew, was a fantastical idea.

"Doug," Gert called. She set the manila folder on the desk and closed it, sealing its contents, an automatic motion. Then she stood up and came from behind the desk.

It was her, all right, only much better dressed. She wore a white silk blouse and black pants, low heels, a pearl necklace, diamond studs in her ears, a slim gold watch. She had certainly been slumming on the ferry. He was embarrassed at the idea of him as he was mixing it up with her.

"Hey," he said shyly.

"I am so happy you decided to come down." She extended her hand.

"Yeah, I uh—" Absently he took the hand, pumped once.

"Yes?"

He wanted to ask how this transformation could have happened. What possible, credible explanation existed. But he couldn't ask, not without admitting his earlier intrusion.

"You look pretty solid," he said, "for someone who's off-island."

She smiled: the sweet pride of victory.

"No, as you can see, I'm very much here."

"What if that woman had come up?"

"Denise Brubaker?"

"Yes."

"She wouldn't."

"But what if she had?"

"I've known Denise Brubaker since forever, Doug. She would not have come up those stairs."

"But what if she had?"

She sighed, disappointed, as if he'd failed his first test.

"In that case, other measures would have been taken. There are always other measures available. If you plan well enough. Which I do."

"Okay," he muttered. He felt purposefully humiliated.

"But the main thing to understand is that she would not have come up the stairs. I knew it. And so did Doreen."

He nodded. "She's one cool cookie, that one."

Gert grinned once, but then pocketed the expression, like a secret. She said nothing else about her secretary.

"Tell me about your job."

"What about it?"

She looked at him sharply. My god, Doug thought, she really does know.

"Why do you ask?" he said.

She went back behind the big desk, sat in her leather chair. "Oh, I don't know. Isn't that the natural thing to ask a young man who is starting a summer on the island?"

She motioned for him to take the seat in front of the desk.

"I guess," Doug said. He sat.

"All right, then. Tell me about it." She leaned back, her hand poised against the side of her face, a show of concentration.

"To be honest, it's gone."

Her eyes grew huge and white; her mouth made an almost perfect O.

"Gone?"

"Yes."

"You mean the restaurant?"

"My job."

"How?"

"That's the thing. I don't know. There's a sign taped up saying it won't open until July, under new management."

She shook her head. "That certainly leaves you out, doesn't it?"

"Seriously."

"What a shame." Her eyes said sympathy, but her tone did not.

"Yeah, and I don't get it. When I worked there last summer there was like never a night we weren't packed. No one said a word about money troubles."

She offered a shrug. "Who knows, Doug. Perhaps it had nothing to do with the restaurant at all. Bad investments? A gambling habit? Cocaine? From my experience, restaurateurs are especially flighty businessmen."

He didn't know what to say to that. He'd seen no indication of any bad habits on the owner's part. He'd seen no habits in her at all, except to work doggedly every single night. She had no other life that he knew of.

"Of course, the workers are always the last to know in these situations. Management is set on only one thing: protecting its parochial interests. Often the best way to do that is to keep the *little people*"—she made quotation marks with her hands—"in the dark, even until it is too late. Too late for them, that is."

"But how does that help?"

Her mouth opened broadly as if she were about to laugh. "Well, c'mon now, Doug. Think about it. Let's say whatever crisis the restaurant is in passes—or they manage to hold it off for another summer. Whatever. The restaurant remains open. They're going to need staff. The last thing a struggling business wants to do is to have bring in new, untrained people. You might as well shoot the thing in the head, put it out of its misery. They tell you nothing so that just in case they need you—slight though that chance may be—you will be available. If they whisper to you that the business is going under, the first thing you'll do when you get off the phone is start looking for another job, right?"

"Yes, but what about when the business does go under, and I'm totally fucked?"

Her arms spread to both sides of the room, as if to suggest to him the enormity of what he didn't understand. "Why should that matter to them? They're trying to protect their interests not yours. If you're caught in a lurch just as the season starts, so what? That doesn't affect them. But if they're open and you're not free to work, that does affect them."

"But that's wrong!"

She gave him a sisterly look. "Now, Doug."

"What is it about people who get into management that they're required to be—" He stopped himself.

She waved her hand. *No offense taken.*

"Let's talk about something more immediate—and more constructive." She leaned forward, put her elbows on the desk.

He shifted in his seat. He'd heard the change in her voice.

"While I am truly sorry for your sake that you've received this bad news, I also think it could be one of those situations that—if you want it to—represents an unexpected opportunity."

"Such as?"

"Such as working for me."

Doug wanted not to show his discomfort, but his body, without asking him, went completely stiff. She, meanwhile, followed her words with a reductive smile, covering only a portion of her face.

"I appreciate that, Ms. Gert, but I don't actually get what it is you do here. What are you selling?"

"It's Jeannie, Doug. And I told you that already. Hopes and promises."

He stared at her.

"Okay, maybe I should say we sell illusions."

The answer made the air go out of him; he felt his guts head to the floor and at the same time a shivering vertigo. What she had said and how she said it made a deep, dark sense.

"Let me backtrack. As you surely know, behind its fishing village face, this is an extraordinarily wealthy island."

"Yes."

"Some of the people who live here, and many of those who visit, are among the richest in the country."

"Uh huh."

"But realize that being wealthy is not merely a matter of piling up a stack of financial assets; wealth is primarily a state of mind."

"Oh, I know that, believe me." He fully intended the scorn. His parents were not exactly ostentatious but they were extremely comfortable; and many of the people his parents liked to regard as friends could not be called anything but ostentatious. Through this network, Doug was well aware of the contentiousness and the pettiness of the very rich, especially—like his parents—the newly so.

"Don't misunderstand me," she said sharply. "I am not making a pejorative statement only an analytical one. I am not talking about a superficial personality or attitude. I mean a clinical state of mind."

He shrugged, a hopeless gesture.

"Okay," Gert said, "let's start over. One instructive way of viewing human beings is to think of them as a continuum of needs. Starting of course with the animal: food, sleep, sex. In this country, fortunately, most of us suffer no real worries about these basic needs."

"Most of us."

"That's what I said. Most. Now, after the animal needs what needs are there? Shelter, of course. This too for most of us is a given. And in our economy so too, most of the time, at least historically, is employment. Even if that employment is not always ideal." She looked at him; he couldn't hold her eyes. "Once a person has satisfied these needs, more complicated and frankly more luxurious ones begin to assert themselves. Modern needs we might call them, because before the modern period such needs, for the vast majority of humankind, were not just unfelt but unknown. What needs, you say? The need to feel satisfied in one's occupation; the need for long range personal stability; the need for gratuitous, even whimsical, pleasures and possessions: boats, cars, horses, snowmobiles. Even businesses one doesn't strictly need for financial success but one wants to own for vanity's sake, e.g., professional sports teams. The very wealthy, to an astonishing degree, are able to satisfy virtually all these needs."

"I guess."

"No, Doug. They can. And they do. Trust me. I've lived among them for twenty years."

So have I, Doug felt like saying; but he realized too that there were strata of wealth beyond that of his parents and their friends. For all he knew, Jeannie Gert would consider his parents blue collar thugs.

"If you're saying that the rich can buy anything they want, I don't know if I count that as a virtue."

She stopped, genuinely surprised.

"Have I said anything about virtue? Virtue—or the lack of it—has nothing whatsoever to do with this discussion."

"Okay. Sorry."

She waved it away.

"What the rich cannot control, however, is the impossible."

Doug snorted. "Of course not."

She raised an index finger. "Don't be so quick to laugh. The desire to alter reality—to recreate it on a new track, if you will—runs deep in every human being. Not one of us does not think, perhaps even obsessively, *If only I had . . .* or *If I had never done . . .* or *With just a little more time.* True?"

He nodded, chagrined.

"Well," she continued, "not even the rich can buy back those lost possibilities. Money does not give one power over time or the forces of age; money does not give one power over life and death. Or, even in this technologically advanced era, over space. Most of all, money does not give one power over closed doors in a person's heart."

"That's right, but what does?"

"Illusion," she said.

Doug started to speak but stopped. He nodded: a small, momentary motion.

"There is a way to break the veil, and it's through illusion. For instance, if a man would like to know again the woman he loved at twenty—as she was at twenty—illusion can make that happen. Or know his grandmother ten years dead, in the flesh. A woman might regret spending her young adulthood and middle age in the workforce; she might wish she had accepted a certain youth's proposal at eighteen and started a family. Another woman might wish she had not started a family and instead taken a small but real opportunity to study in Paris. What might have happened to her? Whom might she have met?"

"But what is the illusion going to do?"

"The illusion answers the question."

"But it's only an illusion."

She raised an eyebrow.

"I mean, it's not real," he said. "You know."

"I'm afraid that depends on your definition of reality."

"But it's not true, right? It's an illusion."

Again, she seemed disappointed.

"That depends on your definition of truth. For our clients what we provide is certainly true enough; it is most certainly real. The man who wants to taste the lips of his long lost beloved most certainly tastes lips."

She moved in her chair, satisfied. As if she had singlehandedly settled the question. Dominated it. Doug was not a client, but he felt himself being played for a sucker. That was annoying enough, but the more nagging question was why? What did she care whether he approved of her or not, if he fell for her act?

"But those illusions, they can't really take the place of reality, can they? They can't actually substitute for the real thing?"

"That is a fair, if simple, question. Even an important one. Can illusions convince? Can illusions echo at the bottom of one's soul, so strongly that one feels oneself fundamentally relieved, assuaged, even transformed?"

Doug nodded numbly.

"I cannot give you a comprehensive answer. But I can give you an answer. Which is this: you seemed very disturbed when you first came up here. More disturbed than you are now. You were anxious that Ms. Brubaker may have discovered Doreen's little lie."

"A little anxious."

She smiled. "A little. But what if I were to tell you that the reason I was so certain Ms. Brubaker would not have climbed those stairs is that her name isn't Denise Brubaker but Linda Ryan, a Boston-based actress whose role was only to make a convincing fuss downstairs and then leave."

Doug's mouth opened like a trap door.

"Or I could tell you that her name is Karen Coffin, a famous island crank—actually, she's quite a madwoman—who enjoys pretending to be other people. Doreen was merely going along with the game until Ms. Coffin left, which we all knew she would."

Doug shifted his head. He couldn't look at her anymore. Obviously, he was being ridiculed.

"Or what if I told you that *my* name is not Jeannie Gert but Linda Ryan, and that I am the Boston-based actress, while the real Jeannie Gert enjoys coming into the office and pretending to be a livid ex-customer for the sake of unsuspecting young men like you?"

"Then I would say you are all full of shit, that's what."

She laughed. "A trite personal attack is no substitute for an answer."

"But what would be the point? Why am I so important?"

"The point? I should think that would be obvious. Why are you so important? You aren't. Not really. Only a little. And I caution you to remember that I didn't say any of those possibilities were true. I did not say positively that the woman downstairs was anything but exactly who she seemed to be."

Doug's head was spinning. This was all way too much. He didn't know why he was still sitting there except for the fact that he had no job and, apparently, she was in the process of offering him one. And too there was this woman's—whoever she was—absolute and intriguing certainty of soul, as if she knew everything about him, including what he would say to any question she raised. Her confidence kept him stuck there.

"What matters," she said, "is that while you watched Ms. Brubaker's tantrum you did not doubt for a second that you were experiencing a reality."

"But your customers know what they are getting is an illusion. How can they accept it as real?"

The grin again: smaller, harder. "You'd be surprised how much they accept, and what they believe."

"And they pay for it?"

"Oh, they pay for it. Dearly. We insist on it, upfront. After all, what other choice do they have? Where else can they go to conquer the impossible? We have them over the proverbial barrel. Nor is putting on an illusion an inexpensive proposition. No, it is often quite costly."

Doug nodded. He glanced around the room, thinking again about the elaborate physical changes he witnessed. He needed to ask at least one more question before he could commit; he needed to ask the perfect, most effective, most biting question of all. But it stayed out of his head and off his tongue. Instead he asked another: "So what do you need me for?"

She shrugged.

"At the moment I can't say. I don't know which illusions will come walking through my door. When we call you we will need you, and when we need you we will know what for."

"That's not the most reassuring proposal I've ever heard."

She put her hands on her desk, clasped her fingers together like an old-fashioned movie mogul set to twirl his thumbs. "Do you have another?"

This act of proprietorship finally pissed him off. "Look, I need a regular paycheck. It can't be a once in a while thing, like whenever you feel like calling me. I don't stop existing when I walk out that door. While you're here doing whatever it is you do, I have a life to take care of."

His pique seemed to amuse her, but she let it go. "You will be paid every week for as long as you remain on the island. Until you return to your old life. That I promise you."

The very words "old life" made him blink and swallow hard. He hoped she didn't notice.

"All right, but how much?"

"How much were you getting from your other job, per week?"

He calculated a generous guesstimate. Then at the last second he added a hundred dollars to the figure.

"I can promise you double that."

"Double?"

"Yes. In cash."

"Every week?"

"As long as you remain on the island."

Doug was finding it increasingly difficult to hold her off. Yet he still felt he ought to.

"Starting when, exactly? I don't mean to be rude, but I have almost nothing to live on right now. And who knows when I'll do any work for you."

"You need an advance?" She snagged a ring of keys sitting on the desk. "How much?"

Doug had no idea what to say. What do people ask for in these situations?

"Two hundred bucks."

She located a key, put it one of the right hand desk drawers, and pulled the drawer open.

"Take three," she said. "No, four."

She fingered four crisp, laundry clean bills from the drawer. Big oval pictures of Ben Franklin. She extended them to him as if they were pieces of gum.

"Thanks," he said dumbly. He pocketed the money.

"Not a problem. And don't worry about paying us back. Consider it a signing bonus. But there is one thing more: your contract."

"Contract?"

"Of course. What do you expect? We're as serious as any island employer." From another drawer she withdrew several sheets of paper. She pushed them across the desk. "There you go. Now make sure you read it all thoroughly. Start to finish."

He took hold of the papers with no little trepidation. He remembered the contract she showed him on the ferry, the unsolvable language delivered like a weapon to the head of the customer. If the same language were employed here, he would not know what he was signing to. *I never had to sign a contract at Marconi's.* Maybe that's what he would say; then leave. As he skimmed the contract he saw it was even worse than he feared. Seven pages of wickedly contorted language about which he had no training and no natural inclination. He read and reread the paragraphs on page one for close to fifteen minutes and could make no living sense of them at all. So he tried reading only sentences. This was no better. His head hurt. He understood exactly one phrase, the first: "I _____, having freely entered this employment agreement with The Treasure Box Inc. . . ." Freely? Maybe.

"Where do I sign?" he said.

She was typing something into her computer. She stopped, closed the window, turned back to him.

"Good. You've read it?"

"Yes."

"All of it, start to finish?"

Doug nodded.

"Do you have any questions about the contract?"

He blinked. "No."

"You're sure?"

He nodded again.

"Okay then. Print your name in the blank space on page one; print your name again, sign, and then date it on the spaces provided at the bottom of page seven."

"Page seven?"

"Page seven."

She went back to her computer.

He laid the contract flat on the desk, found the appropriate spaces. He had no pen.

"Pen's on the desk," she said, before he could speak. She was typing again.

Sure enough. How had he missed it? An ornate, gold-rimmed, forest green fountain pen lay naked as a tree branch against the red wood of the desk. He picked it up. It felt warm and considerable in his hand, yet formal too, impressive: the kind of instrument presidents use to sign bills into law or formalize peace treaties. Or to commit thousands of soldiers to their deaths. Doug scrawled his name in the assigned spaces. Beside his signature on page seven he wrote the date. He paused a moment and studied himself down there: his name formed in inky cursive on the long paper.

"Okay," he said, "I'm done."

"You're done?"

She closed the window, turned back.

"Yes." He pushed the contract toward her, right under her eyes. She didn't even glance at it. "So what do I do now?"

She smiled a last time.

"You wait," she said. "You wait. There's nothing else I can tell you."

As relieved as he was to have his job problem solved, in the house that evening he found himself trying to piece together the meaning of what just happened. He wished he had asked her about the transformation. Until that impossibility was explained, nothing about his new employer could make sense. And he was increasingly sure that Gert knew he had entered her building earlier in the day. He remembered the chair in the center of the room, slightly askew. *It was her.* Looking back on his interview, he recognized it in her superior tone, the dual confidence and irony that played in her eyes, the certainty that she owned him. In her mind it was already a done deal. As soon as he answered the phone. Everything that followed was just going through the motions for his sake, so he could believe he made the decision to work for her. The elaborate and insulting pretense that she hadn't already anticipated his reservations, formed an answer to every question, calculated exactly how much it would take to buy out his shipwrecked existence. Before she even called him, she knew he would sign; because she knew that Doug, of his own volition, had visited them that morning, interested and curious. Desperate enough to push open a door and violate an off-limits space. Willing to put up with whatever he found there. Because he had no other options in the world.

The feeling of being owned did not in a little unsettle him. As the evening drew on he drank beer after beer, less out of celebration than consolation. Or perhaps resignation. What the fuck, he finally decided, in a last effort to reclaim himself. It's just a job. If I don't like it, I can quit.

Doug heard nothing for three days. He started to wonder if he was misremembering the interview with Gert, their agreement. But every time he opened his refrigerator he saw the bottles of Cisco Pale Ale he'd paid for with his advance. The beer certainly felt real enough in his mouth. Damn good, in fact. So too was the three hundred dollars stashed in the bedroom bureau. All he had to do was open the drawer, stare at the cash, and he grew calm. *That's real green. It does what green does.*

He almost called her to make sure he'd heard her right: that he would get paid in a week, like every other employee. He couldn't believe they would pay him for doing nothing but drinking beer. He wondered if he ought to start looking for another job in case the call didn't come. But in the end he decided just to wait a little longer. That is, after all, what she asked of him.

When the phone rang, it was dark. He didn't know if it was a.m. or p.m., the deep middle of night or an hour before sunrise. He also didn't know where he was. When he first sat up, he thought he was in his old room in Amherst and his alarm had sounded; then, for one inexplicable second, he imagined he was in the belly of the Hyannis-to-Nantucket ferry, that in the levels above him were hundreds of anonymous vacationers enjoying ordinary pleasures denied to him. The phone rang again. By the time he got to it, he was back inside his body.

"You are needed," a woman said, as soon as he picked up the

phone. It might be Gert, but he wasn't sure. The voice also sounded a bit like her secretary.

"Now?"

"Yes."

He stood numbly for a moment, staring out his living room window at the three or four visible stars. They were there, but without their usual ocean clarity. His mouth was dry and swollen; his head pulsed, as if grain were being poured through his ears.

"What does that mean?"

He heard a breath: an annoyed, impatient articulation.

"Come in," she said.

"Now?"

"*Now.*"

Silence.

"You are needed."

It was Gert, he decided, but her voice was different, as if ninety percent of who she was—or who he thought she was—had been stripped away, leaving this breathy insistent consciousness on the line.

"What do I do? What do I wear?"

"That will be taken care of."

Silence.

"Just come in. Hurry."

"All right." He waited. There had to be something else to say.

"Goodbye," she said.

It was just after three a.m. when he parked his car on South Beach Street. There were no other cars. There were no lights on in any of buildings, including 1452. Not a soul was on the sidewalks. It occurred to him that he might be the victim of a practical joke. An initiation rite. But he couldn't know until he tried the door. He heard and saw nothing as he stepped on the walk. He went to the door; he stood for whole moments just listening. Nothing at all. The building was obviously empty. He must have misunderstood. He should go home. He should go back to sleep. He didn't try the knob, but he did ring the doorbell. Just so he could say he'd done it.

A thick, black, vertical line appeared, blacker than the air around it. He saw no one.

"Inside," a leathery voice insisted. Male.

He moved forward and the door swung back. A thin, female hand encircled his wrist, pulling him.

"You are a college student in a coma. You were hit by a delivery van. Now you are in the hospital. It is thirty-six hours since the accident. You cannot move, even to open your eyes. You especially cannot open your eyes. You cannot see, cannot hear, cannot speak. You cannot move. You are very near death."

She pulled him further into the room. As his eyes adjusted to the darkness he realized that other people were there. Perhaps as many as a dozen.

"Get in the bed," the woman said.

It felt exactly like what it was supposed to be: a hospital bed. Coldly and efficiently durable; firm against his back. Proper but not inviting. The top portion of the bed, where his upper body went, was set at a gentle angle.

"You must be changed," the woman said. Before he could think, he felt four pairs of hands assault him. They removed his shoes, unzipped his pants, pulled off his sweatshirt. Behind these hands and the bodies they belonged to were a ring of other bodies who, as it turned out, held flashlights. The flashlights came on all at once: focused squarely at his eyes, blinding him.

"Hey," he complained.

"Shut up," someone whispered. The first male voice. "You're comatose, remember?"

Doug nodded and went limp. They removed the rest of his clothing and put a hospital gown around him. Someone behind him shoved him to an upright sitting position and held him while other hands tied the ties at the back. They let him go; he fell lamely against the pillow. They hoisted his legs by the knees and stuck them under the bed covers. They brought the top sheet and blanket all the way up his chest, to his chin. They fastened something to his left arm: awkward and plastic, too heavy not to notice. Apparently, it connected him to a machine. He felt and barely smelled something in the air then, something actual and ethereal at the same time, a condensed texture tickling his nose and entering his lungs. A vaguely sweet, damp smell; out of place. Doug shivered under the covers and realized what it was. Mist generated by dry ice. It continued to billow; it settled hugely around the room and about his bed like sheer fabric. He felt like he was living inside some mildly perverse and unimaginative rock video, a tacky Hollywood rendition of pagan sacrifice.

"You're comatose," the first voice said. "That means you keep your eyes closed and mouth shut. Starting now."

At that instant he heard a car outside. He heard voices: particular and human. He couldn't help himself. He half-opened one eye. Someone's flashlight remained on and from that single weak illumination he could tell the room had been rearranged again. The office furniture and pictures were gone. The computers too. He opened the other eye. He moved his head a centimeter to the left. The floor looked like linoleum. That's why it had felt so strangely hard against his feet when he entered. Various medical paraphernalia brooded in the corners: wires, cords, bags, tubes, mirrors, pumps. A heavy industrial curtain blocked half of the front section of the room; it eliminated the window and shortened the space considerably.

The flashlight moved. He shut both eyes just in time; then he felt the blaze against his face, interrogating him. Maybe there was a whisper. Someone moved. A head was near his shoulder. The male voice spoke directly into his ear.

"Play your part, pal, or you're fucked."

Doug squeaked a tiny assent in the rear part of his throat, but did not visibly react, even to nod. He played his part.

The voices were right outside the front door. Then the door opened. Pairs of feet came in. There were a few moments without words, as if the group were waiting for the assembly to begin.

Overhead lights came on all at once. Doug could feel them, hospital bright, through his clenched eyes.

"Now, Mr. Cox," a concerned male voice intoned, "we'll give you some time with your son."

There was a nearly invisible sound, some movement of fabric, perhaps the curtain. Then an entirely different voice.

"Oh, god. Larry! Larry!"

Doug heard movement. A man's arms encircled his body; a thick, coldly sweating head was on his chest.

"Larry. Oh, Jesus." A second later the man was crying, a horrible wrenching jag of tears. This was a person with no experience in crying and thus no control over it; the air of it ripped forcibly through his lungs.

"Mr. Cox," the other man said. "We'll leave you alone for a few minutes. I'll just wait outside. Call me when you're done. If I don't answer, I'm in another patient's room. In that case, just ring the nurse." The head on Doug's chest moved in a nod. "Thank you," the head muttered.

There was a modest commotion as everyone else—at least it sounded like—left the room. The man waited, still holding Doug's breathing body, his head on Doug's chest.

When the sounds of the people were gone, the man's head came up. He leaned in close to Doug's face. Doug smelled onions and paprika. And lots of whiskey.

"Larry, it's my fault you ended up like this. I shouldn't have yelled. I shouldn't have driven you away." Briefly, as he found his way to words, the man became less barbarically desperate. He began to stroke Doug's forehead with a heavy, sweating paw. He pushed back the hair at the front of Doug's skull. He tried to run his hand through it. When he sloppily kissed Doug on the cheek, Doug nearly broke the game. His disgust almost outweighed his fear. Almost. Somehow, he managed not to move.

"The last thing your mother said to me was, 'You realize you have no idea where he's off to.' And I—I really can't believe I said this, Larry, but I did—I told her it didn't matter. I said to her: 'I don't care.'"

The man broke down again into a mess of clutching and bawling. He eventually grew so weak and inarticulate that he fell to the floor, a heap beneath Doug's body, crying and condemning himself. Now Doug couldn't resist. After all, there was no one else in the room. He cracked one eye. Immediately he saw, coming from the ceiling, the bright assault of light. He closed the eye. It looked like any old hospital room ceiling. Nothing like the ceiling of the room he'd seen before. But the mist from the dry ice was still evident, casting an unreal haze everywhere, accenting and reflecting the garish white tint of the light overhead.

What would happen now? What was supposed to happen? Doug lay still, both eyes perfectly closed.

After a few minutes, the man stood up.

"Okay, Larry, okay." He sounded pathetic, wheezing. He sounded ill. "There's nothing else for me to tell you. You're here because of what I did, not from what you did. All I can ask is your forgiveness. You don't have to give it; I'm only asking. And we've both got to hope that these good doctors know what the hell to do with you. I'm hoping with all my heart—all my everything—that you can hear me now and understand. They say people in comas can still hear. That's what I'm hoping. But maybe someday, hopefully, I'll be able to apologize to you with your eyes open. I'll ask again for your forgiveness, and you'll be able to answer me. Boy, if that could happen—if that day happens, Larry—you know, I won't even care if you forgive me or not. Because I'll have you back. That's all I want now. I want you back, and I want you to hear me say I'm sorry. That's all. But I'm saying it now, even if you can't respond. Because maybe at least you can hear. I'm sorry. I'm sorry. I'm sorry."

The man moved. His head was closer. He spoke in whisper.

"Did you hear that, son? Did you hear me say, I'm sorry?" A long pause, as if he were examining every inch of Doug's face. Now Doug worried. Wouldn't this poor bugger see? Was the spell broken? Might he turn furious?

"Okay," the man said. "Okay." Then Doug felt lips on his forehead—a salty, stinging sensation, as if he'd been branded. The man squeezed Doug's hand. Then he kissed it.

"Amazing. You're so warm. You're warm just like everything's normal. Like none of this ever happened. Like you could just open those eyes right now and talk to me." Again, Doug felt the man studying him; he kept his eyes clenched tight.

"All right," the man said. "I know. Enough of Dad's tears. That's just what you need, isn't it? I'll check on you again, Larry, tomorrow morning. And every day after. Every day. I'm gonna monitor these people and make sure they're taking care of my boy. Okay, Larry? Daddy's here, little boy. Your daddy's here now."

Doug received one more kiss. Briefer, less wet. A last heavy hand through his hair. "I love you, Larry." Then silence. Then a single tired sigh, as big as the room.

"All right, doctor," the man called. "I think I'm ready."

The door opened instantly. Smart professional shoes sounded against the linoleum.

"Are you sure, Mr. Cox? There's no rush. These are your visiting hours."

"No, I'm done. I can go."

"As you wish. Come out this way."

"Sure. Thank you. So much."

"Not a problem, Mr. Cox. This is why hospitals allow visitors."

The door opened; the two of them left. Doug was alone. But he followed orders: He lay still under that garish beacon, too disturbed by what had just happened to do anything else. Minutes passed. He heard a car start. The car pulled away. Another minute. The front door opened. The hospital light went out. He heard a crowd of feet coming through.

"Get up," a woman's voice said, as if it were stupid of him to still be lying there. He couldn't tell for sure, but he thought it was the woman he heard before, when he first came through the door. It might even be Gert's voice, but he didn't think so. It seemed younger and thinner, more brittle.

Doug sat up in the bed. The light remained doused.

"Put these on."

A soft lump landed on his hip. His clothes.

"Leave the gown."

He opened his mouth. He wanted to say something, but she cut him off. "Get dressed, will you?" He pushed himself to the floor and began untying the gown from his back. He tossed it at his feet. It took only a few moments to put his clothes back on. Meanwhile, around him people moved: changing their own clothes. Then all the movement shifted. It went in another direction. The door opened. More than a half-dozen dark heads passed through into the dim early morning. The last person, a svelte form, turned back to him.

"Leave," she whispered. Then she closed the door.

When Doug made it back out on the street he didn't know what to expect, except that after the grotesque masque they'd just performed whatever was there surely would be changed. Twisted out of normal recognition. But what he saw, more startling than any other possibility, was nothing new at all. The street looked no different from when he had entered the building. Other than his own, there were no cars. And there was no illumination except the same two meager streetlights, one close overhead, the other dozens of yards away. The stars, save for a spare one or two, were blocked by a muzzy coating of cloud. Every storefront remained black. He felt the scratch of a thick, sea-fed breeze against his cheeks, but in the vast omnipotent silence Doug could hear nothing at all, not even the ocean against the nearby Children's Beach. But, of course, he remembered, at the Children's Beach there was never a tide anyway.

As soon as he woke, Doug drove to The Treasure Box. He had to check on it; he had to verify the reality of what he'd seen in that earlier, mist-coated glare. It was nine-thirty, only hours since the crew had vacated the premises. He fully expected to see the interior of the building dressed up as a hospital. But when he entered he saw a room that looked precisely the same as the afternoon he'd signed the contract. The walls were pale blue and the carpet was back, along with the computer stations and the framed pictures and the secretary's desk. And Doreen McAlister herself. She was talking on the telephone when he walked through the door. A graying and unhealthily thin man, fortyish, was at one computer station, at the other an overweight olive-skinned teenager clad in a red and silver sweatsuit. The girl sucked on a Fruit Smoothie as she marveled at something on screen.

When the secretary hung up, Doug approached.

"I need to see Ms. Gert," he said.

She stared at him so directly Doug expected she was about to make a crucial announcement. Then she blinked. The look was gone. There was something altogether strange about this woman. Her hair was too blonde and too clean, her skin too clear, her eyes too transparent a shade of blue. Her face was stiff beyond professionalism, beyond even humanness. She suddenly seemed not a pretty local girl, but an industrial creation, a compound formed of chemicals and ingenuity: joined in a mixer, heated in a vat, poured into a mold and allowed to cool.

"Ms. Gert is off-island today," she said.

"Oh, come on. You don't really expect me to believe that."

She blinked again but didn't answer.

"What happened to this room, anyway? A couple of hours ago it looked like a hospital."

She gave him a quizzical stare, as if she could have no idea what he was talking about. As if she thought him mad.

"I'm serious. The walls were white. At least they looked it. The floor was linoleum. All this furniture was gone. There were machines around my bed. I mean the hospital bed, which was about . . . there. I think."

Her look changed to something closer to pity.

"I was working for Ms. Gert," he protested. "I was doing a job for her. One of her illusions. Now I need to talk to her. You better let me."

Doug realized he was being observed by the thin man and the girl with the Smoothie. He better cool it if he wanted to get anywhere with Doreen McAlister. Likely, her no comprendo act was meant to throw these potential customers off the scent. Illusions, he knew, are ruined once one meets the actors behind them, even if one knows, going in, that they are illusions. Last summer he'd seen a recognizable, A-list movie star meandering on Centre Street. He followed her into a boutique to get a closer look, only to discover that this famously beautiful woman, in ordinary light, was plain.

"Please," he said, under his breath.

He didn't know precisely what he would say to Gert, but he needed to express his disgust with the whole enterprise. He wanted to tell her how much his skin crawled when that man put his head on his chest, breathed hot remorse into his skin, kissed his face. All this on less than an hour's notice. What if he hadn't answered the phone? What if he'd been stinking drunk? What if he had followed his instinct and shoved the man away? Just thinking about the illusion made him want to shower, to wash off the tacky built-up residue of emotional prostitution. Whatever they did here—whatever they claimed to do here—was wrong. It was sick. They were using people. Whoring their feelings.

But better, Doug knew, to keep it professional. Keep it from becoming an argument. He wasn't the right man for the job. That's what he would tell Gert. *You need someone else. I can't do this.*

"Ms. Gert cannot speak to you," McAlister repeated, "since she's not here."

He opened his mouth. Despite himself, he was going to yell.

"What's your name, sir?" she said.

She certainly knew it, but he told her anyway. She nodded primly and opened a drawer. She extracted a 4 X 6 index card.

"Ms. Gert left a message for you." Doug hesitated but took it. The letters were in a woman's spidering, aristocratic handwriting: black ballpoint pen.

You performed passably. Now wait. Payday is Friday.

He held the card against his hip, ashamed. He wanted to speak but didn't. This robot girl wouldn't tell him anything. She was programmed against it. He turned and walked to the door. He stopped at the stairs, just like that woman the other day. Like her, he stared miserably up their length, too much the coward to do anything else. He looked and listened, but there was no hint of noise. All he saw were clouds passing over the skylight.

He expected no calls for a few days. He'd have a chance to cool down and settle in—or reconsider. He went to Jetties for the afternoon, trying to remember he was on vacation, to feel again whatever it was that made someone move to Nantucket. But the charade of the morning put a black tinge over everything he saw. All about him—the beach, the water, the scattered, sorry knots of people—looked corrupt, phony, duplicitous. He had been exposed to the heart of some father's secret guilt and saw the man try to expiate it with silly playacting. This beach, Doug was sure, held other, worser, blacker secrets: the acts of phony, self-centered, manipulative people. Who here had murdered? Who had extorted money? Who had left his wife and kids? Who had ended someone else's dreams, mercilessly and for no other reason than the desire to cause pain? Every one of these people had a history and a demon.

The imagined sins closed in around him, folded on top of each other as securely and invisibly as fish scales. Stinking just as bad. Even the sun—which finally broke through around three—failed to encourage him. He walked to his car feeling the long summer ahead of him: just another kind of doom.

The phone was ringing when he got home.

"Hello?"

"You are needed."

"Now?"

"Yes."

His mind was a beehive, but it was no use asking questions.

The front door of The Treasure Box was closed. The shutters were drawn. He knocked. Nothing. He rang the doorbell. He waited. No one answered. What was going on? He had been called, after all. That was certain. He could not just walk away, as he hoped to do that morning. He knew that now. No, he was supposed to do something. It occurred to him to try the knob. It turned; the door swung inward. Doug gasped.

The place was changed again, maybe the strangest transformation yet. The walls were dark wood paneling; the mute carpeting replaced by rusty orange shag. Instead of office furniture and computer terminals the room held a dingy living room ensemble, if you could call it that: an enormous padded couch, a love seat, two heavy lounge chairs, all covered in a stained and threadbare tweedy fabric. These pieces, placed around a long dark coffee table, occupied the center of the room.

Doug could see a picture book or two stacked on the coffee table as well as a few days worth of junk mail, a disassembled newspaper, and a scattered assortment of magazines. The only titles he could make out were *Bass Fisherman* and *Popular Mechanics*. An orange Tupperware bowl full of potato chips sat on top of one magazine; beside this two open beers: Carling's Black Label. On the far end of the couch some clothes were piled: generic gray sweatpants and a blue plaid flannel shirt. A note was placed on top, but in the low light he couldn't quite make out the thin lettering. He walked over. Then he could read: *Put these on*. He did so, indifferently, as he continued to examine the new room.

A few feet from this furniture, closer to the left hand wall, was an enormous, woody television console resting upon a utility table. The rabbit ears of the set were stretched so wide as to look not like a V but two arms grasping for opposite sides of the room. The television was off, the screen a dewy blackness. Back where the secretary's desk should have been was a pool table and a small wet bar. On the wall above the pool table hung a clock advertising Schlitz beer. To the right of the clock was a bulletin board with dozens of buttons pinned into its cork. Most were political. From where he stood Doug could not make out the grainy black and white faces imprinted on some of them, but he could read the lettering—mostly in bright red and blue: *Eisenhower '56*, *I Still like Ike*, *Nixon for President*, *Goldwater '64*, *Nixon's the One*, *Reelect President Nixon*. On the other side of the clock an American flag was pinned to the wall, its stars and stripes loud against the deadly brown paneling. But the flag was starting to sag at the corners, creating wrinkly waves at its center.

Doug waited, standing, for minutes more in the silence. As best he could tell, no one else had showed up for work. Finally, he sat on the couch. He noticed that beneath the *Popular Mechanics* was a *Sports Illustrated* and under that, he guessed from the exposed bottom half of the cover, a *Playboy*. The newspaper was the *Chicago Sun-Times*, dated Sunday, September 10, 1972. Final edition. "Israeli Syrian Jets Duel." "Russia beats U.S. in Olympic case 'long count.'" "City hit by major blaze on west side, at river." On the carpet, at his feet, was the newspaper's *Parade* magazine from the same date. A crew cut, fiftyish man with a straight nose and crinkled, leathery face fixed a twinkling stare at the camera. His closed-mouth smile suggested he knew a lot more than he would ever tell. Behind him, sitting on long wooden benches were a collection of men, women, and children, aged from infant to senior. All of them, dressed in overly bright, wide 70s vestments, were either smiling or laughing. "Acting Director Lewis Patrick Gray III and Family" the cover read, and beneath that message, in even larger letters: "Can A Nice Guy Be Head of the FBI?"

Doug heard movement overhead. Clumsy, undisguised, wooden sounds. Then he heard feet on the stairs. He turned on the couch to receive his second biggest shock of the evening. He actually recognized the person who, reaching the last step, was about to set foot on the shag-covered floor: Denise Brubaker, the angry customer from days before. Except she was dressed very differently: in a heavy green turtleneck and peach colored polyester pants. She moved differently too. None of the charge and anger from before—no red in her cheeks, no frustration glinting silver in her eyes beneath a cap of butchy hair. Now she sashayed almost dreamily, her hand coasting along the banister, a mealy smile on her mouth and a fixed brightness in her eye. If he had to name a word, Doug would say she looked doped. Her hair was discernibly straighter and redder. She wore ridiculous blue eye shadow and peachy-pink rouge.

Brubaker reached the bottom, turned with that same easy motion, and stopped. She showed him the smile in full.

"Sorry about that," she said. "You know how beer goes through me."

Her bright gaze fixed on the Tupperware bowl.

"Why haven't you eaten any of the chips? I got your favorite."

Doug studied the bowl. They were just chips.

Then he understood. He was inside Brubaker's illusion. She was paying for this. The set. The buttons. The magazines. His performance. All he could do—all he was supposed to do—was play along. He would have to figure out his role as he went.

"Thanks," he said. He leaned forward, reached into the bowl. He tasted one. Just a chip. "Great," he said.

That expression of hers changed for a millisecond. Her eyes were clear and awake, her smile appreciative, even relieved. He had joined the game, and she was glad. Then she went dreamy again.

Brubaker came forward with a few over dramatized steps: sly, cocky motions, her hips leading her legs. She sat next to Doug, uncomfortably close.

"So what did you say Dad told you?" she said. She stretched her right arm across the back of the couch.

"Dad?"

"Something like if he caught you messing up while he was gone he'd whup you."

"Right."

Her face became clownish, an easy effect with all that make-up. Her voice went mocking and low, a bad imitation of a man's.

"If I hear anything about you—anything at all—I'm gonna whup you till you can't see straight. Then I'm going to kick your ass out my door."

She chuckled, shook her head. She leaned in. Her hand, as if by accident, touched his knee.

"You know," she said softly. "He's just jealous of you. He can't help it. He's like an old trained dog. I learned about that today in psychology."

"Really."

"Sure. Mrs. Hamlin was saying how there was this guy, this scientist, who was trying to show how behaviors, good and bad, can be conditioned into the brain. They don't necessarily come from who we are or what we really want. His point was that we can substitute unsocial behaviors with social ones, not by changing people but by just conditioning them to adopt the better behavior. Right? Mrs. Hamlin said he tried it out with dogs. In a little while he got them freaking out just because of a bell he rang. Before the experiment, the dogs didn't give a damn about the bell. Why should they? He rang it; they just lay there. But he conditioned them to freak out. At least on the surface, which is the same thing."

Doug couldn't look at this woman. She was far too close. Her leering, overly made-up face was only inches away. He could smell perfume now: a sugary, apricot scent.

"Right?" she said again. She rubbed his right shoulder: a single, expeditionary movement. "Hmmm?"

"I guess."

"So I said to myself, that's dad. Dear old dad. Maybe it's the firehouse or maybe it's *his* dad or maybe it's mom, but for some reason he can't help but be an idiot. He's conditioned that way. A conditioned idiot. No matter what he's doing. So just think about how pathetic he is, not how scary."

"Do I look scared?"

Doug wasn't trying to be complicated. He just wanted a clue as to what was the heart of this illusion. What was expected of him? And for how long? But apparently this remark surprised Brubaker. She looked at him warily, even annoyed, an actress not sure where her partner is going with the scene. Finally she moved her arm down an inch, so that it was settled around his shoulder.

"You're so big now, almost sixteen. You could whip his ass if you wanted to."

Doug shrugged; stared at his feet. He was not, no matter what, going to turn his face to hers. But he wasn't going to run either, not yet. He would wait it out. With the bare ends of her fingers Brubaker began playing with his hair.

"You know, Bobby, I hear a lot of what the girls say. Girls talk, if you didn't know."

He nodded stiffly.

"Oh, they talk," she said, even softer now. "They talk more than boys." She paused; Doug thought he heard her swallow. "They talk about you."

Doug blushed, for real.

"There are a lot of girls who think you are a dream. And I don't just mean those stupid sophomores. I mean seniors. Girls like me. Grown women. They've noticed you too."

She was leaning so far into him that he felt the push of her middle-aged breasts against his shoulder. She kept tousling his hair. Her voice had turned cloying, the same saccharine musical lilt one might use on an infant. And all the while that grotesque scent poured from her: filling his ears, his eyes, his nose.

"You're a big boy. You have your own fan club of women. You don't have to worry about daddy, or any grown man. You're all grown yourself. You're just as much as a man. Maybe even more."

She moved her arm away, brought it back to her own lap. For a moment, as her breasts pulled away, as her arm retreated, Doug felt air again, and with it relief. But then she moved the arm to a new spot: his leg. Her hand rested on his thigh.

"Do you ever think about girls, Bobby? What kind of girls does a man like you like?"

Doug didn't answer. It wasn't just that he was terrified now, though he was. He knew that whatever answer he gave, if he even had one, wouldn't matter. This bit was a monologue.

Brubaker moved her hand along a certain key spot on his lower body. Atop the thin, flexible covering of the sweatpants, the hand made slow, practiced motions. Against himself, against all he was and wished for and ever expected from himself, Doug felt an erection starting.

"So many girls adore you. They talk about your hair and your smile. They talk about your big, round shoulders. And they talk about your eyes. God, do they ever talk about those bedroom blues. But, you know, those girls at school, you have to watch out for them, Bobby. They don't know you. Not like I do. Not like we know each other. All we've been through, you know with mom and dad. You and I, we're like a team."

She stopped moving her hand, but kept it on top of his now full erection. As if to keep track of the thing. Although he was not looking at her, and had not for moments, he knew that she was smiling at him. He felt satisfaction, even victory, coming off her in waves along with the perfume. She leaned in again, those breasts against his shoulder.

Doug was actually paralyzed. His head said *I should run* but at the same time he had no will, or the will he had was tied along with his body to this place, as if with a cord. Against the fact of this horrid performance was the knowledge that he was getting paid for it. For this and for whatever else might happen. He was paid to be here and cooperate. It was a job, not life. Not life at all. Not even a reenactment necessarily. A simple sick fantasy. It didn't finally touch him. It didn't finally matter. And too—perhaps most strongly of all—was the fear of what they might do to him if he walked out.

"Hmmm," she breathed out lazily. She put her head on his shoulder, while that hand stayed exactly where it was. When she spoke again, it was in a conspiratorial whisper. "I think you're a dream too. Don't tell anyone I said that, though. Let it be our own special, private secret."

Doug swallowed. He tried to nod.

"Good," she said. Then she reached inside his sweatpants, all the way down, and found him there. So that was why he had been made to change. No zippers, no buttons, no belts. This is what it had been about from the start. Her hand moved rhythmically along the length of his phallus: testing it, knowing it, becoming its familiar. And as much as this shocked him, Doug felt his body surge as she rubbed; he felt moisture grow on his skin; he felt the center of him swell with an unstoppable liquid flame. She cupped all of it with her hand and rubbed even more.

"Go ahead, Bobby," she whispered. "Go on. You deserve it, sweetie."

Doug couldn't help himself. In a few seconds it was over.

Brubaker chuckled fondly. "Oh dear. Oh Bobby. We must clean you up, shouldn't we? Let me clean you up, sweetie."

But first she leaned in and gave his shoulder a wet, lingering kiss.

"That was fun," she said into his ear. "We should do that again, don't you think? I mean, the next time it's only us here holding down the fort?" She chuckled again, but sarcastically. "And who knows what else we might be able to do?"

She stayed there, close beside him. If she didn't move right now, Doug might not be able to control himself. He might not be accountable for what he would do.

"Okay. I know. You wait here. Let me run up for a washcloth."

She moved off the couch and started girlishly for the stairs, a happy excited energy propelling her steps.

"Just wait here, sweetie. You leave it all up to me. It will be my pleasure."

He didn't look at her as she went, but he heard her taking the stairs quickly, more than one at a time.

When she was gone, Doug let his head fall to his chest. He couldn't believe he was sitting there, his dick spent and shrunken, limp like a worm inside the sweatpants, leaking drops of leftover sickness. He couldn't believe he was sitting in this evil place, in these soiled clothes, letting himself be literally diddled. His head was as sticky as his armpits, his stomach felt curdled, his vision blurred. He wanted dearly to move but felt like a dead man. As if a valve in his body had been open and his essential life drained away. And all in himself that he respected—the very little he did—lost too.

He stayed in place for the longest time before it struck him that Brubaker wasn't coming back. He hadn't heard a sound in the building since she reached the top floor. He listened more carefully. He waited a minute. He heard nothing from upstairs. He stood up slowly, steadying himself when he got on both feet. He removed the sweatpants and the underwear and the shirt, left them in a smelly heap next to the sofa. He put on his own underwear;

he put on his jeans; he put on his t-shirt and U Mass sweatshirt. He put on his Reeboks. He walked to the door. When he made it outside, he vomited.

Doug did nothing but drink until he passed out on his couch. He stirred at three in the morning, wide awake, his body overheated, his mouth dry, his teeth hurting, his breath toxic. *Just let them try to call now.*

He rolled for minutes searching the one position where he wouldn't be too hot to sleep. Failing that, the one position where he wouldn't be so aware of the anvil of a headache crashing against his temples. No luck. Doug made his way to the bathroom. He drank five glasses of water, as cold as he could make the faucet go. After the fifth glass he felt human enough to turn on the light. He fished around under the sink and found a half-used bottle of aspirin, missed by whoever had last cleaned the house. He couldn't know how old the aspirin was or who had used it last. *Probably shouldn't take these.* A tiny piece of consciousness waving a mousy flag. Doug wasn't about to listen. He'd drunk five glasses of water, so he took five aspirin. He turned off the light immediately, before the sight of the red-eyed, unshaven, wire-haired sloth in the mirror could scare him any further.

First thing in the morning he would return to The Treasure Box. He would quit. He would give Gert her blood money back. Then he would leave the island. After all, he still had the return ferry ticket, if nothing else. As soon as he could get his Jetta on the road in Hyannis he would drive to Andover and beg his dad for a job. For just a year. Whatever kind of job his dad cared to give him, doing whatever his dad wanted done. He wouldn't complain; he wouldn't make excuses; he would put up silently with whatever shit his dad cared to dish out at him: accusations, insults, unwhispered whispers, direct attacks on his character. It didn't matter. He could take it. He could take any and all forms of abuse from a simpleton like his father. That was nothing compared to this.

He walked in without stopping, without ringing, without knocking, without looking in the window. He was surprised to find the door unlocked at eight-thirty a.m. He was more surprised by what he saw. The office was only half-assembled, like a collection of toys dumped out of a box and left stranded on a living room floor. Only one computer station was in place. Four others were sitting cock-eyed in the middle of room, cords dangling errantly, not plugged into anything. Only one framed poster—Cairo—was hung in place, and it tilted. The others were stacked against the wall. The secretary's desk was in place, and her telephone, and her typewriter. But the computer was missing. Also the clock and the nameplate. The plant was sitting in a different spot on the desk. Doug spied one ball point pen and one pad of legal paper. Next to the legal pad sat a fat cardboard box. Whether the box was being packed or unpacked he couldn't tell.

The strangest change of all was the person occupying the desk. Jeannie Gert herself sat in her secretary's chair, talking on the telephone. Just the person Doug came to see. But even she looked different: no pearls, no makeup, no silk blouse. She wore a baggy blue dress that might have come from a superstore, if there were a superstore to be found on the island. She seemed merely surprised on first noticing him; then her eyebrows knotted. Her whole face squinted at him even while she continued her conversation in a level voice.

"Yes, we can arrange that," she said.

She listened.

"We can arrange that."

Her eyes bore two holes into Doug's face.

"I'll tell her. Yes. I'll tell her. Okay. Goodbye."

Before the phone reached its cradle she spoke.

"You were supposed to wait."

"I quit," he said.

Of all the reactions he thought this announcement might fetch, what she gave him wasn't included. Her anger slid away like syrup; now she seemed merely bored. She rolled her eyes, turned to the typewriter. She dismissed him with a fluttering right hand.

"You'll have to talk with Ms. Warner. Or Ms. Gert."

He could only pause so long before speaking.

"I am," he said.

She plucked at the typewriter keys, her eyes focusing downward amateurishly. "Upstairs," she said.

Doug took the stairs slowly, his legs calcified by a growing dread. The boldness which had propelled him just minutes before had all but evaporated. Already that seemed like someone else's emotion, someone else's determination. Doug had no idea who he might see when he reached the top of the stairs, but regardless he knew he'd be better off going in another direction. But which?

The office looked exactly the same. All the same, that is, except that Doreen McAlister sat behind the desk, a letter in her hand, a pile of envelopes by her elbow ready to be opened. She glanced at him, a shine of delight in her eye. Then it was gone. She kept reading.

"What are you doing up here?" Doug said.

McAlister said nothing. She finished the letter, then turned to a paper shredder behind her and destroyed the document at once.

"What's going on?" Doug said. "I thought you were that bitch of a secretary."

McAlister afforded him a thin, toothless smile.

"You thought," she said. "Which tells me I played my role well. As did Doreen."

"You're Doreen."

She laughed.

"So," he said, "you mean . . ." He pointed a thumb downstairs.

"She has a lot of promise, don't you think? More than a lot of our recent hires. More than you. Although you're not all bad. At least that's what Jeannie says."

His head was so full of questions, and those questions were so thickly contorted, he couldn't get one out to begin. He gave up trying, at least for the moment. All of him was desperate to know why: why the duplicity, why the confusion. But he knew that if he started down that road he would likely end in a dark forest, not sure of the way out, none of his essential questions answered, turned expertly aside from his original destination. He resisted the temptation and stuck instead to his first purpose.

"Speaking of employment, I'm quitting. Today. Right now."

The woman, whoever she was—Doug couldn't help but still think of her as the secretary—took the announcement steadily. She didn't laugh, but neither was she bothered. Her blue eyes blinked once. Then she nodded. She signaled to the chair in front of her desk.

"Sit down."

"You can have your money back. I don't care." He'd brought it all with him, what was left. He put his hands in his pockets and took out two fistfuls of coins and bills. He set them on the desk. She refused to look.

"Sit down," she repeated.

He did so, but then realized that by complying he had lost his bodily advantage, the only one he owned. She had castrated him with a single request.

"You can't quit."

"Why?"

"Because your contract says so."

"Like hell it does."

She raised an eyebrow. "You did read your contract, didn't you?"

Doug coughed. The bluster was all but spent. "No," he mumbled.

She smiled. She reached into a desk drawer, pulled out a manila file folder. She flipped through document after document, until she found his contract. She turned to the last page, showed it to him. "Is this your signature?"

"Yes."

"Good. At least that's clear. As well as legally binding."

She looked at the document again, found the passage she wanted.

"I, the undersigned," she began, "understand that I may not of my own free will and volition terminate my employment with The Treasure Box, Inc. On signing this contract I forfeit the right to terminate my own employment. Only the owners of The Treasure Box, Inc., named herein, may terminate my employment and only when it is in the best interests of The Treasure Box, Inc."

"That's a crock. I've never heard of anything like that."

"You signed the contract."

"But I didn't know."

She raised her head, her neck and back and shoulders more stiff, more regal even than when she was Doreen McAlister. She had anticipated just such a statement from him.

"That you did not know the terms of your own contract as

you were signing it is your own fault, not this business's, and such ignorance hardly forfeits the contract's legality. You were instructed to read the document thoroughly. You were given time to do so. Subsequently, you were asked if you had any questions regarding the contents. Then the question was repeated to you. In case you had hopes of denying any of those facts, let me inform you that we videotaped the entire procedure and have multiple copies stored in a distant facility. Would you like to see a video of yourself signing your contract?"

"No."

"Would you like to see Doreen tell you to read the contract thoroughly, *from start to finish*?"

"No."

"Do you want to see Doreen say directly to your face, *Do you have any questions about your contract?*"

"No." He knew damn well he'd signed the thing. And he also knew what Jeannie or Doreen or whoever she was had said. What this woman was ignoring was that the contract was impossible to read, purposefully so, especially in its first page, as if front loaded with opacity to wear down any examiner. To defeat them by page two. The fatal passage she read from page seven was about forty times clearer than any on page one.

"The thing is," he said, "and you know this: No one understands that crap. No one really reads it. There's nothing to do but sign. Have you ever read any of that legal garbage that comes up when you install a computer program? Of course not. You just say 'Agree.' Because no one can understand that stuff. If you waited till you understood it, you'd have to never use a computer again. So you just say 'Agree.' It's the same thing with your contract."

Her smile was tighter, but just as sure of victory. "Speak for yourself, Mr. Durkin. Not all of our employees are so careless. I, for one, read every word of that 'legal garbage' as you put it. Because it *is* legal. It carries lawful and binding force as soon as you put your name to it. I'm afraid it doesn't matter why you didn't read your contract; the contract is still binding whether you read it or not. It is binding, provided your signature is attached and was voluntarily given. Which clearly it is and was."

She raised the page again for him to look at. He didn't.

"You can't just make people stay."

"We 'make' them live up to the terms of their contract."

"Then I'm going to break my contract."

"I don't think you want to do that."

"Don't tell me what I want to do. I want to break my contract."

She emitted a small, superior sigh—exactly how old was this woman?—and hesitated a moment, as if considering which of the numberless convincing ways she should use to tell him that it was impossible for him to do what he wanted.

"Mr. Durkin, the consequence of breaking one's agreement with The Treasure Box, Inc. is also spelled out in the contract. Should I read that consequence to you?"

Seeing her look, Doug shook his head.

"I didn't think so," she said. "What I'd rather discuss is why you wish to break your contract at all."

Doug felt himself slipping in the chair. He rested his feet firmly on the floor and pushed, but he never—no matter how many times he tried—could get any higher.

"Because I can't do this," he said. A resigned, exhausted voice. He had nothing to hope for but her mercy now, which wasn't a hope. "I can't be a gigolo for some perverted middle-aged woman."

"You mean . . ."

"Mrs. Brubaker."

She smiled again. "So you found the illusion as distasteful as she did."

Doug could only stare. "What?"

"What's surprising to me is that, if my information about men is correct, the kind of 'favor' provided you last night ranks highly among male sexual pleasures. I would have expected someone like you to enjoy it."

"Not with her! Holy crap, she thought I was her brother. I mean she wanted me to be her brother."

She smiled again; this time complete, undisguised joy. She lifted the receiver of her phone and touched a button.

"Doreen, is Jeannie still down there? Okay, tell her to come up." She put the receiver back in its cradle. "Funny you should say that.

From what I've been told, whatever disgust you purport to have felt hardly got in the way of your enjoyment."

Doug blushed. He dropped his head. He saw again the image of himself down there on the sofa: wet, limp, alone. Humiliated. The worst minutes of his life. And yet it was true. He had been aroused. How could he possibly make her understand? The sensation was a separate matter, nothing he, or any man, could control. And just because you have the sensation doesn't mean it's not at the same time the worst thing that's ever happened to you.

He heard footsteps on the stairs. Seconds later, someone else was in the room.

"Mr. Durkin, I'd like you to meet Jeannie Gert, co-owner of The Treasure Box, and, coincidentally, my life partner."

Doug was astonished to see Denise Brubaker; that is, the woman he thought was Denise Brubaker—the woman who not long before had been rubbing his cock with her bare hand—standing four feet from him, a lanky grin raking her face.

"Hello, Doug," she said.

"I don't get it."

"And my name," the blonde woman continued, "as you surely have figured out by now is Leigh Warner; second co-owner of The Treasure Box."

Warner signaled to Gert. Gert went to the other side of the desk, where Warner gave her a quick squeeze around the waist. Gert lay her arm across Warner's shoulders.

"What you two put on last night was an illusion requested by a client. Jeannie volunteered to act, once it became clear that she could perform better than anyone else available."

Doug didn't hear any sarcasm in her voice, which scared him far worse than if there had been. Gert bowed her head at the praise.

"We were being watched?" he said.

Warner blinked at him. Her old blue-eyed secretarial expression.

"We were being taped," Doug said.

"Mr. Durkin," she said, almost sympathetically.

"Oh my god. You people are sicker than I thought. This dyke and I were acting in a skin flick?"

Warner snorted. "Hardly. We sell hopes and promises, remember?

It's on our sign."

"Doug," Gert said. "I can assure you that none of what we did yesterday will be seen at some triple-X playhouse. If that's what you're worried about."

"But it will appear on a screen somewhere?"

The women looked at each other.

"The customer who paid for the illusion has the rights to it," Warner said.

"So it's porn."

"Don't flatter yourself, kid," Gert said. Her face had lost all sympathy. She looked again very much like Denise Brubaker. "What we did was completely forgettable. Both of us were fully clothed, except for maybe a minute when you had your pants down. And your Guy, let me tell you, is perfectly ordinary. No one is going to get all hot and bothered watching him. In fact, no one would want to watch our silly charade except for the gentlemen who paid for it and for whom it has considerable personal meaning. No one else gives a darn about your sorry dick. I don't. But of course I'm biased." She turned and kissed Warner on the lips.

Doug blushed, not at the kiss, but at her assessment. His eyes went to the floor.

"There's so much going on in the universe, Doug," Warner said, "that you can't even begin to comprehend. Best I can tell, the only thing you ever spend your attentions on are beer and boobs. Stop being such a typical sperm spreader, and you might appreciate what we do here."

"How can I appreciate anything when all you ever do is keep me in the dark? What the hell was that secretary act for? Or her—being the angry customer? And those people at the computers downstairs. Were they phony too? How do I know you're not lying about this 'gentleman client'? How do I know you just didn't want to see me with my pants down? Is this whole office, everything it does, just one big act put on for me?"

The two women smirked identically.

"How am I supposed to care about this business when it's probably nothing but a hoax?"

"That's a hard term," Gert said, "for a splendid production."

"I think the term fits."

"Oh do you," Warner said. "Do you now?" She got up from her desk. She took some steps in the direction of the big window over the sofa, as if to check movements on the street. She stopped. She turned back at him.

"Let me ask you something, since you're feeling so sure of yourself. When you go to a movie, do you stew and fuss in your seat over the fact that you are being shown something that is phony, to use your word: something produced, something purposefully engineered to convince you of a reality that isn't so? Or do you allow yourself to be drawn you into the illusion and let it work on you, perhaps even respecting it more for being artificially created?"

"When I go to a movie I know what I'm getting, and I'm paying for it."

"Exactly. So do are our customers."

Doug's posture collapsed under the force of her authority. He had no idea how to respond. That wasn't the point, what she said, not 'exactly.' Not for him. As far as her logic went it was airtight, yes. But something was missing. And whatever that else was made the difference between right and wrong, cruelty and cooperation. But he couldn't think of it that second. Stuck and sulking, ashamed and overmatched, he couldn't get his mind around the crux of the matter. He couldn't bring up the words he needed to defeat her.

"But why me," he said. "Why go to all that trouble to fool me?"

Warner didn't hesitate.

"That's our business. Not yours. All you need to know is that your talents, if you will, fit precisely the current needs of The Treasure Box, Inc. That's true of anyone we call an employee. You are performing more or less up to your ability, about as well as we anticipated. But you are also resisting us, which too we expected. Your performances would improve if you stopped resisting."

Something she said struck him. He remembered the ferry ride.

"That woman downstairs."

"Doreen," Warner corrected. Her forehead crinkled with annoyance. This woman, the real boss, deeply detested him. Not until that moment, that expression, did he realize just how much. It was as if she could barely stand his smell. She moved back to the desk.

"She was lying to me from the first moment I met her. Before I even talked with her, when I saw her reading that stupid book, she was already misrepresenting herself."

Neither woman reacted.

"She was a plant. She was put there for me to meet."

They looked at him. They shook their heads, but unconvincingly.

"And my job too. Did you put Marconi's out of business, just so I would be available? How long have I been in your sights?"

A whole other explanation for his college failures suggested itself. The suddenly impossible examinations, the cold-shouldered professors, the inevitable low grades. He couldn't believe their reach went that far.

"Did you manufacture all those tests I bombed this year? Or those lousy papers I bought? Who else is in your pocket?"

"Paranoia blinds," Warner said tonelessly. "It blinds famously."

"Or it opens your eyes."

Warner shook her head; she looked at her partner. Gert shrugged. Warner rested both hands on the desk, intermingling her fingers. She stared down at him like a grade school teacher.

"No," she said, "it just blinds." Then: "But the bottom line here is that whether or not your questions have merit, they are none of your business. Why we do anything is none of your business."

"Like hell. You shut down a perfectly good restaurant just so you can get your paws on me—"

"Stop! What you think you know and what the facts are make two very different realities. You don't serve yourself well by inventing certainties out of what are only assumptions. You'll only become more frustrated, more unhappy, and less useful."

"Useful to you."

"Yes," she said, "to us."

Her directness disarmed him. He tried to plead.

"But why can't you just tell me what the fuck is going on?"

"First of all, your repeated use of expletives does not impress us. In fact, it only shows us just how much polish you need before you are truly a worthy employee of this company."

Gert nodded at her partner's words.

"Second, to answer your question, and to borrow a famous phrase from our government, you will know what you need to know as soon as you need to know it. Anything beyond that is none of your business."

"And if I refuse to cooperate?"

"You can't. It's in your contract."

"It's in my contact that I have to let an ugly, middle-aged dyke give me a hand job so some invisible customer gets his rocks off?"

Neither woman took the bait. He should have known.

"Of course," Warner said, "those are not the words used in your contract, but in essence the answer is yes. You are not within your rights to refuse any assignment given you by The Treasure Box, Inc. Unless you want to face the consequence of breaking your contract."

Doug said nothing. He had nothing left. All he could do now was withhold.

Finally, Gert spoke. "Very little of what we do has a sexual element, Doug. It all depends on the client. It's possible that you may work for us for years and never have anyone touch you again. On the other hand, it could happen tonight if duty calls. Leigh's point is that you can't refuse. Whatever the illusion calls for, you do it. Even if that means letting me give you a hand job."

It sounded as if she were about to say something else, something more, but she stopped herself. He recognized that in the moment this woman, and perhaps her name really was Gert, was treating him more kindly than he deserved.

Doug shuddered: his stomach, his shoulders, his legs. Warner glared at him, ecstatic in his confusion, in his near total collapse. It was as if the woman wanted revenge for him ever believing she was a secretary.

"How long?" Doug said quietly.

"Your employment with Treasure Box ends when Treasure Box says it does. I can't tell you when or if that time will ever come."

"If?"

"If."

"I thought this was a summer job."

"It's a job, yes."

"And it's summer," Gert added.

Warner smirked. "It may be your job for quite a long time. If that suits us. It is in your contract, after all."

"I didn't read my contract."

"No one ever does."

"But she promised!"

Warner sat up perfectly straight. She showed the most ruthless smile he'd seen yet, a smile so omnipotent it almost read like sympathy.

"Yes, she promised."

Doug shuddered and went cold. He couldn't look at her anymore. At either of them. His gaze tended to the floor but then, finally, for a stretch of moments, through the far window above the couch. There he saw only formless blue air offering him nothing, not even the body of a cloud. What he wished he could see was the inside of a ferry boat as it moved away from the island. Or, better, from the upper deck of that vessel, the landscape of Nantucket town center: its two tall church spires, its shingled and clapboard buildings, its tiny inns and cobblestone avenues growing smaller, less remarkable, less specific and more blurred, finally disappearing into the fulvous shroud of an island fog. He wished he could see his parents again. Or his two friends. But he knew now they would never make it in, not to this Nantucket, a Nantucket where—through some slipway in the universe's ocean—he found himself trapped in an implausible office. He even wished he were back at U Mass, staring at some squirrelly professor's final examination, not knowing how to begin. An exam he could never pass, if anyone could. But, that's the thing, he thought. Somehow someone always did. And not only pass, but kill it. In every class, no matter how impossible the test, one person always got a hundred. But never him.

16139204R00174

Made in the USA
San Bernardino, CA
19 October 2014